# FEAR—AND DESIRE . . .

Colter turned his head and glanced at her. "You've got to be hungry. Are you stupid or just plain stubborn?"

Their eyes met. Instead of the violent stormy gray from the day before, instead of the cold promise of death, she saw curiosity.

"Just stubborn," she said, risking the truth.

"I thought so." He smiled.

She blinked in astonishment. She hadn't seen him smile before. His lips curved up to reveal white teeth and an easy grin. Tiny lines creased the skin by the corners of his eyes. He was handsome, she thought, startled. . . . The dark shaggy hair and hollow cheeks still made him look dangerous, but his smile changed everything.

Her mouth tilted up in return . . .

## Praise for Susan Macias's
### *Tender Victory*:

# SWEET ESCAPE

## SUSAN MACIAS

DIAMOND BOOKS, NEW YORK

This book is a Diamond original edition,
and has never been previously published.

SWEET ESCAPE

A Diamond Book / published by arrangement with
the author

PRINTING HISTORY
Diamond edition / August 1994

ISBN: 0-7865-0025-5

Diamond Books are published by The Berkley Publishing Group,
200 Madison Avenue, New York, NY 10016.
DIAMOND and the "D" design
are trademarks belonging to Charter Communications, Inc.

PRINTED IN THE UNITED STATES OF AMERICA

10  9  8  7  6  5  4  3  2  1

*To Suzanne Forster,*
*a great friend and writer,*
*who encouraged me to "just go for it."*
*You're the best. Thanks for everything.*

# Chapter 1 ═══════════

"Get ready to move 'em out," one of the buckskin-clad wagon-train scouts called as he rode down the line.

Maggie Bishop shifted excitedly on the seat of her spring wagon. "How much longer?" she asked. They'd promised to "Move 'em out" an hour ago.

The scout reined in next to her and politely tipped his hat. "Any time now, ma'am. You'd best be gettin' your man here with you. Wouldn't want to be leavin' him behind."

Maggie looked at the weathered face of the old man and smiled. "I don't have a man with me."

"So you're the one."

He didn't say it as if he were pleased. No matter, Maggie told herself. "I paid my money, just like everyone else."

The scout studied her, then drew his horse in a wide circle and looked in the back of her open wagon. "How far you planning to go?"

"Just to St. Louis. I'll have to work for a year to earn enough money to go west next spring."

Knowing eyes met and held hers. "You ever been on a wagon train before?"

"No." She tilted her chin up slightly. "I'll manage."

"How are your hands?"

"My hands?" She released one of the reins and glanced at her left palm. Farm work had strengthened her muscles, but the leather from the reins had rubbed her raw. A row of blisters had formed on her tender skin. "What about them?"

"You should be wearin' gloves, little lady."

"Thanks for the advice." Green as she was, even *she* had known that. Gloves would have been nice for protection and to ward off the morning frost, but they were a luxury she couldn't afford.

The old man shrugged as if to say he'd done his best. "By the time we get to Missouri, you're gonna have calluses to last you a lifetime. Ma'am." He tipped his hat to her and rode off.

Maggie stared after him and shook her head. Calluses were the least of her problems. She pulled her shawl closer around her shoulders. The morning was chilly. Spring was late this year, but the wagon train couldn't wait for fine weather. They wouldn't have waited for her either, she thought, remembering how she'd barely made town the previous day. Between purchasing her few supplies and convincing the members of the wagon train that a single woman traveling alone wouldn't be a hardship, she'd been kept busy. But that was behind her now. She was here. And she was going west.

"Let's go now," she said softly, barely able to contain her excitement. Sebastian, her horse, flicked his ears at her comment. Hers was the only wagon pulled by a single horse, but Sebastian was big and strong, and he would carry her safely as far as she needed to go. Her provisions were on the meager side and not enough to tire him.

Around her, the noise increased as people prepared to leave. Children raced around the wagons, families huddled together in tearful farewells. There wasn't anyone to see Maggie off.

She glanced over her shoulder at the small town, barely visible in the morning haze. Even though Edward was several miles away preparing to plow the fields, she half expected to see her brother-in-law come storming out of the mist to claim her. She shook her head and sat straighter in her seat. It didn't matter if he did; she wouldn't go back to the farm with him. He could threaten her all he wanted, she wasn't afraid of him anymore. Maggie raised her chin defiantly. She wasn't ever going to be afraid again.

"I'm doing it, Alice. I'm really here, ready to go. Oh, but I do miss you," she said, wishing her sister were here with her. They had planned this trip together, had saved for over two years to get the money they needed to travel, but it hadn't been enough. In the end, it had been the sale of Alice's pigs that had given Maggie the amount she needed to buy the supplies to get her to St. Louis.

They had hoped to take the pigs with them for food or barter. Maggie chuckled. Alice would never have willingly left the animals behind; they were her pride and joy. Maggie's good humor faded. Alice was gone. She'd died a few weeks into the new year. Her dying request had been for Maggie to go west alone.

So here she was. And when Edward figured out she wasn't coming back from her trip to town, he was going to be furious. No doubt he would—

"Don't make a sound," a man said quietly.

Maggie jumped and turned toward the voice. She hadn't heard anyone approach her wagon. With all her thoughts of Edward, she half expected to see him standing next to her. When he wasn't, she sighed in relief and gave the tall, broad-shouldered man a quick smile. He held a fat bedroll under one arm. Leather saddlebags hung over his left shoulder. A black beaver-felt hat hid his features from view.

"I'm sorry," she said, shifting slightly on the seat of her spring wagon. "You startled me."

"I said don't make a sound," he repeated.

"But why—"

Her gaze lowered from his shadowed face to his chest, then to the pistol in his hand. The muzzle pointed directly at *her*.

She drew in a gasp of air. "What do you want?" she demanded, too stunned to do more than stare at the weapon gleaming dully in the weak morning light.

"Quiet." He reached for her.

Instinctively, she jerked away from the man. Even as she struggled to rise and jump off the other side of the wagon, his hand shot out and grabbed her wrist, holding her fast.

His bedroll hit the ground with a thunk. He ignored it.

"Don't move," he commanded. He glanced at the field.

While townspeople and children milled together, twenty wagons formed an uneven line ahead of her. Her wagon sat at the very end, bringing up the rear. With all the noise and activity, no one noticed the drama being enacted so close by.

Maggie stared at his hold on her. Fingers bit into her skin, squeezing hard but with little visible effort. She twisted in his steely grip; it did no good. Despite his warnings, she tried to scream, but the tightness in her throat and a sudden flash of fear left her unable to do more than whisper.

"Leave me be," she said, trying again to pull herself free. The effort caused his hand to tighten, and she knew he was strong enough to snap her bones.

"Get down."

Another scout, one she hadn't met yet, rode by. "We're ready to get going, ma'am," he said, glancing briefly at her and the man standing beside her wagon before riding off.

Maggie opened her mouth to scream for help, then heard the unmistakable double click of a gun hammer being pulled back. She looked down. The muzzle was less than two feet from her, concealed by the sleeve of the stranger's thick coat.

This is a dream, she told herself, even as sweat dotted her back and her palms. Soon she would wake up in her warm bed on the farm.

"Get down," the man ordered, tugging on her arm. "Slow and easy. You do anything to attract attention—I'll kill you."

"With all these people here?" She looked at the wagon thirty feet in front of hers. In some part of her mind, a voice warned her that it was foolish to argue, but she could no more control her tongue than she could stop the frantic pounding of her heart. "They'll hear you if you shoot me, and then you'll hang."

The stranger's grip on her arm didn't loosen. "Lady, I've got nothing to lose."

Maggie was too frightened even to pray. She allowed her assailant to pull her to the edge of the seat. When he released her, she gathered her skirt and petticoats in one hand and with the other clutched the side of the wagon for balance. Despite the trembling in her limbs, she would run as hard and as fast as she could as soon as her feet touched the ground. Surely no man would shoot a woman in the back.

Even as the comforting thought occurred to her she knew it was a lie. Men were animals—capable of anything—and this one had already told her he had nothing to lose.

Don't think about that, she ordered herself. She hated the familiar, bitter taste on her tongue and tried to use anger to battle her growing terror. She'd promised herself not to be afraid.

As if he sensed her resolve, the man used his free arm to encircle her waist. She hadn't expected him to help her down, and it upset her balance so she fell heavily against him.

His chest and legs were as hard and unyielding as the grip of his hand had been. In that split second before she gained her footing, she looked up. She had an impression of harsh, angular features, an unshaven jaw, then their eyes met and she felt the breath leave her lungs.

He would hurt her, or anyone, and never give it another thought. After the war, Edward had described what it was like to see death in a man's face. She'd never quite understood him—until now. The stranger's eyes showed no trace of emotion. They were cold and empty, as if no soul resided behind the flesh and blood. A killer without conscience.

"Walk away slowly," the man said. "Don't look back. Don't make a sound." His voice, low and powerful, frightened her as much as his words.

Leave? But her wagon contained all her belongings. "I—"

He pressed the barrel of the gun into her side. The round muzzle jabbed between her ribs. "Go!"

She took a step, then hesitated. She thought about the carefully hoarded gold pieces tucked in the corner of her

trunk. They were all that was left from Alice's pigs. The
music box she'd carried from Ohio had once belonged to
her mother. It sat safely in a burlap bag filled with straw.
There were her cooking pot bought from the German family
on the next farm, her provisions calculated to last until
she arrived in Missouri, her copy of the *Prairie Traveler*.
Everything she owned in the world was in that wagon.

He would kill her if she tried anything. She would die
anyway, without her horse and supplies.

"I won't leave," she said, coming to a stop. "This is
my—"

He moved so quickly, she couldn't figure out what he'd
done. One minute she was prepared to fight him for her
possessions, the next he whirled her around until her back
rested flat against his chest. One arm, more like a band of
steel than flesh and blood, pressed under her breasts and
held her in place.

"Quiet!" he whispered in her ear, his breath warm in the
cold of the early-spring morning.

She looked up, but he was staring beyond her to something happening on the far side of the field. Several men
on horseback had joined the wagon train. He stared at
them and cursed. She stiffened at the shocking word whose
meaning she only vaguely understood.

"How the hell did they find me?" the man muttered
softly. He cursed again, then looked at her. Gray eyes, the
color of dawn on a cold day filled with rain, met her own.
She ceased to breathe as he weighed the value of her life.

Maggie closed her eyes rather than watch him decide her
fate. There was no one to mourn her, she realized with a
pang of sadness. No one to mark her passing. Perhaps not
even God.

No! She would not die like some cowering animal. She
opened her eyes and stared at him, defying him with her
gaze.

"Get in the wagon," the man commanded, releasing her
and pushing her toward the seat.

She stumbled slightly, then regained her balance. Why
get back in the wagon? He'd just dragged her out of there.

"Take the reins." He tossed his saddlebags and bedroll into the back, then climbed in after them. A rifle had been slung over one shoulder, hidden from view. He slipped the leather strap down his arm.

"Is this all you have?" he asked as he squatted down and stared at her meager possessions.

"I'm only going to Missouri for now. I'll head to California or Oregon next spring."

He dismissed her with an impatient shrug.

From his crouch he began to rearrange bags of flour and grain. His saddlebag disappeared under a sack, his bedroll filled an empty corner. His actions confused her until she realized he was making a place for himself to hide.

Her first thought was to bolt. While the man was occupied she could escape. But the wagon and Sebastian were all she had.

He paused and looked at her. "I said, get in."

A coldness crept through her. Even as her legs shook and her knees threatened to buckle, she gripped the sides of the wagon and pulled herself into her seat. Keeping her gaze on the man, she blindly reached for the knotted reins.

He picked up the burlap bag containing the music box.

"Don't you touch that," she said without thinking. "It belonged to my mother."

He looked down at the sack as if calculating its value, and she knew with a sinking feeling he would toss it over the side.

Abruptly, he thrust the bundle under the seat. "Store valuables here," he said. "They'll stay dry."

Before she could respond, he dropped to the floor of the wagon and disappeared under the straw and the provisions. He pulled the rifle in after him. Where there had been a man, now she saw only her belongings. She reached behind her and touched the now protected burlap bag. Why had he done that? He was commandeering her wagon. He'd threatened to kill her. She shook her head. None of this made sense.

Once again the double click of his pistol warned her he was nearby. "Don't say anything to anyone," he said,

his low voice taut with tension. "Stay to the rear of the
formation. Go two miles down the road, then turn west
through the forest. Don't talk to me until we're clear."

She nodded her agreement, then, realizing he couldn't see
her, said, "I understand."

The straw behind her rustled slightly.

Maggie struggled to untie the reins. Trembling fingers
fumbled with the thick leather straps. Her horse, Sebastian,
pricked his ears and tossed his head. "Steady, boy," she
said. "It'll be a few minutes yet." She swallowed uncomfortably, afraid the man would think she was disobey-
ing him. "I'm talking to the horse," she whispered. "I
always do."

Silence.

"I didn't want you to think—"

The straw rustled again.

Around her, townspeople milled and called out farewells.
Less than twenty feet in front of her, a family with seven
children prepared to move out. The youngest, a boy of six,
hung over the back of his wagon and shot her a grin.

"Are you going to follow us?" he asked.

"Yes." She forced herself to smile. "I'll be right behind."

Help was so close, she thought frantically. She could
call out, except she had seen the man's eyes for herself.
She believed he would kill her as easily as a barn cat
killed a mouse. What did he want? Where was his horse?
Why, oh why had he chosen *her* wagon? Because she
was the last one in line, or because she was a woman
alone?

A couple hundred feet ahead the first families clucked
to their oxen and began to move slowly. The still-frozen
ground prevented dust from rising to choke those in the
rear, but the smell of animals and too many bodies circu-
lated like a lazy haze.

Turn west, the man had said. Away from the people,
away from the wagon train. Would he kill her there? He'd
have to wait until they were out of earshot, or they would
hear the gun. Perhaps he meant to slit her throat. She'd
heard of Indians who could kill—

"Stop it," she whispered fiercely to herself. "Don't think about it. Don't think about anything." She was driving the wagon because she had no choice. She would be prepared, though. When she had a chance to escape, she would take it. She hadn't come this far to lose everything now. "I'm not afraid. I refuse to be afraid."

The wagon in front moved forward slowly. Maggie flicked the reins and Sebastian took a step. The cart lurched, resisting the pull as if it had become stuck. Her horse took another step, tugging harder, and they rolled free. The journey west had begun.

Maggie looked ahead at the slow-moving wagons. How many nights had she lain awake planning for this moment? She had imagined the excitement, had anticipated a welling of freedom. She'd never thought she would be trapped in her wagon with a dangerous man holding her captive at gunpoint. She swallowed, then took a deep breath.

Oxen were better for the journey, she reminded herself in a desperate attempt to forget the weapon and the man behind her. A team of four or six. But she'd never driven oxen. One horse was all she could manage and afford. Did she have enough flour? Maybe she should have bought another sack. Would he kill her? *Don't think about it.*

Up ahead the wagons slowed. The men she'd noticed across the field rode up, shouting commands to halt. Maggie frowned. One man in a Union uniform looked like the leader. He issued orders she couldn't hear, then the half dozen men with him split into groups of two and began to walk along the wagon train.

They were looking for her captor! With an involuntary movement, Maggie glanced over her shoulder at the straw. Even to her, nothing looked out of place. If she hadn't known better, she'd have said the man had jumped off and disappeared. But she knew differently. She could almost feel the cold pressure of the gun pointing at her body.

The straw behind her rustled slightly. Should she say something? Had he heard the command to stop? Should she warn him? Maybe he would make a run for it.

"There are men," she said softly, not daring to turn around. "They're stopping everyone."

No response.

The wagon in front slowed and she pulled on the reins. Sebastian snorted his displeasure. The two men assigned to the rear of the wagon train moved closer. One was tall and thin, with a slicker covering his body. The other, tall but heavyset, rode bareheaded despite the temperature. Seven wagons ahead, they reined in and spoke to the driver.

She couldn't hear their questions. The stocky man dismounted and disappeared into the rear of the lead wagon. Most of the travelers had protected their belongings with bows and double osnaburg covers; she was the only one without. Seconds later the man appeared, shaking his head.

Maggie nibbled on her lower lip. What was she going to say?

"They're looking for you in each wagon," she said desperately. "One by one. They'll—"

"Quiet," her captor said at last. "Don't tell them anything. They might get me, but I'll get you first."

She shuddered. "I won't." She stared straight ahead, not moving, barely daring to breathe.

The procedure of searching was repeated twice more. On the fourth time, a mere two wagons ahead, they spoke to the driver. Again she couldn't hear, but this time she saw the driver shaking his head, refusing them access. The thin man, who had remained on his horse, quickly pulled a gun and held it to the driver's temple. The stocky man entered the wagon.

Instantly a woman screamed. The wagon shifted, as if something had been thrown or dropped, then there was a flash of skirts and a woman appeared at the back, clutching the baby she'd been nursing to her bare breasts.

The stocky man paused beside her, his hungry gaze devouring her nakedness. One dirty hand shot out to touch the skin and he laughed as she shrank back.

Maggie swallowed. The scene of a man terrifying a woman was too familiar, she realized as panic threatened. She wanted to run, but the fear she'd been fighting held her firmly in its grip. Her legs shook too much to support her weight.

In front of her, the children were already emptying out of the wagon, leaving it free to be searched. The thin man didn't even bother to speak to the driver; he simply nodded and urged his horse forward until he was even with her. Don't be afraid, she silently told herself.

Once again sweat dampened Maggie's back. The moisture chilled her. She wanted to scream, to confess, anything to keep those men and their dirty hands away from her.

"Ma'am," he said politely as he reined in his mount and tipped his hat. "Have you seen a stranger here today?"

"I've been living on a farm a little ways from here," she said, her voice trembling with every word. "Most of these people are strangers."

He nodded thoughtfully, then leaned forward and looked into her cart. "Not many provisions for the trip."

"I'm not going all the way to California," she said. "Just to Missouri."

"And your husband?"

"I'm . . . alone."

His brown eyes assessed her thoroughly. Maggie fought the urge to draw her shawl closer around her body. She wished she'd had the money to buy a gun. Of course she didn't know how to use one, but it would have given her a measure of protection.

"A pretty lady like you?"

"I'm a widow."

The lie seemed to please him, for he smiled. "The war?"

She nodded.

"We lost a great many men. I was luckier than some."

The stocky man had finished searching the wagon in front of hers. He jumped to the ground, then mounted his horse and waited impatiently for his friend. "Come on, Wilson," he called. "Have you searched that one yet?"

Wilson ignored him. "I almost died at Vicksburg."

"I'm sorry."

Now, she thought. Jump off the wagon and run. Wilson would give chase. When he caught her, she would explain about the stranger. But the thought of his partner, the dirty hand that had touched the nursing mother's breast, held her fast in her seat. A man who would do that in public was capable of doing anything in private. She knew firsthand. Wilson, the thin man in front of her, had done nothing to stop it. He might think Maggie was pretty, but he wouldn't protect her. They would never believe her innocence.

"I hope you won't mind if I just poke around in your wagon." He reached for the rifle strapped on the side of his saddle.

# Chapter 2

Maggie wanted to protest, but what was she supposed to say? She could only watch helplessly as the soldier pulled his rifle free and leaned forward to jab it into the straw. When he found the man, he would assume she was an accomplice. Her fingers tightened on the reins.

"Excuse me, sir—" she began, only to be cut off.

"Zachery! Wilson! We've found him." The uniformed officer rode toward the end of the wagon train and motioned for his men to follow.

The tall man paused, his rifle muzzle barely resting on the straw. "How?"

"Gant found his horse's tracks."

"He sure James is still on it? I wouldn't put it past him to turn the animal loose."

The officer shook his head. "Tracks are too deep. Come on, man. We can't let him get away now."

Wilson shrugged at Maggie and smiled. "I'm sorry to have to leave so soon, pretty lady." His brown eyes danced. "Perhaps when I pass through Missouri, I'll stop by to say howdy."

Relief spilled through her and she could do little more than nod. He whirled his horse around and rode toward the group of waiting men. Then they all turned south and spurred their horses on. Within minutes there was nothing left except the murmur of conversation and the crying of the woman two wagons ahead. Maggie clutched her thick shawl and wondered whether the cold in her bones came from the temperature or her fear.

The families at the front of the wagon train began to
move at once, following slowly in the wake of the men.
Maggie clutched the reins tightly and tapped her foot until
it was her turn to urge Sebastian forward. The horse moved
briskly, as if eager to get under way. Maggie tugged to hold
him at a walk. She was going to have to turn off the road
in a few minutes. Go a mile or two, the man had said, then
turn west. Better to start putting distance between the rest
of the train and herself now. They would think she was
slow, or that she was turning back to town. No one would
care enough to investigate where she'd gone, she thought
regretfully. She'd only joined up that morning. The man in
charge had tried to convince her not to travel alone. They
would all think she'd changed her mind about going along
with them. No one would think to ask what had happened
to the Bishop girl.

Maybe she *didn't* have to leave the wagon train. She
could just keep following the wagon in front. Perhaps the
road would widen and she could pass the slower convey-
ances and move into the middle of the line. Yes, that's what
she would do. He would be caught then . . . or would he?
There had been an officer, six men plus the one that had
found the horse. At least eight men searching for one.

As the cart continued to roll forward, the space between
her and the wagon in front widened gradually. No one
noticed; they were too busy talking about what had just
happened. At first she'd been able to hear the speculations,
then the conversations became indistinguishable murmurs,
and finally faded altogether.

Thick trees with their snow-filled branches closed all
around her. This part of the forest quickly gave way to
more farms, but she would be turning away from the cleared
ground. Trails crisscrossed the area; her small wagon would
have no trouble passing. Despite the bare branches, once
she left the main road, she'd quickly be lost from view.
Piles of snow, bushes, and the trees themselves formed an
impenetrable screen.

To her right, the trail widened slightly and a path jutted
off in a westwardly direction. No snow had fallen in almost

two weeks. The tracks in the trail—perhaps from a farmer's cart or someone stocking up on firewood—looked several days old.

Now, she thought. She either had to follow his instructions or make her break for freedom on foot. She shifted in her seat. She rebelled at the thought of abandoning her possessions. As long as she was alive and still had her wagon, she had a chance to escape and make her way to Missouri.

Maggie pulled on the reins and urged Sebastian toward the smaller path. He turned obediently. With a last glance at the wagon train, she saw that no one had witnessed her departure, and within a few seconds, they were lost from view. She was alone with the stranger.

Colter James knew the moment the woman left the main road and turned off into the forest. Beneath him, the wagon rocked slightly on the rougher path and the wheels crunched through ice and snow. Dust and grit from the straw burned in his eyes and lungs. He covered his nose and mouth with the edge of his jacket and forced himself to breathe slowly. It didn't help much. The dryness coated his throat. The need to inhale fresh air, to cough or drink cool water to ease his throat, tormented him. He stiffened, fighting the involuntary urges. He was too close to the wagon train to risk giving away his presence.

The sounds of the wagon train disappeared, leaving only the quiet of the woodlands. Birds chirped, branches rattled in the slight breeze. Something small, probably a rabbit or fox, dove through the underbrush. No other people populated this section of land.

Colter waited another three minutes, then eased into a sitting position and brushed the straw off his head and shoulders. As he glanced around the forest, taking in the trees, the narrow trail, the woman's stiff back, he inhaled deeply.

He released the hammer on his gun and slipped the weapon into its holster. Petty and his men would search for hours before finding his horse.

Earlier that morning the patrol had been less than two
miles behind him. It had been dumb luck, the first such
in months, that had led him to a wagon full of flour and
a way to escape. With a couple of sacks tied to her saddle,
Siren would lead the men after him on a merry chase. The
extra weight would make her hoofprints deep enough to
fool them into thinking she still carried him. When they
found out she didn't, they wouldn't know where they'd lost
him. Hell of a price, he thought. She'd been the finest horse
he'd ever owned. He'd hated letting her loose. But with
Petty and his men so close behind, he'd had no choice.

It had been risky going into Chicago, but he'd never
thought he would run into someone from his old regiment.
News of his arrest had spread quickly, as had word of his
escape. Bad luck, bad timing, and a bad decision on his
part. He'd gotten away with his life and little else. What
was he supposed to do now?

He turned toward the woman sitting on the wagon's
seat. Two years ago he would have killed anyone who
got in his way. A year ago he would have briefly considered letting that person live, then dismissed the idea
as impractical. Today he didn't know what to do. The
war had ended, but the killing went on. He was tired
of the blood and death, yet he would do what he must
to survive. He looked back at his prisoner. She sat in her
seat as stiffly as a broom handle. He could smell her fear.
Better to kill her here and be done with it. He reached for
his pistol, then paused. She was a woman. That changed
everything.

"Slow down," he said.

She started, as if the sound of his voice had been unexpected. "W-what?"

She whirled to look at him, her face going pale. The
reins slipped from her hands. Her horse tossed his head, neighed,
then tossed it again, as if testing the hint of freedom. The
bridle clinked. Colter rose to a crouch and moved quickly
toward the seat.

He was too late. The horse began to trot, then canter,
then gallop.

"Stop, Sebastian," the woman cried. She leaned forward to grab the reins, but the leather straps slipped from the seat and flapped and bounced against the ground.

The wagon rumbled along, the four wheels spinning quickly, too quickly. Colter swung one leg over the back of the seat, then the other. The woman shrank from him. The horse thundered around a curve in the path. A low branch hit the side of the cart, pushing it off-balance. The right wheels rose slightly at the widest point of the turn. Colter flung himself at the rising side, using his weight to force the wagon down.

The right front wheel rolled into a hole in the ground and he was tossed into the center of the seat. The woman clung to the seat back, doing her best to hang on. Again the wagon rose on two wheels and threatened to overturn.

The woman screamed. He turned and saw her foot slip off the footboard. Her body shifted as if she were being sucked toward the ground. He held on to the raised side with one hand and grabbed her arm with the other. The wheels hit the ground, then bounced up. The woman sank farther down. Colter gritted his teeth and pulled. She stopped slipping. The cold air slapped at his face, freezing the skin and making his eyes water. Across his shoulders and back, the muscles tightened and burned in protest. Still he held on to her. He looked to the front. There was another turn up ahead, this one to the right.

"Can you reach me with your other hand?" he called.

She followed his gaze. In that split second he watched her weigh her fear of death with her fear of him. If she let go, she would fall and be crushed by the wheels. If she hung on—God knows what she thought he would do.

Slowly, her free hand came up and clutched his arm. Her fingers dug in right below his elbow. The grip was stronger than he'd expected. The wind tugged at her hair, loosening it until it flowed out behind her.

The horse plowed into the turn, barely slowing as he trampled over a broken branch lying in the path. The wagon jerked up and down, then repeated the motion as the four wheels rolled over the obstruction.

The woman cried out, "I can't hold on."

Colter braced himself and, as they reached the turn, began to pull. Their weight shifted through the curve. The back wheels skidded slightly, and he was able to pull her toward the center of the wagon. But suddenly she stopped, her upper body draped across the seat, her legs still dangling off the side.

"I'm caught!"

He looked at her face. Blue eyes pleaded.

"My dress," she screamed, straining frantically, one hand holding on to his arm, the other pulling at her skirt. "In the wheel."

In a flash he pulled the knife from his boot. Her pale skin blanched white. "What are you doing?"

Her blind terror hit him like a blow to the belly, but he kept moving toward her, bending until he crouched over her prone body. The hem of her dress caught in the spokes, winding tighter and tighter with each turn of the wheel. The horse began to tire and the wagon slowed, but not fast enough.

He wrapped his arm around her legs. Inch by inch, the wheel pulled her down. He reached out and slashed at her dress. The razor-sharp steel cut through the fabric. He released her and she scrambled to the center of the seat.

Colter returned the knife to his boot. The horse slowed to a trot, then began to walk. Sweat and foam coated the animal's back. Up ahead the trail narrowed. More branches crowded into the path. At last the horse took a shuddering breath and stopped.

Colter jumped to the ground and collected the reins. After tying them, he circled the wagon to check for damage. The wheels were intact, none of the spokes bent. He studied the axles, then shook the sides. Nothing broken that he could see.

Now what? He was over two hundred miles from where he had to be. He'd lost his horse and his saddle. He had money to buy another, but—he glanced around; he doubted folks around this farm country got many strangers buying mounts—he would be remembered. He'd come too far to let Petty and his men pick up his trail now. When they realized they'd been had, they'd spread out, looking for—

He shook the sides of the wagon again. They sure wouldn't be looking for a farmer's cart. He moved to the horse and eyed the animal curiously. Big, but strong. He bent over and ran his hands down its long legs. No swelling. He was in good condition for a farm animal. Colter patted the damp back and murmured soothingly. The animal jerked its head up and down, blowing heavily and rattling the bridle. Then he quieted. Colter checked his teeth and stroked his nose. The horse could make the trip with no problem; the wagon would provide cover. The situation was manageable. Except for the woman.

He held on to the bridle and stared at her. She sat in the center of the seat. Her hands clutched the wood as if she expected to be torn from her place. The breeze caught the ruffled edge of her white petticoat. On one side of her dark skirt, a ragged half circle reaching from ankle to knee had been cut away. He'd never thought much about women's clothing. Whores spent most of their time in underwear designed to arouse as well as to provide easy access. He'd heard men joking about the clothes women wore, that it was often easier to go under than through. But he'd never seen a real lady undress.

His eyes narrowed as he studied the flapping petticoat. Underneath there seemed to be another. How many layers did the woman wear? His gaze drifted up to her chest. Here the dark woolen fabric clung to what it concealed, emphasizing her waist and breasts.

Loose strands of hair fluttered around her face and shoulders. In the sunlight, the color was blond with streaks of gold. His gaze moved to her heart-shaped face. A spot of red stained each cheek and he realized she'd been watching his perusal. A wariness joined the apprehension in her eyes as if she feared for more than her life.

He was back where he'd been before the horse had spooked. What to do with the woman. He couldn't let her go; they were too close to town. She'd easily find Petty and his men and tell them about him. It would only be a

matter of days, maybe hours, until they picked up his trail.
It seemed the best solution was to kill her.

She straightened in her seat and stared directly at him.
He'd been told his expression was as unreadable as a block
of stone; it hadn't been a compliment. But the woman
knew exactly what he was thinking. She began to rise to
her feet.

He moved slowly around the horse, with each step calculating how far the sound of the gunshot would carry.
Expecting her to dart the other way, he prepared to duck
around the animal. Instead, she turned and threw herself
into the back of the wagon. Why would she—

His rifle!

Colter cursed his forgetfulness. He knew better. If he'd
been this careless in the field, he would have been killed
in the first skirmish.

The woman dug frantically in the straw. He raced to the
opposite side, where he'd hidden the weapon. She looked
up and realized she'd picked the wrong half to search.
Once again, terror drained the color from her face and
widened her eyes. She swallowed slowly, the movement
emphasizing the slender length of her neck.

She was pretty, he thought with surprise. Young. And
untouched by the horrors that wove together the fabric of
his life. His hand closed on the smooth, cool barrel of the
rifle. He pulled it free from the straw. The woman drew in
a breath.

"No," she whispered.

He opened the breech and reached for the bullets he kept
in an inside pocket of his coat.

# Chapter 3 ═══════════

"No," Maggie said again, louder this time, as if she could convince him by volume alone. The man ignored her and loaded a long, lethal-looking cartridge into the rifle.

She was too stunned to pray or plead. She knelt in the back of the wagon and watched the man prepare to kill her. A few memories of her childhood flashed through her mind, visions of the happier days, before her father had died and her mother had been forced to move the family to town. She recalled the endless conversations with her sister, how they had talked about escaping and traveling west together. But in the end, Alice had refused to leave her husband—she'd been too strong to break her marriage vows she'd made before God, and too weak to survive the rigors of childbirth.

The man snapped the rifle closed.

"No!" Maggie screamed, rising to her feet. She had promised herself not to be afraid.

She unknotted her heavy shawl and threw it at Sebastian. It slapped him on the side of the head and he reared. As the man went to grab the horse she flung herself over the side of the wagon and fell to the ground. Pain shot up from both knees and her palms scraped against the icy dirt. She felt his footsteps as he began to circle around toward her. She pushed to her feet. Sebastian sidestepped; the man hesitated. She grabbed her torn skirt and petticoats at midthigh and hauled them out of her way. Then she fled toward the trees.

Bushes blocked her path. She darted through them, feeling sharp branches scratch her face and tangle in her hair. She had gone about ten feet when she heard him behind her.

"Let me go," she screamed, digging deep for speed.

He caught her arm and spun her toward him. She slammed hard into his chest. All the air rushed out of her. She stumbled back, clutched at her midsection, and tripped over a tree root. The man reached out to catch her, but she jerked away from his hand and fell to the mud-soaked ground.

She landed on her hand and left hip. Instantly, the melting snow soaked through her skirt and into her petticoats. She fought to draw in a breath. Her body ached, but it was nothing compared with the burning of her lungs. At last the cold air filled her. She inhaled twice more before risking a glance at the man.

He stood in front of her, the loaded rifle cradled in his arms like an infant. When she'd first seen him, a hat had concealed most of his features. Now he stood bareheaded. Thick dark hair hung shaggily to his shoulders. Cold gray eyes met hers. No emotion flickered there, no compassion or regret or even triumph. That frightened her most of all.

"What will you do with me?" she asked, when she could no longer stand the silence.

"Kill you."

"No!" She struggled to her feet. "No, I've done nothing to you." The fear swelled inside, but she forced herself to stay strong. She made herself meet his lifeless eyes and defy him. She sensed a predator's instinct about him: while he might respect strength, he would unmercifully destroy the weak.

He took a step toward her. She stood her ground. They were so close she could see the individual whiskers darkening his cheeks and jaw. Hair fell across his forehead. The strands gleamed in the late morning. Thick lashes framed his eyes. She glanced down, afraid to witness the coldness. A faint scar bisected his chin. Thin, firm lips pulled into a line of disapproval as his gaze rested on her face.

He reached out toward her and she flinched. He paused for a moment, then gently touched her cheek with his finger. When he drew back, she saw the streak of blood on his skin. Her blood. He rubbed his thumb and forefinger together as he studied her.

She squared her shoulders. "I'm not afraid."

"Then you're a fool. And a liar."

She was lying, and her words sat heavily on her tongue, but she screwed up her courage and lied again. "You can't kill me."

He raised his dark eyebrows as if surprised by her spirit. "Why?"

"Because it's wrong."

"I've already told you, I have nothing to lose."

"I have everything to lose." She swallowed. "But I will not fear you."

The silence between them seemed to stretch on forever.

"All right," he said at last, and took her arm. "I won't kill you for now."

Colter pulled her through the bushes to the wagon. The horse stood where he'd let him. There wasn't much time, he thought grimly. Petty's tracker, Gant, could have found Siren by now. If so, his men would spread out to cover the area. He needed to get away, and fast.

He gripped the woman's arm, but all his attention went to scanning the brush and trees. Were they out there? He strained to hear the snap of a horse's hoof cracking a branch, listened for the silence that would warn him another traveler lurked nearby.

Nothing. According to the forest, he was safe. For the moment.

Something pushed at his arm. He glanced down and saw the woman trying to shrug off his hold.

"I can stand on my own," she said icily.

He released her.

She pulled her arms close to her body and shivered. Blood dried on the angry scratches across her cheeks. A streak of dirt covered her chin, but underneath, her skin paled with cold and her lips trembled. Mud and snow soaked one side of her dress, and the dampness from the hem had climbed up past her knees. The dirty petticoat showed through the half circle of cutaway cloth flapping in the chilling breeze. She would freeze to death if she didn't get warm and dry.

"Take off your dress," he said.

Big eyes, wide and fringed with dark lashes, got bigger. The woman backed up a step. "No," she whispered, her hands going to her collar. "No. You can't do that. I'd rather die."

He slowly looked the woman up and down. "You're wet and cold. Put on something dry. We're moving on in two minutes, whether or not you've finished changing."

She stared up at him. Freckles scattered across the bridge of her nose and dotted her cheeks. Color flared on her skin, then drained away.

"You do have a spare dress?"

"Yes." She remained in place and looked at the wagon. "Two. In there."

"Get one."

She walked around him toward the cart. In the back sat a small trunk. She lifted the cover and pulled out a light gray dress. The fabric appeared finer than the one she wore now. The pale color and delicate lace at the collar told him it was a churchgoing dress.

"The other one is cotton," she said, by way of explanation, although he'd asked for none. "This is wool."

"Now you've got one minute," he said, folding his arms across his chest.

She held the dress to her. "Turn around."

"I don't have time to chase you again. Change your clothes or I'll do it for you." He thought about pulling out his gun to emphasize his point, but he didn't like to make empty threats.

"I can't," she said softly, retreating until she pressed against the wagon. "Not with you watching."

Her eyes pleaded. How many before her had done the same? he wondered. How many times had he watched a man beg for his life and then refused him mercy? But

she wasn't a man—or even the enemy. Her presence here
was an accident. Maybe that was why he'd decided to
spare her.

In the deepest darkest part of him, he knew keeping her
alive was a mistake that might cost him his own life. But
there had been too much death, caused by himself and others. He was tired of washing away the souls of the dead.

Colter moved past her, ignoring the way she shrank away
when he brushed by. He began to sort through the items in
the wagon.

He knew the exact moment she realized this was as much
privacy as she could expect. The woman draped the clean
dress over the side of the cart and, with her back to him,
began fumbling with the buttons on the front of her damp
bodice.

Even while he cataloged her provisions and calculated
how long they would last, he kept track of her. The dress
slipped off her shoulders and down her arms, pooled for a
second at her waist, then she pushed it to the ground and
stepped out of it. As she reached for the dry garment he
shook his head.

"The petticoat, too. It's soaked."

She froze for a moment, then drew her hair over her right
shoulder. With trembling fingers she released the fastening
at her waist. The petticoat joined the dress on the ground.
There was another, cleaner and dry, still covering her lower
body down to her shoes. The chemise left only her arms
and a bit of her back bare to his gaze. Yet her embarrassment radiated out like a tangible beacon of humiliation. He
knew no man had seen her undress before.

A virgin who traveled with no weapon, no companion.
She was the worst kind of fool.

Colter snapped her small trunk closed. She jumped. While
she stepped into the clean garment and hastily plunged her
arms into the sleeves, he found his bedroll in the corner
and pulled out a thick blanket.

Squinting, he stared up at the sun. Four, maybe five
hours of daylight left. His stomach rumbled. He hadn't
eaten since yesterday, but food would have to wait. There

was no time to build a fire and the woman hadn't packed any dried meat. Did she plan on hunting for her meals? He permitted himself a small smile at the thought. Then three birds flew suddenly from a tree and soared across the sky.

"Let's go," he said. He took a rope from his pocket and approached her.

She stared at him blankly.

"Hold out your hands," he said.

"Why?" She glanced at the rope, then tucked her hands behind her back. "You're going to tie me up?" She sounded outraged. "Like a milk cow?"

"It's that or kill you."

A shudder raced through her. "I won't run away."

"The hell you won't."

He reached for her arms. She swallowed and thrust them out in front of her. He stared at her bare wrists, her pale skin and small bones. He fingered the rough rope.

"Do up your cuffs."

She glanced down at the sleeves, then up at him. Without saying a word, she unfastened the three small buttons on each cuff. He secured the rope tightly, but made sure it pressed on cloth, not skin. Her confusion was as audible as a question. He saw no reason to point out the differences between surviving and being intentionally cruel.

He herded her toward the seat, then lifted her up. The reins rested on the opposite side. Her dress and petticoat lay on the ground where she'd left them. He picked up the garments. Warmth from her body lingered in the fabric. Her scent drifted to him. He inhaled, sealing the fragrance forever in his memory. She wore no floral water, bathed with cheap soap. He inhaled again. Whores always smelled of cigars and whiskey. This woman smelled of something sweet, something— He shook his head. It didn't matter.

With a flick of his wrist, he tossed the dress into the back, then spread out the petticoat on top to dry. With a last look around at the forest, he boarded the wagon and picked up the reins. He clucked at the horse and the animal began to walk.

The woman sat huddled in her corner. She'd pulled on her shawl, but it offered little protection against the temperature. The sun was already moving toward the west; the day was as warm as it was going to get.

"There's a blanket," he said, jerking his head slightly.

She looked over her shoulder and saw it resting on the straw behind the seat. "Thank you." She sounded surprised.

And why not? He was a stranger to her. He'd threatened to kill her. Up here, farmers wouldn't need to keep loaded guns at their side. The war had left the land untouched, the families missing men, but not their ways of life.

She half turned in her seat and awkwardly reached for the blanket. Her tied hands made it difficult to unfold the length of wool, let alone pull it around her. She shook it several times, but only succeeded in startling the horse.

Colter grimaced and grabbed the blanket from her. With a quick impatient gesture, he flung it across her shoulder. She tugged the blanket tightly around her body, then scooted closer to the far edge of the seat.

He terrified her. Better for both of them, he thought, forcing himself to listen to the noises of the forest. The horse walked on. For almost two hours the clip-clopping of the hooves and the rustling of unseen animals soothed his racing thoughts.

He knew how Petty had tracked him this far. He'd used an army scout. Elijah S. Gant. He was one of the best trackers in the army, hell, in the country. Colter should know; he'd taught the man. Which meant he knew how Gant worked. Not much of an advantage, because his former student knew how he worked as well.

The odds were even. If eight against one could be considered even. So where did that leave him? With an old farm horse, a wagon with no cover, and a woman who'd turn him in first chance she got. Getting rid of her would make his life a whole lot easier.

"What are you going to do with me?" she asked, reading his mind for the second time that day.

He snapped the reins and urged the horse into a trot. They couldn't travel too many more hours today. Might as well get as far away from town as possible. First chance he got, he'd turn north and then—

"Aren't you going to answer?"

He picked up his hat from the seat and set it on his head.

"Those men," she said, her voice quiet as if she feared they were still nearby. "They're after you. What did you do?"

He pulled his hat lower.

"Aren't you going to say anything?" she asked. A tremor rippled through her words. "I can't not know. What are you going to do with me? Where are we going? Are you going to kill me? I don't even know your name." She paused and gulped. "Let me go. I won't tell anyone about you. I swear. Leave me here. I'll probably get lost and die in the cold tonight. You won't have to worry about me anymore. Just say something!"

He raised his leg and rested his heel on the top of the footboard. After transferring the reins to his left hand, he placed that elbow on his knee and turned toward her.

Her long hair fanned over the blanket. The sun caught the strands, turning them to a mantle of gold. Soft, he thought with surprise. Her hair looked soft and sweet smelling. Had he ever touched a woman's hair? By accident, perhaps, as he took his pleasure. But never on purpose.

Her eyes darted away, then back. Weariness bracketed her mouth.

"James," he said.

"James? James what?"

"Colter James."

She repeated the name twice, as if seeing how it fit, then she nodded. "I'm Margaret Anne Bishop."

He raised one brow.

"Maggie," she said.

He shifted until he faced front again. Maggie. He didn't like knowing her name, though it didn't matter if she knew his. If Petty ever found her, a description would be enough.

The horse trotted on, its hooves thunking on the frozen ground. In another few weeks this trail would be thick with mud. But between then and now there would be several storms, probably even snow. He shot the woman a glance.

"What?" she asked, catching his eye.

He shrugged. "You're alone."

"So? Why does everyone say that?"

"Everyone?"

"The scout for the wagon train. And the other people heading west. Most of them didn't want me along. They said they had no use for a woman traveling alone. That I'd be a burden. That I should wait for my family." She sighed and let her chin drop to her chest.

"You have no family."

She stiffened. "That's not true," she said, the slight tremor in her voice belying her words. "I've got lots of relatives. In fact, they're expecting me to meet up with them in a couple of days. They'll come looking for me."

He didn't reply.

"If you let me go, I won't—"

"You're lying."

She hunched down lower on the seat. "If you think I don't have family," she whispered, "you'll kill me."

"Family or not isn't going to make a damn bit of difference."

"Is that supposed to make me feel better?" Her voice cracked on the last word.

"No."

"Then why'd you say it?" Another quaver shook her voice.

"It's the truth."

He looked more closely. A tear trickled down her cheek. She brushed it away quickly and straightened.

He'd seen women cry before. When the battles had raged close to farms and small towns, they'd huddled in their homes until the fighting was through. Then they viewed the scarred earth, the dead, the dying, and their sobs had painted the churned battlefields with all the colors of pain and loss. He'd watched wives move through the bloated remains of the fallen, searching for a familiar face, pausing over a mangled body to wonder if it had once been a loved one. He'd seen widows and mothers trying to dig a single grave in a field beside a house. Once he'd stood on the edge of a clearing while a pregnant woman and eight children buried a cloth-wrapped body. Neither money nor wood could be spared for a coffin. All they had to offer was their tears.

"I'm not afraid of you," Maggie said, her chin raised defiantly. Dampness darkened her lashes. Her full lips pulled into a straight line.

Despite the scratches and dried blood on her face, despite her tied hands and her bruises, she sat stiffly on the seat. She was his prisoner and yet she spat at him like an angry kitten.

"You should be."

She flinched as if she'd been struck, but she didn't back down. "Why? Are you going to kill me later?"

Was he? Not if she didn't give him reason. But she didn't need to know that. He settled more comfortably on the seat and stared straight ahead.

"It'll be dark soon," he said. "We'll make camp at the next stream."

"Camp?"

"Eat. Sleep. Rest the horse."

"Out here?"

"You're the one who was taking this open wagon to Missouri. Where did you plan to spend the nights?"

"That's not the same thing."

Sebastian's ears cocked toward them, as if he were following the conversation. Colter relaxed slightly, knowing the horse would alert him to strangers.

"Those men," she said softly. "Won't they be looking for—"

He glanced at her. He wasn't sure what she saw in his expression, but it was enough to silence her.

"If you do anything to give me away, I'll slice you open from belly to throat and leave you to drown in your own blood."

She gasped and shrank back as far as the seat sides would let her. "I won't give you away."

"Just so we understand each other."

"I understand," she whispered.

They rolled through a shaft of sunshine. The alternating light and shadow highlighted then shaded the woman's features. But even the forest gloom couldn't erase the lines of misery and terror. Her hands opened and closed convulsively. Her body shook slightly. He knew men who'd cracked under less pressure. But this lone woman hadn't.

An emotion stirred within him, dusty and unfamiliar at first, but then he recognized it. Respect. It had been a long time since someone had surprised him like this woman. Years. The feeling had been dormant since Alexander had risked his life to save a stranger.

Colter couldn't let the woman go. Scaring her was an easy way to keep her in line. Fear was the first rule of war. He closed his ears to the sound of her rapid breathing and closed his mind to the voice that reminded him the war was long over.

# Chapter 4 ═══════════════

Maggie shrugged off the blanket and stared at the small clearing. In less than an hour it would be dark. The man—Colter James—unhitched Sebastian and led him to the narrow stream a few feet away.

Now, she told herself. Now, while his attention was on the horse. He wouldn't notice if she jumped off the side and made her way into the trees. And froze to death, she thought as she rose slowly to her feet. Every muscle in her body ached. What hadn't been pulled when the wheel caught her dress had been jolted or scraped by her jump off the wagon and her aborted escape attempt. Joints had stiffened during the afternoon and bruises swelled while the cold seeped through to her bones. Despite the thick blanket, she hadn't been able to get warm. If she survived, later that night she would find an opportunity to get away. For now, she was too tired, too sore, too hungry, and too defeated.

She grabbed the side of the wagon with both hands, wishing he'd untied her before seeing to the horse. With her wrists bound, it was difficult to brace herself for the jump down. She shifted her weight forward awkwardly and crouched.

"Hold it!" he called.

Colter left Sebastian drinking at the stream and walked quickly toward her. Before she could figure out what he was going to do, he swept her up in his arms and set her on the ground. When she gained her balance, he released her.

She nodded her thanks, not daring to speak. If she said anything, her voice would shake. The shaking would remind her she was a prisoner. The questions—what to do next, what would become of her—would begin, and this time she might not be able to shut them out. Better to be silent. At least then she could pretend not to be afraid. He remained in front her. She could feel his stare, but didn't dare raise her gaze past the middle of his chest. She couldn't best him physically, and the image he'd painted an hour before, her cut-open body lying alone and in agony, remained fresh.

Colter took both of her tied hands in his. She wanted to protest, to pull back and demand he not touch her, but she saved her strength. There was a greater battle to be fought if he tried to bed her.

"These must hurt," he said, uncurling her fingers and studying the dirty scrapes across her palms.

"Not much."

He held her firmly, but without causing pain. Rough calluses brushed against the back of her hands. He could have crushed her bones, she thought, noting the strength in his long fingers. It was early spring, yet he was tanned, as if the skin had been permanently darkened. By contrast, her fingers looked slender and fragile, though the redness and blisters showed she'd spent little of her life idle.

"Your face is scratched." He released her fingers only to reach up toward her cheek.

She stiffened and turned her face away. He paused with his hand outstretched, then cupped her chin and forced her to look at him. Again he held her securely, but didn't hurt her.

"I'll untie your wrists."

Hope flared, though she fought to keep it from showing. With her hands free she would be more mobile. When she'd regained her strength, she would—

"Give me your word you won't run away."

He'd pulled his dark hat low on his forehead, but she could still see his eyes. They stared into her soul and offered little except the promise of violence in return.

"You have my word."

The lie tasted bitter. Her mother had taught her to tell the truth, she thought. But surely this didn't count.

Working quickly, he unfastened the ropes at her wrist and tucked them into his coat pocket.

."Don't go out of my sight," he said, turning to Sebastian.

She rubbed her wrists and stretched her fingers. In her gray dress, the long sleeves protected her skin from the rope. She recalled how he'd made sure she fastened the cuffs before he tied her up. Why had he bothered?

She glanced around the clearing. The trail lay to her left, the stream in front. Behind and to her right were thickets of trees and bushes. She wouldn't try to make her escape until nightfall. But there were other things she needed to take care of.

"I must—" She paused, not sure what to say. "I'll just go over here for a few minutes," she said cautiously, moving toward the screen of growth.

"Don't go anywhere."

He led the horse to a patch of new grass and hobbled him for the night. Maggie shifted her weight from foot to foot. "I'm not running away," she said sharply. Heat rose to her face. Why was she making it so difficult?

Colter rose and approached her. When he'd first threatened her, she'd been sitting in the wagon. Since then, she hadn't had much of a chance to think about his height. With darkness rapidly falling, her body aching, her stomach rumbling, and her bladder full, she realized he towered over her. The top of her head barely skimmed his chin.

"You need to relieve yourself," he said flatly.

She resisted the urge to deny the truth and offered the barest nod.

"This way." He walked toward the trees on her right.

"What?" He couldn't mean to accompany her.

"Follow me."

"But I can't—"

"Do you have to go or don't you?"

"I—"

He stopped and spun to face her. "You're not going into the forest by yourself."

"Why? I won't get lost."

"I don't trust you."

The heat in her cheeks flared hotter. "I gave you my word."

"I know."

The insult hit her like a slap. "Mr. James, I assure you I do not give my word lightly." She conveniently ignored her plans to escape that night.

"Right." With that, he resumed walking.

Maggie hesitated a moment, then picked up her skirts and hurried after him. About a hundred feet from the clearing, Colter stopped and pointed toward a tree. "On the other side of that tree."

"What?"

"I'll be right here." He folded his arms over his chest.

Maggie felt her mouth drop open. "But you can't mean to stand there and watch!"

"Take it or leave it."

"I'll leave it."

Before she could take a step back to camp, he grabbed her arm. "Don't be a fool.

"You're embarrassed." He spoke the words softly, as if the possibility had just occurred to him.

She stopped without turning around. "Of course." She closed her eyes and sighed. "Please."

"I won't look."

She glanced over her shoulder, but Colter James was staring up at the tree branches above them.

"Do you promise?" she asked.

He glared at her then, as if warning her not to push her luck. She gathered her tattered dignity around her and moved toward the tree he'd pointed out. The wide base offered a modicum of privacy, but hardly erased the fact that a man stood less than ten feet away. But need overcame her fear.

"I'll hear you if you try to run," he called out.

"I'm done." She stepped from behind the tree.

He looked at the sky and frowned. "It'll be dark soon. We need to take care of your cuts and get a fire started."

As calmly as that. As if this sort of thing happened every day. Perhaps to him it did. She remembered the men who had come after him. The stocky one who had touched the nursing mother's breast. So far Colter James had not molested her in any way, but it would be night soon—and it was in the darkness that true beasts stalked their prey.

As they made their way toward the camp Maggie tried to memorize her surroundings. If she made her escape tonight, she'd have to move quickly and silently. He'd expect her to head toward town, so it made sense to go in another direction. But she wasn't sure what settlements lay around here. She could walk for days and never find a farm or village, and freeze to death or starve.

All thoughts of escaping fled when she stepped into the clearing and saw the stream. She'd had nothing to drink since morning. Instantly, her mouth grew dry and her throat scratchy. She hurried toward the flowing water.

Clumps of snow lined the muddy bank. A few chunks of ice floated along the surface. Her feet sank into the wet earth and she glanced down and frowned. Colter walked right up to the edge of the stream and squatted down. He was wearing boots, of course. After placing his hat on the ground behind him, he leaned forward and dipped his large hands deep into the coolness and brought handfuls of the liquid to his mouth.

Maggie moved upstream a couple of feet, stepping carefully on some small rocks to try and avoid most of the mud. The water was more shallow here. With one hand, she held her skirts out of the stream. She bent down and used the other to scoop up her drink. Her hair fell over her shoulder and the ends trailed into the stream, but she didn't care.

The first taste, icy cold and almost sweet, coated her tongue and numbed her lips. The second soothed her throat. She drank slowly at first, then faster and faster as if she had to fill herself before she was pulled away. Nothing had ever been this wonderful. A single drop clung to the side of her mouth. She licked it away with her tongue. Water splashed on her hem and her hair blew against her. She smiled. Her fingers dangled in the stream. She could stay here forever.

"Don't drink too fast," Colter said.

She turned toward him. In those few seconds of pure-
ly sensual pleasure, she'd forgotten about her situation.
"Why?"

"You'll get sick. Take a break, then drink more in a few
minutes. We should see to your hands and face anyway."

"I'll be fine." She looked down at her palms. She flexed
her fingers and winced at the pain.

"Come here."

She moved slowly, one step at a time, until she stopped
where he indicated. The fear returned, heavy and thick like
a cape that weighed her down.

He pulled a faded red kerchief from an inside jacket
pocket and dipped it in the water. "Your face," he said
as he reached toward her cheek.

Maggie froze in place. "I can do it."

"You won't be able to see what you're doing."

The damp cloth pressed against her skin. Instantly it
burned. She flinched. He paused.

"Go ahead," she said, through a tightened jaw.

Each blot stung. This time she forced herself to be still.
She'd rather die than show weakness.

Their close proximity again pointed out the difference in
their heights. Her eyes were level with his throat. Dark
whiskers rode the underside of his jaw, then stopped. His
coat hung open. She breathed in cautiously, remembering
how Edward would go months in winter without bathing.
By spring, his odor filled the house. But this man smelled
of horse and earth, soft scents pleasantly bound together by
breezy night air.

Colter worked efficiently. And gently, she realized as
he wiped a spot beside her mouth. She wondered what he
thought as he ministered to her. Why he bothered.

"There." He put one finger under her chin and tilted her
face toward the rapidly fading light.

"Thank you," she said, stepping back from him.

Their eyes met. She searched his quickly, praying she
would not find desire. She glanced down, unsure if her
prayers were answered. As always, the steely gray depths
gave nothing away.

"You know how to start a fire?" he asked.

"I've been cooking since I was a child."

His grunt indicated he was unimpressed. "There's plenty of wood here in the clearing. Put it there." He motioned to a dry spot on the far side of the wagon. "You have matches?"

"Of course."

He walked off without saying another word.

Maggie moved stiffly, every aching muscle protesting her arduous day. She gathered the wood beside the stream, careful to keep her now clean palms free of splinters. Colter searched through the wagon and found Sebastian's blanket and supply of grain.

After she'd collected enough wood, she piled dry leaves and twigs together, then collected the glass bottle containing the matches.

The breeze that had followed them all day whipped up suddenly, snapping the corner of her shawl and sweeping her hair across her face. After brushing it away, she glanced around the camp. She needed to get her hair out of her way. He'd spread out his wet kerchief on the side of the wagon to dry. She couldn't use that. Somehow asking for the use of the ropes he'd tied her with seemed like tempting fate.

She'd lost all her hairpins during the wild ride. There were extras tucked in a corner of the trunk, but she had a feeling that pinning her hair up again would be a waste of time. Better to tie it back and be done with it.

Maggie stared down at the petticoat still stretched out on top of her damp wool dress. One of the ruffles fluttered in the wind. She set the matches back in the wagon and fingered the white cotton. That would do fine. She tugged on the ruffle, but the tiny stitches didn't budge. She'd sewn this herself; she should feel some measure of pride at her workmanship.

Before she could yank the seam again, the man appeared at her side. He moved with the silence of a predator.

"What are you doing?" he asked.

"I need a length of cloth to hold my hair back."

He pulled the knife from his boot and sliced off a foot of the ruffle, then handed her the fabric and put the weapon away. "Start the fire."

Apprehension made her fingers clumsy as she tied the knot. After gathering the bottle of matches, she hurried to her stack of leaves and twigs.

The cork was stubborn at first. She worked it back and forth until it finally came loose with a pop. She shook a match onto her palm, then set the bottle on the ground next to her. After lighting the match, she held it to the kindling. The dried tinder caught immediately. The breeze swept around her and stirred up the tiny pile. She cupped her fire, protecting it, then blew gently to fan the flames. They stretched up, sipping her breath, then flickered and died.

"You blew too hard." He stood across the clearing, with his hands on his hips and his feet braced on the frozen ground. Despite the rapidly falling temperature, his coat hung open. "You sure you know what you're doing?"

"Yes." She gathered more leaves and another match. It took her three tries, but she managed to get the fire going.

When the flames crackled around the logs, Colter took a bucket from the back of the woman's wagon and returned to the stream. He picked up his hat and set it on his head, then filled the bucket and carried it to the fire. She sat where he'd left her, huddled by the burning wood. Her body shook slightly and she held her hands out for warmth.

What the hell was she doing out here all alone? he wondered. Maybe in the wagon train, with other people around to help, she might have survived, but on her own, she would be hopeless.

He kicked a large rock over to the fire and moved it into the flames. After setting the bucket on top, he looked around until he saw a fallen log.

"Stand up," he said.

She obeyed without question, although her movements were slow and awkward, as if every muscle hurt. He knew the feeling. She was stubborn, but she wasn't a complainer.

He thumped the side of the log with the heel of his boot.

"What are you doing?" she asked.

"Getting us something to sit on. The ground's still frozen. But I don't want some critter crawling out to spoil my dinner."

"Critter?" She turned her head from side to side, searching in the rapidly growing shadows. "Such as?"

He almost smiled. "Nothing big enough to do more than scare you."

She visibly relaxed. "Can I help?"

"Start supper."

He bent down and began to push the log toward the fire. It resisted at first, then it rolled across the uneven ground. About two feet from the flames he stopped and anchored it with a small rock at each end.

"I don't have much," Maggie said as she looked through her supplies.

"I know." He watched her pull a couple of cans out of her wagon. "You planning to hunt for your meals?"

She shook her head. "I paid extra when I joined the wagon train. They promised to supply me with a portion of whatever they hunted."

"You believed them?"

"Of course." She looked surprised. "Why would they lie?"

"Ever occur to you they might have brought several weeks' supplies with them? They might not have hunted right away."

She measured out a bowl of flour. "I know people brought smoked meat and bacon. But I couldn't afford—" She busied herself closing the bag of flour. "I was planning to get by."

"I'll hunt tomorrow. Tonight dried meat will have to do."

The sun dropped behind the trees. A faint glow still lit the sky, but most of the light came from the fire. She stood on the far side of the wagon. Her features blurred in the shadows.

"Will I still be with you tomorrow?" she asked softly, as if she feared the answer.

# Chapter 5 ═══════════════

Colter ignored her question. "If you're going to make biscuits, get started. I'll handle the coffee."

She picked up her bowl and a wrought-iron bake pan, then walked the few steps to the fire.

Colter swore under his breath. He didn't need any of this trouble. Petty and his men were close. The only reason he hadn't insisted on a cold camp was that Petty and Gant would assume he'd get as far away as possible. Even if they thought he was in the area, once they saw wagon tracks, they'd keep going. They knew the rule: Colter James would rather kill a man than travel with him. For once, his reputation for being the meanest, coldest son of a bitch in the army might save his hide.

So what the hell was he doing traveling with a woman?

He grabbed the coffeepot and stalked off to the stream. After filling the pot, he stood on the bank and watched the sky darken. Slowly, the stars began to appear. He studied the constellations, using their placement in the early-spring evening to confirm his location. They said heaven was north of north. He didn't believe in heaven. Only in hell. And hell was a six-by-six prison cell. No window, no light. No freedom. Not that he would spend any time in prison if Petty found him. Colter knew the major would have him dancing at the end of a rope. Orders were orders.

The sounds of the forest changed as the night animals appeared to investigate their surroundings. The snufflings and low hoots reassured him. There was danger in silence.

41

He should return to camp. The smell of the baking biscuits drifted to him and made his stomach growl. If he
stayed long enough, maybe the woman would run off and
he could forget about her. But she wouldn't; not yet. She
was too cold and hungry to stray far from camp. He'd have
to go after her if she did run. They were still too close to
town. She could make it back, and if she did, she could
send a message to the nearest military post. They'd notify
Petty and he'd be on his way to a hanging.

The woman was right. It was his own fault for picking
her wagon.

He returned to the camp and added coffee to the pot, then
set it in the fire. She sat on the log and opened a can.

"It's corn," she said.

"Fine."

"The biscuits are almost ready."

He pulled out his saddlebags and removed two pieces of
dried meat. The fine leather bags stamped with his initials
reminded him of the saddle he'd lost. He'd spent a month's
pay, ordered it special from Mexico. Still, he could get
another one. It was the horse that was irreplaceable.

The vision of Siren, proud, strong, spirited, pulling some
farmer's plow, made him cringe. Maybe she'd find her way
to someone who would appreciate her. But no one else
would know how many times she'd saved his life. How
her nose for trouble had made her shy away at just the
right moment so the bullet whizzed past his body instead
of through it. He'd had two horses shot out from under him
in the first three years of the war. Siren had been a gift. A
well-bred mare straight from a South Carolina plantation,
saved for the master and stolen for the enemy.

"The biscuits are done."

Colter returned to the fire and sat at the opposite end of
the log. Maggie used his kerchief to grasp the pan and drag
it off the heat.

"I've only got one plate," she said, motioning to the lone
tin plate resting on the log between them.

He shrugged and dropped a strip of meat in the center.

"And one fork."

He pulled out his knife. "Not a problem."

"But the corn."

He took the can and dumped half onto her plate. "What's left?"

"Where do you want your biscuits?"

He pierced one on the end of his knife. "Anything else?"

She shook her head.

He bit into the biscuit. The hot bread threatened to burn his mouth and he swallowed quickly. He blew on the remaining section, then tasted. Light, fluffy. Nothing like the hard lumps of dough he usually choked down. He chewed slowly. When he finished, he looked to see how many were left. Only then did he become aware of the woman watching him.

"Not bad," he admitted, reaching for the coffeepot and pouring them each a cup.

"There's more." She offered the pan again.

He took another biscuit and was surprised to see a slight smile curving the corner of her full mouth.

"Have you been on the road long?" she asked.

"Why?"

"Just making conversation. I've been traveling several days, Mr. James. I'm a little tired of my own company. Don't you ever feel the need to talk to someone?"

"No."

She took a tiny bite of the dried meat. After chewing it a moment, she grimaced and put the rest of it back on her plate.

"We're having nice weather," she said, trying again.

He grunted.

"I noticed a few of the men after you were in uniform. Did you serve in the army?"

He glared at her. She seemed unaffected.

"My brother-in-law stayed out of the fighting as long as he could," she said. "He joined the volunteer fire department. That gave him a deferment for a time. But in the end he had to go."

"Everybody fought," Colter said.

"So you *were* in the military." Her voice rang with triumph.

He scooped up another knifeful of corn. That bit of news was less than useless.

"What did you do?"

He didn't answer.

"You have saddlebags. Therefore you must have owned a horse. The cavalry? Did you leave before you were mustered out? Can't you go back? I'm sure they'd understand. You could—"

"I killed people."

"What?"

"When I was in the army. If someone asked too many questions, I killed him."

"I— Oh! I—" She saw him eyeing the last biscuit and grabbed it for herself. "You're trying to scare me. It's not going to work."

He knew he could reduce her to a trembling mass of fear in less than a heartbeat. He didn't. He admired her spirit. He might have had to kill to stay alive, but he'd never found pleasure in the job. He would let her believe she was safe with him because he hadn't decided she wasn't. If she was strong enough, she just might make it after all.

They finished the rest of their meal in silence. Colter ate the corn from the can, fishing out the kernels with the end of his knife. The coffee chased away the salty dryness of the meat. When he drained the last of his drink, he stretched out his feet and wished for a cigar.

Colter needed a plan. He knew where he was going and about when he had to be there. Petty had an idea of where he was going, but no idea about the timetable.

"I have peaches." Maggie held up a can. "For dessert. Would you like some?"

His mouth watered. Peaches? He'd just spent the winter in flea-bitten hotels, existing on a diet of watered whiskey and dried meat, and she had peaches?

"Sure." He swallowed.

She shook the can. "What did you do in the army?"

His eyes narrowed. He glanced at the can, then at her determined features. Not bad, he thought grudgingly. "Scout."

"I don't understand."

"I scouted for the North. Went south and looked for troop movements, investigated rumors of equipment shipments."

"By yourself?"

"Most of the time."

"Were you ever caught?"

"Once."

"So you know what it's like to be a prisoner."

Their eyes met. The flickering fire shaded everything with red-and-yellow light, illuminating half her face. She pleaded, silently, eloquently. As he refused to give her any sign of remorse, any indication he'd been moved by her words, she drew herself up and stiffened.

"I see," she said.

"No, you don't."

She waited, but he said no more. He thought she might return the can to her wagon. He wouldn't blame her. But she began to open it with maddening slowness. He fought the urge to jerk it from her and pry off the lid with his knife. She finally removed the cover and used her fork to pull out one glistening peach. Then she offered him the can.

Colter wiped his knife on the side of his trousers and reached it inside. The fruit floated in a sugary liquid. He pierced one piece. The sweet scent rose up and he inhaled deeply. He raised his knife quickly toward his mouth and licked off the moisture. The fruit was smooth on the curved outside, rough and meaty where the pit had been removed. He took a bite. Canned fruit never had the flavor of that just picked from the tree, but he hadn't had any kind of a peach in almost two years. He chewed slowly, then, unable to stop himself, quickly finished the rest.

He glanced down at the can, where four more halves floated. He returned them to Maggie, but she shook her head.

"I don't want any more." She made a great show of splashing water from the bucket onto her plate. "I'm full. Go ahead."

Would he, in her position, have been as generous? Easy question, easy answer. No.

When he'd finished his dessert, he stacked more logs by the fire. From the corner of his eyes, he saw her hovering by the edge of camp.

"Go," he said abruptly, the moment of privacy his thanks for the peaches. "I'll count to forty. If you're not back by then, I'll find you. You ever try to sleep hog-tied?"

"No."

"It's damned uncomfortable."

"I understand." She darted into the underbrush.

What was he supposed to do about the woman? He couldn't let her go. Petty was too close. The best solution, the only solution, was to kill her. Simple and easy—she wouldn't even know what happened. But he couldn't. It had nothing to do with her and everything to do with himself. He'd gotten too old, seen too many dead. It wasn't easy anymore. He remembered too much. Besides, she was a woman.

Those dark hours in prison, before he'd escaped, had taught him that he did value life, especially his own. He'd still kill without hesitation . . . if there was a reason. Margaret Anne Bishop hadn't done anything except get in his way.

Unfortunately, if he kept her, he'd be responsible for her. Still, there was no other choice to make. Until he could let her go without risking her life or his neck, he was stuck with her. Though God only knew what he was supposed to do with her.

Maggie hovered in the bush. The cold seeped through her wool dress, through her skin, until her very bones seemed to quake. The iciness she felt had less to do with temperature than it had to do with circumstance. And fear.

He waited. For her. She knew what would happen when she returned to camp. She knew what he wanted. What all men wanted. Closing her eyes did little to erase the memories. The wardrobe doors had prevented her from seeing the horror, but the sounds—she cupped her hands over her ears—nothing could block them out, even now. Her heartbeat thudded loudly, echoing against her palms, but it didn't cover the past. The rustle of bedclothes, her mother's pleading for gentleness, the rhythmic groans, the clink of coins hitting a metal dish.

She thought about praying for escape or, at the very least, strength. She didn't. In the past so many important prayers had been left unanswered. Her plight would be of no concern to the God who had turned His back on her mother and sister.

Slowly, she took her hands from her ears. The night sounds once again intruded. Some winged creature fluttered close to her face and she ducked out of the way. Her heart continued its thundering beat. How afraid could she be and still live? He would come for her. He'd threatened to make her sleep hog-tied. Would she be allowed to sleep at all?

She hadn't gone far from the camp and the scent of the fire led her back. Within ten steps, she could see the flickering flames. Her throat thickened as she tried to swallow. Her mouth grew dry. Colter sat on the log, exactly where he'd been when she'd left. He might not have moved, except— Her gaze darted around the campsite and she saw the two bedrolls laid out by the fire. She took another step, barely daring to breathe, not allowing herself to hope.

"You were long," he said, not bothering to look up.

She stared at him. His hat hid his face from view. The thick coat added bulk to an already broad and strong frame. He could crush her like a mosquito if he chose to. She suspected her life had as much value to him.

"You going to stand there or are you going to lay down?"

His voice startled her into movement. She circled around the camp, keeping as far away from him as she could. When she approached the bedrolls, she saw they were stretched out on either side of the fire, at an angle. Clothing had been folded to provide pillows, and the top of the beds were little more than two feet apart.

Colter rose and began to approach her. Maggie took one step back and then another. She clutched her shawl tighter around her body as if the knitted length of wool would provide protection against him. Her muscles tensed. One of his hands reached into his coat pocket. She scanned the ground for a weapon. A rock, a stout branch, anything.

He pulled out the ropes he'd used earlier. "You going to behave?"

She shook her head wildly. Her hair, tied back with the ruffle from her petticoat, flapped against her shoulders like a lash.

"I won't let you," she cried out, barely able to speak past the lump in her throat. She stumbled backward until a tree halted her progress. Terror clawed at her chest and made it impossible to cry, impossible to breathe.

"What the hell are you squawking about?" He looked from the ropes in his hands to her chest, where her crossed arms and the shawl provided scant protection. He stared at her face, then met her eyes.

The fire was at his back, leaving his expression in shadow, but hers fully exposed. She blinked several times, trying to calm the fear, knowing that emotion would only inflame him. She'd heard the things that men did in the dark.

With a mumbled curse, he reached out and grabbed her wrist. He jerked her forward, forcing her to follow him, until they stood next to her bedroll. Then he dropped her hand.

"Give me your word you won't try to escape."

She stared at him, unable to comprehend the question.

He shook his head impatiently. "I'll tie you up if you don't answer."

"I—I won't run." She spoke softly, forcing the words past the tightness in her chest and throat. An unimportant lie, she told herself, even as she felt guilty. She'd always tried to be truthful. This was different, she told herself. This was about staying alive.

"You move and I'll hear you. You try to run and I'll find you."

She didn't doubt him. "I understand."

He nodded once and stuffed the ropes back into his coat pocket. Turning on his heel, he stepped into the shadows. "Get some rest. We leave at dawn." Then he was gone.

Maggie sank to her knees, ignoring the hard ground and the dampness that instantly began to seep through her Sunday-best dress. Relief came slowly, creeping out like a shy forest creature, not quite trusting of human largess. He didn't— He hadn't— She shook her head, not sure what to believe.

A rustling in the bushes told her of his imminent return. Quickly, she pulled back the blankets and lay down, rolling into a tight ball. Even as she closed her eyes and forced herself not to move, she felt the oilskin he'd put down to protect her from the ground. As he walked past her toward his own bed, she pulled the blanket tighter around her shoulders. Her fingers touched the second layer he'd added. It was the blanket he'd tossed over her while they'd traveled through the forest. She opened one eye, and then the other. Slowly, quietly, she turned toward the fire and looked up.

Their eyes met. He'd removed his hat, and his thick dark hair tumbled over his forehead. He lay on his side, facing her, his weight supported on one bent arm. He reached forward. She gasped and started to slide back. He picked up a log and tossed it onto the fire. Sparks flew up into the black night.

"I've never raped a woman." With that he turned onto his back and shut his eyes.

She allowed herself to relax slightly. Resting her head on her arm, she curled up tighter and tried to get warm. The smell of wood smoke, so clean and comforting, chased away the fragrance of fear. He hadn't touched her. Who was this man? What kind of animal taunted, then cared for its prey? She fingered the extra blanket he'd given her. Why hadn't he killed her? There'd been ample opportunity. After all the miles they'd driven today, he could easily fire a gun without being discovered.

The image of her dead body lying on the edge of the road wasn't pleasant and she pushed the thought away. On the fire, a log hissed and cracked in two. One half rolled to the edge of the flames. The new configuration allowed her to see him clearly. Already his breathing had deepened, as

if he'd fallen asleep. She trusted that as much as she would
trust a quiet but wounded bear.

Firelight danced across his features, illuminating them,
then casting them in shadow. Dark hair, carelessly cut,
reflected the light. The strong line of his profile caught
her attention and she studied the straight line of his nose,
the firmness of his jaw. For an animal, he cared for himself
well. No unpleasant odor emanated from him. No grease
tamed his hair. He hadn't shaved in several days, but the
stubble didn't take away from his cleanliness.

She closed her eyes, not wanting to think like that. He
was her captor; he might still kill her. Despite her efforts
not to look at him, she continued to see him in her mind, as
if his form had been imprinted on the inside of her eyelids.
She shook her head angrily. This accomplished nothing, she
reminded herself. She'd promised herself not to be afraid.
What was important was her escape. How was that to be
managed?

She thought about the men she'd seen riding after him.
The stocky one who had touched the nursing mother's
breast. She shuddered. The taller one, Wilson, who had
tried to flirt with her. At least eight against one. Colter
James didn't have a chance. Then she recalled his stealth
and cunning. He'd already made one escape from them,
with little trouble. Perhaps *they* were the ones who didn't
have a chance.

# Chapter 6

Maggie hadn't planned to sleep. She'd thought she would lie still until she was sure Colter was asleep, then make her way out of camp. Once she reached the forest, she would be safe; the night was too dark for him to follow.

Instead, she found herself coming slowly awake. It was the cold that roused her. The top blanket had slipped to the ground, leaving her shivering. She blinked several times to clear her vision. The fire burned low. Across the dying flames, her captor continued to rest on his back. His slow, even breathing indicated he slept, but she wasn't sure. With a man like him— She sighed. She had no choice but to try now. He had looked weary from their journey and from whatever had gone on before. She could only hope that the men who chased after him had tired him.

She sat up and pulled the blankets around her shoulders. Several pieces of wood sat in a pile. She added two to the fire. Better to keep him warm than have him wake from the cold as she had. The logs cracked. She held her breath, but he didn't stir. She counted to a hundred.

The flames illuminated a small portion of the clearing. She could just make out the large shadow that was Sebastian. As her fingers flexed and released with her nervousness, she stared at the horse. If she could unhobble him, she would be able to escape without fear of Colter catching her. With the men after him, he wouldn't dare stay in one place very long. In a couple of days she'd be able to come back for her wagon. Then she could start her journey to Missouri.

She rose quietly. Keeping the blankets around her, she took a single step and listened. His breathing didn't change. Her heart thudded so loudly in her ears, she wondered that she didn't wake the dead. She took a second step. The night noises continued. The thought flashed through her mind that she had, for the first time in her life, broken her word.

The moment of conscience made her stumble on her third step. She saved herself before she completely lost her balance. Her quick exhale created a small cloud of fog. She froze and listened to the night. Better to be alive and a liar than dead and honest, she told herself. It wasn't her nature to surrender. Perhaps that is why she had survived and her sister had died. She shook her head. Her sister had died because she hadn't had the strength to bear Edward's stillborn child. Right and wrong seemed so simple on Sunday morning, she thought, remembering how she'd pleaded with her sister to leave her husband and come west. Alice had refused, smiling through her pain. "My place is at my husband's side," she said, even as her lifeblood had flowed away.

Maggie pulled her blankets tighter around her shoulders. Her fingers clutched the top covering, the one Colter had provided. She could lie but she couldn't steal. She let his blanket fall to the ground as she took another step.

The double click of the pistol stopped her instantly.

"Going somewhere?"

She spun to face him. Colter had raised himself up on one elbow. The light of the fire allowed her to see the gleaming steel of the weapon. The muzzle pointed directly at her heart.

She dropped to her knees. Colter cursed. The harsh words passed over her head. She didn't understand the meaning and she didn't want to. In spite of the cold and the defeat, she felt ashamed. She'd given her word. It made no sense; the man was a killer. But to knowingly lie . . .

She risked glancing up and saw that he'd tucked the pistol into a holster at his side. Her relief was short-lived as he pulled the ropes from his coat pocket.

"I had to try," she said.

"You shouldn't have given your word."

He raised one dark eyebrow and waited. She released the blanket and held out her hands. He secured the ropes around her wrists. Strong fingers pulled the cuffs of her dress to protect her skin. She noted the kindness, but it made no sense to her. She believed that he would still kill her, but the fear that he would take her against her will, at least this night, had faded.

He grabbed her upper arms and hauled her to her feet. After picking up the two blankets, he pushed her toward her bedroll, then stood there until she lay down. He arranged the coverings over her, then returned to his own bed. In the distance, an owl hooted. Colter's breathing deepened and slowed. Life was all around her. Hunters and hunted. She felt as alone as a single star in a black night sky. Each moment she was a prisoner took her farther and farther away from all that she knew. She began to wonder if she would ever find her way back.

Colter stirred the fire and tossed on another log. After filling the pot with water, he added coffee then set it next to the bucket already heating. He worked silently, from habit rather than design, having made no decision about waking or not waking the woman. He did his best to ignore her. Yet time after time his gaze strayed to where she lay curled up under the blankets.

Only the top of her head and part of her face were visible. A few strands of dark blond hair drifted across her forehead and the makeshift pillow. The cold, or some dream, made her shiver slightly as she slept. The restless stirring of her arms indicated that even in sleep she resisted the ropes.

She was his prisoner.

Colter sat on the log and stared into the fire. It was all going wrong. They should never have found him in Chicago. He should never have had to sacrifice Siren to make his escape. And the woman—what the hell was he doing with her? He'd never taken anyone prisoner before.

During the war he killed those who got in his way and left alive those who didn't. He rewarded his helpers and ignored the innocent. He should never have taken her wagon.

Other options had been available, if only he'd taken the time to think them through. He couldn't let her go and he wouldn't kill her. He thought about the contents of her wagon and shook his head. The stupid woman should be grateful he'd come along; she wouldn't have survived a week on her own, even with a wagon train. He'd saved her from the grave and saddled himself with a problem that could have him dancing from a short rope on a tall tree.

She stirred slightly and he looked back at her. Her eyelids fluttered, then opened, revealing irises the color of a spring sky. Clear blue for once, untainted by fear. She blinked, confused, then sucked in her breath.

He crouched down beside her and waited. Using one elbow as leverage, she raised herself into a sitting position and held out her hands to him. He untied the ropes. She started to pull her hands back, but he stopped her with a firm grip on her forearm. Beneath his palm, her muscles leaped and stiffened. Her fingers curled into tight fists. He didn't bother to glance at her. Instead he unbuttoned one cuff of her light gray dress and rolled up the sleeve.

Rope burns had formed in the night. They looked red and tender. He released that hand and turned to the other. Again he unbuttoned the cuff and rolled back the sleeve. These burns weren't as raw or as wide. On the inside of her wrist, where the rope hadn't rubbed away any skin, her pulse thudded visibly. He released her, grabbed the ropes, and rose to his feet.

"The coffee's almost ready," he said, and walked to his bedroll.

He heard her stand, then walk toward the bushes. He gathered up his blankets and the oilskin, then moved to do the same with hers. Her scent remained behind, a combination of cheap soap and fear. And something else, he thought, rolling the blankets into a neat bundle. The unique fragrance of her skin. Not unpleasant, perhaps vaguely pleasing. Still, the scent troubled him until he realized he was reacting to what was missing rather than to what was there. Unlike the whores he'd bedded, she didn't smell of smoke and sweat, stale passion and sickly-sweet perfume.

The coffee boiled. He poured them each a cup, then reached for his saddlebags. After removing a small bar of soap and his razor, he poured some heated water into a bowl. He left the rest in the bucket for her along with a clean rag, and made his way to the stream.

Ice clung to the bank. He broke through the new patches, then squatted down and lathered the soap. He shaved without a mirror, having learned the hard way that the glint of reflected sunlight could be seen from miles away. He feared prison more than cutting his own throat. The war had forced him to become proficient at surviving. He dropped his coat onto the ground away from the stream, then stripped off his shirt and splashed the water over his chest and arms. After lathering the soap, he cleaned himself, rinsed, and shook himself off. The cold air raised bumps on his flesh. He rubbed dry, then quickly slipped into his wool shirt and pulled on his coat. The concern from the night before, even the regret, was lost in the rightness of being alive.

After returning the razor and soap to his saddlebags, he picked up his cup of coffee and turned toward the fire. He froze. The woman—Maggie, he thought, for the first time using her name—sat with her back to him. Her long hair concealed her body. She hadn't removed her dress, but from the alternating thrusts and juts of her elbows, her ablutions were no less thorough. At last she dropped the rag into the bucket. After buttoning her dress, she picked up a hairbrush.

He sipped the coffee and stared. With long strokes she swept the bristles through the gold-blond length. She had to tilt her head to reach the very bottom. The ends dangled to her waist. Sunlight caught the handle of the wooden brush, then moved to caress the swaying strands. She moved rhythmically, lifting the brush and pulling it down. Soft, he thought. Her hair would be soft and smooth as the

belly of a fawn. The fingers of his free hand curled toward
his palm.

He'd never seen a woman brush her hair. He knew he
must have watched his mother, but she'd died so long ago
that all his memories had been lost. The horrors of war left
room for little else but pictures of suffering and death.

He'd never married, never courted, never bedded a lady.
Whores didn't brush their hair while a customer spent hard-
earned coin. He'd seen and touched and tasted the most
intimate parts of a woman—for a price. A time or two a
certain brunette in Washington had offered him a second
poke at no cost save her own pleasure. But the ritual of a
woman's daily grooming was a mystery.

Maggie switched her brush to her other hand and began
to stroke the left side of her head. Colter continued to
watch. He didn't know the rules of polite society, suspected
that she would object to his perusal, but didn't care. She
was his prisoner.

Even as the thought formed he recalled his own imprison-
onment— the way they'd stripped him naked, beaten him,
and left him shivering in his cell. He felt the rage at the
lack of freedom, the outrage at the indignity, the frustration
of not claiming death on his own terms. He turned away,
set his coffee cup on the edge of the wagon, and walked
to the horse.

"Whoa, boy." He patted the animal's face, soothing him.

"His name is Sebastian."

Colter nodded. "You called him that yesterday."

"Thank you for the coffee."

She spoke quietly. He didn't have to strain to hear the
words, but she didn't make any effort to raise her voice.
From what he'd observed, most women liked to talk. Even
those he'd paid for had expected conversation after he'd
taken his release. He continued to stroke Sebastian's face.
But instead of the heat of the horse's thick coat, he felt the
warmth on the inside of Maggie's wrist.

"There's dried meat for breakfast," he said, jerking his
head toward his saddlebags.

"I'll just have coffee."

He moved beside Sebastian and removed the blanket covering him. "You're no good to anyone if you starve."

"What good am I now?"

He looked at her then. She'd pulled her hair away from her face and caught it in a braid. The thick rope hung over one shoulder, tied with the ruffle from her petticoat. Although her face and hands were clean, dirt smudged the bodice of her dress, and mud darkened the hem. She shivered as he studied her. His flash of annoyance was squelched when he realized she was freezing. "Put on your damn shawl and sit by the fire."

"Don't you want me to cook something?"

"No time. We've got a long way to go. If you don't want meat—" He drew in a deep breath. She was his responsibility. It wouldn't do any good not to kill her outright and then let her die slowly because she was too stubborn or too stupid to eat. "Eat something canned."

She moved to the log and sat on the edge, facing the flames, her back to him. "I'm not hungry."

"Son of a bitch."

"You say that a lot. What does it mean?"

Colter scooped out a measure of oats from the bag in the wagon. "Nothing."

"But if it doesn't mean anything, why do you say it?"

"It keeps me from taking out my temper on those around me."

She looked at him over her shoulder. "You mean you're being *nice*?"

He remembered now why he preferred to travel alone. "Yeah. I'm being nice."

Sebastian made quick work of his breakfast. While the horse ate, Colter packed up the few items they'd used. He checked the dress that he'd spread out to dry yesterday. It was still damp, but her petticoat could be worn. He tossed the white ruffled garment over his shoulder, then fingered her dress. His knife had cut away a huge half circle of fabric. Even when the dress was dry, it would be unsightly. He had a feeling that his prisoner would object to wearing it, even if it was warmer than her Sunday best.

"You have needle and thread?" he asked without turning to look at her.

"Yes."

Good. When they made camp later, he would cut up a blanket and she could sew in a piece to fix the skirt. With one quick tug, he pulled a blanket free from her bedroll and tossed it on the wagon seat. After removing two pieces of dried meat from his saddlebags, he walked over to the fire. He held out one. She grimaced and shook her head.

Both pieces went into his shirt pocket. "We're moving out. You got any last business to take care of?"

When he glanced at the bushes surrounding the camp, she flushed and shook her head. "Thank you, I'm fine."

"Here, put this on. It'll help keep you warm." He tossed her the petticoat.

Maggie grabbed the undergarment and looked pointedly from it to him. With a grunt of irritation, he squatted down in front of the fire and turned his head away.

From the corner of his eye he saw her rise slowly and set her coffee cup on the ground and her shawl on the log. He dashed the remaining contents of both their cups and the pot on the fire, then tossed dirt on the dying flames. Anyone with a scrap of tracking ability would be able to figure out how long ago camp had broken. He could only hope Petty and Gant didn't come by. He stared up at the pale sky. The sun had barely risen above the horizon and the forest was in shadow. The way his days had been going, he was due for some good luck.

He glanced back at the woman and swore. She jumped at the sound of his voice.

"Stop staring at me!"

"What the hell are you doing?"

She'd pulled the skirt of her dress up around her waist and was holding it with one hand. The petticoat he'd given her hung around her knees. She used her other hand to try to ease it up and over her other undergarments, but the ruffles underneath kept catching. Near as he could tell, they'd be here another hour if he left her alone.

He surged to his feet. She gasped and jumped back, stepping on one of the ruffles and losing her balance in the process. He leaned forward and grabbed her arm to steady her. She trembled in his grasp.

"Lady, bedding you this cold morning, with my stomach empty and eight men looking to go to a hanging, is the last thing I give a goddamn about."

She blinked twice and looked up at him. "Stop swearing at me. I'm not afraid." She jerked her arm free. "I'm cold."

"The sooner you finish here, the sooner you can be in the wagon, wrapped in a blanket."

"I'm doing the best I can."

"It's not enough." He grabbed her skirt and pulled it up to her armpits. "Hold this."

She tried to loop one arm around the fabric.

"Both hands."

"Sir! I demand—"

"Do it!" he growled in her ear. She did it.

Her breathing increased. If she inhaled any deeper, she was going to pop the buttons down the front of her dress. Indignation radiated from her. Colter almost smiled. If she kept this up, she wouldn't have to worry about being cold. Her temper would keep her warm.

He reached down and took hold of the waistband of her petticoat. Yanking it up to her midsection, he twisted it sharply, freeing the garments underneath. A single ruffle stuck out from below. He shoved his hand down her skirt and smoothed it flat. As his palm brushed against her backside he heard an audible "oof" of air, but she didn't say anything. He pulled the waistband tight and secured the first button.

The warmth of her body burned against his fingers. The unexpected feel of her curves against his palm had made him think of her—for the first time—as a woman. No, he'd thought of her as a woman before. The contact made him aware of her sexually. It was what she'd feared all along.

The second button refused to slide into its hole. He wrestled with it for several seconds, then muttered a complaint about acting like a lady's maid. All the while awareness licked around the edges of his consciousness. Her scent, the narrowness of her waist and back, the heavy skirt resting on his forearms. Damn her. With a quick jerk, the button slid into place.

"Hurry up," he said, allowing his temper to show in his words.

Maggie released her skirts, then swiveled to ease them into place. As she reached for her shawl he pulled the ropes out of his jacket pocket.

She dropped her shawl. "Please don't. I won't run."

"We know what your word is worth. I don't have time for this."

She tucked her hands behind her back. "I swear. Please. I'm sorry about last night. I had to try."

"You'll try again."

"Not today."

Blue eyes pleaded. She bit on her lower lip, her white teeth a contrast to the deep pink of her mouth. He stared at her mouth, the shape, the way the corners turned up slightly. Damn it all.

He took a step toward her. She stepped back.

"Lady," he said, "you can make this easy, or you can make it hard. Argue with me and I'll tie your hands *behind* your back. By the end of the day your shoulders will feel like they've been wrenched out of their sockets. You fight the ropes hard enough and they will have been."

"You're cruel."

"You're not the first to say so."

She stepped back and clutched her hands together at her waist. "No! I'm not a cow to be pulled along behind. I won't let you tie me up. You can't treat me this way. It's not right."

He blinked several times. "Lady—"

"Maggie. My name is Maggie." Her blue eyes flashed defiance.

He moved closer; she moved back an equal amount.

"I don't care who the hell you are," he said softly. She swallowed at his menacing tone. "I don't have time for trouble. You're going in that wagon, and I'm tying your wrists."

"I'll go quietly in the wagon. I'll stay there as long as I have to. But you won't tie me."

Was she stubborn or just plain stupid? Frustration made him wish he could just cuff her and be done with it. But he'd never liked bullies and hadn't felt the need to act like one before. He wouldn't start now.

Her strong façade began to crumble. Her mouth quivered and her hands shook as she laced her fingers together. Two more seconds and she'd acquiesce. She drew in a deep breath. But instead of folding, she tilted her chin up. The first rays of morning sun caught the smoothness of her cheek and the faint dusting of freckles. A single tear hovered at the corner of her right eye. That damn pointed little chin moved a notch higher.

Colter shoved the ropes into his jacket pocket. He tossed her shawl over her shoulders, then took her arm and led her to the wagon.

"Don't make me regret this," he said.

Before she could interfere, he gripped her waist and shoved her onto the seat. Her shawl fell forward. He reached up to push it back in place. His thumb brushed across the side of her breast. She stiffened. Her eyes widened and all the color drained from her heart-shaped face. Heat poured into Colter, racing from that single point of contact and collecting in a hard and growing need. He cursed again.

He stalked away and finished hitching the horse. After taking a last glance around camp, he stepped into the wagon. He didn't want to take the time to erase the signs of their camp completely. Besides, Petty and Gant would expect him to travel alone and on horseback. He glanced over his shoulder at the clear set of footprints. Obviously a man and a woman had spent the night here. The officer and the tracker would take one look at those footprints and move on.

He snapped the reins and the horse began to move forward. Maggie sat on the far edge of the seat, clinging to the side.

"You fall out, the wagon's going to roll over you."

She cast him a questioning glance, then inched toward the middle. He grabbed the blanket between them and threw it over her.

"We're traveling by some farms today," he said. "Don't plan on screaming."

"I won't. I told you, I'll stay as long as I have to. I won't give you away."

He grunted in response. There was no reason to believe her. He had a bad feeling he would regret his moment of softness. Yet even as he tried to ignore her the sweet scent of her drifted to him in the morning air.

She was his prisoner, he reminded himself. Nothing else. He'd killed more people than he could remember, endured more, seen more than any man should. The war had left him empty of anything but the need to live and die on his own terms. He didn't care about the woman. He couldn't. Caring would kill them both.

# Chapter 7 ═══════════════════════

Elijah S. Gant urged his horse forward through the underbrush. Snow lay all around; the chilly morning added an icy cast to the slowly dissolving mush. The frozen hoofprints stood out as crisp cuts on the dirty ground. Colter James had passed this way in the night. Gant squinted against the bright sunlight and shifted in his saddle. At least his horse had, Gant amended. Despite his earlier claim to his superior officer, he no longer thought the escaped criminal rode his prized horse. The hoofprints were deep enough to indicate that the animal carried a large man, but Gant wasn't convinced. Something in his gut told him the horse was riderless. That instinct had saved his ass too many times for him to ignore. He frowned. It was the one thing he and Colter James had in common. That and the fact that they were both damn fine trackers. The best. Now the student hunted the teacher.

Soon, he thought, running his hand down the smooth barrel of the rifle he carried. Soon there would be only one.

"See anything?" Major Petty called from behind.

"Just the trail we were following last night. Looks like he went through the forest, heading south."

"South?" Petty sounded annoyed. "But we've just come from there."

I know, Gant thought. The change in direction had been the first clue that James had abandoned his mount. Up ahead a dark pile in the center of the trail caused him to slow, then stop his horse and dismount. He squatted down and stared at the mound of horseshit. The second clue, he thought triumphantly. He'd been right; James had parted company with his horse. A horse carrying a rider continued moving while it relieved itself. The tidy pile meant the horse had stopped; therefore there wasn't a rider.

"Find anything?" Petty asked, reining in his horse.

Gant stared up at the officer. Despite the weeks they'd been on the trail, the major looked as clean and starched as a store-bought shirt. His boots gleamed from careful polishing, as did his mount. A heavy wool coat hid his blue uniform, but Gant knew the sleeves and pants were perfectly creased. With his thick blond hair and rugged features, he'd been popular with his men and the local ladies. Gant stared at his blue eyes and sucked in his breath. He hated everything about Petty. He would have ignored the major's question, would have dared to show his contempt, but Petty was his superior. Besides, along with shiny buttons, Petty's uniform boasted a row of medals won in battles Gant had done his best to avoid.

"Just that James came this way." Gant poked a stick into the fragrant pile. A tiny wisp of steam escaped. "Not that long ago."

He rose to his feet. No point in telling the other man that the horse was alone. If he played his cards right, he would have James's horse for his own. One thing about the tracker, he had the luck of the devil. Or rather, he'd had it for a time. Gant thought of the small cell Colter James had escaped from. Guess Lady Luck'd had other things to do when her favorite son had been charged with killing all those men. Well, James wasn't going to see the inside of that jail cell again. When they caught him, they would hang him from the nearest tree. Gant mounted his horse, then lovingly stroked the rifle by his thigh. Maybe. Or maybe Gant would shoot him in the gut and watch him die slow. He kicked his horse sharply.

It was past noon when they came into the clearing. A bay mare stood alone under an oak tree and nosed through the snow, searching for food. Three fifty-pound flour sacks rested on her saddle. Behind him, Gant heard Petty swear.

"How does he do it?" Petty asked. "He's always one step ahead of us."

Gant didn't like the grudging respect in the major's tone. "He killed those men and almost got away with it," he said. "That kind always has cunning. He's dangerous. We should shoot him on sight."

"No!" Petty frowned. "No one is going to shoot him unless it's absolutely necessary. My orders are specific. Colter James is to be captured, then hanged by the neck until dead. You understand that, Captain?"

Gant tugged his hat low over his eyes. He waited as long as he could, then answered, "Yes, sir."

Behind Petty, the rest of the men watched the exchange. They all liked and respected Petty. Gant knew he was merely tolerated because of his tracking skills. The men stayed away from him. Except for Zachery. Gant sought out the bareheaded heavyset man. Zachery liked him because Gant let him have his way with the women they found. Zachery preferred good women because it was easy to make them scream. Gant liked watching. Zachery had told him about the nursing mother on the wagon train. About how he'd touched her breasts and felt the warm, moist milk. If they found Colter quick enough, they were going to track down the wagon train and find that woman. Zachery wanted to take her while she nursed her child. He wanted to hear both her and the baby screaming together. Gant wanted to see the fear in her eyes.

He urged his horse forward until his gelding came alongside the bay mare. James's mount looked up from her grazing, but didn't try to run.

"Easy, girl," Gant murmured. He slid off his horse and grabbed her reins. With a quick jerk, the rope tying the flour sacks came loose and they tumbled to the ground. He ran his hands over the custom-made leather saddle. All the way from Mexico, he thought. It was as beautiful as the mare.

"We'll take her with us," Petty said.

"I'll ride her." Gant pulled his saddlebags and the rifle from the other horse.

"Why does *he* get to ride her?" one of the men asked.

"My horse has a bad leg." Gant looked up and dared them to challenge him. The last gaze he met was Petty's. Unlike the other men, the major didn't look away. He seemed to weigh the cost of the mare over annoying his tracker. Gant didn't care what the decision was. Either way he would take the mare. If Petty pissed him off, he would leave and find James on his own.

"Fine." Petty wheeled his horse around to face the direction they'd come. "We have to find his trail again. What do you suggest?"

Gant swung onto the saddle and settled in. The bay perked up her ears as if listening for instructions. Sitting in the other man's saddle, feeling the warmth of his mount between his legs, Gant could taste the victory.

*You think you're better than me, Colter, but I know you. I know you're going to make a mistake, and when you do, I'll be there.* First Alexander's rifle and now Colter James's horse.

Gant smiled and looked at Zachery. "The wagon train. That's where he lost us. We'll pick up the trail there. He's heading north or northwest. We'll find him."

He barely touched his heels to the mare. She leaped forward, her gait strong and sure. Damn, she was a fine animal. The best he'd ever ridden. The sun warmed his back as they headed up the trail. In a few days, maybe a few hours, Colter James would be dead. And his knowledge, knowledge that made Gant lie awake at night shivering in his own sweat, would die with him.

Maggie winced as the wagon rolled over another rut in the rough path and she bumped into the unyielding wooden seat back. Between the ice and snow and the muddy patches of clear ground, the wagon jerked and skidded as much as it moved forward. Beside her, Colter James sat straight, swaying slightly with the movement. He held the reins in his hands and gazed forward while she clung to the sides and darted quick glances all around.

She'd never been in the wilderness before. All her life

she'd been surrounded by some sign of people. First on the farm, then in town when they had lived in Ohio. Even after her sister had married Edward and they'd moved out to be with him, there'd been neighbors within a few miles. But here there was no one. Even the noises sounded different. Louder. Birds flew overhead and unseen creatures rustled in the shadows. The steady clip-clop of Sebastian's trot echoed against the ground.

She stared at the tall oaks and maples that made up the thick forest. Beyond the first few feet of foliage, everything faded into shadow. Occasionally she caught glimpses of snow-covered land that would probably thaw into meadows. But they hadn't passed any signs of life.

He could kill her now and no one would know. No one would hear the gunshot or find her body for weeks, maybe years. She shut her eyes tightly against the picture and prepared to blink back the tears, but they didn't come. The fear that had been her closest companion for the last twenty-four hours seemed to be lifting. That didn't make sense. She glanced at the man. Maybe it did, she thought, studying his strong profile. He'd pulled his hat low over his eyes. His chin jutted forward. From this angle, she couldn't see the scar that bisected his skin there. Either he didn't notice her studying him or he didn't care. He continued to stare straight ahead.

Maybe it did make sense, she thought again. If he'd planned to get rid of her, he would have already done so. And he hadn't tied her up. She flexed her hands and released the blanket so that it fell off her shoulders. The midday temperature had risen above freezing. Even her feet were beginning to thaw. She swallowed against the dryness in her mouth. Her gaze dropped to the canteen on the seat beside them. He hadn't offered and she hadn't asked. She swallowed again.

"Take it," he said.

She looked up at him, but he continued to stare straight ahead. "What?" she asked, her voice hoarse. She cleared her throat.

"A drink. If you're thirsty. That's what it's for."

How did he know what she was thinking? The canteen
lay between them. She worried her lower lip, then reached
out with one hand, prepared to pull back if he made a
move. But he didn't. Her fingers closed around the cold
metal and she drew it to her. After unscrewing the cap,
she wiped the opening with her shawl and took a small
drink. The icy water coated her tongue and throat. It tasted
sweet and clean, despite being in the canteen. She darted
Colter another glance. When he didn't return her look or
make a comment, she raised the container to her lips and
drank greedily.

When she was finished, she wiped the back of her hand
across her mouth. Her stomach growled loudly. Before she
could screw on the top, he reached out to take the canteen
from her.

"Done?" he asked.

"Yes. Thank you."

He drank without wiping it clean. He drank slowly,
tilting his head back and letting the water pour into his
mouth. She watched his throat move up and down as he
swallowed. He'd shaved, she realized with some surprise.
His tanned skin looked smooth. He dropped the empty
canteen onto the floorboard and reached into his jacket
and pulled out two pieces of dried meat. Without saying
a word, he offered her one.

Just the sight of the shriveled beef made her shake her
head. She would rather starve. "No, thank you." But her
stomach had other ideas and rumbled again.

Colter turned his head and glanced at her. "You've got
to be hungry. Are you stupid or just plain stubborn?"

Their eyes met. Instead of the violent stormy gray from
the day before, instead of the cold promise of death, she
saw curiosity. "Just stubborn," she said.

"I thought so." He looked at the meat, then back at her.
And smiled.

She blinked in astonishment. She hadn't seen him smile
before. His lips curved up to reveal white teeth and an easy
grin. Tiny lines creased the skin by the corners of his eyes.
He was handsome, she thought, startled by the realization.

The dark shaggy hair and hollow cheeks still made him
look dangerous, but his smile changed everything. Her
mouth tilted up in return.

"I'll hunt for fresh meat tonight," he said, turning his
attention back to the trail they followed.

"I have more canned vegetables. And peaches."

He nodded. It was as if the smile had never been. But she
didn't mind, Maggie told herself as she pushed the blanket
off her skirt. She didn't mind at all.

They rode for another hour, then Colter suddenly reined
in Sebastian and stared intently at the bushes on the side
of the road.

"What is it?" she asked.

"Quiet!"

He tied off the reins and jumped down from the seat.
After crossing in front of the horse, he crouched down
and studied the ground. Maggie peered past him, trying
to see what he was looking at. There was a low-lying
bush, a grove of trees, a bit of snow, and some decaying
leaves. What could possibly interest him? He rose to his
feet and moved silently into the forest. Within two steps
the shadows swallowed him. Maggie stared after him and
counted her heartbeats to pass the time. Suddenly she sat
bolt upright. He was gone! She could escape!

She slid over to his side of the seat and reached for
the reins. Before she touched the strips of leather, Colter
reappeared at the side of the road. His cold gray stare froze
her in place. He didn't say a word; he didn't have to. The
handsome man who had smiled at her only a short time
before was gone; the hunter had returned.

# Chapter 8

Colter approached her purposefully. Panicked, Maggie tugged at the knot holding the reins secure. He broke into a run. She stood and started to jump out of the wagon. He caught her as she dropped to the ground, grabbing her right arm and forcing it behind her. She screamed at him to release her, then cried out in pain as he jerked her wrist and forearm higher up her back.

"Let me go!" she shrieked.

Her hip bumped against his rock-hard thighs. She jabbed at him with her free elbow. He shoved her against the wagon; her chin barely cleared the rough wood. Her breasts mashed painfully against the side. She kicked out, but he avoided her feet. Before she could catch her breath, he'd tied her hands behind her back. The ropes scraped her bare wrists.

"No!" she screamed. "Let me go!"

"Shut up, dammit." He grabbed her arm and turned her to face him. "You shouldn't have tried to get away."

He pulled her alongside the trail. She stumbled beside him, trying to jerk free. She tripped on a rock. His fingers bit into her arm, digging deeper when she lost her balance. She started to go down, but he hauled hard until she regained her footing. He stopped in front of a sapling. He took another length of rope and looped it around the tree. She squirmed to get away from him, but couldn't break his hold on her arm. What was he doing? He turned her until she faced him and shoved the rope between her bound wrists. The knots at her wrists tightened. He secured her with her back to the tree.

Realization dawned.

"You can't leave me here!" Her voice shook. She stared at the unfriendly wilderness. Dear God, better that he would kill her quickly. "Why? Not like this. You can't!"

"Stop!" he commanded.

She drew in a breath and bit down hard on her lower lip. Her body trembled. Her knees threatened to buckle, then did, and she sank to the ground.

"No," she whispered, staring at the cold snow-covered earth. "No."

Colter leaned forward and took her face in his hands. He raised her chin until she was forced to look at him.

"There is a trail," he said slowly, as if she were half-witted. "Of a wounded animal. Probably a deer. I'm going to find it. We'll have fresh meat tonight. If you're quiet, I won't gag you."

Icy dampness seeped though her clothes and chilled her skin. She stared into his eyes, searching for the man who had smiled, struggling to find a trace of compassion. Nothing, she thought. Nothing but gray darkness and the promise of death. She tried to turn away. His hand held her in place. Strong fingers cupped her chin and grazed her cheek. His thumb brushed against her jawline once, then a second time. She twisted away from the contact.

"Do you understand?"

She nodded.

He looked up at the sun. "I'll probably be an hour. Maybe longer." He unhitched Sebastian and led the horse across the trail and into the trees.

Maggie stared after them, trying to see into the foliage. One second they were there, then they were gone. He'd left the wagon. Panic subsided slowly as the thought penetrated. He'd left the wagon. He *was* going to return to her. She wouldn't die.

Relief made her giddy. She tried to stand, but her knees shook so badly it took her three attempts until she was upright. At last she was able to balance by leaning against the sapling. Her arms ached where he'd held her. The ropes rubbed against her bare skin, but she was safe.

She glanced around the area between the wagon and her tree. Nothing special, she thought. Snow, leaves, small bushes. She walked forward quickly, but was jerked to a halt by the rope. The muscles in her shoulder screamed their protest at being pulled back.

Maggie circled the tree. The loose rope allowed her to travel completely around the sapling, but her forward movement was limited to about three feet. Her fingers couldn't reach either of the knots. He'd thought of everything when he'd secured her. She glanced at the top of the sapling, but the tree grew several feet above her head. She forced herself to walk faster. If she couldn't untie the knots or lift the rope over the top, she was stuck. But at least she was safe for the moment. That's what mattered. When he returned . . . She fought down a shudder. If he chose to abandon her, there was nothing she could do.

The urge to scream built up inside. Maybe someone else would hear. Then she remembered the look in his eyes. If she angered him, he would kill her. She knew that as well as she knew her own name. Maggie sank to the ground and shifted to get comfortable. She wasn't ready to die.

Alice had had such dreams for the future; they both had. Alice was gone; it was up to her to make the dreams come true. Survival was all that mattered. Strength, she told herself. Strength and patience. She glanced up at the sky. She should enjoy this time without Colter James around. At least she wasn't afraid.

Maggie leaned her head back against the tree and closed her eyes. She must have dozed, for when she awoke, the sun had moved far toward the western horizon. The temperature had dropped. Her shawl offered scant protection against the coming night and the blanket was where she'd left it, in the wagon.

The wagon. At least that was still there. She looked all around, but didn't see any sign of Colter or Sebastian. How long had she been asleep? Shouldn't they be back by now?

She tried to stand. Flames of pain shot through her arms and shoulders. Her thigh muscles shook as she forced herself upright. She tugged against the ropes, but the coarse bindings didn't budge.

In the distance something howled. An answering cry from the glade behind her caused her to spin around and peer into the forest. What before had been the rustling of small animals became the purposeful stalking of a hungry predator.

"Colter," she called out softly.

No answer.

Maggie pulled harder against the ropes. The tree shook but didn't bend. The pain in her shoulders increased, as did the chafing on her wrists. She felt moisture trickle down her palms. What if he didn't come back? What if something had happened to him? What if he was dead?

She shivered, but with her hands tied behind her back, there was no way to keep warm. She was hungry and thirsty and scared and hurting. Tears threatened, but she blinked them away.

She heard rustling behind her and spun to face the noise. Something small and furry bounded deeper into the forest. She caught her breath. What if someone else found her? She remembered the men who had searched the wagon train. She remembered the heavyset man—Zachery, the officer had called him—who had touched the woman's bare breast. Another shiver racked her body.

"Colter," she cried out again.

The silence from the trees, broken only by the faint call of a bird, mocked her fear.


The deer had traveled farther than Colter expected. He left Sebastian tied to a tree by a patch of new grass. While the horse fed he moved silently between the trees, following the trail of broken branches and tiny drops of blood. By the hoofprints, he suspected the animal had broken a leg. It wouldn't last the night. The wolves would be circling before the sun had fully set.

He walked quickly, sacrificing silence for speed. The muddy trail showed the animal moving slower and slower as its strength bled away.

He came upon the deer suddenly. It crouched beside a tall oak tree. One leg jutted out awkwardly, bone breaking through the skin. Its whole body shuddered with the effort of each breath. Wide brown eyes flared in panic and pain. It struggled to get to its feet and escape. Colter pulled his knife free and killed the animal quickly. He returned for Sebastian and loaded the deer on the horse's back. The old gelding snorted his displeasure at the smell of blood. Colter patted his face.

"An extra measure of oats tonight," he promised.

Sebastian picked his way through the underbrush. Colter stared up and tried to judge the time he'd been gone. The sun was already descending. The woman would be getting worried, he thought as he picked up his pace. And cold. He thought of the dried meat in his shirt pocket. And hungry. He almost smiled. Stubborn fool. She'd rather starve than eat something she didn't like.

He continued back the way he'd come, but instead of tall trees and snow, he saw again the fear in her eyes as he'd tied her. The unfamiliar cloak of regret folded around him, drawing tighter with each breath. He didn't have the time or the patience to keep tying and untying her. They were certain to come to a farm or some type of settlement. What was he supposed to do with her then?

Hell, what was he supposed to do with himself? He could buy a horse from a nearby farm, but he'd risk being identified to Gant and Petty. He could let the woman go. No. He shook his head. She would turn him in for sure. What reason would she have not to? In her position, he would—

One sound, different from the rustling and murmurs in the forest, caught his attention. He drew Sebastian to a halt and listened intently. There it was. Again.

The cry of a woman. Maggie.

He quickly tied the gelding to a tree and took off at a run. Instead of following his original trail, he angled east so that he emerged from the woods about forty feet back from where he'd entered. Maggie stood where he'd left her. Alone.

He released the breath he hadn't known he'd been hold-

ing. For a moment he'd thought she was in danger. He
stepped closer. She pulled on the ropes that held her fast.
Tendrils of hair had escaped from her braid and fluttered
against her face. Her shawl had fallen into the muddy
ground and her skirt was wet. He walked closer, deliberately stepped on a twig, and snapped it. She spun toward
the sound.

Her face blanched. For an instant her eyes held the same
expression as the deer's had, right before he'd killed it.
Maggie cried out his name, lunged toward him, only to be
brought up by the ropes. She sagged against them.

"I thought you were gone," she said, her voice edging
on hysteria. "I thought something had happened. There are
noises, in the woods. I thought that man had come back.
The soldiers. I called for you."

He grabbed her shoulders to steady her and she winced.
He cursed himself for tying her hands behind her back
instead of in front. He'd done it without thinking. During
the war it had been the only safe way to secure the enemy.
But she wasn't his enemy, although he was hers.

"Hush, Maggie," he said. "No one's going to hurt you."

He waited for her to recoil from his words. Who else did
she have to fear if not himself? But instead of withdrawing,
she seemed to gather strength. Her trembling lessened.

"You came back," she said. The wildness faded from her
eyes. She straightened and he let go of her shoulders. His
fingers curled tight into his palms as the warmth from her
body and the delicate structure of her bones imprinted itself
in his mind.

"I found meat."

With a last shuddering breath, she shook off the remains
of her fear. Her chin tilted up and her spine stiffened.
"Untie me."

He pulled his knife from its sheath and reached behind
her. In the second that it took the sharp blade to slice
through the ropes, she leaned against him. He absorbed
her slight weight and forced himself to ignore the images
that sprang to his mind.

The ropes dropped to the ground. As Maggie brought

her arms to her sides and rotated her shoulders, she cried
out in pain. She stared down at her hands. The ropes had
rubbed the skin completely raw. Blood trickled down her
palms and dried on her fingers.

Colter stared at her injuries and felt as if someone had
kicked him in the gut. He'd never meant to hurt her. Had
never meant to scare her into thinking he'd abandoned
her. He should apologize. He drew in a breath to speak
the words, but she raised her eyes to his. The accusation
there silenced him.

The knife still in his hand, he squatted down in front of
her and lifted the hem of her dress. She took a step back.
When he reached for the ruffle on her petticoat, she stood
still. He sliced off a length of cotton. He'd been in such a
hurry to find the deer that he hadn't thought about what
might have happened to the woman. To Maggie. What if
wolves had come along? It was unlikely, but they were a
long way from the small farming town she'd been so intent
on leaving. Anything could have happened. It would have
been his fault.

He got a canteen from the wagon and soaked the length
of cloth, then slit it in half and wrapped the cool rags
around her wrists. She winced, then stood mute for his
ministrations. He recognized her stillness for what it was:
exhaustion.

"Here."

He offered her the water. She took it awkwardly, wincing
as she tried to raise her arms. He took the container back
from her and held it to her mouth. She parted her lips.
Tilting the canteen, he allowed the water to trickle into her
mouth. When she'd drunk her fill, he closed the container.
A single drop of water clung to the corner of her mouth.
The tip of her tongue swept it away.

She shivered. He picked up the shawl where it had fallen
onto the muddy ground. The knitted wool was less than useless. His meager attempts to make her comfortable didn't
erase what he'd done.

"I've got to get Sebastian," he said abruptly.

"Where is he?"

"I left him in the forest when I heard you call."

She nodded and started to shuffle toward the wagon. He watched her take small steps. Her arms hung stiffly at her sides as if the effort of clutching them in front of her chest would hurt too much. He caught up with her in a single step. He swept her up in his arms and carried her to the wagon. She stiffened against him and began to protest, but before she could say more than "What are you—" he'd settled her softly in the back of the wagon. Straw cushioned her. Sacks of flour supported her back. He grabbed the blanket from the front seat and spread it over her.

She clutched at the coarse wool and stared at him. "What are you doing?"

"I'll get the deer and wrap it in oilskin. It can ride up front. Sleep."

One strand of gold-blond hair drifted across her face. He wanted to reach out and tuck it behind her ear. He wanted to feel the silky smoothness between his fingers. But most of all he wanted her not to be afraid.

"I won't kill you," he said abruptly.

Wariness joined the surprise and fear on her face. "Why should I believe you?"

He thought about telling her that despite what had happened to him, he was still an army officer and officers didn't lie. Except they did. He thought about telling her that he'd seen too much death in his life. That his conscience didn't have room for one more soul. He could have said that he'd never killed a woman, never cheated a whore out of her money, never spoken rudely to a lady. Hell, he'd never spoken to a lady at all, until her.

He studied her heart-shaped face. The circles under her eyes. The dark lashes that framed so much emotion. He looked at the freckles, so pronounced against the pallor of her skin. Her mouth, the quivering corners the only indication that she still trembled. Would pretty words that he didn't know how to say convince her? In the end, he only had the rawest of truths.

"Believe me, Maggie Bishop. Believe me because I haven't killed you yet."

# Chapter 9

Maggie forced herself not to look away. He stared down at her with such intensity, she thought she might be blinded by his gaze.

"Yet," she repeated. "That's not much."

"I give you my word."

"What's that worth?"

She expected him to get angry, or to stalk away. She didn't expect him to smile. Again the flash of white teeth and the crinkling around his eyes took away from the ruthlessness of his features. She'd barely adjusted to his expression when the smile faded.

He left the side of the wagon only to reappear with a canteen. He dropped it beside her.

"Your life," he said. "My word is worth your life."

And then he was gone.

She raised herself up on one elbow and watched him disappear into the forest. For a moment she thought about jumping over the side of the wagon and escaping. To what? To the freezing cold? To certain death? Better to wait until she had a plan, or at least supplies. If she could take Sebastian and the wagon, all the better. She hadn't come this far to die now.

She shifted on the straw and grimaced at the pain in her shoulders. She would be sore for a few days. She settled back on the straw and thought about Colter's words. He was right; he hadn't killed her yet. In a funny way, that made her trust him. Also, he hadn't tried to take her into his bed.

She closed her eyes against the old memories, but they rose up and threatened to engulf her. She'd been nine when she'd learned what her mother did to pay for food and the roof over their heads. It had been a cold day, like this one, only it had been raining. Her mother had tried to send her outside. There was nowhere to go and stay dry. In desperation, the older woman had forced her into the large wardrobe in the corner. Maggie opened her eyes and made herself look at the trees, the sky, anything but the past. It didn't help. Not even Colter appearing, leading Sebastian, could erase the flow of memories. She could hear the pain in her mother's voice, see the shame in her eyes.

"It's a game, Maggie," her mother had said between her tears. "If you're very quiet, we'll be able to buy meat for our supper."

So she'd huddled in the corner of the wardrobe and listened to the sounds. The low muffled tones of a man's voice. Her mother's higher answers. Silence, then the squeaks of the old bed. The noises from that afternoon and a hundred others like it blurred together. Once, curious, Maggie had pushed open one of the wooden doors and stared out. What she'd seen—a strange naked man doing awful things to her mother—had made her ashamed and terrified. When Edward had made Alice cry out in the night, Maggie had known what he'd done to her. What all men did.

"Are you all right?" Colter asked.

His question drew her back to the present. She looked at him and nodded. He'd wrapped the deer in oilskin and tucked it on the footboard.

"We'll travel another hour or two," he said.

He adjusted his hat, then climbed into the wagon. With a flick of the reins, he urged Sebastian to walk and then trot along the narrow trail.

It was about an hour before dark when they stopped for the night. Maggie rose to her feet and climbed onto the seat, then stepped down to the footboard. Her back and shoulders felt stiff, but the discomfort was bearable. Her wrists pained her the most. Blood had dried on her hands. She felt dirty and tired. Before she stepped down, she checked to make sure the music box was still tucked under the seat in its burlap bag. If she ever escaped, she would take her only treasure with her.

Colter tied off the reins and came around to where she stood. Without saying a word, he moved close to her and reached for her waist. She rested her hands on his shoulders. He lifted her down and set her on the ground. There was nothing possessive about his touch; he released her as soon as she gained her balance.

She stared up at his face, trying to see his expression despite the hat shading his eyes. She studied the square jaw and the scar bisecting his chin. The firm mouth that rarely smiled.

"Will you really not kill me?"

"Yes."

"Then why keep me prisoner?"

He removed his hat and slapped it against his thigh. He looked past her. "I need your horse and wagon until it's safe for me to buy a mount."

"What happened to your horse?"

"I had to let her go."

"Why?"

His gaze dropped to hers. "I won't kill you."

"Those men? They were after you?"

"Yes."

"Why?"

"I'll let you go when I can." He replaced his hat. "We need firewood. Gather as much as you can. I'll dress the deer. We'll have fresh meat tonight. I'll smoke the rest."

With that he turned and walked away.

Colter had carried the deer down to the stream about a hundred yards from the wagon. He returned with a bucket of water. He started the fire in about half the time it would have taken her, then set the bucket on a flat stone and left to prepare their meal. Maggie collected another armful of wood. After checking to make sure the flames burned hot, she walked toward the flowing stream.

The path curved, hiding the camp from the water. She stopped a few feet upstream from where Colter worked.

She washed her hands and face. She left the makeshift bandages in place. She'd replace them when the water had heated.

Colter was busy with his task and didn't look up when she made her way back. She unpacked the utensils necessary for dinner. As she lifted out the cast-iron pan she saw his saddlebags. She set the pan on the ground, then glanced over her shoulder toward the trail. Colter wouldn't come back for several minutes. Straw covered part of the leather bags. She brushed it away, exposing the fine leather stamped with his initials. Again she glanced over her shoulder, then reached forward, unfastened the buckle, and lifted the flap.

Dried meat, a small bottle of spirits, a pair of socks, more rope, and a spare shirt. She sighed. She'd been hoping for an extra gun. Just a small one. Silly really. She didn't know how to use one. She turned the saddlebags over and opened the second pouch. Another shirt, some extra bullets. She slipped a few into her skirt pocket. Her hand dove in deeper and touched a bag containing coins. She pulled it out. The bag sat heavily on her palm. She thought of the few dollars she'd managed to save. He had a hundred times as much, maybe more. She pulled open the drawstring and looked inside. Coins glinted. Tilting the bag, she poured some onto her hand and stared at them. They felt cool against her skin. He would never notice if she took a few, she thought.

Without even trying, she remembered the sound of a metal coin hitting a small dish her mother had kept by the side of the bed. She had performed horrible acts for less than what one of these would buy.

Maggie stared at the money in her hand. With this many coins she wouldn't need her wagon or Sebastian. There was enough here to set her up with a whole outfit—six or eight oxen—and provisions to last all the way West. She could take the coins and run. She could—

One by one she dropped the coins back into the bag. With each clink, she flinched. It didn't matter what they would buy; she couldn't steal them. Stealing was worse than lying and she could barely bring herself to do that.

She was transferring water from the bucket to the cooking pot when Colter returned. "I cut venison steaks," he said, dropping them into a pan she'd left beside the fire. "And pieces to dry."

She added another log to the blaze and sat back on her heels. "Aren't we leaving in the morning?"

He nodded.

"There's no time," she said. "It takes a few days to smoke meat. We don't even have a smokehouse."

"It's easy." He handed her a length of oilskin filled with strips of meat. After sorting through the wood she'd gathered, he picked up two sticks. "Take these green branches and stand them up like this." He poked them into the ground over one side of the flames. Both were about two feet long with a V at the top. "Lay another across and fold the meat over. Keep the heat steady but low. They'll be cooked and dried by morning."

She helped him drape the meat over the cross branch. "If you say so."

"It's this or nothing."

As Colter had expected, she looked up at him and wrinkled her nose. "Not much of a choice."

"There's some edible grubs at the base of these trees."

Her slow sweet smile caught him like an unexpected left hook. His head snapped back and he had to stand quickly to hide his reaction.

"You're teasing me," she said.

"No, the grubs are real."

"I believe you, but I'll settle for dried meat." She walked over to the wagon. "I've got canned tomatoes. We can have the steaks plain tonight and tomorrow I'll make a stew." Maggie turned and looked inquiringly at him.

He nodded, then picked up the empty bucket. "I'll get more water."

His long stride ate up the trail, but even after he'd filled the bucket, he stood beside the stream. He'd never lived with a woman. Not since his mother had died. He barely remembered her. The domesticity of this arrangement felt as strange and uncomfortable as a new pair of boots. She was his prisoner. Until it was safe for him to buy a horse, he was stuck with her. If she didn't cause too much trouble, they would both get out of the situation alive. He would clear his name and make his way back to Tennessee, to that land he'd found during the war. The valley by the river. He would live the rest of his life the way he'd lived the last fifteen years: alone.

He returned to the camp and caught Maggie holding her skirts over the fire. When she heard his footsteps, she stepped away from the flames and dropped the damp cloth back around her legs, but not before he saw the long slender curve of her calves.

He set the full bucket on the rock in the fire, then walked over to the wagon.

"You said you had a needle and thread."

"I do," she answered. "Why?"

"That dress is soaked."

"My other one has a big hole on the side."

"Could you use a piece of blanket to fix it?" She joined him at the wagon. He dug around and found the dark blue blanket he wrapped around his rifle. "Would this do?" he asked, handing her the blanket.

"It would do fine."

He grabbed the wool dress and laid the skirt over the side of the wagon. Then he sliced off a large piece of the blanket and handed both to her. As he went to return the rifle to the straw, he moved his saddlebags. The top flap came loose. He looked up and drilled Maggie with his gaze. He'd left the flap fastened.

She didn't have to say a word. The flush began at the collar of her light gray dress and climbed steadily to her hairline.

"I didn't take anything," she muttered, staring at the piece of blanket in her hands.

"But you tried?"

"Yes."

He fastened the saddlebag shut and moved toward the fire.

"Colter?"

He turned. She held out her hand. He walked over and stared at the five bullets resting on her palm.

"There's no gun in my bags," he said.

"I know."

He took a guess. "You don't even know how to fire a gun."

She looked up at him. "Is it hard to?"

He shook his head impatiently. "What the hell are you doing out here alone? If the wolves don't have you for supper, some man is going to find you, strip you naked, and—"

She paled, either at his harsh tone or his words, and he bit off the rest of what he'd been planning to say. She swallowed.

"Dammit, Maggie, where's your family?"

"I don't have any."

She thrust her hand toward him and dropped the bullets onto his palm. Then she picked up her dress and hurried toward the fire. He followed slowly. She kicked a log over to sit on. While he positioned the pan with venison steaks close to the flame, she threaded a needle.

"There must have been someone," he said quietly. He felt her look up at him, but he kept his attention on their dinner. "You told Wilson you were a widow."

He glanced at her. She sat hunched over her dress. She laid the piece of blanket under the cut in the cloth and matched up the edges. One side stuck out too far. He leaned over and handed her his knife.

She looked from the handle pointing at her to his face, then back. "Thank you."

"And the dead husband?"

"There isn't one."

"Why'd you lie?"

She shrugged. "People expect a woman my age and traveling alone to have lost a man or to be meeting one." She began to sew.

"But you didn't marry?"

"No. My sister did. Alice." She looked up and smiled. "She wanted to get married, even though—" Her smile faded. "Anyway, when Edward asked, she said yes."

"Edward?"

"My brother-in-law."

The words came out casually, but he heard the disdain behind the tone. "Why don't you like him?"

"I didn't say—" She jabbed the fabric with her needle and sighed. "He wasn't kind."

"Did he beat her?"

"Sometimes."

Anger flooded him. He'd never understood a man's need to hit a woman or a child. "Did he beat you?"

Her fingers slowed in their task, stopped, then resumed the tiny stitches. "You'd better keep an eye on those steaks. They'll burn if they're too close to the fire."

Automatically, he checked the meat, then moved the pan a little to the left. So Edward had hit her as well as his wife. Colter's hands tightened into fists.

"Where's your sister?"

"She died a short time ago."

"Children?"

"They died, too." She glanced at him out of the corner of her eye.

"Are *you* married?" she asked.

"No."

He tried to picture having a wife, a home to come back to, someone who gave a damn about whether he lived or died. Some of the men he'd met had married. A few had lived long enough to father children. He tried to imagine what couples did with each other day after day. It had to be more than sex that drew them together, something more that kept them in the same place. Was it children? Habit? After his mother died, his father had never brought home another woman. Of course, he'd been gone most of the time, trapping in the mountains. When he was home— Colter automatically rubbed his cheek as if the pain of the blows could still be felt.

He jiggled the pan. The smell of wood smoke and cooking meat blended in the night air. Around them night birds and nocturnal critters moved through the forest and rustled the new growth.

"Where'd you grow up?" he asked.

"Ohio," she answered. "We had a farm."

"You're a long way from home."

"I'm going further."

"What's out West?"

She tied a knot in the short thread, then cut the ends with his knife. After measuring out another length, she threaded the needle. Only then did she look up. "It's away from here."

Firelight danced in her blue eyes, turning them the color of a midnight sky. Orange and red flickered on her skin. Her full lips quivered as she tried to smile. She lifted the dress and turned it to sew on another section. She winced with the movement and drew his attention to the bandages around her wrists.

"I'm sorry, Maggie." He motioned to her injuries. "I'm sorry about you getting scared and hurt. I didn't mean that to happen. I saw the deer tracks and . . ." His voice trailed off and he looked back to the meat. "Sorry."

"Thank you." She bowed her head. "Colter."

By the time they'd finished dinner, the second bucket of water had heated. Colter collected their few dishes.

"Your dress mended?" he asked.

"Yes." Maggie held it up. The blanket was a couple of shades darker than the original fabric, but she could wear it.

"There's water," he said, nodding at the bucket. "I'll go down to the stream and clean the plates. You wash up here and change your clothes."

"But I—"

"I'll be gone ten minutes. You got anything you don't want me to see, you have it covered by then."

She stared at him and nibbled on the corner of her mouth. More hair had escaped from her braid and tumbled around her shoulders. The long curls draped down the front of her bodice. One strand curved over her right breast. The light caught her hair, turning it gold and making his palms itch. She was pretty enough, but it was her hair that made him

think things that would send her running from him again.
She continued to stare.

Her woman's scent drifted to him. The sweet musky
fragrance pleased him. Then he frowned. It was different.
He inhaled sharply. Yes. A change. It was almost time for
her cycle.

"You know," she said, "you always give orders."

"So?"

"Were you an officer in the war? You never *ask* me to
do anything. I'm trying to decide if it's a habit or if you're
naturally bossy."

"Does it matter?"

She glanced at the fire, as if weighing her words, then
looked back at him. Her chin jutted forward and up. "Yes."

He fought the urge to smile. "A captain."

"Should I call you that?"

He remembered the last time someone had used the title.
It had been in the prison, when five guards had come into
his cell and attacked him. He'd been stripped, spread-eagle
over the back of a chair, and held down by three men. Murder was to follow their sport. A guard had been unbuttoning
his trousers and calling him "Captain" when Colter broke
free and turned on the men holding him.

He withdrew from the memory. It didn't matter anymore.
He'd killed two guards and possibly a third. The remaining
two had been left for dead. He'd escaped and headed north
that day.

"No," he said, turning away. "Don't call me that."

He strode to the stream. A quarter moon illuminated the
path. After washing the dishes, he rinsed off his face and
stared up at the stars.

They would come for him. Petty, and that bastard Gant.
They would find him if he wasn't careful; he'd trained his
former student too well. Why? he asked himself for the
hundredth or thousandth time. Why had he been set up
for murder? Was it because he had a reputation for being
a cold-blooded killer? He'd earned it honestly. How many
others had been forced—by the war and circumstances—to
do the same? Who had killed Alexander and the other men

in that regiment? There'd been no evidence linking anyone to the crime. It hadn't been robbery; the only thing taken had been the rifle. Who had fingered him as the killer? And why go to all the trouble to arrest him and put him in prison, then send in a guard to commit murder? It didn't make any sense, unless the real killer thought Colter too dangerous to be put on trial. But why?

He knew he'd never get all the answers, but that didn't matter. All he had to do was stay alive long enough to get to the meeting place and find the one man who would swear to his innocence. An easy enough task. Or it should have been. Except Gant was breathing down his neck and Petty was anxious to attend a hanging. If only he hadn't been spotted in Chicago. If only he didn't have the woman to deal with.

The woman. He bent down and scooped water into his palm and drank the cool liquid. He thought about Maggie's hair, the way it flowed down her back, the colors it reflected, the scent of it, and how it would feel against his skin. Had he ever seen anything that beautiful before?

His body responded to the images his mind produced. He shifted his position to accommodate the growing hardness between his legs. Women like her, the gentle acts they required, were as far out of his experience as sailing an ocean. If she were a whore, he would buy her services. She might even tempt him to return. It had been a long time since he'd felt desire burning through his gut. Easy enough to ignore the need. Like all bodily functions, the urge to mate could be controlled and suppressed. It wasn't about the woman, he told himself. It was about doing without.

He rose to his feet and collected the clean dishes, then waited another five minutes before returning to the fire. Despite his claim of giving her only ten minutes, in the end she had twice that. It's not that he didn't want to see her creamy skin. He drew in a breath and banished the image. He didn't want her to be afraid. There'd been too much fear, too many dead along the way. Men in unmarked graves, mourned only by the earth and the seasons.

He paused at the edge of the clearing. Maggie sat in front of the fire, brushing her hair. He would give her a quarter of the money she coveted for a touch of those golden strands. He would sell his soul to claim her body for a single night, to ease the ache that had nothing to do with desire and everything to do with how long he'd been alone.

He stepped into the circle of light and set the clean dishes in the back of the wagon. No point in making the bargain; he had no soul to sell.

# *Chapter* 10 ═══════════

Maggie tied the braid and tossed it back over her shoulder. She adjusted the skirt of her dress. The patch worked; the circle of the blanket blended with the fabric already there. She didn't care if the match wasn't perfect; at least she was warmer in the thick wool.

Something moved in the darkness. She started, then relaxed as Colter dropped the dishes into the wagon and approached her. He loomed large in the firelight, his dark hair hanging over his forehead, almost to his eyebrows.

"How are your wrists?" he asked.

She glanced down at the dirty strips of cloth. "Better."

"We should change the bandages."

She picked up the knife beside her and raised her skirt to expose the petticoat. Only a third of the bottom ruffle was left. Before she could bend over and hack it off, he stepped next to her and crouched down. With her sitting on the log, they were almost at eye level. She handed him the knife.

He slit the length of cloth, sheathed the knife, and began to unwind the dirty cloth from her wrists. He worked quickly, without comment.

"You've done this before," she said, more because she was nervous than because she wanted to talk. He was so close to her. Although he hadn't threatened her virtue, his masculine presence made her uneasy. The first bandage came free and she winced as he peeled it away.

"Men got wounded in the war."

"What about you?"

His gaze flickered to her face, then back to her hands. "Once."

"Badly?"

He shrugged. "I lost a lot of blood. It looked worse than it was."

"I see the doctors managed to save you."

He worked on the second wrist. "I was in South Carolina. Not many doctors wanted to help a Yankee officer."

"What were you doing there? Were you a spy?"

Silence.

"Who nursed you?" she asked.

"A slave."

"Why would he risk himself for you?"

"I asked him the same question."

"What did he say?"

"That I owed him a debt."

"Did you pay it?"

Colter slit the length of ruffle in half. "I tried."

"What happened?"

He grasped her palms and turned her arms toward the fire. She resisted him for a second, then forced herself to relax. The raw burns had stopped bleeding, but looked ugly. Staring at them made the wounds hurt worse. Maggie turned away.

"We'll bandage them tonight," Colter said. "Tomorrow or the next day let them air out. They'll heal faster." He brushed his thumb against the damaged skin. She bit her lip and forced herself not to wince. "You'll carry a scar on this one. Maybe on both."

He shifted and her knees bumped his midsection. The warmth of his body chased away her chill and his impersonal manner helped to ease her fears.

"Scars don't matter," she said.

He wrapped the bandages quickly. But instead of releasing her hands, he looked up at her. He'd left his hat in the wagon. The fire illuminated half his face. The dancing flames cast uneven shadows on the lines and hollows of his cheeks. Stubble darkened his jaw. Gray eyes were steely in the night.

"Maggie, I never meant—" He looked down at the bandages. Long fingers held her loosely; she could have pulled away. His thumbs swept across her palms. She jumped slightly as an unfamiliar shiver shot up her arms. He moved back instantly.

"I'm sorry," he said, standing.

Was he sorry for the scars or for the way he'd touched her? "There's still some coffee left," she said.

He held out his cup.

"Where are you from?" she asked. "Your people, I mean."

He took the cup and tasted. "The mountains, west of here."

"Where?"

He shrugged and took a sip.

"Your family? Do you still see them?"

"All dead."

He spoke with such lack of feeling that she hesitated to offer sympathy. So, they had that loss in common. A chill passed through her. She held her arms tightly to her waist. In the distance, an owl hooted. The far-off sound made her feel even more alone.

She stared out into the night, to where Sebastian dozed. Was Colter telling the truth when he said he would let her go as soon as he was able to find another horse? How long would he keep her? Could she wait? Should she risk another escape? He was a man; all men were dangerous.

Colter tossed the rest of his coffee into the bushes. "It's late," he said, then took a deep breath. "We'll have rain in two days. Maybe three."

"Are you sure?" she asked.

"Yes." He walked over to the wagon. "I'll get the bedrolls. Don't be gone long."

She rose and headed to the nearest grove of trees. How did he know about the rain? Edward had been able to predict it, but only the day before. She inhaled, trying to smell what he had. There was only the earth and the forest and fire. He was guessing, she decided, even as she tried to remember which trunk contained her slicker.

* * *

"So James is heading for Canada," Major Petty said as he rode next to Gant. "I wonder what's there for him."

Not Canada, Gant thought, someplace else. Not what; who. Captain Colter James had gone in search of the one man who had the power and prestige to help him. Worse than that, the man was the alibi James needed to clear his name. Petty didn't need to know that, and Gant had no intention of telling him. As long as they found James before he found his friend. If they didn't, if they failed, Gant was a dead man. The hunter would become the hunted. Gant looked at the rifle. Sweat popped out on his back, but he forced himself to glance casually at his superior officer.

"Looks that way, sir." He said the last word just late enough to make Petty stiffen in his saddle.

"Why Canada? Why not Mexico? He was stationed near the Mexican border before the war. Makes sense to go to where he knows."

James isn't going to Canada, Gant thought, although he wasn't ready to share that piece of information, either. He didn't know where James was meeting his friend, but it was somewhere north of here. Could be in a city or out in the wilderness. Anywhere. It didn't matter, Gant told himself. He would be there. Ready. If he could lose Petty and the other men along the way, all the better. Then he could kill Colter James himself. He glanced at the rifle again and touched the smooth wood. Yes, he would kill him with this rifle.

He smiled as he thought about his former teacher squirming under the cold steel gaze of the gun. Maybe he would take Zachery with him. He could use the backup. James was a bastard through and through. He couldn't be trusted. Once Gant had killed James, he would reward Zachery for his loyalty. They could stop at a few nearby farms for sport.

Gant thought about the woman they'd used the night before they'd left Chicago. She'd been a pretty blond thing with huge tits that had quivered with her fear. Zachery had taken her twice, once from behind, plunging where no man

had thrust himself. Her screams of outrage and the blood
running down her pale thighs had made Gant hard. He'd
leaned closer, studying the look in her eyes and the teeth
marks Zachery had left on her nipples. The knife made her
scream louder. Those plump white breasts bounced with
each cry. He'd rubbed himself faster and faster, expelling
his seed as Zachery had slit her throat. The white sticky
flow had spurted onto her chest, and his moan of satisfac-
tion mingled with her death rattle.

The memory sent heat rushing to his cock. He squeezed
his legs and the bay mare leaped forward. What a beauty,
he thought, easing the pressure. She responded instantly
to his every command. The horse slowed and he patted
her neck. He could hardly wait to see Colter James's face
when he learned Gant had his mount. The soft-mouthed
mare had been his prize possession, the only thing he'd
ever cared about.

Patience, Gant told himself. He couldn't afford to let
Petty know the truth. A mistake, something said in haste,
could ruin his chances for getting James. Worse, his own
life would be at risk.

He studied the trail, then raised his head and sniffed
the air.

"Rain," he announced. It would make James harder to
track, but the weather would slow him down. He was either
on foot or had some farmer's old nag. He would find him.
It was just a matter of time.


As Sebastian drank from the stream Maggie moved
around the small clearing, stretching the stiffness out of
her legs. Overhead, storm clouds threatened. She glanced
up.

Colter followed her gaze. "Rain tonight."

"Right on time," she said.

As he'd promised two days before, they were about to
get wet. She looked into the back of the wagon and found
the slicker she'd pulled from her trunk.

"We'll make camp early," he said. "An hour or two
shouldn't make a difference."

She nodded, then picked up the reins and led the old gelding back to the wagon. Colter hooked him up. A gust of wind swept through the clearing. Maggie shivered. He reached in back and grabbed her blanket, then tossed it to her.

"Thank you."

Her politeness was a habit. He never acknowledged the words, but she felt better saying them. As she gathered the length of wool around her shoulders, he squatted down and studied the ground.

"What is it?" she asked.

"Wagon wheel."

She joined him and stared at the wooden spokes. "Is it cracked?"

"Loose. It wobbles."

"Can it be fixed?"

The brim of his dark hat tipped slightly. After four days of traveling with him she was beginning to understand his spare language. He still held her prisoner, she still thought about escape, but the fear had faded until it was simply something in the background, like the buzz of flies on a summer afternoon.

"Two-hour job," he said. "I don't have the tools. It's not the wheel—that'll last long enough—it's the tracks."

She bent down next to him and looked at the ground. Two deep ruts rolled along the narrow trail and marked their passage.

"Every wagon makes tracks," she said, confused. Had he thought they'd moved across the muddy ground without leaving a mark?

"The left rear wheel wobbles." He jiggled the rim. "Damn."

"But I don't—"

He stood up suddenly and towered over her. "Every wagon leaves tracks, but a loose rear wheel is distinctive— easily followed." He stared off into the distance.

She straightened. He held his body perfectly still, as if he could see beyond the small glade. His powerful chest rose and fell with each breath. His mouth pulled into a straight line. The clean jaw—shaved each morning, despite their days on the road—clenched tight. She didn't have to see his eyes to know they'd be steely gray and cold as death.

They stood close together, close enough that she could have reached out and touched his arm. She knew he was completely aware of her, that he would grab her if she started to run, but he ignored her and looked back the way they had come.

"You're worried about those men," she said. "The men who were looking for you."

He didn't answer.

She moistened her lower lip and clutched the blanket tighter around her body. She had to try again. She *had* to know. "Why are they after you? What did you do?"

He didn't say anything for so long that she turned and started toward the front of the wagon. She reached the seat. Before she could grab the side and pull herself up, he said, "I escaped from a military prison."

She spun to face him. "I thought you were a captain in the army?"

"I am."

"Then why were you in prison?"

He walked over to where she stood. Large hands grasped her waist and lifted her into the seat. Her blanket dragged and he pushed it in after her. Then he looked up. The watery sun pierced through the cloud cover and illuminated his face. His gray eyes absorbed the light and reflected nothing back.

"I'm accused of murder," he said, as calmly as he'd told her about the rain. "Eight men. Shot in the back."

He'd taken the seat next to her and clucked at Sebastian to walk on before she'd had the chance to form a whole thought. Murder? Eight men? She swallowed and shot him a glance from the corner of her eye. Dear God, he couldn't be telling the truth.

But he was. She knew it, sensed it.

Eight men, dead at his hand. She slid closer to the edge of the seat. The fear that had faded with the passing days returned and threatened to suffocate her with its weight.

She grasped at the collar of her dress and eased it away from her throat, but that didn't make breathing any easier.

Eight men. He'd killed eight men.

Her hands clenched and unclenched at the blanket she'd pulled tightly around her. The wagon moved on—she didn't know in what direction. Mindless prayers went out to a God she knew wouldn't listen. She was alone with a killer.

She shouldn't have asked, she told herself. Better not to know. She thought about the conversations she'd had with Colter James, the meals they'd shared. When he'd smiled at her, she'd thought him handsome. He was nothing but a cold-blooded killer. Eight men shot in the back.

"You asked," he said abruptly, as if he could hear her thoughts.

"Yes," she murmured softly, afraid to answer, afraid not to.

She felt those gray eyes boring into her. She didn't even have to turn and look at him to see his expression. His anger radiated out and scorched her, as if she'd moved too close to a raging fire.

Nausea churned in her stomach and with it a cramping from her monthly time. She'd have to change her rag soon. Did she dare ask him to stop? Would he want to know why? A flush crept up her cheeks as she thought about having to explain that particular problem to a man like him. Back at the farm, she and Alice had been careful to hang their washed rags on the far side of the house. Even in winter, they'd kept what was private out of Edward's sight.

The cramps increased and she wrapped her arms around her midsection. Just forget it, she told herself. Forget what he said. Stop picturing the dead men lying on the ground. Stop!

She forced herself to stare at Sebastian's neck and the way his head bobbed with each step. The up-and-down motion soothed her, and time passed.

Early afternoon, Colter pulled the wagon to a stop at the top of a rise. The trees had thinned out some and patches of snow-covered meadow showed from between the trunks.

The trail had widened a few miles back. Maggie stared at the ground and wondered if she really did see another set of tracks or if her imagination was playing tricks on her.

Colter tied off the reins and stepped to the ground. At the top of the rise, he squinted into the sun and inhaled deeply.

"Smoke," he said, without turning around. "There might be a farm close by."

She didn't say anything. Could she find help? Even as the thought formed she knew she wouldn't have a chance. If she tried to run, he would catch her in about three strides.

"We need provisions," he said.

Again, she didn't respond.

He turned and started back toward the wagon. She shrank against her seat, but he ignored her and went to work on the leather straps holding Sebastian to the wagon. When the old horse stood free, Colter dug in the back and pulled out his saddlebags and his rifle. Then he stopped beside Maggie.

"Get down," he said.

Now. He was going to kill her now. Surprisingly, there wasn't any fear. There wasn't anything. He grabbed her arm to steady her until she gained her balance on the muddy ground. His hand left an imprint of heat on her skin. She shivered.

He slung his saddlebags over one shoulder. With his free hand, he gripped her chin and forced her to look at him.

"Stay here," he commanded.

She stared, but didn't speak.

"I won't be gone long. If you give me your word, I won't tie you up."

She couldn't speak. She tried but no sound came.

"Dammit, woman, are you listening to me?" Fire flashed from gray eyes. She hadn't known flames could burn so cold.

Slowly she nodded.

"You'll stay?"

She nodded again.

He studied her another minute, then turned and walked

over to Sebastian. With one quick, fluid movement, he sprang on the gelding's back and urged the animal through the forest.

"I'll be back in an hour or so," he called over his shoulder. "If you get cold, start a fire."

Why would a murderer care if she was cold?

He and the horse disappeared down the sloping hillside. She watched the changing patterns of light on the mushy snow and forced herself to count to one hundred.

A tremor racked her body. Then a second and a third. Her teeth chattered. When she was sure Colter was gone, relief swamped her and her knees felt weak. Impulses swept through her. Escape! Go! Now!

She'd taken three steps in the opposite direction from his when she brought herself up short. No. She couldn't just run away with nothing but her clothes and one blanket. She wouldn't survive the night. She had to plan. Food, matches, another blanket.

She frantically gathered together her supplies and tied them up in her shawl. She slung the awkward bundle over one shoulder and held it in place with her arm. With her other hand, she grabbed the precious burlap bag containing the music box. The combined weights left her off-balance, but she forced herself to turn away from the wagon. It would have been easier if he'd left her Sebastian, or at least the saddlebags, so she could have taken some money. A feeling of guilt swept over her. She *would* have taken the money, she told herself. She would have forced herself. Survival was what mattered.

They'd passed a stream a while back, she remembered. She'd go until she reached it, then follow the water. When the road began to angle down, she stumbled and almost dropped the burlap bag, but didn't bother to look back at the wagon.

She'd walked for almost ten minutes before she realized she was really and truly free of Colter James. She lifted her head, and for the first time since Alice had died, she laughed.

# *Chapter* 11 ═══════════

Colter swore as the sun sank lower in the sky. He was late getting back to the woman. Again. After what had happened to her the last time he'd left her, he was concerned about how Maggie might be faring. He shrugged off his concern. There were enough supplies in the wagon to keep her warm and dry until he got back. She could make a fire. He smiled. It might take her half a dozen matches, but she would eventually get the damn thing going.

Overhead, clouds swarmed together. Rain. He could taste it. Just a matter of a few hours until the downpour started. Spring weather, he thought. Finally. He was that much closer to freedom. Stay alive, he told himself. If Petty and Gant didn't find his trail in the next few days, he would be safe. Then he would head straight to the meeting place and clear his name. Afterward he would let the woman go.

He adjusted the pair of rabbits he'd shot for their meal. The smoke he'd smelled had turned out to be an abandoned fire used by a farmer to heat his midday coffee. The field had been empty when he'd found it, but the cleared brush had told him there was a farm nearby, maybe more than one. In the morning he would go closer and see what they had to offer. He had money to buy almost anything. A horse would be nice. Provisions. He glanced at the pair of rabbits hanging down. At least they had fresh meat for dinner. He inhaled the scent of rain and urged Sebastian to hurry. He'd seen something else during his exploration; he had a surprise for Maggie.

One side of his mouth lifted up in a smile. He imagined the look on her face when he showed her what he'd found. Suspicion would darken her blue eyes to the color of a midnight sky. She would approach cautiously, like a skittish mare, then she would go all quiet and give him that look that made him feel—

The smile faded. He cursed long and loud as he remembered how he'd left her a couple of hours before. Sebastian tilted back his ears as if trying to understand the words. She'd angered him with her infernal questions and he'd lashed out at her. Told her the truth. He shook his head. Not all of it. Just enough to put the fear of God into her. He told himself she deserved it; she didn't have any right to pry into his life. So he'd deliberately scared her until she'd hunched up on her seat, all stiff and barely breathing. He'd hated her then, for making him act like the animal he was. He'd hated himself more for being that way in the first place.

He urged Sebastian up the hill and through the thin grove of trees. The wagon stood where he'd left it. He realized he'd half expected it to be gone. Stupid, he thought. How was the woman supposed to move a wagon all by herself? Still, in the back of his mind, he'd thought she might try to escape.

"Maggie," he called out.

No answer.

He remembered the dull fear in her eyes when he'd left, and cursed himself. He should have reassured her, told her the truth about the murders. Pride, he thought. He'd hoped she would figure it out on her own. He was getting soft and foolish. He swung down from the horse and prowled around the wagon. The woman was his prisoner, nothing more.

He called out her name again. And again there was no answer. A vague feeling of uneasiness came over him. He hesitated before searching the surrounding brush. It was her time; if she was tending to her female needs, he didn't want to embarrass her. As he continued to circle around he realized she was gone.

He returned to the wagon and searched the back. A blanket was missing, the bottle of matches, along with the bundle she kept tucked under the seat. She'd run.

"Fool woman," he muttered.

For a second he thought about letting her go. If the wolves didn't find her tonight, the rain would probably make her sick and weak and they would get her in the end. Either way he would be rid of her. He pawed through their supplies again. She'd left both oilskins and most of the food. She'd been limited by what she could carry.

"But she took the burlap bag," he said aloud. "What could be that important?"

Sebastian pricked up his ears.

"Damn."

Well, if she wanted to run off on her own, let her. He reached for the lines to hitch the horse to the wagon, then dropped them on the ground. Three long strides carried him past the wagon to the trail and he studied the way they'd come.

There. On the side of the road. Footprints. Small and clear. He could even see where she'd stumbled and almost dropped what she carried. Let her go, he told himself.

The wind picked up. He felt the damp chill through his thick coat. All she had was her shawl and a blanket. Cursing the woman, the weather, and whatever fate brought them together in the first place, he mounted Sebastian and turned the horse toward the trail. He would find her. When he did, he was going to kill her for being this much trouble. If the wolves didn't get to her first.

Maggie set her bundles on the bank of the stream. No matter how many times she told herself he wouldn't be able to find her, she kept looking back over her shoulder. Even as she forced herself not to scan the grove of trees behind, she felt a shiver up her spine. Someone or something was watching her.

"You're being silly," she said aloud. "No one is there. Even if Colter James decides to come after you, he probably hasn't gotten back to the wagon yet."

The words sounded brave and sensible, but the tremor in her voice made her bite her lower lip and wonder if she'd made a terrible mistake. Maybe she should have stayed with the wagon and taken her chances there. Maybe she should have waited for another time to escape, when she was stronger and the weather was better. Maybe she—

"No!" she said firmly, not allowing her voice to shake. "This may be the only chance I have."

Her arms ached from the heavy bundles and her shoulders still felt stiff from being tied to a tree. The wounds around her wrists throbbed. She was cold.

And he would come for her.

It wasn't logical to think that, she told herself. No doubt he would be grateful she had left. He would go on without giving her a second thought. After all, now he had Sebastian *and* the wagon. He would travel faster alone. But men chased him and she knew his name and face. She could turn him in. He would never let her escape. He would stalk her as quickly and successfully as he'd stalked the wounded deer.

She glanced over her shoulder and peered into the brush. Nothing. Her gaze dropped to the ground. Standing out as clearly as a freshly painted church on a street full of saloons were her footprints. The tracks showed where she'd entered the small clearing. They blurred at the edge of the stream where she'd gone up and down the bank, looking for the driest spot, then ended at the place she now rested. A blind man would be able to find her.

She *had* to escape. She had to live. But how?

The stream rushed past her. She picked up her canteen and filled it. The icy water flowed into the container and over her hands. Again she stared at the tracks, then back at the stream. Maybe, she thought, and rose to her knees.

Several tree branches littered the ground. She selected a slender long section of wood about the length of her arm, stuck it into the water, then pulled it out. The wet part, darker by several shades, covered more than two thirds of the branch. She eyed the far bank. The distance from here to there was about double the width of her wagon. No doubt the stream widened in parts and grew deeper. Could she risk it?

She glanced back at her tracks. Could she not?

If she could use the water as cover, even for just a quarter of a mile, he would never be able to find her. The stream wouldn't leave any tracks. She would be safe. Tomorrow she would find those farms and ask the people there to help her.

Once her decision was made, Maggie worked quickly. She hitched her skirts up to her waist and pulled all the fabric to the front. By twisting it, she managed to bind the cloth into a long coil. When she'd looped the blanket containing her supplies over her right shoulder, she picked up the burlap bag and held it with her left arm. She wedged the coiled skirt between the bag and her chest. The heavy packages made her stride awkward and the twisted dress pulled at her hips and waist. With her pantaloons exposed, she felt naked to the world. And cold. But there wasn't any choice. If her dress got soaked, she would freeze to death. Taking a deep breath, she stepped into the stream.

A loud gasp escaped as the frigid water swirled around her ankles and instantly soaked her shoes. Another step brought the level up to her knees. The stockings and the legs of her undergarments clung to her skin. Icy fingers of cold crept up to her thighs and her teeth began to chatter.

A third step placed her foot on a rock. The stone shifted and she started to lose her balance. With her free right hand, she grabbed for an overhanging branch. The bare twigs clawed at her palm, but she managed to hold on. The cold deepened. Slowly, she forced herself to move forward, against the current, pulling at branches to help her progress. If Colter tracked her to the bank, he would expect her to go downstream. It would be easier to travel that way, but by going upstream, she wouldn't have to go as far to lose him.

Another step, then another. The stream curved and she kept moving forward. Her entire body vibrated with cold. Her fingers turned blue. Her legs grew heavy and her feet slipped on the slick creek bed. When she started to go down, she reached to the trees for help. The first branch she caught tore away from the trunk and landed on the bank. She yelped and went down on one knee, almost dropping the burlap bag. Water swirled around her waist and saturated her dress. She grabbed another branch. Slowly, fighting against the current and her own fatigue, she pulled herself upright. Her arms trembled, especially the one holding the music box. She wanted to drop her supplies and the box. She wanted to lie down in the stream and let the deadly water strip the lifeblood from her body.

She gasped for breath and found herself too weak to draw in much air. With the next step, she couldn't feel her legs or her feet. She tried to open and close her free hand, but it hung loosely at her side and refused to obey. She took a step, then another. The stream widened and flattened. Finally, she saw a relatively dry bank. The rocky bed changed to mud. She forced herself to move forward. One more, she thought. One more step. When the stream retreated to lap around her ankles, she let herself fall forward onto her knees. The music box tumbled from her arm and rolled onto a pile of dead leaves. Her blanket filled with supplies hung against her side.

Crawl, she ordered herself. She crawled until she was free of the water. Her body shook with icy spasms. Her teeth clattered together. Muscles tightened in protest and her midsection cramped.

Rolling on her back, she stared up at the sky and panted in exhaustion. The gray color and lack of light confused her until she realized clouds obscured the sun. A chilly wind swept through the trees. Rational thought returned, and with it, awareness of her predicament and the bone-numbing cold. First she had to find a place to camp. Next she needed to make a fire. If she didn't get warm, she wouldn't survive.

Gritting her teeth against the pain and shaking, she rose to her feet. Her skirts tumbled around her legs. One side remained dry, the other clung to her in thick wet folds. Her undergarments stuck to her skin as well. Her feet felt as if they were blocks of ice. After picking up the burlap bag containing the music box, she shuffled away from the stream to search for a small clearing.

She found it about twenty paces directly west. She squinted up at the sky. At least she thought it was west. She was so turned around. She set her bundles on the ground and clutched her arms to her chest. She needed to collect wood and start a fire. Everything else could wait.

Each of the places they'd camped on previous nights had provided plenty of firewood. This small section of the forest was no different. Branches littered the muddy ground. She collected several large chunks of wood and a few twigs for kindling. Later she'd gather enough for the night, but now she needed to get warm. Her hands shook so much, she could barely open the bottle containing the matches. All her fingertips were blue, her palms a ghostly white. She fumbled with the thin matches, dropping three before she managed to get hold of one. She struck it, but her violent shaking made the flame quiver, then die. She tried again. And again.

At last a few leaves caught fire, then the twigs, and finally the branch. She huddled on the ground next to the growing flames. Mud soaked through her dress, but she didn't care. When the fire crackled and spat embers, she held her hands out to the warmth. The first pains were so sharp, she thought she'd been burned. But she couldn't find a mark on her pale blue flesh. It was, she realized, the blood coming back to her fingers. She raised her arms toward the heat. This time she muffled her cries as the cold was forced out of her hands.

Only when she could move her fingers without pain did she rise from the ground and survey her camp. Her throat felt dry and scratchy; her stomach rumbled. She needed to eat.

After untying her bundle of supplies, she surveyed her meager belongings. She'd forgotten a cooking pot and a knife. She had no canned foods, only some dried venison and a few biscuits from last night. Without the pot, she couldn't make coffee—not that she'd brought any—or heat water. She reached down and moved the bread. She'd brought a metal bowl. That would have to do for heating water. She looked around for a flat rock. Colter always set one in the fire for them to cook on. She spied a likely stone and walked over to it. It was heavier than it looked and she had to strain to lift it. Moving in quick shuffling steps, she carried the rock to the fire and dropped it.

And put out her fire. Maggie stared at the scorched wood. A few embers glowed, but the warm flames had disappeared. Had the rock been too big? She tried to remember what size Colter had usually used. Big enough for a pan. Maybe the fire had been too small, or hadn't caught on enough.

It took another two matches and several branches to get the flames going again. Her feet still felt like they were encased in icy blocks, but she couldn't do anything about that now. She didn't have spare shoes or stockings, and she couldn't walk around barefoot. The best thing would be to get settled, then take off her shoes and sit with her toes close to the heat.

As Maggie collected more wood she struggled against exhaustion. It was the cold, she thought, and fear. Mysterious sounds filled the forest, cracklings she couldn't identify. She started at each one, spinning around to peer into a shadow, jumping so high once, she lost her balance. Animals called and cooed. Large nameless creatures trod softly on the ground. Once she thought she saw a man, but when she cried out, the shape turned into a misshapen, burned tree trunk.

She dropped her load of wood beside the fire and went back to gather another. Three more trips produced a pile of fuel, but she doubted it would last the night. She hadn't had to work this hard when she'd been with Colter. Even though she had been collecting the initial supply for the past few days, Maggie remembered that he had always helped later. He brought back the large logs that burned so long. He collected the water and started the coffee and cooked the meat.

She returned to the woods, venturing farther into the coming darkness. It wasn't that late in the afternoon, but the sun had disappeared behind a wall of clouds and she doubted she would see it again until the morning. The wind picked up. In the distance something evil howled to the coming night. She clutched the blanket closer to her body and shivered. Her skirt clung with each step. Everything ached, but she had to go on.

It was another hour before she had a pile of wood big enough to last the night. Her feet had thawed enough to hurt. She'd raised three blisters on her left hand and lodged a splinter in her right one. But she couldn't rest yet.

She retreated behind one of the trees and attended to her needs. Low in her belly, her muscles cramped with her monthly flow. She rinsed her used rags in the stream, then draped them over a log near the fire. After filling the canteen with water, she poured some in a bowl and set it on the rock in the fire. Hot water was almost as good as coffee, she told herself. While it heated she chewed on a biscuit.

Darkness bled onto the land, covering the trees and staining the sky black. A howl split the night. From the other side of the stream came the answer.

Maggie huddled closer to the fire and eyed her pile of wood. It would last, she told herself. It had to. In the morning she would feel better. She would follow the stream back, find the road, and go looking for the farms. She would be safe there.

She forced herself to finish a biscuit, but pushed away the meat. She would have it in the morning. The hot water warmed her insides, but the lack of taste made her grimace. Coffee, she thought. She would love a cup of coffee. And peaches. Or tomatoes. A stew with spices and fresh meat.

Tomorrow. She would be safe and fed. This ordeal would be over. She would never again have to fear that Colter would kill her.

She wrapped up the rest of her food and started to make a bed for the night. She stared at the two blankets. She'd forgotten an oilcloth. The damp and cold would seep in for sure, she thought with dismay. How could she have forgotten? What else had been left behind?

Overhead, lightning flashed, followed by a crack of thunder. She winced. The storm Colter had foretold. She'd also left behind her slicker.

She moved closer to a large tree and hoped the branches would protect her from the worst of the storm. As she closed her eyes she remembered Colter's scorn when he'd told her she wouldn't have survived in the wagon train. At the time she hadn't listened to him. As she held her hand against her empty stomach and fought the tears, she knew he was right. She'd been raised on a farm, had spent the last five years growing vegetables and cleaning and helping Alice. What did she know about the wilderness? For her, food came from the ground each year, with the regularity of the seasons. Chickens and cows provided a supply of eggs and milk as well as meat. She'd rarely been hungry, had never had to search out her next meal. Even Edward at his drunken worst hadn't made her as fearful as the howls of the wolves did.

The rain began slowly. One drop hit her nose, another rolled down her cheek. She grabbed the burlap bag and tucked it next to her, then clutched the matches under the blanket. Even huddling next to the trunk didn't protect her from the elements.

Where was Colter? Had he given up looking for her? Had he even tried? She struggled to remember why she'd bothered to run from him. He'd killed those men, she thought, and waited for the wave of fear to sweep over her.

Nothing. She realized she would gladly risk being with him at this very moment rather than face the storm and the wolves. But he is a killer, she argued with herself. He said so. He said he was accused of—

She blinked. And thought. It was important to get it right. Had he said he'd killed them? She exhaled sharply. No. Accused. That was the exact word. Realization dawned, and with it the feeling of having made a terrible mistake. What if he hadn't actually killed them? She'd risked her life for nothing. He'd promised not to kill her, and so far he hadn't. Not once had he hit her or threatened to take her to his bed. He'd fed her and—she fingered the patch on her skirt—cared for her.

Another bolt of lightning lit the sky. The answering thunder brought a chorus of howls. They were closer than ever. Maggie shivered under the tree. She was at the mercy of any wild animal, man or beast. She knew nothing of surviving in the open. Colter was right. She wouldn't have made it on the wagon train. She'd been a fool. She would be lucky if she made it through the night.

The rain poured down, mingling with her tears, soaking through her blankets. She thought about praying, but knew it was too late for that. So she called out over and over, saying his name as if it were a talisman against the fate she'd brought on herself.

"Colter, where are you?"

# Chapter 12 ═══════════

Colter stared at the muddy banks and swore. Circling Sebastian around twice didn't change what he saw. She'd gone into the stream.

What the hell was she thinking about? Didn't she know how quickly a person could freeze to death in water that cold? He shook his head. Of course she didn't know that. She didn't know anything about surviving in the wilderness. She was as useless and unprepared as the green troops he'd watched being slaughtered for five long years.

He glared at the footprints. He had to give her credit. Going into the stream made her harder to track. So if the cold didn't kill her, she had a fair chance of getting away. Not from him, of course, but from another tracker. Colter urged his horse into the rapidly flowing water and hoped the soft roaring sound wasn't what he feared. He would find her, all right. He would find her and beat some sense into her. If he didn't kill her first.

Sebastian snorted his displeasure as he stepped cautiously into the frigid stream. Colter ignored him and scanned the banks. It would be dark soon, and the storm was coming. He had to find her before the water washed out her tracks. The current picked up within a few feet downstream of the place she'd entered. Water surged around the gelding's legs and brushed the underside of his belly. The banks of the stream turned high and rocky. Even as Colter looked for a trace of Maggie—a bit of cloth, a broken branch, footprints—he braced himself to find her floating facedown in the water. The muffled roar grew and he knew without following the stream that it turned into rapids.

He drew Sebastian to a halt and stared at the rocky banks. If she'd come this way, she was dead. The current was too strong; even the gelding had to shift to maintain his balance. Raindrops splattered. Colter adjusted the slicker around his shoulders and pulled his hat lower over his eyes.

It was over, he thought, turning the horse and letting him make his way upstream. His problem had been solved with little or no effort on his part. He should be grateful. Nothing to be done now but wait out the rain. It was getting darker by the minute. Soon he wouldn't be able to see a damn thing.

He tried to force the picture of Maggie's lifeless body out of his mind, but it refused to go. He hadn't wanted to kill her, at least not after the first day. Hadn't meant to make her suffer. It had been bad luck on her part that she'd been last in that wagon train. Too much death. His hand tightened into a fist as he fought the urge to strike out.

He'd been twelve when he'd first seen a man killed. Fifteen the first time he'd done the killing himself. A neighboring tracker had been mauled by a bear and left bleeding and broken in a mountain valley. Even now Colter could see the dark pool of blood on the ground and the bright colors of the wildflowers that bloomed in the warm summer afternoon. The man had screamed his agony, had begged Colter to put him out of his misery.

Sebastian reached the spot where they'd entered the stream. Colter stared at the tracks on the bank, then up at the rapidly darkening sky. He should forget her. What was done couldn't be undone. But the memories of that man's cries for mercy echoed in the rain. Colter had tried to stem the bleeding and offered to get a doctor, even though he knew the closest one was three days' ride away. The man had continued to beg until his throat grew dry and his cries hoarse. His hands had clawed at the ground, then reached for Colter.

It had taken only one shot. A single bullet to the head. He'd been too close when he'd fired, and bone and brain had splattered over his pant legs and the wildflowers. He'd heaved his breakfast, retching until there was nothing left. He'd run away and never told a soul what had happened.

So much blood on his hands. How many others had he killed? Most he'd never known, but their ghosts wouldn't let him forget those nameless faces. Now a woman. Maggie Bishop. He would offer a prayer for her passing, but he doubted God would be willing to listen to him.

Maybe she'd gone upstream.

The thought tore him away from the past and he narrowed his eyes. If she'd been smart enough to use the water as cover for her tracks, she'd probably realized that most people automatically went downstream. It would be like her to do the unexpected. He kicked the gelding, and Sebastian surged forward.

The rain grew heavier, the current rougher. He could barely see. Water pooled on the brim of his hat and dripped down. As soon as the sun set, he would lose what little light he had. There had to be a clue, something to tell him she'd gone this way.

He was about to turn back and take cover for the duration of the storm when he spotted a tree branch lying on a bank. It had recently been torn away from the trunk. He closed his eyes and pictured about where the branch would have been if still attached. Then he checked the depth of the stream on Sebastian and pictured Maggie's height. Yes, she could have grabbed it and torn it off.

Lightning splintered the sky like a rifle shot; the boom of the thunder followed on its heels like a ricochet. Colter glanced around and turned Sebastian toward a grove of trees. They took shelter under the smallest. There was nothing to do but wait out the storm. With the wind, the clouds would pass quickly, leaving the moon to light his way. If she'd gone upstream, if she were still alive, he'd find her.

The howling of the wolves woke her.

The deep-throated calls carried through the forest and echoed off the trees. Maggie opened her eyes and peered into the darkness. For several seconds she didn't remember where she was or why she was so cold. She must have fallen asleep. How long had she been dozing? She shivered and shifted against the tree. As she clutched her blanket closer to her body, she realized the wool covering was wet, as was she.

The storm. She remembered the bright flashes of lightning and the bone-jarring crashes of thunder that followed. And rain. It had pounded her, soaking through her scant protection and putting out her fire.

The fire!

She glanced around the small clearing. With the faint moonlight, she could make out the remains of her fire and the pile of wood she'd placed nearby. Everything dripped.

A shiver racked her body, then another. Her teeth chattered. Her legs felt thick and numb, her head ached. She had to start a fire, she told herself.

Tree bark poked through her clothes and jabbed her right shoulder blade. She forced herself onto her knees and crawled the short distance to the pile of wood. Tossing the top pieces aside, she picked a couple from the middle, where they had a better chance of staying dry, and set them on top of each other. The corked jar had kept her matches dry. She shook out a couple onto her palm, then glanced at the container to count how many remained. Her eyes widened. Three? She counted again. Three matches plus the two she held in her hand? She couldn't survive with only five matches.

The combination of fear and cold made her hands tremble even more. Her fingers felt thick and clumsy. Tears threatened, the moisture blurring her vision.

She was going to die. Out here in the wilderness, where neither man nor beast would mourn her soul, she was going to die. She struck the first match. In the distance, a howl cut through the night. She dropped the flame and it sputtered and went out on the wet earth. She carefully lit her second and carried it to the piece of wood. A sliver on the log caught, flared brightly, then died.

"Oh, please," she prayed, not caring that God had abandoned her. "I don't want to die. Not like this."

Before she could reach for her third match, the wolf in the distance howled again. The answer came quickly, from a place nearby. Maggie gasped and sprang to her feet. She wanted to run but didn't know which way led to safety. She grabbed a piece of wood and held it like a weapon. Another wolf cried out, this one practically behind her. She spun to face the sound. Silence, then a rustling to her left. She turned toward the noise, but could only hear her own labored breathing. She backed up so the thick tree was behind her.

She peered into the darkness, trying to see the animals. An eerie yipping warned her they were closing in. The high-pitched sound grew as the wolves drew closer.

"No!" she screamed.

She grabbed a second branch and used it to bang against the first, hoping the noise would drive the wolves away. Another growl. She wanted to start the fire; the flames would be her best protection. But she didn't dare risk exposing her back.

She circled around the tree, keeping the trunk at her back. In the watery moonlight she caught a flash of yellow eyes, then they disappeared into the gloom. The pat-pat of paws on damp leaves echoed loudly. Her legs shook so badly, her knees threatened to buckle. She continued to bang the wood together, not caring that her arms ached and her palms grew raw.

One of the wolves broke through the underbrush and approached. She fought the urge to run and made herself lunge toward it with the wood, banging vigorously. Rather than flee, it crouched down as if ready to pounce. She didn't dare move any closer.

"Get away," she screamed as tears flowed down her face.

The taste of fear and death coated her tongue. The stink of the animal threatened to gag her. All her dreams, her entire life, had come down to this moment. Caught like a wild animal in a trap, she could only watch the wolf move closer. It huddled low, gathering itself together to leap. She thrust the wood in front of her, like a shield, and braced herself for the impact and the pain of ripping teeth.

# Chapter 13 ══════════════

Maggie screamed as the wolf flew toward her. A loud gunshot knocked her on her rear. The animal fell lifeless at her feet. She dropped the wood. Her gasps sounded loud in the stillness, then she heard the other animals scurrying for cover. She pulled her knees toward her body and rocked back and forth. Branches rustled behind her. She circled around and rose to her knees. At first she thought the wolves had returned, then the shadow became a man, and the man became someone she knew.

"Colter!"

She lurched to her feet and raced to him. Every step shot pain through her legs, but she didn't care. He loomed large and forbidding in the night. His hat hid his face from view. In one hand, he held the rifle that had saved her life. She threw herself against him and wrapped her arms around his waist. He was warm and alive and here. He'd saved her life.

She tried to tell him about the stream and the rain and the wolves. Her legs grew weak, but she clung to him, never wanting to let go. Shivers racked her. The heat from his body made her want to be closer while the strength of his hard muscles eased her fear. She could barely speak, but she continued with her half-coherent tale until she felt him grasp her upper arms and hold her away from him.

"You hurt?" he asked.

His question made her stop for a moment. She collected herself and shook her head. "Cold and scared, is all."

She smiled shakily. "You saved me. I knew you'd come. Thank you."

"Don't thank me," he said, his voice low and angry. "Right now I can't decide whether to beat some sense into you, or just shoot you and be done with it."

She reached up toward his face. He jerked his head back, but she continued to stretch up until she could grab his hat and pull it off. She blinked and felt the tears trickle down her cheeks. His gray eyes met hers. The lack of expression there was comforting in its familiarity.

"If you were going to kill me, you would have just left me out here to die. I do thank you, and there's nothing you can say to stop me. Thank you, Colter James."

He snorted. "Why'd you run?"

Because he'd killed eight men. The thought crashed in on her and she dropped his hat. "I was afraid."

"Of me?"

"Yes."

"Good."

She remembered something. "I'm not afraid now," she said, wondering if he heard the quaver in her voice.

"Oh?"

"You said 'accused.' You didn't say you killed those eight men."

He looked over her head and shrugged. "Means the same."

"Does it?" She shook her head. "Maybe for some people, but you're very careful about what you say. If you'd killed them, you wouldn't have bothered to try to make the truth pretty. You wouldn't waste the time. You didn't kill them."

"You sound sure."

"I am."

He pulled the knife out of its sheath and held it in front of her. "You willing to stake your life on that, lady?"

She stared at the blade. Moonlight caught the sharpened edge. She thought about the frightened young woman who had been kidnapped at gunpoint. She thought about the miles she'd traveled with this man, the things he'd taken the time to teach her, and how much she still had to learn. She thought about the taste of fear and death as the wolves had circled so close to her.

She took a step toward him and stopped when the knife point hovered inches from her chest. "Yes," she said. "I'm willing to risk my life on that. You might be a bastard, but you didn't kill those men."

"Son of a bitch." He sheathed the knife and strode past her. "Better get this fire going," he said. "The wolves will be back." He bent over and grabbed the dead animal by its hind legs and dragged it into the forest.

She crouched down by the pile of wood and emptied the last three matches onto her palm. She lit one and held it to the narrowest end of one log. A tiny flame flickered along the wood. She breathed on it, cautiously encouraging the fire to grow and dance along the fuel. Colter returned with an armful of wood.

"We'll need more to keep them away," he said, crouching down next to her.

She nodded.

"Running away. Damn fool thing to do."

She stared at the small fire. "I know. I wasn't thinking." She turned to look at him. He hadn't bothered to put his hat back on, and his hair hung down across his forehead. He looked cold and threatening and she couldn't believe she'd actually embraced him. Embarrassment flared, and with it, her temper. "It's your fault anyway, so don't get angry at me."

"My fault?" He turned those gray eyes on her. "How d'you figure?"

"You deliberately tried to scare me."

"You're the one who asked why those men were after me."

"You didn't have to make it sound so awful."

"I told the truth. You're the one who insists on that."

"You could have been more delicate."

He raised one eyebrow. "How do you make breaking out of prison after being accused of murder sound delicate?"

"You could have told me you didn't do it."

He didn't have an answer for that. His silence soothed her temper. A sudden howl made her stiffen.

"More than a mile away," Colter said, feeding the fire with another log.

"They were so close," she said, shaking at the memory. "I thought they were going to get me for sure. There were so many of them. With the rain, I'm surprised they could smell me, or hear me, or whatever they do to find their prey."

"It's your time."

"Pardon me?"

He rose to his feet and walked over to the log where her washed rags had been stretched to dry. After the rain, they were as wet as before.

"They smell the blood. On you and these."

He scooped up the clean strips and dropped them into the fire. The flames sputtered and sank, then rose up and consumed the cotton. The heat on her face didn't come from the blaze, but from the embarrassment roaring through her body. She stared at the ground and wished it would swallow her whole.

"They came sniffing around night before last," Colter continued. "But the fire was big enough to keep 'em back. How many more days you have?"

He couldn't be talking about this. Her mother had barely been able to explain the changes Maggie had experienced the summer she turned thirteen. Even Alice hadn't commented on her monthly, except when she wasn't feeling well.

"How did you know?" she asked quietly.

"The smell."

Her head jerked up. "I wash."

"On your skin. Your scent began changing a few days back. I knew it was your time. You started two days ago. How much longer?"

"Two more days."

"We'll collect extra firewood when we make camp."

The small tremors that had rippled through her body became one massive shake. Her teeth clattered loudly.

"We need to get you warm."

Colter kicked the log closer to the fire and reached down to grasp her arm. She thought about flinching from his touch, but she didn't have the strength. She allowed him to lead her to the log. As she sat, her hand brushed against his. He jumped.

"What the hell?" He took her fingers in his and squeezed. "You're frozen." He touched her sleeve. "And wet. You forgot your slicker, along with everything else."

"I was running away. I didn't have time to pack for every contingency."

"Fancy words won't keep you alive or warm."

"Neither does nagging."

He stared at her for a moment. "For a woman who damn near got eaten by a pack of wolves, you've sure got a lot of fight left in you."

"Thank you." She risked a smile.

The corner of his mouth twitched slightly, and she figured that was as good as he was going to give her. He dumped more wood on the fire, then left her alone and went to settle Sebastian for the night. Her stomach growled. She reached for the venison she had left and choked down a strip of meat.

The storm had passed, but the temperature continued to drop. Even with the fire blazing away in front of her, she couldn't get warm. Her hands shook, and she couldn't feel her feet. Pulling the blanket around her didn't help because it was soaked through.

Colter returned and silently handed her a flask. When she hesitated, he ordered her to drink. She uncapped the silver container and sniffed.

"Spirits!"

"It'll warm you from the inside out."

"But I've never had them before."

"If you stop being so foolhardy, you won't have to have them again. Now drink."

She took a tiny sip and gasped when the liquid burned her tongue and throat. "Tastes nasty."

"More," he ordered as he sat next to her on the log.

She obeyed, then coughed and handed him the flask.
He stuck it in his coat pocket. "Any part of you dry?"

She glanced down. "One side of my dress is only a little
damp."

"I didn't bring any spare clothing, except one of my
shirts." He continued to study her as her eyes widened.
"Would you put that on while your dress—"

"No!"

"Didn't think so."

Without warning, he took her hands in his. His rough
skin felt warm against hers. He checked both sides and
brushed his thumb against a red raised bump.

"What happened?"

"I got a splinter carrying the wood."

"You get it out?"

"Yes."

"How are your wrists?"

"Healing."

He chaffed his palms back and forth until her fingers
began to tingle, then itch, and finally sting. "That hurt?"
he asked.

"Yes."

"Good."

She stared at their joined hands. She wasn't afraid. Tired,
cold, worried about where she'd end up, but not afraid.
Even with the night around, knowing the wolves were still
close, she trusted Colter to take care of her.

"Better?" he asked, releasing her hands.

She flexed her fingers. They moved easily. "Much."

He rose from the log and collected a bundle he'd dropped
next to the fire. First he unrolled an oilskin and stretched it
out by the flames. Then he tossed down two dry blankets.

"Can you walk over here, or do I have to carry you?"
he asked.

She stared. "One bed?"

"Looks that way."

Her stomach lurched. "I'll be fine here."

He grunted. "I'm not interested in your skinny, shivering
body. Get over here before I tie you up for the night."

She glared. "I'm not skinny."

"Lady—"

"Maggie."

He rubbed his forehead with his hand. "Maggie. It's past midnight. We're going to be up at daybreak. I'm tired and cold and wet. I've spent the better part of the day tracking you. I'm not a patient man." He drilled her with his gaze. "Move."

She worried her lower lip. One bed. A picture of her mother with that naked man on top of her flashed through her mind. Every part of her screamed to run. He was a man; all men were dangerous. But she'd said she wasn't afraid.

She glanced at him. Shadows stained the half circles under his eyes. The lines had appeared between his eyebrows. He *did* look tired. He *had* rescued her. And he could have taken her many times before. She rose and shuffled over to the makeshift bed. Each step made her wince as her frozen feet screamed their protest. Gingerly, she knelt on the far edge of the oilcloth. Colter leaned over and pulled her into the center. He tugged off the wet blanket and draped it over the log. After slipping a dry one around her shoulders, he grabbed her skirt and lifted it above her knees.

She shrieked and tried to scramble away. "No! Don't hurt me! Please, not that. Anything but that."

"What the hell are you squawking about?" Colter sat back on his heels and glared at her.

She paused on the edge of the oilskin and tilted up her chin. "I'd rather die."

"Fine with me. I'm getting in the mood to kill you."

She clutched the blanket closer to her chest. "I won't let you have your way with me."

"Is that what this is about? You think I mean to bed you?"

She nodded cautiously.

He turned his head away and mumbled something she couldn't quite hear. The only words she caught were "ladies," "trouble," and "goddamn whore." She didn't know whether to be insulted or laugh.

He reached for her foot. She pulled it toward her.

"Can you feel your feet?" he asked.

She tried to wiggle her toes. "No."

"Unless you want to lose your foot to frostbite, you've got to get warm and the blood flowing again. I don't want to bed you, Maggie Bishop. I've never been interested in shy virgins scared of their own shadows. Now cooperate with me, or so help me God, I'll beat you within an inch of your life."

If the angry tone of his voice hadn't convinced her, the uncharacteristically long speech had. He reached for her foot. She fought the urge to run only because she knew she'd only fall on her face if she tried to stand up.

He worked quickly on the laces, then eased the shoes off her feet.

"I'm going to have to take off your stockings," he said.

She swallowed. "I—I'll do it." She pulled up her skirts to midthigh and rolled down the fabric. Her embarrassment was almost enough to warm her. As soon as she dropped the thin undergarment on the oilskin, she folded her skirt down to her ankles.

Colter took the shoes and stockings and set them on the log by the fire. He returned to sit close to her. Before she could protest or speak or even think, he pulled her feet onto his lap.

"This may hurt," he said, and began rubbing the chilled skin.

At first, shock kept her in place. She blinked several times, but couldn't erase the picture of her small white feet in his large tanned hands. Those long fingers she'd watched performing other tasks around the camp swept from heel to toe on each foot. Rough palms rubbed back and forth, creating heat.

He bent his head slightly, as if the task absorbed him. Stubble darkened his cheeks and jaw, adding to his dangerous air. She could see the pistol he wore at his waist, the glint of the knife in its sheath. To his left, the rifle lay within reach. He folded the dress back a few inches and began to rub her ankles. A tingling began as the blood flowed into frozen skin.

He handled her as gently as a mother handled her newborn child, held her as securely, soothed her as thoroughly. The tingling deepened, becoming something more than the thaw. He acted as if . . . She shook her head. No, that wasn't possible. Yet the thought persisted. He acted as if he didn't hate her. Almost as if she were a person. Except for Alice, and before her, their mother, she'd never mattered to anyone. Colter could have left her to die. He'd known the wolves would find her. He could have gone on and made better time without her. Yet he'd come back. Because she could have told the men after him where he was, she thought. And yet—

Some small feeling stirred inside. A feeling that whispered he might have come after her out of concern. His thumb rubbed the underside of her big toe, then swept down and across her arch. She jumped. He looked up questioningly.

She shrugged. "I'm a little ticklish."

One thick eyebrow raised. His thumb brushed across the sensitive curve. She stifled a giggle and tried to twist away. "Stop it!"

He grinned.

She told herself to smile back, to say something, anything, but she could only stare. In his gray eyes, where there had been nothing but cold emptiness and death, humor gleamed. The creases by his eyes deepened, softening the danger, but not erasing it. A tiny shiver—the kind that had nothing to do with temperature or season—rippled through her belly. Who was this man? What price did he pay for those infrequent smiles?

His thumb moved again. She laughed.

"Stop tickling me," she said, and succeeded in pulling one foot free. She tugged at the other, but he held her fast.

"Don't be afraid, Maggie," he said, the grin fading. "Not tonight. We have to keep you warm. I won't hurt you. I give you my word."

His word. He'd promised not to kill her, and now he
swore—at least for this night—not to abuse her body. She
believed him because he'd never lied to her before. He lowered her heel to the ground and reached for his saddlebags.
From one side, he pulled out a clean shirt and quickly wrapped it around her feet. She wiggled her toes and
sighed.

"Thank you," she murmured.

Instead of answering, he piled more wood on the fire.
When the flames blazed up toward the sky, he moved alongside of her on the oilskin.

"We need to sleep," he said.

She nodded and told herself not to be concerned. He'd
given his word not to hurt her. For tonight at least.

With one fluid movement, Colter eased her down on the
ground. She immediately turned away from him and used
her arm as a pillow. She felt him draw the blankets up over
her, then settle himself next to her. Instantly she stiffened,
as if by sheer force of will she could keep them from
touching. She hadn't braided her hair that morning, had
instead simply pulled it away from her face and tied it
with the length of ruffle. Now his warm breath fanned
the back of her neck and stirred the loose strands against
her cheek.

"The point is to share body heat," he said, then looped
one arm around her waist and pulled her firmly against
him.

Maggie gasped. From shoulders to calves, he pressed
next to her. As he was taller, his feet hung past hers,
and when he shifted, his chin bumped her head. She'd
never been this close to a man, had never been surrounded
by such intense heat. She lay there like a starched board,
barely daring to breathe. Gradually, she became aware of
his heartbeat thudding slowly against her back. The arm
around her waist remained in place, but held her loosely, giving her the illusion of being able to escape if she
needed to.

She would never sleep, she told herself, but at least she'd
stopped shivering. Thoughts raced through her mind. The

memory of her flight and the almost disastrous end made
her stare into the darkness, looking for wolves. Even as she
told herself Colter would protect her, he removed his arm
from around her.

The sudden lack of weight on her midsection should have
made her feel safer. Instead, she felt chilly and abandoned.
And confused. He was a man. All men were dangerous, he
more so than most. And yet . . .

As heat invaded her body, muscles began to relax. She
stiffened them again, telling herself she didn't dare let her
guard down. But her thoughts grew tangled. Colter's even
breathing soothed her further. She'd walked so far today,
had faced so much. She'd almost died. But he'd saved her.
She didn't know anything about the wilderness, she thought
sleepily . . . would have to learn to survive on her own . . .
would ask . . .

Colter stared into the fire as Maggie drifted off to sleep.
He felt the exact moment she relinquished her tight hold on
herself and sagged against him. Her back pressed against
his chest; her curvy backside burrowed into his thighs.
From the top of her head down to her delicate ankles, they
pressed together. Except for one part, he thought, shifting
uncomfortably.

From the moment he'd touched her bare feet, he'd grown
hard with wanting. Between the darkness and her innocence, keeping his arousal hidden had been easy. Even
now, all he had to do was tilt his hips slightly and she
would never feel his erection or know what she'd done
to him.

A log cracked on the fire and sent sparks shooting up
into the night. He raised himself up on one elbow and
stared down at her face. The flames cast dancing shadows
across her skin, making the pale softness appear as if her
expression changed with each flicker. The scent of her
body—he inhaled—filled him. Even with her time, she
smelled clean. Innocent. He remembered the look in her
eyes when he'd told her he wasn't interested in shy virgins.
It was only part of a lie. He never *had* been interested in
virgins. Still wasn't. Except for this one.

It wasn't regret, he thought, feeling the darkness invade his midsection. Wasn't pain or remorse. It was—

Maggie stirred in her sleep and moved her head forward. One long strand of hair slipped off her shoulder and onto his arm. He stared at the length of hair and remembered how it had fascinated him. As she slept he picked it up and watched as it curled around his finger.

Soft. Too damn soft. He rubbed the strand between his thumb and forefinger. Soft and sweet enough to die for. Carefully, so as not to wake her, he moved his hand closer and touched the hair cascading over her shoulder. He raked his fingers down the length, closing his eyes as the cool silk slipped along his skin. A small knot caught on a callus at the base of his thumb. She stirred slightly, and he froze in place.

For five minutes he stayed in one position, ignoring the cramping in his shoulder. When her breathing deepened, he released her hair and lay beside her. She snuggled close to his head, her rear brushing his hardness once. He bit back a groan.

He'd promised not to hurt her. Promised to see her through this night. He would find his way out of this hell and let her go as soon as he could. The pain in his gut tightened. Twisting a single strand of her golden hair around his finger, he fought the weakness that not only put him at risk, but threatened both their lives.

# Chapter 14 ═══════════

Sebastian's soft snuffling woke Maggie. The big gelding stood close to her head and pushed at the dead leaves, searching for new growth underneath.

"No food for him, no coffee for us," Colter said from behind her.

She rolled onto her side and blinked at him. He squatted by the fire, warming his hands. No coffee or horse feed? But they had plenty in the wagon and . . .

The memories returned. Maggie pulled the blanket up to her neck. They'd slept together last night. With his shirt covering her feet and his body warming hers, she'd quickly relaxed. Too quickly. But nothing had happened. He'd kept his word.

She sat up slowly and pushed her hair out of her eyes.

" 'Morning," he said, and handed her a cup. She looked at it. "Hot water."

She wiggled her toes, then stared at the ground. Her dry shoes and socks lay neatly beside her.

"How do you do that?" she asked.

"Do what?"

"Move so quietly. Know exactly what needs doing. How did you find me in the middle of the night during a storm?"

He shrugged. "War has a way of teaching a man to survive. If he doesn't learn, he dies."

She sipped the hot water and grimaced. Telling herself it was better than nothing didn't make it taste good.

He stood up. "Get yourself ready. It'll take us about two hours to get back to the wagon. If the rain hasn't mired it in mud, we need to get it out of the center of the path." He turned toward the stream.

"Colter?"

He paused.

"Could I learn to survive? Could you teach me what I need to know so that I can make the trip west?"

He stepped around slowly until he faced her. Dark eyes probed hers, looking for secrets but giving none in return. "You set on making that trip?" he asked.

She rose to her knees and nodded. "When you let me go, I'll make my way down to Missouri. I'll find work, and in the spring I'll join a wagon train and go west."

"What's out there?"

"I don't know. I just know I have to try to make something of my life. I promised my sister—" She looked down at the cup of hot water and back at him. "I promised Alice I'd find happiness and live for the two of us. We'd always talked about going west. Maybe Oregon or California."

"You'll never make it alone."

"I know that now."

She set the cup on the ground, then scrambled to her feet. He knew how to survive. He knew enough to make her journey easy. If only he'd teach her. She thought of the few dollars she'd managed to save and knew that wasn't enough to convince him. Compared with the amount he carried, it was a meager offering. He already had possession of her wagon and horse. He'd promised to return them, and she believed him, but they weren't much of an attraction. For a second a picture of her mother—naked with a smelly man writhing on top of her—filled her mind. As a woman, she did have one thing that Colter might want, despite what he'd said about skinny virgins. She felt herself flush. Better to die, she thought. What did that leave her?

"I have a proposition," she said loudly, wondering if he could hear the quaver in her voice.

He tipped his hat slightly, urging her to continue. She cleared her throat and tightened her hands into fists.

"I won't give you away. I won't tell anyone about you. I won't try to escape or be any trouble to you. I'll do the

cooking and help more with the camp." How did he keep
his face so expressionless? She stumbled on. "In return,
you'll teach me to survive. You'll help me learn enough
so that I can go west with the wagon train and not be taken
advantage of. You'll teach me so that I can find my way to
Missouri."

"Or I could just shoot you here and leave you for the
wolves."

"You won't. You gave your word."

He took off his hat and hit it against his thigh. "You trust
the word of the man who kidnapped you?"

He had a point there. She raised her chin slightly. "Yes."

"Damn fool woman."

"Do we have a deal?"

She knew she sounded desperate, but what choice did she
have? He was all that stood between her and certain death.
What would happen to her when he finally let her go? She
was in the middle of the forest. She would have to find her
way to a town, then south. A few lessons in direction would
be a help. Some hints on building fires and finding berries.
Her fingers curled tighter and she buried them in the folds
of her skirt.

"Just enough to survive, Colter. Surely you can spare that
much."

A breeze tugged at her hair. The tie hung halfway down
her back. She pulled it off impatiently, and the long strands
blew out behind her. A flash of sunlight made her squint.
She heard his sharp intake of breath, then he spun on his
heel and strode away from her. Her jaw dropped. She lifted
her skirt and hurried after him. She stepped on a sharp rock
and yelped, then brushed the stone away.

"Colter? Where are you going? Are you going to help
me?" She caught up with him beside the stream. As her
bare feet absorbed the chill of the earth, she shifted slightly.
"Colter?"

He shoved his hat on his head and stared at the opposite
shore. "You would have to do everything I tell you. No
more running away, no more shaking every time I look
at you."

Relief made her knees weak. "Agreed."

"You'll listen and learn. No arguing."

"Fine. I'm really grateful—"

He turned quickly and grabbed her shoulders. For a second she stiffened, then she forced herself to relax. He studied her face. "Didn't you worry that if I bothered to come after you last night, it would only be to kill you?" he asked. His fingers bit into her skin.

"Yes."

"And you still want my help?"

She nodded.

"In God's name, why?"

"You're all I have," she said simply.

He released her. The smile started slowly and soon spread to a grin. Then she heard a sound that made her stare. He chuckled. The chuckle became a laugh. The deep throaty sound was contagious. She found herself giggling, then laughing with him.

He looked down at her. "I can't decide if you're crazy or brave as hell. I sure didn't plan on this when I broke out of that prison."

"I didn't plan on this when I left the farm."

They stared at each other. The gray in his eyes softened slightly.

"Deal?" she asked, holding out her hand.

He took it slowly and shook. "Deal."

"Will you teach me to use a gun?"

"No." He turned and walked away. "I'm leaving in ten minutes. Get your shoes on before you freeze."

But the gruff words didn't dishearten her. As she hurried toward a clump of trees she hummed under her breath. He was going to teach her to survive. She'd come this far. There was nothing left to stop her.

Gant urged the bay mare forward. She leaped over a fallen log, then cantered down the narrow path. Zachery's gelding followed closely behind.

"We'll go another couple of hours, then we'll make camp," Gant said.

Zachery grunted in return. The damp weather hadn't helped anyone's temper, and the enlisted man's was shorter than most.

"We've got two days till we have to meet up with Petty and his men," Gant continued. "In the morning we'll head northwest. If there aren't any signs of Colter James, we'll have to join the others as planned."

"If there are signs?" Zachery asked.

Gant smiled. "If we get lucky, he'll try to escape capture. Be a shame to have to shoot him in the back."

"Thought you preferred the belly."

Gant studied his companion. Even in the cold, Zachery didn't bother with a hat. His thick coat added to the bulk of his stocky body. Barefoot he towered over most men. Despite his large size, he had a small head and dark slitty eyes. Gant suspected he might have some foreign blood in him, but had never been drunk enough to risk asking.

"A belly shot would suit me just fine," Gant said. "But we'll have to take what we can get. The way James's luck is running, we'll probably have to turn him in to the major for a hanging."

"Dead is dead."

"Maybe." Gant grimaced. He wanted his enemy to suffer. But more than that, he wanted him silenced. What if James said something to Petty, and what if the major believed him? Gant's throat tightened, as if he could feel the rope closing around his neck, and he tugged at his collar.

Their narrow trail widened into a path. "Rain's destroyed most of the tracks," Zachery said, glancing at the muddy ground. "Only the deepest ones are still there."

They paused and stared at the ground. A few wagon ruts remained visible.

"Farmers," Gant said. "Went in the last couple days. Heavy wagon, single horse." He pointed at the barely visible imprint. He leaned over to study the mud. "Loose rear wheel there. He might be on the side of the road up a ways. Wouldn't want him to spot us."

Zachery grinned. "In case we get lucky?"

"Yeah." Gant tightened his knees and the mare walked forward. "Maybe we should split up tomorrow. Cover more ground." He looked at his companion. "We don't have time for trouble."

Zachery frowned. "I ain't had a woman—"

"As soon as we get James, you can have as many women as you want. This isn't the place. The farmers will know each other. If you were to get caught—"

"I ain't been caught yet." Zachery grinned, showing a missing bottom tooth.

"Your luck is bound to run out. The last thing we need is the men around here riding hell-bent for your hide. We'll get James, then we'll head to one of the towns. No one cares about whores."

Zachery grunted. "Don't like whores. They smell bad and don't scare easy enough. They want to be paid for killing 'em."

Damn. Just like Zachery to start thinking with his cock. "We have to be in a big city to find a lady. We'll take one when we get back to Chicago."

Zachery looked dissatisfied.

"You go northwest," Gant said. "Along this trail. I'll head more north. We'll meet up tomorrow night. If you find James, don't approach him."

"You saying I ain't a good enough shot to get him in the back?"

"I don't want anything going wrong. We'll find him, then figure out the best way to take him."

"You're the captain."

"It'll be worth it," Gant promised.

"Better be. When we get to Chicago, I want a girl. No more than fourteen this time." The enlisted man licked his lips. "A virgin. Gonna stick it to her till she screams loud enough to wake the dead."

Even as he stroked his erection Gant wondered if Colter James would be able to hear her cries.

# Chapter 15

They stopped at the wagon long enough to boil water for coffee. Fortunately, the rain hadn't soaked into the ground, so the wheels didn't stick in the mud. Once Sebastian had been hooked up, Maggie placed the pot of coffee on the floorboard between them. She set two cups on the middle of the seat and started to climb on.

"Wait," Colter called.

He covered the narrow trail in two strides and gripped her by her waist. Through the still slightly damp dress, the layers of petticoats and undergarments, he could feel the warmth of her body. That same warmth had kept him awake most of the night. He felt her gaze on his face, noted the gentle smile, but didn't return it. Every part of his body screamed for release. Even now, a throbbing settled between his legs. But not by a breath would he let her know. Desire, like other physical reactions, was easily controlled. Besides, he had no use for a woman like her. A lady. She was a complication he didn't need or want.

He set her on the seat and tucked her skirt in around her. She smiled her thanks. He ignored the smile and her, turning quickly to check that Sebastian's lines were clear. After climbing up next to her, he grasped the reins and flicked them.

As the wagon rolled, Maggie gathered her blanket around her body, then picked up the coffeepot.

"This is going to taste wonderful," she said, and handed him a cup.

He took it without speaking. His silence didn't deter her. "I'm glad it's not raining," she said.

"Rain tonight."

"But the sky's perfectly clear. How can you tell?"

"Smell."

"A storm?"

He grunted.

She sipped her cup. "Did you find any farms yesterday?"

He thought about the plowed field. "No, but they're close by."

"Will you try to get provisions today?"

"Maybe. We'll have to make camp early to stay out of the storm. It'll rain all night. Probably for a day or so. If I can't buy food, I'll hunt something."

He thought about the two rabbits he'd shot. He'd left them by the wagon when he'd gone off to find Maggie. They'd disappeared by the time he returned with her this morning. No doubt the same wolves that had threatened her had found them. A small price to pay, he thought, then told himself he was a fool.

He thought about Petty and Gant, and then about the dead men. Why had they been killed? Nothing had been stolen except a rifle. He frowned. It wasn't just the murders. It was specifically Alexander's murder. Colter had brought him north from South Carolina. And for what? To dig ditches for the Union army, then to die only a few months into his freedom? Shot in the back like a thief. He rubbed the reins between his fingers. Or like a slave.

Maggie set her empty cup on the seat between them. "Tell me something about the forest. How do you find your way?"

It seemed easier to answer her questions than to wrestle with his own. He wouldn't find any answers today. Besides, he'd agreed to her bargain. So, as they rode northwest, he explained about using the sun and how it moved in the sky from season to season. As he talked about the stars he wondered what the real price of their deal would be. Why had he agreed? He glanced at Maggie while he spoke.

Maybe it was because he was tired of seeing the fear in her eyes.

"I don't think I'll be able to remember very many stars," she said, then bit her lower lip.

"I'll help you find the North Star," he said. "That'll be enough."

"Can we practice tonight?"

He shook his head. "Storm's coming."

"Oh, I forgot." She tapped her heel on the floorboard and rubbed her skirt. "I barely got dry, now I'm going to get wet all over again."

"You won't get wet."

"But if it rains—"

He lifted the corners of his mouth. "You won't get wet."

She bounced with impatience. "Why?"

"It's a surprise."

"For me?"

She sounded pleased, but uncertain. Wide eyes met his. Delight colored her cheeks. The combination of excitement and apprehension hit him low in the belly. No one had taken the time to surprise him as a child, at least not pleasantly; he shouldn't be shocked that she'd suffered the same fate. But dammit, Maggie deserved more.

"Yeah, Maggie. For you."

Her laugh cut right through him, down to the black part of his soul. Her pleasure mocked him. He'd seen women smile during the war. Wives who came along with their husbands and camped nearby. He'd seen the families spending afternoons together. Eventually, he saw the same women cry out their pain, keening with sorrow over a broken and lifeless body. Maggie had asked him to teach her to survive. He would do what he could, but it would take so little to snuff out her life. An angry bear, a poison root, a pack of wolves.

Or a man. Her greatest fear. He would do his best to help her meet the challenges of nature, but who would protect her from the evil of man? Who would save her from a bullet meant for him?

He looked away from her. He couldn't do a damn thing about their situation. They were stuck with each other until he could buy another mount. And he was in no rush to do that. Riding in this old wagon was the safest way to travel. Gant could walk right across their tracks and not know how close he'd come to his prey. Easier to stay alive that way.

Around them, birds flew overhead and called to one another. The soft breeze, not yet cold from the coming storm, rippled around them. Maggie leaned over the back of the seat and dug for her hairbrush, then loosened the tie at the base of her neck and shook her head. He told himself not to watch, ordered himself to look away. He would have succeeded if the sun hadn't caught the wavy curls and turned them to gold.

He raised one boot to the top of the footboard and leaned forward, resting his forearm on his knee. He studied the trees on either side, noticing the grayish brown lumps that would blossom to leaves. He saw rabbit tracks in a patch of snow and thought about stopping and going after the animal. But Maggie took the brush and drew it from her scalp to the ends, and he was lost. When the soft silky length fanned out, then fluttered slowly down to her back, when she tossed her head and the clean fragrance drifted over to engulf him in a sensual prison of need, he turned and stared.

She smiled up at him. "I forgot to braid it last night. I've got tangles everywhere."

He remembered her hair drifting across her shoulders and onto his hand. He remembered the feel of the strands on his skin and the way a curl had twisted around his finger, as if the golden length were alive. He gripped the reins tighter.

This morning, when she'd pleaded with him to help her, he'd been ready to turn her down. Until the sun had glinted off her freed hair.

It wasn't just about beauty even as he acknowledged he'd never seen anything as wonderful as her hair. It wasn't just because she was a woman, even though his groin tightened convulsively at the thought of bedding her. It was the innocence. The realization that no man had seen or touched what he coveted. That she'd defied him, bargained from her captive position. That she remained, despite her

fears, unbroken and whole in a world left scarred by killing
and war.

He'd ridden north after he escaped from prison. Had
passed through Maryland and Pennsylvania and seen the
land. All the small brush and fields had been trampled to dust
or destroyed by cannon fire. Trees stood like stark wounded
sentinels, with broken branches and bullet-riddled bark. Few
buildings remained near the main battlefields. Thousands of
footsteps erased all signs of unmarked graves.

Maggie continued to stroke her hair. The slow, sensuous
movements battered at him. He had no fear of succumbing
to the growing desire. It was enough to watch and want.
For as long as she brushed her hair to torment him, he
was alive.

"Are you going to look for those farms today?" she
asked.

"There isn't time before the storm. Maybe tomorrow or
the next day."

"Can I come with you?"

His gaze narrowed. "Why?"

She studied the brush in her hands. Her silence length-
ened. He waited.

"I get frightened when you leave me alone," she admitted
at last, her voice very small.

"You can't come with me."

She looked up. Her blue eyes flashed with indignation.
"We made a deal. I'm not going to run away, Colter. I
swear."

"It's not that. I don't want us to be seen together."

Delicate eyebrows drew together. "I don't under—"

He cut her off. "It's better if the men following me think
that I'm alone. If a farmer tells them about me and I *am*
alone, they won't look for a wagon. They'll assume I'm on
horseback and not find me."

"Oh."

He drew in a breath. "And if they don't know about you,
there won't be any trouble when I let you go. You wouldn't
get far if the army knew you were helping me."

"Oh." Same word, but this time she sounded pleased.

She dropped the brush in her lap and reached up to braid her hair. Her raised arms drew the fabric tight across the front of her dress and outlined her breasts. They would fill his palms, he thought, swallowing. The full curve of the undersides looked to be a perfect fit. His fingers curled around the reins and he slammed his raised boot down on the footboard. Maggie, apparently unperturbed, continued braiding.

"Any coffee left?" he asked, through gritted teeth.

She poured him a cup and handed it to him. He grasped it by the handle, careful to make sure they didn't touch. He took a gulp, almost hoping the flare of hot liquid would burn his tongue and distract his thoughts, but the lukewarm coffee moved easily down his throat.

"Colter?"

"What?" he asked sharply.

She returned the brush to the rear of the wagon and finished tying the length of ruffle around the end of her braid. "Why didn't you kill me?" She pulled the blanket around her shoulders and leaned against the back of the seat. "That first day. When I tried to run away into the woods. You'd loaded your rifle. I saw you. But you didn't shoot me. Was it because we were so close to town?"

"You ever see a man die?" he asked.

"No."

"It's not always easy. Some don't want to go. Some go too fast. I've shot men. Slit throats. Knocked one over the head with a rock and threw him in the river. I knew he couldn't swim." He glanced at her. She hadn't moved away from him, but her face had paled. "I don't know how many. I could tell you it was the war, but I'd killed a few before that." He pulled his hat low over his eyes and stared straight ahead. "A man saved my life once. Risked his own, and his family's. Had never met me. Healed me and told me to get out. I left without telling him my name."

"Did you go back?"

"Yeah. Two months later I went back to ask him to spy for me." He swore under his breath, remembering how Alexander had stared up at him with those wise brown eyes. He'd known the risk. They both had.

"Did he get caught?"

"No. He came north."

"So what—"

"He's dead." Colter finished the coffee and set the cup between them. "Nothing's left. That's why I couldn't kill you, Maggie. Because he was gone and the killing got hard. I couldn't take one more life. There's been too much blood. Too many faces staring up from the ground. Too many dead."

She half turned to face him. "I'm sorry for asking and making you remember."

"Doesn't matter."

"What was his name? The man who saved you."

"Alexander." He closed his mind to the memories.

The wagon rolled over a rut in the road. He tightened his muscles to remain in place on the seat. Maggie swayed with the movement and caught the side with one hand. As he fought to forget the past he saw her glance at him. The fear had faded, and he was grateful. He would keep her alive and safe—even from himself—because somewhere he'd lost the will to do anything else.

# Chapter 16

They continued along the narrow track. Sebastian strained to pull them up the rise. At the top Colter drew the gelding to a halt and stared out at the valley that stretched out before them. Oak trees marched along both sides of the shallow hollow of land. Stumps stood where wood had been harvested for cabins, fuel, or plank roads. A few dots of color blossomed where the brave spring wildflowers risked nightly frost and snow.

"There," he said, pointing to one side of the valley. "Next to that grove of trees."

"What?" She peered ahead. "Oh! A building?"

"Abandoned homestead. I found it yesterday. Floor's dry and clear of snow, so the roof and walls don't leak. We'll stay there while the storm passes."

Maggie looked at him, her eyes wide. "Is that my surprise?"

He nodded and looked away, suddenly uncomfortable. "Just some old settler's shack."

"Thank you, Colter." She fairly quivered with anticipation. "We're stopping early enough for me to get a good supper on. I can use the venison. There's a few herbs in my bag."

He grunted.

Maggie ignored his bad temper. A roof and four walls! She sighed as she pulled the blanket tighter around her shoulders. No wolves. No worry about the fire going out. And if the storm lasted through tomorrow, no traveling. She shifted on the seat and wondered if her derriere would recover from the abuse of the hard wagon and uneven paths they'd followed.

Clouds had been collecting for the last hour or so. As Sebastian drew them down into the valley the sky darkened and the wind grew chilly. By the time they reached the cabin, the first drops spattered onto the ground.

Colter jumped down. "I'll take care of the horse. Get a fire started."

He jogged to her side and gripped her waist. With one fluid movement, he lifted her off the seat. As quickly as he grabbed her, he let her go. Rain pelted her head and shoulders, but she stared up at him, searching his gray eyes for the answer to the mystery. How could the man who claimed to kill so many take the time to help her from the wagon?

"Inside," he said, and pointed to the narrow wooden door.

She picked up her skirts and hurried along the few feet, released the catch, and ducked inside. The door swung shut behind her and darkness engulfed her. No windows, she thought with dismay. The only light came from the cracks around the door. She pushed it open, saw a pile of wood in a corner, then used a log to prop the door wide.

From end to end, the cabin was smaller than the enclosed back porch on Edward's farm. A good-sized stove dominated one wall. A table remained, with a single chair. There was one shelf, no bed, nothing personal to say who had lived in this small space. Cobwebs filled every corner, while dust coated each surface. It was dry, at least. Dry and soon to be warm. If the stove worked.

Maggie crossed the room and pulled open the front cover of the stove. She leaped back and shrieked when a mouse darted out and made a dash for the door.

"Problem?" Colter asked as he walked in and dropped their bedrolls in the center of the floor and their cooking utensils on the table.

"No. Everything's fine." She leaned down and looked into the stove. Leaves and bits of cloth formed a nest. She poked around to make sure no other critters remained inside, then loaded in a couple of logs and some kindling.

Colter paused by the door. "Anything else you don't want to get wet?" he asked.

"My burlap bag."

He removed his hat, drew his fingers through his hair, then plopped the hat back on his head. "Must be something important if you took it when you ran off. If you had any sense, you would have taken food or an oilcloth instead."

"I couldn't leave it behind."

He left, muttering something about women. She smiled and followed him. Outside, the rain began in earnest. Dashing toward the nearest grove of trees, she looked for more wood. Along with some sturdy branches, she found a couple with dead leaves still attached. These she used to sweep the floor.

By the time Colter returned, she'd dusted off their lone table and chair and was unpacking the food. Preparing the stew only took a few minutes, then she pushed the pot to the back of the stove to simmer. The shelf contained three candles. She lit two of them and set them on the table. He placed her burlap bag in a corner, then took off his hat and shrugged out of his coat.

The stove worked well, warming the room, so she slipped off her blanket. Their eyes met. Maggie's contentment vanished as quickly as smoke up the chimney. As Colter continued to stare at her the small room seemed to shrink. They were alone in the middle of the wilderness. They had been alone for many days now, but not inside a cabin. He was a man. Apprehension flared.

"There, ah, might be a peg by the door," she said, pointing. "For your jacket and hat."

He turned to look, then hung up both garments. She folded her blanket and set it on top of the bedrolls he'd dropped in the center of the room. Her eyes widened. Tonight! What would happen? Memories of her mother's piteous cries, and Alice's moans of distress mingled in her mind until she wanted to cover her ears to block out the sound. Pictures of that naked man writhing on her mother's body, visions of Alice's bruised body— of her own, from

Edward's heavy blows— filled her. She closed her eyes,
but they didn't go away. The sights and sounds grew and
grew and her heart thundered until she thought it might
explode inside her. A log cracked, like the sound of a
gunshot. She jumped and looked around her.

Colter still stood by the door, his coat and hat hanging
neatly on the wall. Gray eyes studied her, examined her
face, then looked down at her hands. She curled her fingers
into her palms to hide her shaking.

"Maggie?" He said her name as if he'd already called
her several times and she hadn't answered.

"What's in the bag?" he asked.

The low tone of his voice, so controlled in contrast to
her wild imaginings, so calm compared with the galloping
of her heart, brought her back to the present. She took
a deep breath and forced herself to relax. After moving
the bedrolls to one side of the room, she picked up the
burlap bag and set it on the table. There was a moment of
awkwardness as they both offered the other the chair, but
her panic continued to subside. Maggie insisted and Colter
sat down.

"My mother's mother brought this when she came from
Germany," Maggie said, rolling back the burlap and brushing
aside the straw. "I never knew her. When my mother died,
she left it to Alice. Alice left it to me. It's all that I have
from my family." Her smile quivered slightly. "Someday I'll
give it to my little girl. I suppose it keeps us all remembering
the past."

Colter looked at Maggie rather than her treasure. The
fear had faded. Whatever had caught her in the trap of
terror had receded enough that she could smile at him. He
wanted to offer comfort. The need to heal was as foreign
to him as the woman in front of him. She chatted on about
her family's history. He listened to her voice rather than the
words. The sound grew stronger with each passing minute,
the pitch changing as the horrors receded.

What did she fear? And why? Her brother-in-law? He
remembered her admission that the man had beat both her
and his wife. Colter thought about asking where she was

from and, when his business was completed and his name cleared, of paying a call to that particular farm. He brushed the thought away. To what end? Would he kill the man? No. Too many dead fought for room in his small dark soul. Too much blood dripped off his hands already. He wouldn't kill again.

"What do you think?" Maggie asked.

He looked first at her face, studying the creamy skin, her cheeks pinkish now that the blood had returned. Blue eyes sparkled up at him. Long lashes swept down to cover her confusion as he continued to stare at her. The color in her cheeks deepened. He glanced down. On the table sat an old wooden box. Carvings covered the top and sides. Roses entwined, the vines forming large hearts in each corner.

"You risked your life for a box?" he asked.

"Not just a box. A music box."

She twisted something in the back, then lifted the cover. A single soft tinkly note filled the room, then others, until they flowed together to form a melody. His jaw dropped. "What the hell?"

He leaned forward and stared inside. All he saw was a piece of wood anchored about halfway from the bottom. A tiny bit of metal stuck up from one corner. He pressed it. The music stopped. His gaze flew to hers. She smiled.

"I used to listen to it for hours when I was a little girl. When I was sick, my mother let me keep it beside my bed. I'd play it over and over again."

He released the tiny rod. The music continued, the tune getting slower and slower. Maggie turned the box and showed him the key that wound the mechanism. He wound it three times, then sat back and listened. The tune made him think of a waterfall on a warm day, of light and—

He shook his head. He was about to slam the box shut when she moved close and pointed to the false bottom.

"That shelf comes up," she said. "You can see how it makes the sound."

He told himself to turn away. He didn't have time for music boxes. Instead, he tipped the box and caught the bottom strip of wood in his hand. He saw bumps in a rotating cylinder and the metal teeth that made the individual notes.

Maggie leaned over the table, rested her weight on her elbows, and pointed. "That's where the key fits."

They were close enough that he could have touched her face with his hand. A single wisp of hair escaped from her braid and brushed against her cheek. Now that he knew the softness of those gold strands, the way the curls wrapped around his fingers, he wanted to know more. He wanted to bury his hands against her scalp; he wanted to brush the long tresses until they glowed. He wanted to feel them falling against his bare chest as her mouth caressed him. The need threatened to swallow him whole. He closed his eyes, but that only intensified the images and the desire. Maggie reached up and tucked the errant curl behind her ear, never knowing how that unconscious act sank into his belly like an unseen first punch.

"No one remembered the name of the song," she said. "Mama told us the man who wrote it died a long time ago. Bach, I think." She took the false bottom from him and replaced it. "It almost sounds like a piano, don't you think?"

He could only nod.

"I always wanted to learn to play. When my father was still alive, we used to go to church every Sunday." She closed the box and set it in the burlap bag. As she fluffed up the straw she shrugged. "The music was my favorite part. Mama said I might take lessons from the preacher's wife. But then Papa died, and we lost the farm." She carefully closed the bag. "We moved to a different town and stopped going to church."

Her smile faded, and her eyes took on that look of sadness that made him wonder about her past. Her pain doused his desire more effectively than twenty minutes with a high-priced whore.

"I guess I haven't heard a piano played in almost ten years." She shrugged. "Seems a silly thing now."

"It's not silly, Maggie."

She glanced up, surprised. "Kind of you to say that, Colter, but you don't have time for music and pianos any more than I do. I'll get started on our biscuits."

He rose to his feet and took the burlap bag from the table. After tucking it in a corner, he rearranged his saddlebags. Kind? That was one thing he'd never been accused of before. His hard-earned reputation had involved many descriptions, most of them unsuitable for female ears. Cold-blooded solitary son of a bitch being the first that came to mind. He walked to the door and opened it enough to see out. Driving rain covered the sunset. A chilly wind whipped around him.

"Will the storm last through tomorrow?" she asked.

"Hard to say. For the morning, at least. We won't be able to travel till the day after. Roads will be too muddy."

"Are you worried about those men after you?"

He shut the door and turned to face her. She stood at the table, working together the ingredients for her biscuits. Flour covered her hands. Light from the candle softened her features, but couldn't erase her concern.

"Some," he admitted, then wished he hadn't.

"They won't be able to track you in this weather."

"I'm not getting any farther away, either." He paced the length of the room. It took three long steps.

"How many are there?" she asked. "I saw six—no, seven. There was an officer."

"Petty."

She looked surprised. "You know the men who are after you?"

"I served under Petty for almost a year before the war." He kicked at the hard-packed dirt floor. "There's eight men, unless they've added reinforcements. The one you didn't see is Gant." He shoved his hands in his pockets and stared into the darkness. "Captain Elijah S. Gant. Former tracker for the United States Army. Had a command until a few months ago."

"Is he good?"

Colter smiled. "The best."

"But not better than you."

"Not better," he agreed. "Equal. I taught him. We were together almost two years. What I know, he knows."

Maggie shivered as if she were cold. She attacked the dough. "They won't find you. You said so yourself. What with you using the wagon and all."

"Maybe." He pulled out the lone chair and sat down. "If they find me—"

"They won't."

"If they find me," he continued, ignoring her comment, "I want you to take the wagon and head into the forest. No sense in both of us hanging."

"Hanging?" Her eyes widened. She wiped her hands together, brushing off the flour. "You said you'd only been accused of killing those men. Won't there be a trial or—"

"No." He cut her off with the word. "Petty won't risk losing me again. I've already proved a prison cell can't hold me. If they find me, they'll hang me from the nearest tree. No point in you getting involved. Just ride away and don't say anything." He pointed at her hands. "You're making a mess of the flour."

"What?" She glanced down. "Oh. The biscuits." She returned to blending the ingredients. "Could you talk to someone and explain what happened? Maybe I could say something. You've been very kind and—"

There was that damn word again. Kind. She continued speaking, but he didn't listen. Her delicate brows drew together, creating a small furrow in her forehead. He'd kidnapped her, but she was worried about *his* future, or rather his impending death. Had anyone ever cared if he lived or died? His mother might have, before she passed away. His brother? Perhaps, if he'd lived long enough. Colter couldn't remember exactly when the child had died. Somewhere around age three or four, he thought, trying to recall the time of year. Must have been winter. That's when his father's drinking was the worst and the small boy had chafed at being kept indoors by the weather.

A single blow, Colter thought. A swift backhand across the head that sent his brother flying across the room and into the corner of the fireplace. The child hadn't even murmured as he'd slid to the ground. A tiny trickle of blood in his ear and down the corner of his mouth. Perhaps there had been bruises, or some other mark of his brother's death, but all Colter remembered was a small stain on the wooden floor and the silence.

Maggie dropped the biscuits onto the pan, all the while casting him worried glances. The third time she looked up and swallowed, he took pity on her.

"You're right," he said, wondering why she thought it mattered. "I'm sure they won't find me."

"You *are* a good tracker."

He picked up a short log and used his knife to peel off kindling. Maggie continued to prepare their meal. While it cooked on the stove she wiped the table and single shelf, then swept the floor again, using the branch with dead leaves attached.

"You're not doing much but stirring up dust," he said. "It's a dirt floor."

"I know. But it's hard to sit still. I'm a farm girl. There's always chores." She set the branch down. "You could teach me how to use a gun," she said brightly.

He ignored her. After a minute or so she went back to sweeping.

Neither of them would take the single chair, so they sat on the floor to eat their meal. Conversation lurched forward in fits and starts. Colter alternated between restlessness at being cooped up inside this small shack and thoughts about the men after him. He was getting closer to his goal. Another couple of weeks he would meet up with the general and clear his name. Then he would be free. If Petty and Gant didn't find him first.

He dunked the last quarter of his biscuit into his stew and chewed it thoughtfully. Why had he been set up? Sure, he had the right reputation, but he'd never shot anyone in the back. He thought of the sentry in Baltimore, that second year of the war. He *had* shot one man in the back. Man. He shook his head. Boy. Maybe sixteen. *Damn. Don't think about it.* He'd had no choice. That had been the only bridge for twenty miles in either direction. It was get across or be captured. So he'd shot him. Without giving it a second thought. It hadn't been until his time in prison that he'd even thought about the boy at all. One cold night, when he couldn't sleep, the kid's face had appeared, then he'd remembered the whole damn thing.

"You're scowling," Maggie said. "What are you thinking about?"

He took another bite of stew.

She sipped her coffee, then stared at him over the tin cup. "Have you noticed that we have very one-sided conversations?"

"So?"

"I guess knowing how to talk to someone isn't a necessary survival skill. They must not teach it in the army." She offered him the plate of biscuits. The loose strand of her hair teased her cheek and made his palms itch.

He took the roll. "Thanks."

"You're welcome." She sipped again. "It sounds like the rain is slowing up."

As he chewed his food he considered her hopeful expression. "You're not going to give up, are you?"

"I'm sure I don't know what you're talking about," she said, her eyes twinkling.

The shadow of a smile tickled the corner of her mouth. Suddenly he knew if he didn't see all of her smile, he wouldn't be able to draw in another breath. He wanted the fear and all the pain gone, just for a second. He didn't care if this entire evening was an illusion, that a cold wet world waited beyond that door. He didn't even care that eight men rode to a hanging. He had to see her smile.

"I'm sure you do," he said, his voice deliberately low and teasing. Then he winked.

She burst into delighted laughter. "Just when I think I understand you, you go and do something like that." She filled his coffee cup and leaned forward. "Talk to me, Colter James."

So he explained the best way to saddle a horse. She spoke about planting vegetables in the spring. He shared a story about the first time he visited Mexico. Then she brought out the music box and they played it over and over again. The candles burned down to stubs. He loaded more wood into the fire, she cleaned the dishes. He spread the bedrolls out on either side of the stove and they sat on the ground talking.

He studied her face, the smooth pale skin and full lips. The strand of hair still swayed back and forth with each movement and he longed to touch it. To touch her.

He was growing used to the desire. He was probably going to stay hard until he found his ease with another woman. Perhaps even after. But that didn't matter. He could control the wanting. It was her laughter that caused him to ache. The way she looked at him out of the corner of her eye. It was the quick movements of her hands when she talked, and the humor. It was that her eyes darkened to the color of a midnight sky when the fear faded and that she hadn't been afraid since before dinner. The ache in his gut deepened every time she used his name. He didn't understand the cause, but knew instinctively it had no cure.

"The worst part was," she said, continuing with her story, "they couldn't get the same color. There I was, a month before Christmas, and no red wool." She smiled. "So I used green."

He raised his eyebrows.

"I know what you're thinking." She pulled her knees tighter to her chest. "I finished that last sleeve and Alice helped me attach it to the rest of the sweater. Poor Mama. A red sweater with one green sleeve." She shook her head at the memory. "She never said a word about it. Told me it was the most beautiful sweater. She wore it to church that Sunday." Her head dipped toward her chest. "We still went to church in those days."

He didn't have to see it happen to know the light in her eyes had begun to fade. A fierce need filled him. "Did anyone say anything about the sweater?"

She looked up and grinned. "I was too proud to notice if they stared or laughed. I held my mama's hand. I was seven, I think. She wore that sweater the rest of her life."

Soft and sweet, like maple candy he'd had once a few years before. Her eyes met and held his. Her shadows were gone. Without thinking, he reached toward her to tuck that loose strand of hair behind her ear.

He never got close.

She flinched from him, rolling away and coming up on her knees. Her face paled. Her arms crossed over her chest. He felt the same shock and rippling pain as the time he'd taken a bullet in the shoulder.

"Your hair's coming loose," he growled.

She reached up and fingered the curl. "Oh." She swallowed.

He sprang to his feet. "It's late. I'll see to the horse."

After grabbing his coat and hat, he slipped out into the storm. But the rain and the cold meant nothing. Nor did the thought that Petty and Gant could find him at any time. Even if they caught him tonight, his last thought as he dangled from the tree would be the look in Maggie's eyes when he'd reached out to touch her.

The woman who had braved traveling alone across country and stood up to wolves lived in fear of him. Not in fear of pain or death, but of him. It didn't matter that he'd promised not to hurt her, or that he'd saved her life. In their short time together, she'd seen into the blackness of his soul and learned that he had—perhaps through the darkness of war, perhaps before—lost his humanity. He had become a true killer. A hunter of men, moving without thought or conscience. He would never be anything else.

# Chapter 17 ━━━━━━━━

Maggie finished washing the breakfast dishes and set a new pot of coffee on the stove. Outside, water dripped from the eaves of the small shack, but the rhythm had slowed from the previous night. While gray clouds covered the sky, they looked lighter, and she thought the storm might end later this morning.

She set her tin cup on the table and sat down. Colter hadn't spoken a single extra word to her today. He'd asked for a second biscuit, had announced his intention of getting more firewood, and then left. The friendly man from the previous night might never have existed.

Last night. She shivered. She didn't want to think about that. What if he'd touched her? What would have happened? Would he have expected her to share his bed? Would he have made her cry out in pain, as Edward had made Alice? Would he have made her whimper and done those things the men had done to her mother?

Horror swept over her. She couldn't imagine ever wanting to be with a man that way. Colter was so much bigger and stronger than she. She could never physically best him. She remembered the heavy logs he carried every night and the way he moved so quickly and gracefully. The muscles she'd felt when she'd run to him and held on tight while the wolves had circled close by. He could defeat her easily.

And yet he was often kind, she reminded herself. Last night he had winked at her and made her laugh. It had been, she thought with a smile, a pleasant evening. The smile faded. If only he hadn't tried to touch her.

The door opened. Maggie straightened in her chair.

Colter stepped inside and shook off his hat. "Storm's letting up," he said, not looking at her. "I'm leaving."

"What?" She pushed the chair away from the table and rose.

He stared at a point over her left shoulder. "I'm taking Sebastian and going out to find a farm."

"Why?"

"Buy a horse."

"A horse? What for?"

"So I can let you go." He looked at her then. Last night she'd seen laughter and humor in his eyes; this morning they'd returned to gray ice, stealing the light and reflecting nothing back.

Fear clutched her. She wasn't ready to be alone. She hadn't learned enough to survive. "Why now?"

He shrugged.

"Something must have happened. You said it was safer for you to travel in the wagon. What if you're recognized? What if someone remembers you?"

"Doesn't matter."

But it did. "If it's about last night—"

"It's not."

She didn't know him well enough to know if he lied. And she wouldn't be able to find the words to convince him to stay. Her stomach tightened. She felt cold.

"Take me with you," she said. "At least to the farm. I don't want to stay here by myself." *I'm afraid.*

He put his hat on his head. "I'll travel faster alone. There's enough wood. Don't stray far from the cabin."

Then he was gone. The door slammed shut. She ran and opened it, but he'd already mounted Sebastian. The old gelding began walking away.

"Colter!" she called.

He pulled the horse to a stop, but didn't turn around. Rain soaked her dress and hair. "When will you be back?" The real question was if he would bother to come back at all, but she didn't dare ask that.

"Before dark."

"Please let me come with you. I don't want to stay here alone," she repeated. "Colter?"

He kicked Sebastian and rode off without looking back. She stood in the rain until she couldn't see them any longer, then she turned and went inside.

Had she done this to herself? Had her fear of men insulted him? Was he punishing her?

Now what would happen? She didn't know enough to survive on her own. There was barely enough money for her to make it to Missouri. She glanced around the shack. His saddlebags sat in the corner. He'd come back for them, she told herself, and felt relieved. Until then, she would keep herself busy. There was laundry. She could bake bread. While her hands were busy she would think. She'd survived this long; she would make it through whatever else might happen.

Colter paused about a hundred feet from the farmhouse. He'd ridden almost two hours, circling around nearer places until he found one that he felt safe approaching.

Safe. He shook his head. This had to be the dumbest thing he'd done in a long time. If Gant and Petty came around and found out he'd been here, it would only take a couple of days for them to catch up with him. He knew his head start had shrunk considerably. While Maggie and her wagon provided a great cover for him, they also slowed him down.

The best plan would be to return to the shack and stay with the wagon. Then, even if the soldiers crossed his path, they wouldn't know they were close. But he couldn't use the best plan. Not after last night. Not after Maggie had looked at him as if he were about to rape her. His chest tightened. He'd never despised himself more than when he'd seen what he'd become, reflected in her eyes.

Sebastian shifted, and he gave the horse his head. Slowly, the animal moved toward the farmhouse.

Colter glanced around at the flat empty fields. Only a third of what he could see had been plowed. He studied the small house. The porch sagged, and the garden on

the side looked untended. The rain had changed to mist.
Water dripped from the eaves. The front door opened and
a woman stepped out. Five or six small children surrounded
her. At least he was alone on horseback, he thought as he
approached. Even if Gant and Petty talked to the woman,
she wouldn't know about Maggie and the wagon.

The woman walked to the front of the porch and started
down the stairs. Her print dress had faded from too many
washings. The children's clothes also looked worn. But as
he approached he saw they were curious, but not frightened, and they had the happy smiles of a well-fed brood.

He drew Sebastian to a halt. The woman stepped closer
and offered a nod. She was pretty enough. Her blue-black
hair gleamed in the morning light.

"May I help you, stranger?" she asked.

Maggie hummed as she hung the last of her undergarments over the tree next to the cabin. Colter's spare shirts
and socks flapped nearby. The rain and clouds had blown
away, leaving behind bright sunshine. She rubbed her hands
up and down her arms. Not exactly warm yet, she thought,
raising her face toward the sky, but pleasant. She inhaled,
smelling the fresh earth and the promise of spring. Birds
chirped around her. A pair of blue jays soared overhead in
an intricate mating dance.

She opened her arms wide and spun in a circle, around
and around until the sky swirled and she had to stagger
to keep her balance. This was good. This moment. Safe,
fed. No planting to be done, no weeding, no milking. She
untied her braid and let her hair fall loose. The ends swayed
back and forth. She glanced at the sun. It wasn't noon yet.
Colter probably wouldn't return for a couple of hours. She
had time.

Hurrying inside, she glanced at the pot of water she'd left
on the stove. She would need the bucket, and a metal basin.
Within minutes she'd unbuttoned her dress and rolled it
down to her waist. Working quickly, she washed her hair,
then rinsed it with cold water from the nearby stream.
Using a petticoat for a towel, she wrapped the cloth around

her head, dumped the dirty water, and slipped back into her dress. Only then did she pick up her brush and move the chair in front of the fire.

Seating herself, she let the petticoat unwind. She worked slowly, gently pulling the brush through the wet strands. With her eyes half-closed, she thought about being a little girl, when her mother had brushed her hair dry. Later, after Alice had married Edward, the two women had often helped each other wash their hair, then sat together and talked.

Maggie smiled at the memories. She missed her sister, but was finding it easier to remember the good moments with her rather than the suffering they'd both endured. Alice's hair had been lighter than her own. A pure yellow blond that had brought boys running from all the nearby farms. Alice had laughed so easily. Had rarely questioned anything. She hadn't asked how her mother had suddenly been able to afford meat for their meals.

She hadn't known the truth, Maggie thought, her smile fading. She'd had her job at the laundry, waiting on customers. With her sweet smile and pretty face, she'd brought in many eligible bachelors. Maggie had been too young to get a job to help out. That's why she'd been there when their mother had been with those men.

Don't think about that, she told herself. Think of better times. She recalled how carefully Edward had courted her sister. He'd seemed fine enough. When their mother died, he'd let Maggie come live with them.

Maggie shifted on the chair and switched the brush to her other hand. How she'd worried when her sister closed that bedroom door. How she'd listened for the sounds she heard from the wardrobe. But there had been only silence, those first years. Silence, and every nine months another stillborn baby.

Once, Maggie remembered, Alice had whispered about what went on between a man and a woman. Sometimes it was awful, she'd admitted. Fast and painful. But sometimes, when they kissed and talked first, it wasn't so bad. Sometimes, Alice had said, she got a funny feeling inside, as if she wanted Edward to do that thing.

Maggie frowned. Wanted a man to do that? She shuddered. Why? She'd never asked Alice any more questions, and after the death of the next baby, the frightening noises from behind their closed bedroom door had started, as had the hitting. Alice warned her to get out, to find a man of her own to marry. Maggie had refused. She didn't want a man and wouldn't leave her sister alone with a much-changed Edward.

Her hair dried and she continued to stroke the brush through the long strands. Besides, Alice had been the pretty one. Oh, Maggie had been asked to dance at the harvest celebrations, and occasionally at Christmas, but no one had come calling. Sometimes when Colter looked at her, it was almost as if he thought she *was* pretty. Did Colter like her looks?

Asking the question made her stomach jump a little. A tiny shiver rippled down her spine. She knew he would never hurt her. So shouldn't she trust him not to bed her?

Which made her think about last night. He had only tried to touch her hair. She knew that now. He'd reached up to tuck an errant strand behind her ear. A simple gesture.

She had touched him when he'd rescued her from the wolves. She'd run to him and embraced him like a—she lowered the brush to her lap and stared at it—like a wife. She had held her body against his and sobbed out his name. After he'd comforted her, they'd lain together, pressed from shoulder to ankle. He'd never touched her or taken advantage of her in any way.

The memory of how she'd acted the previous night made her ashamed. No wonder Colter had been distant this morning. No wonder he wanted to leave her. She'd insulted his honor. He wasn't like those men who used her mother then left their coins in the dish beside the bed. He wasn't Edward; he would never hit her or make her cry out in fear. She would tell him, she thought with a rush of fierceness. She would explain what had happened to her mother and her sister, and then ask him to forgive her. Surely if he understood her past, he wouldn't leave her alone until she'd learned how to survive.

She set the brush on the table and reached back to begin braiding her hair. A noise from outside caught her attention. She cocked her head and listened. There it was again. A horse. Colter!

She ran to the door and flung it open. She smiled widely. "Colter," she called. "You're back!"

The animal broke through the clearing. She stared at the gray mare, then raised her gaze to the rider.

Her scream shattered the afternoon. The blue jays in the trees squawked and took flight. The stocky rider stared at her, then a slow smile split his dark face.

"Now, ain't this interesting," he said, urging his mare closer to her. "Colter, is it? That wouldn't be Colter James you're calling to? He around here?" He pulled his rifle free of the saddle and looked around.

She stared up at him. Nameless terror swept over her, immobilizing her. She knew this man. She'd seen him that first day. He'd searched the wagons in front of her. He'd touched the nursing mother's breast. Zachery. The officer had called him Zachery.

He looked back at her. "Don't see nothing. Now, why would a man go off and leave a pretty thing like you behind? I'll bet he's hunting you some supper."

Her legs and arms refused to move. It was only when the man sheathed the rifle and started to dismount that she was able to jump back and start to run.

"Not so fast, girly," he said, slipping off his horse and coming after her. "You know where James is, and I aim to find him."

Maggie picked up her skirts and ran as she'd never run before. She drew in a deep breath and screamed for Colter to save her. Zachery thundered behind her. Even as she commanded her legs to move faster, he caught her arm and swung her around in front of him. She collided with his chest.

His fetid breath fanned her face and she shrank back. Dark hair fell over his forehead, much as Colter's did, but there was little else alike in the two men. Zachery's eyes gleamed with an animal cunning and an expression she couldn't read. She squirmed and tugged to break away from him.

"Not so fast," Zachery said, his free hand coming up to touch her loose hair.

She jerked her head away. "Let go!"

"Oh, I like a girl with fight in her. You'll tell me what I want to know about Colter James, but go ahead and make it hard on yourself first."

He slipped his hand down her back and pulled her closer to him. He stank of sweat and foulness and she wanted to retch. The hand holding her arm tightened. She screamed.

He laughed and glanced around the empty clearing. "Gant told me not to make trouble, but you ain't no farmer's wife. Who's going to miss you?"

# Chapter 18

Colter adjusted the bundle strapped behind him. He hadn't been able to get what he'd come for. The widow had no horse left to sell. He'd bought some ham and bacon, yeast, flour at a higher price than she'd asked, and ignored the gratitude in her eyes. He'd been ready to leave when he'd thought to ask about and then purchase her late husband's winter coat.

Colter patted the woolen garment laid out in front of him. It was for Maggie. He was tired of seeing her running around shivering, trying to gather wood to start a fire and cook, all the while clutching that blanket. At least she would be warm. Of course he hadn't solved the problem of leaving her. Without a horse, he would be as vulnerable as a fawn facing a pack of wolves. So Maggie was stuck with him for now. He glanced up at the clear sky. He would sleep outside tonight. It would be cold as hell, but at least he wouldn't have to see her shrink from him every time he got near her. In the morning he would head for another farm in the opposite direction. He had to get a horse.

Sebastian trotted along, his farm-horse gait uneven and shuffling. Without a saddle, Colter had to work to stay on the animal's back. He kicked him into a canter to get back to the cabin quicker. At the top of the next rise, he saw down into the valley. At the opposite end stood the cabin. A few minutes later he could smell the smoke from the fire, and he urged Sebastian to go faster. He thought about how Maggie would look when she saw the coat. Maybe it would make her smile again.

They rounded a bend in the narrow trail. Overhead, birds flew in wide circles and scolded loudly. Then he heard a scream.

The unfinished sides of the cabin's walls bit into her back. Maggie pressed harder as if she could melt through the wood and find herself safely inside. Her cheek throbbed from the strength of Zachery's blow and she tasted blood in her mouth. Mud caked her hands and the front and sides of her dress. She'd fallen when he hit her.

The tall broad man now stood in front of her, grinning. One of his bottom teeth was missing, she thought, staring into his eyes and knowing she would die. He reached forward and placed both hands on her breasts. She screamed again, this time calling for Colter to save her. But she no longer expected an answer.

She grabbed the man's arms and tried to force him back. He laughed and pressed hard against her. He leaned forward and kissed her neck, all the while squeezing and pinching her breasts. The pain and his closeness made her squirm. The smell of his body and breath surrounded her. One of his legs raised up and rubbed between hers. She pulled away, but he pinched her more and she cried out.

"That's it," he said, biting her hard just below her ear. "I want to hear your pain. I want to make you bleed and scream, and then I'm going to stick my cock up you until—"

"Colter!" she called, refusing to listen to this man's filthy threats. "Help me."

"He won't come," the man said.

He wrapped one hand around her hair and yanked her head back. She couldn't help thinking that she'd just washed her hair. Why did he have to keep touching it? If she survived, she would never feel clean again.

"You're mine," Zachery said, and reached down to kiss her.

"Think again."

Maggie gasped at the familiar voice. The words were followed by the slam of a rifle breech being snapped shut. Zachery spun away to face Colter. Before Zachery could reach for his pistol, a shot rang out. He jerked back against her, then fell to the ground. Blood spurted everywhere.

Maggie stared at the body lying at her feet, then slowly raised her eyes to Colter. He stood at the edge of the clearing, the rifle still in his arms.

"You killed him."

Colter let the rifle sag toward the ground. Her words hammered at him with almost the same force of the bullet that had destroyed Zachery. "Yes."

"Thank God." She sank to her to knees and began to sob.

Colter stared at her bent head, at the blood splattered on her hands and the cabin wall. Then he realized what she'd said. He dropped the rifle on the ground and raced to her side. Before he reached her, she looked up and held out her arms.

"Oh, Colter, you saved me."

Then he was holding her tightly against him. Her broken cries shattered him. Hot tears dripped against his shoulder and neck. Her heart thundered against his chest. He said her name over and over, rocking her back and forth. She continued to cry, her body trembling with each sob. Words about threats and fears tumbled out. Her fingers dug into his back. He cupped her head and held her closer. The smell of death surrounded them, but he couldn't let go of her. Mud caked her beautiful hair.

Her sobs lessened, spaced by deep breaths and hiccups. As she calmed, his anger built and turned to rage. Damn Zachery's soul to hell for all eternity.

"I heard a sound," she said, for the first time stringing words together to make sense. "A horse. I thought it was you." She pulled back enough to look up at him. Her eyes were red and swollen from the tears, but the irises stood out, a vivid blue. Her mouth quivered. "I came running outside. I wanted to tell you—" A sob broke through and she squeezed her eyelids shut. A tear escaped. "I wanted to say I was sorry about last night. I didn't mean to pull back. I know you'd never hurt me."

He'd been shot twice in his lifetime. Had a couple of knife wounds and been in countless brawls. But nothing caused him quite as much pain as her confession. He fought the anguish and the need to call out his fury at what had happened to this innocent woman.

"Hush, Maggie," he said. "You don't have to apologize. I shouldn't have—"

"No, it's not you. It's me." She bit her lower lip and shuddered. "He hurt me, Colter. He touched me and told me the things he was going to do to me. If you hadn't come back . . ."

Another tear slipped down her cheek. Without thinking, he moved his hand to cup her chin and used his thumb to wipe the tear away. She didn't recoil from his touch, he thought with gratitude. She simply stared at him as if she could find the ease for her suffering in his eyes.

"I'm glad you killed him," she said. "Is that wrong?"

"No. Men like him deserve to die."

"But you told me you didn't want to kill again."

"He doesn't count, Maggie."

She dropped her chin to her chest. "He touched me." Her shoulders hunched together. "My hair. I'd just washed it. Now it's dirty. And my face and my—"

He had no comfort to give her. Washing away the dirt wouldn't erase the memories. Only time would blur the edges of what had happened to her today. He wanted to lash out at Zachery, and at Gant for choosing such a man in the first place. He'd heard rumors of their joint perversions. If he hadn't arrived in time . . . He didn't allow himself to think of what would have happened.

He rose to his feet and pulled her up beside him. "Go on inside," he said.

She paled and clutched at his hands. "Don't leave me."

"I have to take care of the body."

She glanced down at the dead man. Blood oozed out of the wound in his chest. His eyes stared up sightlessly. "Oh, no." She took two stumbling steps, dropped to her knees, and threw up. He crouched beside her and held her hair out of her way. Her stomach continued to heave. When there was nothing left, he passed her his handkerchief. She wiped her mouth.

"It wasn't like that when Alice died," she said. "And Mama was already gone when I got there."

"It's all right," he said. He helped her to her feet. "Go on inside. I'll be along shortly."

She nodded once and walked to the door. When she disappeared inside, he bent down and grabbed Zachery by the heels and pulled him away.

It took several minutes to find the right place to leave the soldier. Colter didn't give a damn about burying the man. He hoped the wolves devoured him in a single night. A quick search of the area produced Sebastian munching happily on some spring grass. Zachery's horse had run off. Probably when the rifle fired. Colter squatted down and studied the tracks leading up to the cabin. The dead man had traveled alone. But for how long? If Zachery was this close, the others weren't far behind.

Gant would pay, he decided. Somehow, some way, when this was over he would punish the bastard as Maggie had been punished.

He hobbled Sebastian, then returned to the shack. Maggie jumped when he opened the door. She stood in the center of the room. Mud and blood covered her dress. Her face and hands were dirty and her hair matted. But it was her eyes that captured his attention. She was stretched so tight she was about to explode into a hundred pieces.

"I need to wash my hair," she said, twisting her hands together. "Is there hot water? I need hot water."

"Sit," he said, pulling out the chair. She just stood there, looking at him. Slowly, he reached for her hand. She didn't flinch. When their fingers entwined, he pulled her over to the chair and eased her down.

"You'll feel better soon," he told her.

"What about my hair?" Blue eyes focused on his.

After a battle he'd seen strong men wandering around talking about inconsequential things. The trauma of what had happened to them worked on their minds. Maggie was no different. He'd learned to just go along with whatever they wanted. If she wanted clean hair, he wasn't going to argue.

"I'll have to boil water."

"Yes," she said slowly. "I'll need water."

A full bucket sat beside the stove. He picked it up and nearly dropped it when she screamed. He spun around. Maggie stared down at the front of her dress.

"Blood. Oh, Colter, I'm bleeding!"

"You're fine." He placed the bucket on the stove and moved to her side. "It's Zachery's blood, not yours."

She brushed at her bodice, smearing the blood and mud together into a sticky paste. "Get it off me!"

He grabbed her shoulders and shook her. "Maggie, stop it. You're fine. The dress is dirty. If you take it off, I'll clean it."

Tears filled her eyes. "I'm not fine. I'll never be fine again. He wanted to hurt me, like those men hurt my mother."

He leaned forward and pulled her against him. He didn't understand what her mother had to do with this. "Hush, Maggie, I'm here."

"But you're leaving."

"No, I'm not."

She tilted her head back until she could look up at him. "You didn't find a horse?"

"No. I'm going to stay with you until it's safe to let you go," he said. "I give you my word."

She blinked the tears away, and some of the terror disappeared as well. "Your word. I trust that. I trust your word. And you. Help me."

He nodded. "I'm going to turn my back. Take your dress off and wrap yourself in a blanket. While the water's heating I'll go down by the stream and get your dress clean. You'll be fine while I'm gone."

She listened intently to every word. Her blue eyes widened as he spoke of taking off her dress, then she blanched at the mention of being alone.

"But I—"

"You'll be fine," he repeated, knowing he had to be strong for both of them. "Say it."

She swallowed. "I'll be fine while you're gone."

"When I come back, you can wash your hair."

"My hair." She reached up and touched the matted strands. Her eyebrows drew together. "You must be sorry you picked my wagon to hide in."

If he lived for all eternity, he'd never forget the image of seeing her pressed up against the cabin walls with Zachery about to rape her. Every night he would see the terror in her eyes and hear her cries. If Petty and Gant didn't find him and hang him, he would spend the rest of his days knowing his pathetic life wasn't worth one moment of Maggie's pain.

"Yes," he answered, and turned his back.

She stood motionless for several seconds. He listened to the silence. At last the whisper of skin on cloth told him she'd begun to undo the buttons. He clutched his hands into fists and the rage swept through him and left him trembling with impotence. There would be no payment for Zachery's crime, and his trip to hell had been too short to give Maggie ease.

"Here," she said.

He reached back and took the dress without turning around. When he reached the door, he paused. "You'll be fine."

"I know," she whispered.

He walked quickly to the stream. He looked around and found four heavy stones. About ten feet to his right, the water flowed over a flat, wide section of earthen bed before forming a miniature waterfall and narrowing over a cropping of rocks. Using the stones, Colter anchored the dress securely. The flow of the stream carried off surface bits of mud. Soon the rest of the stains would be gone.

He returned to the cabin. At the door he paused, not wanting to go inside and see Maggie. He hated knowing he was responsible for the dull fear in her eyes. Worse, there was nothing he could say to make her feel better, no offering he could make to turn back the events of the last few days and prevent Zachery from finding her.

He reached out and touched the latch. "Maggie, it's me," he called.

"You can come in."

He drew in a breath and stepped inside. The light from the open door flooded the small room. She stood near the stove. In the time he'd been gone, she'd washed her face and hands and pulled a blanket over her body. He scanned her slender shape beneath the rough wool. Without the yards of petticoats and dress, he could clearly see the outline of her body. The blanket gaped at the bottom, exposing long legs covered with pale pantaloons. Her hands clutched the ends of the length of wool at her chest, but he could see the swell of her breasts and the small ruffle of lace at the top of her camisole.

How he ached, looking at her. Not with desire. Not now, with her in so much pain. No, he ached *for* her, with her. He ached for having to see her like this. He'd imagined removing the layers of her clothing, one by one, easing away the feminine undergarments, and touching the delicate skin underneath. He'd thought about claiming her with his mouth and his hands. But he'd never wanted to see her like this.

At last, almost afraid of what he would see there, he raised his gaze to her face. She'd washed away the dirt. His breath caught in his throat, then was expelled with an angry growl. Rage returned. The imprint of a man's hand stood out on her pale cheek. A red swelling bruise defined each finger and the shape of his palm.

"I wish he weren't dead," Colter said, slamming the door shut behind him.

Maggie jumped. "What?"

"I'd kill him again, but slowly, until he suffered enough to pay for this." He motioned to her face. "Then I'd wish him alive again and again to continue killing him."

"I'm sorry for making you kill him." she whispered, and hung her head. "You did it for me."

He moved closer to her until only the table separated them. "I told you, his kind doesn't matter. He's needed killing for a long time."

"I wish I could believe you."

"It's true. Don't waste your pity on him."

She nodded without looking up. He wanted to go to her and offer comfort. He wanted to hold her close until all the horror faded and she remembered nothing except being safe and warm. But he didn't offer the comfort. It wasn't his place.

"I think the water's warm," he said, moving to the stove. She stepped back out of his way. "Do you still want to wash your hair?"

"Yes, please."

"When you're done, you can put on your gray dress. I've left the other in the stream. It should be clean soon."

He poured warm water in the basin she'd left on the table. A second bucket went on the stove. He picked up the jar of soap and handed it to her. She stared at it, and then at him.

"Help me."

Help her? He'd never seen a woman wash her hair, let alone assisted. The simplest course of action would be to wait outside until she was done. She'd washed her hair on her own before. She would manage. But even as he thought about bolting, she arranged the basin next to the bucket and lowered the blanket to her waist.

He didn't run away. He didn't voice his concerns. He simply did as she requested and helped. His hands felt big and awkward as he scooped up soap and rubbed it into her hair. He inhaled the clean scent and knew he would carry it with him always. When several strands fell loose, he caught them. The wet ends felt slick and cool to his touch. He did everything she asked, and one thing she didn't.

He didn't look. Not even when she raised her arms to lather in a second handful of soap. He sensed the front of her chemise tightening across her breasts. Water dripped down her neck and dampened the fabric. The thin cotton would become transparent, exposing the sweet shape of

her breasts and the color of her nipples. But he refused
to look.

Instead, he did as she bade and poured the water slowly
to help her rinse the soap away. He wiped a dab of lather
from behind one ear and ignored the need that threatened,
cooling it with glances at the rapidly darkening bruises on
her face. When she'd twisted her hair to remove the last
of the water, he handed her the petticoat she'd used as a
towel. She wrapped it around her head and straightened.
The blanket fell to the floor. And then he couldn't help
looking.

Her breasts thrust out, the nipples hard from the damp
cloth clinging to their rosy tips. The round undersides curved
upward in a shape designed to fit a man's palm. The ache
returned. He felt ashamed for the flash of desire streaking
through him, like lightning through a night sky. He had no
right to want this woman, or to see her exposed. She trusted
him with her battered self. He would rather die than betray
that trust. He bent down and picked up the blanket, then
draped it around her shoulders.

"Dry your hair," he said, pleased that his voice sounded
normal.

She seated herself in front of the stove. "Is it clean?"
She released the petticoat and her damp hair tumbled down
her back.

"Yes."

She touched a single strand. "It feels clean. I suppose
there's nothing more to wash out." She stared at the brush
he handed her.

"You'll forget," he said, knowing it wasn't true. But she
needed to hear the lie.

"I don't think so."

"The memories will fade."

"Do you forget?" She glanced up at him. Her blue eyes
probed his, looking for answers, demanding honesty. "Or
do you remember the names and faces of the dead?"

He hesitated. "I remember."

"All of them?"

"No. Some I killed without knowing their names."

"You knew this man."

It wasn't a question, but he answered it anyway. "Yes."

"Will you remember him?"

If he lied, she would know. He sensed that and believed it without question. "Yes."

She glanced down at her lap, then up at him. Her mouth trembled. "Because I made you kill him?"

"Because of what he did."

"I'm not sure I'm worth the spilling of blood."

"Everyone has a right to survive, Maggie. Even you."

"Everyone?" she asked. "Even Zachery?"

# Chapter 19 ═══════════

Colter stalked outside without answering and grabbed an armful of wood. He made the trip three more times, until there was enough for the rest of the evening.

"I'll see to your dress," he said, and left.

The slamming of the door made her jump. Maggie forced herself to pick up the brush and drag it through her hair. Everything took so much effort, she thought, wishing she could close her eyes and have this day over. She hoped Colter was right, that the memories would fade in time. She wished she could believe enough to pray. But God had let Alice and her mother die. No one had been punished. The injustice had weighed on her faith until it began to crumble. Now there was nothing left but dust.

Colter returned a few minutes later. As he had earlier, he identified himself before he came inside. She appreciated the gesture even as she resented its cause.

He hovered awkwardly just inside the door. "I'll make coffee," he said.

"That would be nice."

Her position sitting on the floor in front of the stove forced him to step around her. She thought about moving, but it was too much trouble. When he finished his task, he sat in their lone chair and stared over her head.

"Your dress is clean."

"Good."

"I've left it over a bush to dry. I checked the other clothes. They should be dry shortly. Thank you for washing my shirts. You didn't have to do that."

"I wanted to." She felt the tears well up in her eyes and wondered at the cause. Surely it took more than a clean pair of socks or a shirt to make her weep.

He crouched down beside her. "Maggie?"

"Oh, I don't know what's wrong, so don't bother asking. I don't usually cry at all, but in the last couple of weeks I feel as if that's all I ever do."

"I think you're very strong."

She sniffed and looked up at him. He'd removed his hat. Dark hair tumbled over his forehead. For a second she thought about Zachery and how he'd looked, but she forced herself to stare into Colter's gray eyes, and she knew the two men were nothing alike. Stubble darkened his cheeks and jawline. He'd left in such a hurry that morning, he hadn't bothered shaving. He'd left because . . .

"I'm sorry about last night," she said.

"I know."

"I didn't mean—" She twisted her fingers around her brush. "It wasn't about what you think."

"I know." He reached out his hand toward hers, paused, then took the brush from her.

Their eyes met. She glanced anxiously at him, searching his face for clues to what he was thinking. Handsome, she thought with surprise, as she had once before. Attractive enough to turn a woman's head when he walked down the center of town. But it wasn't his pleasing looks that made her relax enough to offer him a half smile. It was the gentleness she saw, the concern, and the memory of his anger on her behalf. No one had worried about her fate in many years.

She wanted to give him something back. She wanted him to know how much she appreciated what he'd done. Most of all, she needed him to know she understood the price he'd paid. She shifted on the ground, turning until her back was to him. She pulled her damp hair together and let it fall straight down. He drew the brush slowly through her hair. She leaned into the movement, letting him pull her head back.

"My mother used to do this when I was a little girl," she

said. "It always made me feel safe. Do you remember your mother?"

The brush slowed, then he resumed the stroking. "She died when I was about six. I have a couple of memories of her voice, but that's all."

She should have guessed, she thought, remembering his coldness their first few days together. Nothing soft or feminine had blurred Colter's masculine edges. She regretted the question and any pain it might have caused him. "I'm sorry."

"It was a long time ago."

Maggie drew her knees up close to her chest and pulled the blanket tight around her shoulders. The heat from the stove soaked into her body. She hadn't realized she felt cold until she began to warm. The tenseness seeped away with the chill, although tremors still racked her body. Flashes of Zachery bending over her made her quickly shut her eyes and want to squirm. Her breasts hurt where he'd abused her. But here, now, with Colter close and the walls of the cabin between her and the rest of the world, she didn't feel quite so terrified.

His hands felt strong and sure where they touched her shoulders and back as he lifted her hair. Each stroke soothed her. She let her eyes drift shut as she concentrated on the slow motions. The scent of his body, clean and pleasant, surrounded her, comforting her with its familiarity. She had survived the attack. The man who threatened her would never hurt her again. All because of Colter. And she had insulted his honor. Her eyes opened. If he hadn't come back . . . She shuddered and refused to let herself think of that.

"Last night," she said, then paused, not sure how to explain.

"You don't have to tell me. I understand."

She stared at the black stove. Dust covered the crevices in the legs. A candle burned on the table. Shadows collected in the corners, but she didn't fear them as much as she thought she might.

"I was nine when my father died," she said. Suddenly she could feel the wind whipping through her, as it had the day they'd buried the man. Snow had threatened. She remembered the cold the most. And the silence of her mother's tears. "We lost the farm and had to move to town, Alice, Mother, and I. There wasn't much money and we lived in a single room. First we ate only twice a day, and then once. Alice got a job working in a laundry. It helped, but not enough."

He reached up and drew her hair out from the side of her head. His fingers brushed her cheek. She winced as he touched the bruise. Instantly Colter froze in place. If she did nothing, said nothing, he would withdraw from her. If she explained her reaction, if she continued on with her story, he would know why she feared him. Had feared him. It would be so much easier not to tell; she'd never even told Alice. But that was the coward's way. She owed him more.

"The swelling is tender," she said, not daring to glance over her shoulder. He got to his feet. She clutched the blanket to her and rose to her knees. "Colter?"

He laid the brush on the table. "I'll be right back," he said, then grabbed the basin and left.

He returned a few minutes later. Snow filled the metal bowl. He tore off a section of her petticoat and soaked it in the snow. Then he handed her the cold cloth.

"Put that on your cheek. It'll help with the swelling and the pain."

"Thank you."

She sat on the blanket and did as he suggested. When he'd resumed brushing her hair, she forced herself to continue. "That summer after we moved to town, I spent most of my time outside. I kept Alice company at her job, or I ran errands for the lady who ran the general store. In return, she helped me with my reading and ciphering." The cloth warmed slightly and she turned it over. The stinging in her face was fading as the cold numbed the skin. "One day I came home and my mother had a stew cooking." She smiled at the memory. "Bread, too. It was the best meal we'd had since we moved to town. I never thought to ask where she got the money."

She hung her head until her chin touched her chest. "My mother was a good woman. She loved my father and my sister and me. She believed in God and prayed every day."

Colter dropped the brush and put his hands on her shoulders. Through the blanket and the thin cotton of her chemise, she felt his strong touch.

"You don't have to tell me this," he said quietly.

"I heard them that winter." Maggie shifted until she could look at him. He leaned against one of the table legs. As she turned, her knee slid between his thighs, but they didn't touch. "It was cold and she had no place to send me. It was a game, she said. I had to be perfectly quiet. A mouse." She forced herself to smile. "I thought it was a game, at first. Then I heard noises." She closed her eyes against the memories, but couldn't block out the sounds. "A man. And my mother. They—" She exhaled slowly and dropped the damp cloth in the bowl. "They did things. I couldn't imagine what. I wanted to ask my mother what was happening, but something made me afraid to. I think it was the sound of the coins hitting a metal dish. I'll remember that forever." She glanced up at him, expecting many things, but as usual his expression remained unreadable.

"I looked once. She hadn't locked the wardrobe door and it swung open a little. I could see them. That naked man on my mother." She tossed her head. The dried hair went flying over her shoulders. She brushed it away impatiently. "My mother sold herself to feed her children."

The tear fell before she could blink it back. Colter reached up and smoothed it away with the tip of his callused finger. "Maggie." His hand lingered on the undamaged side of her face as if he could communicate with his touch what words couldn't say.

She rose to her feet. "They killed her. After years of using her, one of those men came in the room while she was alone and he killed her. I found her body." Clutching the blanket tighter around herself, she began to pace the small room. Colter got up and stood in the corner, out of her way. "I ran to get the doctor, but it was too late. The sheriff didn't do anything." She bit down hard on her lower lip. "They talked about her in the streets. I heard them. Those same men who had paid for her spoke about her as if they were holy and she were the dirt beneath their feet. I hated them. All of them. The good men of the town were going to sell me to a family passing through on their way west. Alice had married by then. She came back and got me."

Colter watched as she stopped pacing and seemed to collapse in on herself. "No one cared that my mother had been murdered. No one cared but me."

The bitter taste in his mouth came from shame and guilt and anger. How many times had he paid for a woman, not caring who she was or where she'd come from? He'd never thought about the circumstances that had reduced her to prostitution, had never thought to ask about a family. A child.

He couldn't even imagine what it had been like for Maggie to see and hear her mother with all those men. His stomach churned. He was as guilty as any of them.

"That's why you frightened me," she said. "From the very beginning I've been afraid that you'd want me to do those things. That you'd force me. Hurt me."

Her long hair flowed around her like shimmering gold. He hated himself for the desire he'd felt for her. He had no right. "I'd never hurt you."

She raised her face until their gazes locked. Blue eyes, dark, troubled, filled with pain, called out to him. It was a small room; he could cross it in three strides. He took a single step. She didn't retreat. Another step, and still she remained in place. When he stood directly in front of her, she tilted her head back. The corner of her mouth quivered in a fair imitation of a smile, then she sagged against him.

He could have carried her for a mile without feeling the strain, but that slight weight pressing against him and the trust inherent in the gesture made his legs weak. Slowly, giving her every chance to withdraw, he placed his arms around her and held her close. He'd comforted her like this before, but always in reaction to danger. She'd clung to him without conscious thought. But this time she knew he touched her. Her hands wrapped around his waist, then moved higher up his back. Her unbruised cheek burrowed against his chest.

Inside, in the dark place his soul dwelt, he felt a sharp stab. It wasn't desire that plagued him. No, the growing hole signaled a much graver threat. Somehow, in the last few days, Maggie Bishop had begun to matter. He who had never risked himself for another, save once, cared about this woman. He would give his pitiful life for hers. Before God, he swore he would deliver her from this danger. At any price, he thought, even as he knew the price would be higher than he could imagine.

She looked up at him, then stepped back and took both his hands in hers. She studied his callused skin, rubbed her thumbs across his knuckles.

"You killed him for me," she said.

Unfamiliar emotions, more frightening than an enemy bullet, ripped through him. He could only nod.

"Thank you." She bent her head and touched her lips to his palms, first his left, then his right.

The fleeting kiss stirred him as no courtesan's touch ever had. Fire raced through him. The flame would burn unquenched. He stared into her blue eyes and knew the trust there would keep her safe from him forever. No one had believed before. He dropped his hands to his side. That wasn't true, he reminded himself. Alexander had believed, and now Alexander was dead.

# Chapter 20

Gant stirred the fire and stared into the darkness. Zachery was late.

He swore out loud, cursing the man and whatever kept him away. Damn it all to hell, if that bastard didn't get back by sunrise, Gant would have to waste good daylight looking for him. He poured himself another cup of coffee. He didn't need this shit right now. They were close to finding Colter James; he could feel it. His old enemy slept near enough that the hairs on the back of Gant's neck stiffened.

Something crackled to his left. He jumped to his feet and pulled out his pistol. "Zachery," he called softly.

Another noise, this more of a snuffling, caused him to relax and return the pistol to its holster. Some animal. Damn, he should have shot it and cooked it up.

He sipped the hot liquid and sat back down. Now what? Time was wasting, but there wasn't anything he could do about it. When Zachery got back, Gant was going to scare some sense into him. He smiled grimly. Not too much; he liked Zachery stupid and mean.

Tomorrow they would continue north. Knowing James's destination helped, but not enough. In this wilderness there were hundreds of paths a man could take. But he'd find him. It was just a matter of time.

Gant inhaled sharply, as if he could smell his old enemy. Oh, yes, Colter James was close. Soon he'd have him in his gun sights. Then he would kill him. And the truth would die with him.

*    *    *

Maggie stirred the pot on the stove. Colter had left long enough to kill a couple of rabbits. The meat simmered and its savory aroma filled the small cabin. The rest of their supplies were tucked in the corner. Tomorrow there would be bacon and biscuits for breakfast. She knew it was wrong, but she was grateful that the woman at the farm hadn't had a horse. Without his own mount, Colter would stay with her a few more days.

The door opened and Colter entered. He carried more wood in one arm and something bulky in the other.

She set her spoon down. "What have you found now?"

He set the wood on the pile, then held out the bundle. "For you." She stared. "Take it." His mouth tilted up in a smile.

She reached out and touched the cloth. Wool. She grabbed the fabric and pulled. Her gaze flew to his. "A coat?"

He nodded. "It might be a little big, but I didn't think you'd mind."

"Of course not." She slipped her arms into the sleeves and pulled it up around her. The thick material felt heavy on her shoulders and the collar rose up past her ears. She fastened the front. Already she felt warmer. The hem fell almost to her knees. "It's wonderful." She spun in the small room and laughed. "I'll never be cold again." She stopped in front of him and looked up. "Thank you."

His gray eyes softened. She would never be able to see into his soul, but for this moment the warmth flickering there was enough. He'd shaved. The smooth line of his jaw and tanned hollows of his cheeks tempted her touch. She reached out her hand, then pulled it back in confusion. What was she thinking of? He was a man; she couldn't *want* to touch him.

But he wasn't just a man, she thought, slipping off the coat. He was Colter.

She hung the coat on a peg next to his behind the door. As she smoothed the sides she repeated, "Thank you."

"You're welcome. I asked if she had any spare dresses, but she didn't."

"This is more than enough." She turned to face him. He stood as he always did, relaxed but alert. His tall, powerful body loomed over hers, but she wasn't afraid. Not of him. "You've already done too much."

He shook his head. "I can't do too much for you. It's my fault—" He motioned vaguely toward her. "My fault."

She didn't want to think about Zachery. "Nonsense. I don't want to talk about anything gloomy. We have a wonderful stew for dinner. I have a new coat. We have a fire." She tapped her foot on the ground. "And music."

Within minutes she'd pulled out the box and wound it. The tinny tune filled their cabin. Colter stared at the contraption. "I've never seen anything like it."

"I know. I'm so glad I brought it with me. I thought about leaving it. I was afraid something would happen to it, but then I realized I couldn't bear to be parted from the memories."

Her hair hung loose over her shoulders. She felt his gaze drawn to the curls tumbling down the bodice of her dress. Part of her wanted to pull her hair back and braid it. Part of her wanted to stand there watching him watch her. Her breathing increased slightly, as if she'd run too far. Her throat felt funny, almost tight, and a lump formed in her stomach. Before she could figure out what was wrong, Colter returned his attention to the music box and wound it up to play again.

They ate their stew with fresh biscuits. A single can of peaches remained. She poured them in the pan and topped them with a flour-and-sugar mixture.

They sat in silence while the dessert baked. Maggie found herself content to lean against the bedrolls and stare into the darkness. Colter whittled wood into kindling. She watched his strong hands move quickly and confidently. Logs cracked in the fire, the sound mingling with the calls of the night creatures. This evening no wolves disturbed the mood.

"We'll leave early in the morning," Colter said.

"Fine. I'm going to make bacon for breakfast." She stretched her arms over her head and smiled at him. He didn't look up. The tightness of his expression troubled her. "You're thinking that you'd be better off by yourself, aren't you?"

"No."

"Colter." She reached out to him. He stopped carving and looked at her. Slowly, deliberately, she rested her hand on his forearm. "Tell me what you're thinking."

"My thoughts aren't fit for a lady's ears."

"I never thought of myself as a lady."

"That doesn't change the fact."

She withdrew her hand and rested it in her lap. She wouldn't get anywhere badgering him. He was the kind of man who would go to his grave with his secrets.

The music box wound down. She rose and turned the key several times, then checked on the cobbler. Another few minutes, she thought, staring at the still-pale crust.

Her face throbbed from Zachery's blow. She reached up and touched the bruise. Even as her fingers traced the imprint she remembered her horror when she'd first seen Zachery in the clearing. The look of uncontrolled lust in his beady eyes. She swallowed thickly and fought the memories. The expression on his face when she'd called for Colter. He had—

Blood rushed to her head. She clutched the back of the chair and squeezed it tightly.

"He was one of them," she said. "Zachery. He was one of the men after you!"

"I know."

"Oh, no!" She spun to face him. Her hand came up and covered her mouth as the realization finally dawned. "They're right here. Close by. They must be, for him to have found the cabin."

"They split up." He nicked off another chunk of wood.

"But the others—"

"Not far behind."

"You're in danger. What are you doing here? Why haven't you run?" she demanded. "Take Sebastian, go. You've killed Zachery. They mustn't find you. I'll be fine by myself. Just go. Now!"

"I'm not leaving without you."

"But you'll travel faster alone."

He studied the piece of wood, then sliced off a sliver by the edge. "No."

"But you have to think—"

"No," he said again, this time more firmly. "I'm not leaving you behind. You're my responsibility and I'll not risk letting Petty and Gant get ahold of you."

"They won't do anything."

"There's a dead soldier lying out there. Can you prove you didn't kill him?"

She sat heavily in the chair. "Then we must leave tonight. This minute. Before they catch you."

"We'll leave early in the morning."

She wanted to argue with him. She wanted to convince him to run, to take Sebastian and ride for freedom. She wanted to pack up their belongings and force him out into the night. She looked at his face. Only the tight set of his jaw hinted at any internal turmoil.

"It's because of me," she said softly. "Isn't it? You won't leave me behind because you promised to keep me safe, and you won't leave tonight because of what happened earlier."

"We both need the rest."

"There'll be a lot of rest if we end up in prison."

He set his knife on the ground and rose to his feet. When he stood in front of her, he reached down and pulled her up in front of him. His hands held hers, his callused thumbs brushing back and forth across her knuckles. "No one is going to prison. Do you trust me to keep you safe?"

They stood close enough that if she leaned a little toward him, they would touch. The frightened little girl inside longed to bridge the distance and feel the warmth of his body next to hers. The woman inside feared the man. "I trust you," she said, wishing she could trust completely.

"If I thought those men were close enough to find us tonight, I wouldn't risk your life."

The top of her head barely grazed his chin. She had to bend her head back sharply to see his face. Firm male lips offered a half smile. She smiled back.

His hands felt good on hers. Warm and safe and comforting. She wanted to cry out in protest when he released her fingers. "I think your dessert is about done."

She sniffed. "I think you're right."

When she'd spooned out the warm sweet and taken her first bite, she thought about the first night they'd spent together. She'd used peaches to barter for information. They'd come so far.

"This is good," Colter said.

"I'm glad you like it."

Or had they? In a way, their situation had come full circle, back to where they'd begun. That first night she'd huddled under her blankets, terrified that her kidnapper would kill her, or worse. Her life had been at risk, because of him. These many days later men hunted the hunter. They were now close enough that she could smell death. Yet he stayed in this tiny cabin and offered her protection, when leaving would surely save him. Now his life was at risk because of her. A mirror image.

They cleaned up the dishes quickly. Maggie went outside first. While Colter was gone she wrapped up the music box and returned it to its burlap bag. Then she stretched out the two bedrolls close to the stove.

The door opened. "Use your coat to keep warm," he said as he stepped inside.

"I will."

She took it off the peg and stretched it out over her blankets. She pulled off her shoes and slipped under the layers of cloth. The coat smelled of horses and tobacco and faintly of a man she'd never met. The combined odors weren't unpleasant.

Colter moved around the cabin, adding wood to the fire, then blowing out the candle. She heard him settle down next to her.

Her breathing slowed and she closed her eyes. Her muscles relaxed. Suddenly an evil laugh filled the tiny room. Her eyes flew open and she stared into the darkness. Nothing. She must have imagined the sound, she thought, trying to calm her racing heart. A hand touched her breast and she inhaled the fetid smell of Zachery's body. She jerked up on one elbow. Despite her attempts to hold back the sound, a moan of distress escaped her lips.

"Maggie, what's wrong?" Colter's calm voice comforted her in the blackness.

"Nothing." She lay back down. "I'm sorry I woke you."

"I wasn't asleep."

It was all in her mind, she told herself. Just a reaction to what had happened earlier that day. She'd had nightmares for months after she'd found her mother's dead body. She would get over this, as she'd eventually stopped having those dreams.

She clutched her arms tight around her chest and forced herself to think of pleasant things. Of the warm spring sunshine and the taste of the cobbler. Slowly she relaxed again, letting her head sink into the folded clothes that served as a pillow.

The shaking began in her legs. Tiny tremors rippled her calves and thighs. They moved up to her arms and chest, and finally her whole body shook. Even her teeth chattered. Behind her, Colter stirred restlessly. She bit her lower lip to keep her teeth quiet and waited for him to yell at her. Instead, she heard cloth rustling. Then a warm body brushed against hers. She jumped.

"Hush," he said, his arm coming around her waist and pulling her tightly against him. His hard chest pressed against her back, his legs, through the yards of her dress, tangled with hers. Warm sweet breath fanned her cheek.

"I'm s-sorry," she whispered.

"No need to be."

"It's just—"

"Hush. I'll keep you safe."

Gradually the tremors slowed and she allowed herself to sag back against him. As her eyes drifted shut she felt a warmth deep in her belly. She tucked one hand under her unbruised cheek and let the other rest on top of his.

This was nice, she thought. Perhaps this was what Alice had meant when she talked about liking some parts of the marriage bed. Colter shifted. Her breasts felt tender from Zachery's abuse, but a slight tingling began behind the pain. Her fingers moved against his hand. He splayed his hand and her fingers slipped between his. She didn't want to sleep, she wanted to hold on to this moment forever.

"Tell me about your family," she said.

He didn't answer for so long, she thought he'd gone to sleep. "They're gone," he said at last.

She wasn't surprised. She'd sensed a connection from the beginning. "So we're both alone."

"You're not alone, Maggie."

# Chapter 21

Colter stepped out into the predawn cold. Maggie slept on by the fire. He deliberately didn't look back at her curled under the blankets and her coat.

Sometime in the night she'd turned toward him. When he awoke, it had been to firm breasts pressing into his chest and her leg thrust between his. His hardness had flared instantly, and he'd backed away without making a sound.

Even with the freezing air swirling around him, the throbbing continued to ache between his thighs. He'd deliberately not put on his jacket. It took a while, but finally the cold won and his need subsided to a manageable annoyance. He shrugged into his coat and went to check on Sebastian.

When the horse was fed and watered, he collected their now frozen clothes. Everything she'd washed early yesterday had dried in the night. A couple of hours in the sun would thaw them. Her dark wool dress was still soaked through. He'd have to stretch out an oilcloth and place the dress on top of it today to dry. At least Maggie had her spare gray.

Maggie. Even as he thought her name pictures of her filled him. She'd been so brave last night, insisting that he leave without her. Her blue eyes had flashed with equal parts fury and indignation. She was determined to protect him. She had about as much hope as a barn cat facing a hungry wolf. No one had ever offered *him* protection. No one had ever given a damn before, except maybe Alexander.

He collected a few more logs and quietly entered the cabin. As he stirred the embers of their fire he thought about his friend. He missed him. Damn fool waste of time. They hadn't seen each other much in the year before Alexander had been murdered. Still the empty feeling persisted. He measured out coffee and water, then set the pot on the stove. He cut several slices of bacon and dropped them into a pan.

Maggie turned in her bundle of blankets, sighed, then raised her head and blinked sleepily at him. Long blond hair tumbled down both shoulders and in her face. She pushed it aside. Being so close to her warm soft body had kept him awake much of the night and he'd used the time to touch her hair. Even now he could feel the silkiness on his palm. He looked away.

"Good morning," he said as he turned the bacon.

"Is it still dark out?" she asked.

"Yes."

"Good. I didn't want you to let me sleep late."

She sat up and stretched. He didn't have to look to know the fabric of her bodice would tighten over her breasts. Stop it, he commanded himself. He'd gone without before.

No, that wasn't it. It wasn't about being without a woman, he thought with regret. It was about being with Maggie. He had a bad feeling that the need was specifically for her. He knew her past, he knew what she feared. He burned for the one woman he could never have.

Maggie stood up and folded the blankets. Then she slipped into her coat. "I'll just be a minute," she said, walking toward the door.

"Bacon and coffee will about be done when you get back."

She left the cabin. He stared down at the pan. Gant was closing in. He could tell by the feeling of unease that had settled on him in the night. They were going to get out of here, but barely ahead of his former student. Even if the wolves had found Zachery's body, with all the tracks left around the cabin, it wouldn't be hard for someone to figure out what had happened. And Gant was no fool.

The old question of why he'd been framed for murder filled him. He wondered if he'd ever find the answer. Eight men, shot in the back. Nothing stolen except for Alexander's rifle. Why those men? Why Alexander? Why take the rifle? What had those men done to deserve killing?

He shook his head. He should know better. Most people needed a reason for killing, but enough didn't. They liked the sport of it. Still, eight men shot in the back wasn't much sport. They'd had their hands tied together and their feet hobbled so they couldn't run. There hadn't been much sign of a scuffle, so the men had known their killer. Who? And why?

He turned the bacon again, then slid it onto two plates. As he studied the meat he thought of the black-haired widow who had sold it to him. If Gant and Petty found the cabin, they would find Zachery. And the woman. She would be able to describe him. They would know he'd killed their man. Would they suspect why?

He'd ridden alone to the farm. The widow didn't know about Maggie. He aimed to keep it that way. Whatever happened, he was determined to get her out of this alive.

The door banged open. Maggie stepped inside. Her cheeks glowed from the cold. "Snug as a bedbug," she said, pulling her hands out of the pockets of the heavy coat and blowing on them.

"Good. Eat." He poured coffee.

They didn't talk through breakfast. While she cleaned the dishes he packed up their supplies. He hitched up Sebastian. The gelding tossed his head and neighed, as if eager to get under way.

"You might not be much to look at, but you're a strong one, aren't you?"

The horse nuzzled Colter's hand. He patted the animal's head and scratched his ears, then went inside for Maggie.

As the first rays of sun crept over the trees, they pulled away from the clearing and out of the valley. Colter thought about going to the farm and asking the woman not to

mention him. He could pay her. Then he thought about
Gant and what he would do if he found out she'd lied to
him. Five or six orphans wouldn't disturb Gant's sleep for
a single night.

Colter turned around and glanced back the way they'd
come. There was nothing to be done about the woman
now. He couldn't take back talking to her. His gaze fell
on the narrow path and the clear marks their wagon cut
in the ground. The left rear wheel wobbled. If Gant con-
nected him with the wagon they'd be as easy to track as
a one-legged bear. But Gant had no reason to. Colter had
ridden to the widow's house on horseback.

On the wagon seat, Maggie wiggled in her coat and
smiled at him. "It's going to be a beautiful day."

She was the most beautiful part of it, he thought as her
blond hair fluttered in the morning breeze. At least she was
safe. For now. He looked around them, at the trees rising on
either side. Most of the snow had melted. Only a few dirty
patches showed through the underbrush. Tracks of animals
crisscrossed through the mud.

"There," he said, pointing at a dainty set of tracks. "That's
a deer. Different animals live in different parts of the country,
but some are in all of them. Usually you can find deer and
rabbits."

She studied the ground as he tried to teach her enough
so that she could survive without him. If Petty and Gant
got too close, he would have to risk sending her off on her
own. Telling himself she'd be fine didn't ease the knot of
worry in his gut.

Gant paused at the top of the rise. A narrow valley
stretched down before him. He saw several paths, a cleared
area, and a small cabin at one end. But no sign of Zachery.

He glanced at the sky. Almost noon. He didn't have time
to waste. He had to meet up with Petty in two days. If he
didn't find Zachery soon, he would have to go on without
the man.

To his left an open field stretched out for about half a
mile. In the distance something moved. He squinted, but

couldn't get a fix on it. Damn. He was about to urge his mare on when the object moved again. It looked like a horse.

With a slight pressure from his knees, the mare leaped forward. What a beauty, he thought as he stroked her mane. He would have to tell Colter how much he'd enjoyed the mare. He would tell him right before he killed him.

Her smooth gait carried them quickly across the field. Through the thin row of trees he saw a familiar horse, saddled and bridled, cropping new grass. Zachery's mount.

Gant slipped his rifle from its sheath on the side of his saddle and looked around. No way his man would go off and leave his horse like that. He listened. The sounds of the birds told him no one else was around. No predator, no other men. He urged Siren close to the other horse and grabbed its reins. The animal snorted and tried to continue eating. Gant stared at the ground, then secured Zachery's horse to a tree and turned his mare in the direction the other horse had come.

It took almost two hours to follow the animal's tracks until they disappeared into the stream. Although he studied the ground carefully, there had been no sign of Zachery. Gant inhaled. Someone had been cooking nearby. Not recently, maybe not since morning, but certainly in the last couple of days.

The mare stepped out of the woods by a small cabin. Gant dismounted and went inside. The stove was still warm. Someone had left within the day. He went back outside. On the dirt path, leading out of the valley, wagon tracks cut through the mud. They looked familiar. He crouched down. Left wagon wheel was loose. He remembered he'd seen these tracks a few days before.

"Is that you, James?" he asked aloud. Squawking blue jays circled overhead, but had no answer for him.

He walked toward the stream, searching for footprints. He found a man's by a flat part of the stream and a woman's footprint a little ways down. He moved in a wider half circle, looking for anything that might identify the owners of the wagon.

Colter James would never travel with anyone. Not unless he didn't have a choice. If it *was* him, at least he was with a woman, and not his friend the general.

A cold sweat broke out on Gant's back as he thought about the general. The man would as soon skin him alive as look at him. Gant glanced up at the sky. Damn. Where the hell was Zachery? They had to find James before Petty and the others did. At the very least they had to find him before he found his friend. If James and the general got together—Gant shuddered—that sunrise would be his last.

He walked away from the stream toward the cabin. Before he got there, he circled around a large oak tree and tripped over a familiar black boot. He pressed against the tree for balance and looked down. He wished he hadn't. He turned his head, took two steps, and heaved his guts out.

Zachery. Or what was left of him after the wolves had feasted on his body. The booted leg was all that remained, except for a few scattered bones and a partially eaten head resting against a rock.

Gant wiped the back of his mouth with his hand. He hurried to his mare and quickly left the cabin. Now he knew what had happened to Zachery.

The mare cantered across the narrow valley. Gant took a swallow of whiskey from the bottle he kept tucked in his coat pocket.

They crested the rise and Gant looked around at the farmland. Some was already plowed, ready to be planted. To the west stood several fields that hadn't been worked. James wouldn't risk stopping here, he thought. Unless he needed something real bad. Gant remembered the wagon tracks. Maybe a horse? He patted the mare. Only one way to find out. But which farm? He glanced down and saw a single set of tracks crossing an unplowed field. He followed them. When he reached the house, several children ran out to greet him. A pretty dark-haired woman walked out onto the porch and shaded her eyes against the sun.

# Chapter 22 ═══════════════

Their luck had changed and it wasn't for the better. Colter stared at the path. Damn. He looked over his shoulder. It didn't matter that he couldn't see Petty and Gant. He *knew* they were there. Behind them. Gaining.

"Are they closer?" Maggie asked.

He didn't spare her a glance. Or an answer. No point in taking out his bad temper on her. She'd done her best to stay out of trouble and not hold them up. It wasn't her fault they were being chased by the United States Army. Hell, it wasn't even her fault she wasn't halfway to Missouri by now.

"Colter?"

His name, spoken with concern and a touch of fear in her voice, made him feel lower than a snake's belly. Damn.

"It's not you, Maggie." He glanced at her and forced himself to smile. "I don't like this country." He motioned to the rolling hills of harvested forest. Where there once had been acres of pine and oak, stretched hundreds of stumps broken by patches of brush and tiny saplings.

"But you can see if anyone's behind you."

"And be seen." He flipped the reins. "I prefer cover. I can track any man anywhere, but this way the odds are too close to even."

"Even? There are eight of them."

"Seven," he said, then wished he hadn't.

For the last two days they'd managed not to speak about what had happened at the cabin. Maggie still suffered in her sleep, but the dreams were short, and usually only disturbed

193

her once or twice in the night. Perhaps that was also contributing to his bad temper. He was growing soft, he thought with disgust. He liked holding her every night. He enjoyed the feel of her body next to his. He liked knowing she had grown comfortable enough with his presence that he could casually pat her back or tug on her braid without her cowering in fear.

"Well, seven against one," she said. "That's so much better. I shouldn't be concerned at all."

He looked at her. Her smile seemed forced, as did her humor. Still, he grinned in return.

"How far are they behind us?" she asked.

His grin faded. He wasn't sure she was ready to hear the truth. Hell, he wasn't sure he was ready to tell it. "Close," he said.

"In days."

She wasn't a fool. Fearless, strong, and beautiful. "Three. Maybe four. But they're on horseback. They'll travel faster."

"How long until they catch us?"

"They won't."

She placed her hand on his forearm. Her fingers tightened. "How long?"

"Three days. They'll catch us in three days."

She turned in her seat. The weather had warmed to well above freezing. They hadn't seen ice and snow since leaving the cabin. She'd pulled off her new coat and draped it over her shoulders. "Why didn't you tell me this before? What are you going to do?"

"Not get caught."

"How?"

"Get where I'm going before they get me."

"Where are you going?"

"To meet a man."

The wagon rolled over a rut. Maggie had to clutch the sides to stay in her seat. She glared at him. "That's it? That's all you're going to tell me?"

"You don't need to know more." He glanced at her. Disappointment clouded her blue eyes. She swept her long lashes down, but not before he saw the emotion.

"I see." She turned to face front, and folded her hands in her lap. A single strand of hair escaped from her braid and whispered against her cheek.

He reached out and tucked it behind her ear. Her skin was warm to his touch. And softer than he could have imagined. It made him want things he'd never known enough to want before. It made him regret having met her, for he knew what it would cost when he let her go. "If you don't know where we're going, you won't be able to tell Major Petty anything."

"You don't trust me." Her lower lip jutted out. "Why?"

"I trust you more than I've trusted anyone."

"Of course. I'm terribly honored by that trust." She sounded bitter and hurt.

"I don't want you to know where we're going so that if we're caught, you won't have to lie. Petty may look like a dandy, but he's not stupid. You don't lie well, Maggie. I'd rather you didn't have to learn to on my account."

There was one thing he wasn't telling her. He didn't want to give Gant an excuse to kill her. The other man would be angry that Colter had been this difficult to find and he would want to take out his temper on anyone or anything that got in his way. Better for it not to be Maggie.

"If that's a compliment," she said, some of the hurt going out of her, "then thank you."

"You're welcome."

"You've mentioned before that you know the men after you. Who are they? How do you know them?"

"I served under Major Petty for a time, during the war. He's a good officer."

"You sound as if you like him."

Colter scanned the horizon. The lack of trees and almost unlimited visibility made him as nervous as a rat on hot stove. But he had to keep going. He squinted up at the sky. Almost due west now, he thought. Just a few more days.

"Petty's all right. It's Gant who's the problem."

"He's the tracker?"

He nodded.

"You trained him?"

"For two years." He thought about their time together and grimaced. "Never liked him. He's—" He glanced at Maggie. Despite what she'd been through with her mother and her sister's husband, she was still innocent about the real evil in the world. Gant's perversions would make a whorehouse matron blush and then vomit. "He's dangerous."

"Why?"

"He won't let anything stop him. Or anyone. No price is too high."

"That must have made him a good soldier."

"Yes."

"Were you a good soldier?"

He should have expected the question. She asked it innocently, her face clear and guileless. He could keep it that way with a lie, or see her shrink from the truth. The hell of it was, he was tired of lying. "The best."

She nodded. Her expression didn't change. "I thought so. But not anymore."

Every time he thought he understood her, she surprised him. He had a feeling that he could know Maggie Bishop for a lifetime and still not understand her. "Not anymore," he agreed.

"So you and Gant tracked during the war?"

"Most of it. Gant got a command the last year. In the Colored Troops."

"Oh. Did you get a command?"

"Never wanted one."

"Did they offer?"

"Yes."

"Then why did you refuse?"

Up ahead Colter saw a ribbon of reflection that signaled they were close to water. "We'll stop there for lunch," he said, pointing.

"Colter James, you are the worst companion I've ever had. Just when we finally start talking, you stop answering questions." She planted her hands on her hips.

"How many companions have you known?"

"What?"

"I'd like a figure so I know just how bad I am. Five? Twenty? Am I the worst of twenty, Maggie?"

"Oh, you, you!" She stomped her foot on the footboard and huffed. "You know what I mean."

"Yeah, I know." She sat so stiffly in the seat he thought her spine might snap at the next bump in the path. "All right. Ask me anything. Except not about the war."

She eyed him suspiciously. "And you'll answer?"

"Yes."

She shrugged out of her coat and tossed it in the back of the wagon. She toyed with the end of her braid. "Have you ever been married?"

"No."

She shifted in her seat until she was turned toward him. She chewed on her lower lip. "Where did you grow up?"

"In the mountains, out west."

She thought for a moment. "All right. Tell me about when you were growing up."

He sighed heavily as his good humor fled. What would she want to hear? That his father was a liar and a thief? That when he was home he drank and beat his kids? The good part had been that he was gone most of the time. Would Maggie like to hear about the first time he, Colter, killed a man? Maybe he should describe his first visit to a whorehouse. Anger threatened. He told himself the person he was angry with was himself and not her. His temper would only damage the fragile bond between them, but that didn't relieve the need to lash out. Still, he wouldn't hurt her. He couldn't. There had to be something pleasant he could tell her. Something to appease her without scaring her back into a cowering huddle. He searched his memory.

"There was an old man," he said at last. "A half-breed. He taught me about tracking animals. How to find them. What to do with the pelts and the meat."

"What did your father do?"

"He was a trapper." He flicked the reins and urged Sebastian to go faster.

"Why did you leave the mountains and join the army?"

Again he didn't answer.

"Colter?" Maggie looked at him.

"You don't want to know any of this," he said.

"But I—"

"My father beat the hell out of me while I was growing up. Once when he was drunk, he hit my younger brother so hard he killed him. I ran away because I knew I was next. Is that enough? Do you want to know more?"

He hunched in his seat, not bothering to look at her, knowing what he would see if he did. She'd been huddled in the corner, her eyes wide and unfocused. He didn't want to know she still feared him. He cursed himself, his temper, and her for asking in the first place.

"I'm sorry I've upset you," she said calmly.

He risked a glance. She stared straight ahead. Her face looked pale, except for the bruise, but other than that, there was no sign of terror. God, he was a bastard.

"You haven't," he said. "It's not you. It's the men after us. It's this shorn forest. I'm not fit company."

They neared the stream. Colter drew Sebastian to a halt and jumped down. He walked around to Maggie's side and held out his arms. Their eyes met. No fear, he thought with some surprise. Just compassion and some emotion he didn't dare name. Just seeing it was like a kick in the gut.

She placed her hands on his shoulders and he lowered her to the ground. When she'd gained her balance, she raised her hand and touched his cheek. "You're a good man, Colter James," she said, then stepped back.

An uncomfortable heat blossomed around his shirt collar. He ducked away. "We'll camp here for an hour or so, then cross the river."

He walked to the nearby bank and studied the flowing water. From shore to shore, the flow measured about fifty feet at the narrowest point, then widened to a hundred a few yards downstream. Past that, rocks jutted out from both shores. No telling how deep the water was. The midday sun beat down on his back. He removed his hat and brushed the back of his hand across his forehead. It was warming up fast. Snow runoff would widen and deepen all the rivers and streams. The currents would flow fast, threatening all who crossed. In fact, the runoff should have already started, but this river didn't look dangerous.

He squatted down and touched the soil. Dry. The banks were flat here. He looked around. Not many trees grew close to the water. That didn't make sense. He moved closer to a stunted oak tree and fingered the bark. About a foot off the ground, several large gouges, more like blows than cuts, showed through the bark. As if something big, or fast moving, had hit the tree.

"What's wrong?" Maggie asked.

"Not sure. This doesn't feel right. The river should be higher." He shrugged but couldn't erase the bad feeling tightening the muscles between his shoulder blades.

"Maybe we should cross first, and then eat. The *Prairie Traveler* says to cross any body of water before settling for the night. In case it rises while you're sleeping." She stared up at him earnestly.

"You been reading your book?" he asked.

She nodded.

"That's good advice." He looked upstream. "And what we're going to do. Make sure nothing's hanging over the edge of the wagon. I can't tell how deep the river is. It might go up past the sides, so pile what needs to stay dry on top."

He boosted her into the wagon back. While she rearranged their belongings he walked up and down the bank. A faint sound caught his attention. He shook his head. Not a roar, more of low rumble. He checked Sebastian's tack and made sure the lines weren't tangled.

"I'm done," Maggie said as she scrambled into the front seat. She set the burlap bag containing the music box between them on the seat.

"Let's go," he said.

She clutched his arm. "Colter, look." She pointed at the river.

"So?"

"That little tree there. It wasn't in the river before, was it?"

He studied the width of the water. She was right. It was wider than it had been just five minutes ago. And the current looked rougher.

"Should we try and go around?" she asked.

"No time. It'll only be worse upstream. We can't cross down there." He pointed. "See those rocks? We'd be crushed, or at least lose the wagon. From the looks of it, we couldn't cross anywhere downstream for at least another couple of miles. We'll have to take our chances here."

"I understand." She looked at him with complete trust. Her confidence made him feel worse.

He didn't want to ask, but he had to. "You know how to swim?"

She shook her head.

Figured. He reached back and grabbed a rope. In the time it took to secure her to the seat, the river had risen another foot. He flicked the reins. Sebastian took a step forward. Water sloshed around his hooves.

"If the river is deep," Colter said, "the wagon will start to float. The current will carry us down some. It's smooth enough and slow enough that we won't turn over. The horse can swim. We'll most likely get lodged by a tree or against the muddy bottom. Just hang on."

With one hand, Maggie gripped the ropes around her waist. There was a slipknot beside him. If he was wrong and the wagon did turn over, he could release her in an instant, then drag her ashore. Her other hand held on to the music box.

"I'm ready," she said.

He took a deep breath. The clean moist air filled his lungs. Drowning was not how he'd planned on dying. He'd seen other men go that way. It wasn't fast or pleasant. Not that there was a good way to die.

"Come on, boy," he called, and flicked the reins.

The old gelding tossed his head in protest, then moved farther into the water. Colter felt the instant the horse began to swim. The leather lines floated and the wagon jerked from side to side. He braced his feet on the footboard and held the reins more firmly. He glanced at Maggie.

She stared back at him. Color stained her cheeks and her eyes glinted with determination.

"I—I'm all right," she said.

Water rose past the wheels and seeped onto the floorboard. Maggie shrieked and held up her feet.

"It's cold!" she said. "It seems all I do is get this blue dress wet."

With a giant lurch, the wagon rose up, swept away by the water. Colter tensed to stay in one place on the seat. They rocked back and forth. Maggie was silent. He didn't have time to look at her.

"You still with me?" he asked.

"Yes."

"If we make it—"

"If?"

"When we make it to a town, I'll buy you a new dress."

"I'll settle for staying dry."

Sebastian continued to move forward, swimming hard against the current. But for every foot he gained, the river moved them downstream three. The wagon rocked and bucked like an unbroken stallion. The contents shifted and banged together. Water sloshed higher and higher. He began to worry that they would sink before they made it across. Small waves lapped at his ankles.

Another foot forward. They were more than halfway across. Despite the warmth of the sun, Colter felt cold. He glanced around, trying to figure out where they would land. They were getting closer to the rocks. They had to reach the bank before they hit the rocks, or they wouldn't be able to save the wagon. He looked upstream.

A large dark shape flowed through the water toward them. A log swirled closer and closer.

"Hang on," he called.

Maggie turned to look. "Oh!"

She clutched the side tighter. He switched the reins to his left hand. With his right, he gripped the slipknot, ready to release her if they tipped over.

The water-soaked log hit the rear of the wagon. The force spun them halfway around. Sebastian nearly went

under. Water sloshed up, soaking Maggie. She screamed
and clutched at the sides with both hands. The wave caught
the music box and carried it into the river.

"No!" she called. She reached for it, but the rope held
her in place.

"Let it go," Colter commanded, tugging gently on the
reins to get the horse headed back toward the bank. Just
another couple of feet and the gelding should be able to
touch bottom.

"No!" She lunged forward struggling to reach the music
box. The burlap bag floated farther away.

"Dammit, Maggie, it's not worth your life."

The box bobbed in the water, dipping below the surface,
then reappearing just out of her reach. She glanced over her
shoulder. "Please. I can't lose it. It's all I have."

He cursed her, then pulled the slipknot. Wrapping the
loose end around his hand, he released enough line for her
to hang over the edge.

"A little more," she called back to him. "I can't quite . . .
get . . . it. It's starting to sink. Hurry."

He released more line. Sebastian scraped the bottom. The
jarring motion sent her falling toward the stream. Her skirt
dipped into the water.

"Colter!"

He dropped the reins and grabbed the rope with both
hands. The slick footboard made it hard to keep his balance.
Slowly, he began to pull her back.

"Wait." With one last stretch, she grabbed the bag. "Got
it."

He pulled hard, jerking her to safety. Sebastian gained
his balance and heaved on the wagon. Colter felt his feet
slip out from under him. He went to grab for the side,
realized he was holding the rope, and released it so Maggie
wouldn't be pulled down with him. He reached for the seat
back, lost his grip, and fell into the river.

# Chapter 23 ════════════════

Maggie clutched the soaked burlap bag to her chest. The slight splash made her turn around.

"Colter!"

She screamed his name. The place where he had been sitting was empty. The rope tied to her waist dangled off the side of the wagon.

"No! Colter!"

She tossed the bag into the back of the wagon and peered over the side. Nothing. She called again. Several feet away she saw his hat floating. Sebastian continued pulling the wagon up the side of the bank. The winded animal lurched to a stop and Maggie found herself falling out of the wagon into the river.

She landed on her back. Water surrounded her and she didn't dare breathe. Panic threatened, and with it the knowledge that she was going to die. She opened her mouth to scream. Water filled her mouth. No! Not that. She mustn't inhale.

Then she realized her hands were clutching the muddy bottom. She pushed off and struggled to her feet. Her head broke through the surface and she spit out the dirty water. She drew in a deep breath. The river lapped around her thighs.

Colter! She had to find Colter.

"Where are you?" she called out.

His hat still floated several feet away. She walked toward it, using her hands like paddles as she made her way through the rising water. Mud churned, making it impossible to see anything below the surface. Her dress clung to her legs. Every step was an effort. The wet wool dragged at her, pulling and tugging, its weight threatening her balance. Her feet slipped on the smooth bottom.

As she grabbed the hat she realized it would have come off his head when he fell. She tossed the hat on the shore. She had to find him. She took a step, only to be brought up in midstride. She looked behind her. The rope was still attached to her waist, and the loose end had tangled up in the wagon. She jerked it free.

"Maggie."

The faint call came from the rocks a little ways downstream. "Colter? Where are you?"

She kept close to the bank and moved forward. She saw the sleeve of a familiar flannel shirt. As she came around a slight bend she saw a fallen tree and Colter clinging to the side.

"You're all right! I was so worried." She tried to hurry toward him, but her dress worked against her.

He held on with one arm. Most of his body lay under water; his chin barely cleared the rippling surface. A gash split one side of his face. The current tugged at him. His grip slipped.

"What's wrong? Can't you get up?"

"Caught. Can't hold on," he gasped.

"No. Don't let go. Here." She tossed the rope toward him even as she made her way through the river. Her legs ached from the cold. Her heart pounded. It was like being in that stream all over again. Only this time Colter wasn't going to be able to come save her. She had to save herself and him.

The rope slipped past him, but he made no move to catch it. There were only ten feet between them

"Hang on," she demanded. "Don't you dare let go."

"Empty the wagon," he said, his voice barely above a whisper. He slipped a little more and the water lapped at his mouth. He coughed. "Horse pull it out then. Go south."

"I'm not going anywhere without you." She began to cry in frustration. Every step was torture. The water weighed her skirts down. She started to slip. She jerked the fabric up as high as she could and regained her balance. When she looked up, he was gone.

"Colter!"

She flung herself toward the tree. The river caught her and carried her the last couple of feet. When she reached the slippery bark, she grabbed hold with one hand and reached under the surface with the other. She felt his back. She pulled with all her might. His head rose above the surface.

"Hang on," she ordered.

"I'm caught." The water filled his mouth. "Can't get loose. Save yourself. Take the wagon—" He went under again.

"No!"

The river lapped around her midsection and was still rising. She pushed hard against the tree. It barely moved, but that was enough. Colter again surfaced.

"Help me," she cried. Her wet braid clung to her back, her skirts made movement impossible. "I can't do it alone. Here." She thrust him the rope.

"I'll pull you down." His gray eyes pleaded with her. "Don't die, Maggie. I didn't come this far to kill you, too."

"I'm not going to die and neither are you." She worked at the knot around her waist. When it was free, she tucked one end in his hand. "Hold this."

Taking a deep breath, she ducked under the tree. Just being underwater was enough to make her heart pound faster than ever. She wanted to scream, to breathe, to return to the surface. Death was so close that she could taste it. She forced herself to keep going. Colter depended on her.

When she thought her lungs were about to burst, she resurfaced on the other side of the tree. Leaning over the waterlogged bulk, she tied the end to the rope, then made her way to the bank. The mud and water sucked at her. With her last strength, she pulled herself free.

"Don't die," she pleaded. "I'll get Sebastian and he'll pull you free. Just hold on for a little longer. Please, Colter, I don't want you to die either."

A wave lapped over him. His head went under. She moved to jump back into the river when he came up again, this time a little higher than before.

"Hurry," he said.

She ran to the wagon. Sebastian stood, his sides heaving. He'd managed to pull the wagon out of the river. She worked feverishly, undoing the lines that held him in place. Her cold fingers could barely work the buckles. Please, God, she prayed. Let me be in time. Useless prayers, she thought, then prayed them again.

At last the old gelding was free. Maggie walked him over to the fallen tree. Colter still lay in the water. The rising river covered most of him. Only the top half of his face lay uncovered.

"If I pull the log away, will you be able to swim?" she asked.

He answered with a slight nod.

She tied the ropes to Sebastian, then urged the horse to pull. At first nothing happened. At last the log moved a little. With a huge heave, he lurched forward and the log jerked loose with a sucking sound. Water swirled around. Colter went under.

Maggie raced to the edge of the bank. She took a step in, then another. With the mud, she couldn't see anything. Had she been too late?

There! A hand. She went down on her knees and grabbed his arm. He clutched at her skirt. Slowly, inch by inch, she helped him ashore. When he was at last free of the river, he turned and fell on his back. His eyelids fluttered and he exhaled her name.

She hunkered down beside him. "You made it."

"You should have saved yourself," he muttered.

"You're welcome." She smiled and wiped the hair from his face.

"Maggie." He gripped her hand. Gray eyes stared intently into hers. "We need to get out of here. Now!"

"What? I have to build a fire and get us both dry. You've swallowed a lot of water, there's a cut on your head, and who knows what else. We have to rest."

"No. Gant is right behind us. There's no time." He struggled into a sitting position. "Son of a bitch." He rubbed his temple and touched the cut. "I don't know what hit me, but it was big." He shook his head and groaned. "Help me up."

She sat back on her heels. "No. You're in no shape to do anything. It's too dangerous."

He glared at her. Water dripped from his hair. His head was already puffy and discolored. But he managed to look mean enough to make her think twice.

"They will find us," he said slowly, as if she would have trouble understanding the words. "If we don't keep moving, it will be tomorrow instead of in four days."

"But you're hurt."

"I've been hurt before. I know it's not bad."

She worried her lower lip. Despite the bright sunshine and warm temperature, her wet clothes made her cold. She shivered. "I don't think—"

"Dammit, Maggie, what do I have to say to convince you? If they find you with me, they may kill you." He rolled onto his knees, then supported himself by pressing on one bent leg, and rose slowly.

She stood beside him, ready to help if he fell. He staggered a few feet, braced himself, and stood upright.

"Hitch up Sebastian," he said. He made his way to the edge of the river.

She led the gelding back to the wagon and secured him. In the time it had taken her to pull Colter free, the water had risen another two feet and sloshed at the back wheels.

"Come on, boy," she said, pulling on the bridle.

Sebastian heaved against the muddy ground and jerked the wagon up onto dry land. Sweat lathered his sides, and his ribs bellowed with each breath. She pulled off the tattered remains of her petticoat and ripped it in half. One section she tossed in the back, the other she used to wipe the horse's damp sides.

"Poor boy," she murmured. "This is harder than plowing. You've been very brave."

Her hands shook as she worked. All she could think about was Colter standing beside the river. She wanted to go to him and force him to lie down. But the stiff set of his shoulders and back warned her away. This was all her fault. How could she have been so stupid? Colter had told her to let the music box go. Why had she tried to save it? What did it matter compared with Colter's life? She'd nearly killed him, all because she hadn't been willing to let go of the past.

When Sebastian was reasonably dry and his breathing had slowed, she patted him one last time. From the clean half of her petticoat, she tore off a length to form a bandage. Taking a deep breath, she walked over to Colter. He stood staring at the current as if the rapidly flowing water would give him answers.

"Here." She thrust out the length of cloth.

He took it and pressed it against his cut.

"I'm sorry," she said.

"Forget it."

"No. I didn't listen to you, and you almost died." She wrung her hands together and stared at her wet shoes. "Please forgive me."

"There's nothing to forgive." He continued to look out at the river. "You thought you were losing something important and you were willing to do anything to get it back."

"Not hurt you."

A silence stretched between them. Finally he turned toward her, reached out, and touched her chin. She raised her head. His gray eyes met hers. No warmth flickered in the gray depths, but no anger either.

"I understand," he said. He lowered the piece of cloth to his side. The cut stood out raw and jagged on his tanned face. "Forget it."

She curved her palm around the hand touching her chin. "Thank you." His fingers moved against hers. He felt cool to the touch. They were both soaked. "You're right," she said. "We'd better get going. Sebastian is pretty tired. I don't know how far he'll be able to go today."

Colter released her. "An hour or two should do it. Look." He pointed at the river.

The water flowed faster, visibly rising on both sides of the bank.

"What's happening? A flood?" she asked.

"Step back." He motioned her to retreat several feet. "Listen."

She heard a faint rumble. No, that wasn't right. She cocked her head. A thundering noise, so low she could barely hear it, but growing. "What's that sound?"

"Logs. Hundreds of them. That's what's wrong with the river. It's been dammed. Now they're releasing the water and the logs, carrying them downstream to the mill." He squinted into the sunlight. "Let's go."

He took a step and almost fell. She glanced up at his face. "Oh, Colter." The color had fled until his ashen skin matched the cold gray of his eyes. He looked ready to collapse.

"I'm fine." He stepped again and went down on one knee. "Damn."

She bent beside him. "Let me help."

He grimaced. "I'll crush you."

"I'm stronger than I look."

"Sure. So's a rat. That doesn't mean it can carry a man."

"I'm bigger than a rat." She took his arm and looped it around her shoulders. She wrapped hers around his waist. "Stop talking and concentrate on getting to the wagon."

It was like trying to lift a house. His strength fled rapidly. She got him upright, but he sagged against her. Her thighs trembled and her knees threatened to buckle. She forced herself to stagger forward. Colter tried to help. She felt him collect himself in spurts of energy. The load would lighten for a few feet, then he would lean on her again and she would fight going down.

When they reached the wagon, she stared at the high seat. There was no way she could lift him up there. She left him leaning against the side. Her steamer trunk was heavy, but she managed to wrestle it over the edge and carry it over to him.

"You must get in the wagon," she said. "Colter, I can't do this. Use the trunk for a step. You have to pull your-self up."

"I'll try," he grunted, and took hold of the seat back.

Inch by inch he dragged his body up. She leaned against him, pushing with all her might. Her body ached. A slight breeze chilled her through her damp clothes. At last his foot hit the footboard. With a final lunge, he pulled himself into the wagon and collapsed on the seat.

Maggie climbed up the opposite side and stared at him. His eyelids were closed and his breathing shallow. He looked pale, but not as gray as before. She shook him. "Colter?"

No answer.

For the second time that day, she prayed. *Make him live, Lord. Please. He's all I have. Don't let him die. Not now. We've come so far. Keep us safe.*

Tears of frustration burned her eyes, but she brushed them away. He was unconscious. That wasn't dead. Not yet, anyway. She jumped down and looked around. His hat lay on the bank where she'd tossed it. She went over and picked up the wet felt. The first log floated into view.

She stood on the shore and stared at the cut trees racing down the river. They came slowly at first. Just the one, then a few seconds later another. Then they came in clumps of three and four. Finally the entire river, for as far as she could see, was covered with logs.

A smile tugged at her lips. She gave in to the impulse, then giggled softly. The giggle turned to laughter. She glanced around at the exposed land Colter had hated. Hun-dreds and hundreds of trees had been cut down. If the loggers went to all the trouble to dam the river, they must have that much wood or more to float down. It could take hours. Or days. It was, she realized, the gift of time. God was keeping them safe.

She looked skyward. "Thank you," she mouthed, then wondered if she were being foolish. Her faith had betrayed her so many times in the past. And yet— She clutched the wet hat to her breast. It felt good to believe, even for a few minutes.

As the logs clattered together she returned to the wagon. Colter lay as he'd fallen. His color remained pale, but he was breathing, at least. He was right. They had to get out of here.

She climbed into the seat and adjusted Colter's head so that it rested on her lap. She brushed his wet hair off his face. After flicking the reins, she braced herself for the jerk forward. Sebastian walked slowly. She let him pick his way. She wasn't sure where they should be going. She held the reins with one hand and with the other stroked Colter's face.

"Be all right," she whispered over and over again. "Don't die. I need you to be with me. Colter, please."

He stirred on her lap.

"Colter?"

He murmured something.

"What? What did you say?"

"West."

# Chapter 24

Maggie turned the horse until he walked directly into the afternoon sun. Within another mile they left the harvested area and entered the forest that Colter favored. In the shade the temperature dropped. She could only see the sun between the branches. New foliage made it difficult to keep track of their direction, and with only a narrow path to follow, she couldn't always go exactly west.

Colter continued to lie still. Occasionally he muttered words or phrases. She tried to listen, but nothing made sense to her. Her fingers grew numb from the cold. Her body shook. He, too, was set on by tremors. What was she going to do? Had she saved him from the river only to have them both die now? Her throat tightened and she wanted to scream.

Stop! she commanded herself. Colter had taught her many things in the last few days. She could do this. She had to. His life depended on her. Taking a deep breath, she forced herself to stay calm.

When she was sure they'd been traveling two hours, she began to search for a small clearing near a stream. She left the wagon and walked on foot until she saw a flat area for their camp. She led Sebastian as he pulled the wagon through the dense foliage. Overhead, birds fluttered and screamed their protest at the invasion. But the tiny creatures didn't seemed alarmed. That was good, he'd taught her. Most likely they were alone in the woods.

She unhitched the horse and hobbled him in a section of new grass. After filling a bucket with water, she left him and began to collect wood. On the seat, Colter stirred restlessly. He would be as cold as she was, maybe colder. Between the drenching and his injuries, he needed to get warm.

Dry kindling, leaves, small logs. She studied the mound in front of her and lit a match. It caught. Hungry flames consumed the small bits of fuel and began on the logs. She could have sobbed her relief, but there was no time.

Working quickly, she gathered enough wood so that she wouldn't have to leave to collect more until nightfall. After rolling over a stone for cooking, she set it next to the fire, but not on it. She couldn't move it until the flames were high and burning larger logs. Next she spread out a bedroll and filled the coffeepot with water from the nearby stream. Only when everything was ready did she approach Colter and touch him.

He jerked upright when she shook him. His eyelids fluttered, but he didn't seem to be seeing her.

"We have to get you down," she said.

"Cold."

"I have a fire going. Help me, Colter. Just slide down. It's only a short distance to the bedroll."

He moved obediently. She'd expected him to fight her. When she touched his face, she realized there wasn't any fever. He stepped off the wagon seat and fell to the ground. She half dragged him to the bedroll. Once there, he collapsed on his back.

"Colter?"

He raised his head slowly and grunted.

"I'll be right back."

She moved to the far side of the wagon and pulled out her gray dress. She stripped off the soaked blue one, her chemise and pantaloons. Shivering naked in the afternoon, she pulled on fresh undergarments, then the gray dress. She left her damp hair hanging in its braid. She could deal with that later. Colter had a spare shirt and socks in his saddlebags. She collected those, the remaining blankets, and his flask of spirits. As she scanned the contents of their wagon for what else she might need, her gaze fell upon the wet burlap bag.

The music box. Shame filled her. She wanted to pick up the bag and toss it into the woods. All this was her fault. If she'd just listened to him, he would be fine now and they would both be safe. Because of her selfishness, their lives were in danger. She turned away and returned to the fire.

Colter lay on his side, facing toward the heat. He'd pulled his shirt off one arm and it sagged down his back. She dropped her supplies beside him, settled on her knees, and touched the wet cloth. Her breath caught in her throat.

"Oh, dear God, what happened?"

He didn't move. She pulled the shirt away. From his shoulder blades down to his waist faint scars crisscrossed his muscled skin. He stirred, and the thin, puckered lines rippled like an obscene design. She'd seen marks like this once in her life. A neighbor had employed a former slave. She'd come calling and seen the man working in the garden. His bare back had glistened with sweat. The scars had made her feel sick. He'd told her about the beatings that had produced them.

Now, as she stared at Colter's back, her stomach clenched and her head felt light. Who had committed such a crime?

"Maggie?"

"I'm here."

"Cold. So cold."

"I'll help you."

She bent over and rolled him so that she could remove the wet shirt. She pulled off his boots and socks next. His trousers presented a problem she didn't know how to deal with. He opened his eyes long enough to stare at her, then unbuttoned his pants and stripped them off. She averted her eyes as she handed him a blanket. He tossed it over his lower half, then lay back down on the bedroll.

The fire flared hot and bright. She moved the flat stone into the flames and set the coffeepot on top. Taking the softest blanket, she turned back to Colter, prepared to rub him dry.

She'd seen Edward without his shirt once or twice. Other men occasionally worked half-naked in the summer heat. But seeing Colter this way was something very different.

Broad shoulders blended into a muscled chest. Light hair covered him from just below his throat down his stomach, where it narrowed and disappeared under the blanket. A star-shaped scar puckered on one shoulder. He shivered. She bit her lower lip and reached out to touch him. She rubbed the soft wool gently across his arm. He didn't move or even open his eyes. Maybe the shock of his fall in the river had made him go to sleep. She didn't mind. Better for him not to be watching her right now. She rubbed a little harder. Still he didn't move. His silence gave her courage. She pressed the blanket over his chest and began to massage him with both hands. She rubbed and kneaded until her palms tingled. She pulled back the cloth and saw his skin glowed with a rosy tinge.

She reached out her hand and touched the center of his chest. Warm. She sighed in relief. She was about to cover him completely when she again looked at the scar. A bullet wound? The reddened skin was about the size of a half-dollar. Slowly, as if he would stop her if he knew her intent, she touched her fingertip to the center of the scar. She thought of the marks on his back and sadness flooded her.

She shifted until her knees pressed against his side. Stubble darkened his jaw. She touched the firm line, moving her finger back and forth. The movement caused a faint rasping sound and she smiled. She liked the feel, so different from her own face. She studied the wound on his forehead. It had stopped bleeding, but still gaped open. He probably needed stitches, she thought, then shuddered. She would wait and ask him later.

A single lock of hair tumbled down. She brushed it back, smoothing his dark hair over and over again. Bending closer, she cupped his face in both her hands. Handsome, she thought.

"Mama would have liked you," she said aloud. "Alice, too. You're a fine man. I'm so sorry about the music box. I never meant for anything bad to happen."

Her eyes filled with tears. It seemed that all she ever did these days was cry and get wet in streams and rivers. She smiled. A single tear dripped onto, his cheek. She moved her finger to brush it away, then paused. She glanced around the glade to make sure no one was watching. She looked at Colter, but his eyelids remained firmly closed.

He was a man; all men were dangerous. But there was something about him. Something different. He'd risked his life for hers, had told her to save herself. He'd killed for her. She could never repay the debt.

Slowly, she lowered her head and kissed away the tear. She tasted salt and something else. Something wonderful that could only be him. She glanced at him, but he didn't stir. She kissed his cheek again, lingering longer this time. His skin was warm beneath her lips, his beard stubble prickly. She kissed his other cheek twice, then slipped down until their lips touched. The fleeting contact made her stomach lurch and her palms grow damp. She'd never kissed a man before. One had tried once, but she'd been too afraid. It wasn't horrible, she thought with surprise.

She bent down and kissed him again. His mouth felt firm, yet soft. She held the pose, blinking, sensing there was something more to do, but not sure what. His chest swelled against hers as if he were drawing in a deeper breath. She sat up instantly, feeling guilty and slightly wicked. The coffee was almost brewed. She drew a blanket up around his shoulders and busied herself drying his feet.

When the coffee was ready, she called his name. He didn't stir. She poured a cup and held his head up on her lap.

"Drink just a little," she said. "It'll warm you from the inside."

He took a sip without opening his eyes. She remembered the brandy, poured in a splash, added a second for good measure, then offered him the cup. Taking small sips, he drained it. She released his head. He rolled on his side. Soon she heard his deep, even breathing.

She was concerned about injuries to his lower body, but knew she would never have the courage to lift the blanket and look. She checked his wet trousers for blood. Nothing. A nearby log provided a spot to dry his clothes and her undergarments. She stretched an oilcloth on the ground and spread out her dress. His pistol was in the wagon, under the seat where he'd been keeping it when they rode during the day. It was soaked. Did water affect it? Were the bullets wet as well? She didn't know how to open it, or fire it, so she tucked it in a corner of the wagon. In Colter's boots she found a knife. She carried it with her as she did her chores. If she had to, she'd defend them as best she could.

"Alexander!"

She spun at the sound of Colter's voice.

"Alexander!" he called again.

She rushed to him. He'd rolled on his side, away from the fire. Sweat beaded his brow. She wiped it away. "Hush. You're safe." She hesitated, wanting to offer comfort. "Alexander is safe, too." Her words soothed him and he slipped back into a dreamless sleep.

He'd mentioned the name before. Alexander was the man who had spied for him and had saved his life. Why did Colter call out for him? She added more wood to the fire. His blanket had slipped down in back and she reached over to pick it up. She paused when she saw the scars. His angry words came back to her. "My father beat the hell out of me."

She pulled the blanket up around him and tucked the edge under his shoulder. How could a parent do such a thing to a child? She wanted to weep for his pain, but her tears wouldn't erase the memory. How many times had she wondered at the nature of this man? He wore his ugly secrets well.

She poured herself some coffee and settled down next to him. With one hand, she stroked his face. With the other, she held the knife. She would protect him while he healed. He stirred restlessly. She murmured words of comfort and bent down to kiss his brow. His hand came up and captured hers. She held on and swore never to let go.

\*     \*     \*

"Where's Zachery?" Major Petty asked.

Gant tugged his hat lower as he steered the bay mare through the camp. "Dead."

"What happened?"

"I don't know. We split up. Zachery never returned. I went looking for him and found what was left of his body. I think he was shot."

Petty raised his blond eyebrows. "By whom?"

*Whom?* Gant fought the urge to sneer. "Colter James."

That got the reaction he wanted. Petty looked stunned. Gant dismounted and strode over to the fire. One of the soldiers grabbed his horse. Gant poured himself a cup of coffee and gulped it down in one swallow. He'd had to ride most of the night to get back to the main camp. As it was, he'd arrived six hours late. But Petty had waited. Gant had known he would.

"How do you know James killed him?"

Petty stood next to him, his blue uniform freshly brushed. Gant glanced down and grimaced. Even the other officer's boots gleamed. How the hell did he manage to keep so damn clean when they were in the middle of this godforsaken wilderness? Who was he trying to impress?

"He was seen. A farm woman—"

Petty frowned. "I find it hard to believe that Colter James would allow himself to be seen."

Gant didn't like being cut off like that, or having his word questioned. "She didn't spot him. He stopped to buy supplies."

"What did he want?"

Gant grinned and glanced at the bay mare. "A horse. He was riding one, an old farm horse. No saddle. He bought food."

Petty turned away from the fire and paced the camp. "That doesn't make any sense. Why would he take that kind of risk? For flour? Hardly. And if he already had a horse . . ." He rubbed his blond mustache thoughtfully.

Gant thought about how he'd like to kick Petty in the balls and watch him writhe on the ground. Actually he'd rather watch the major while several men held him down and another few stuck him up the ass.

"Wilson," Petty called. "Get out the map. Gant, let's try to figure out exactly where James is going."

*I know where he's going, you stupid son of a bitch.* He followed his superior to the lone tent. Inside, Wilson pinned a map to one wall.

Petty traced a line from Chicago north. "Where is the farm?"

Gant pointed. Petty followed that line north. "This doesn't lead anywhere. If we go west . . ." His finger moved directly west. "St. Paul?" He looked at the tracker. "Would James go to a city?"

Gant wanted to say no. Of course that was where James was headed. He'd known for weeks. Petty would figure it out sooner or later.

"Looks that way," he said grudgingly.

"I wish I knew why he was going there," Petty said, rubbing his clean-shaven cheek. "He can't escape us."

*He can meet the general,* Gant thought, fighting the sick feeling in his stomach. He looked at the map. They were close, but not close enough. A man alone on horseback would make good time.

"You said he was trying to buy another horse?" Petty asked.

"That's what the lady told me." Lady. Gant wanted to laugh. She'd been a widow, all hot and hungry for a man. He'd seen it in her eyes. Too bad about Zachery. He'd told the other man not to make trouble, but suddenly he was itching for a little of his own. He would have liked to see her blue-black hair spread out on a pillow. She had had a nice voice. *Wonder what it would have sounded like when she screamed?*

Petty unpinned the map and rolled it up. "He's close and we're getting closer. Wilson?"

The lanky corporal stepped into the tent. "Yes, sir?"

"Tell the men we're breaking camp." He turned to Gant. "We'll get him within the week. Perhaps I'll wire ahead to the local sheriff."

*Perhaps.* Gant sneered silently. Maybe when he took out James, he would accidentally shoot the major. But instead of feeling excited at the prospect, he tugged at his collar, as if the rope were already beginning to tighten around his neck.

# Chapter 25 ═══════════════

Colter wanted to tell whoever was sitting on his head to get the hell off. He shifted to get away from the pressure, but moving only made it worse. He thought about opening his eyes. Instead, he contented himself with a groan followed by a sound cursing whatever was causing the pain.

The results were unexpected. A sweet voice assured him that he was fine— all the while, gentle fingers stroked his face and bare shoulder. He opened his eyes.

Maggie bent over him, her face soft with concern. The hands touching him belonged to her. Her touch tugged at his memory, but before he could figure out what it all meant, she brushed her fingers against his bare shoulder again. Bare?

He sat bolt upright. The blanket fell to his waist. Holy mother of— He was naked.

He looked at her sitting next to him. "What the hell is going on?"

She placed her hand on his forehead. "Good. You're still cool. I was so afraid of a fever. There's no medicine or doctor. I didn't know what I was going to do."

He jerked away from her touch. "I don't care about a fever. Where are my clothes?" He glanced around at the camp. It was unfamiliar. Slowly it was coming back to him. The river. Falling in the water. Something big hitting him. He reached up and felt the gash on his head. "Where are we?"

She smiled, then poured a cup of coffee. "Drink this. You'll feel better. I've made a stew. I had to use the

last of the meat. I don't know how to use your rifle, so
I couldn't hunt. Besides, I don't think I'd actually find
anything to kill. Even if I found it, well . . . killing it . . ."
She shrugged. "I don't think I could. It was bad enough
with the chickens back on the farm."

She continued to ramble for several seconds, stopped
suddenly, flushed, and stared at her lap. She was wearing
the gray dress again. He remembered her jumping into the
river to rescue him, even though she couldn't swim. He
remembered trying to get her to save herself and that she
wouldn't leave him.

He looked around at their camp. Sebastian munched on
new grass on the far side. A pot bubbled on a bright fire.
His trousers and undergarments had been stretched out on
a log nearby. He glanced up at the sky. Almost dark.

"How long was I asleep?" he asked.

"About two hours. How do you feel?"

"Like I was hit by a cannon." He stretched his legs
under the blanket, then rotated his shoulders. "Nothing
broken, although my head hurts like hell. What happened?
I don't remember much after you pulled me out of the
river."

She knelt next to him, darting him glances. When their
eyes met, she quickly turned away.

"You were right about the river," she said. "I watched
some logs come downstream. There were hundreds of them.
I think those men after you will have to go around."

"Good. That gives us a couple of days." He frowned. "I
hope it's enough."

"It will be."

"Maybe." He squinted up at the sky. "It'll be clear tonight.
I'll be able to get our position. Do you know what direction
we rode in?"

"West, I think. Once we got in the forest, it was hard
to tell."

"You've done fine." He picked up the coffee and took a
sip. "Maggie, could I have my trousers, please?"

"They're still wet."

"I'm getting up, with or without them."

She flushed a deeper red this time and scrambled to her feet. The pants came sailing toward him. She made a beeline for the wagon and ducked behind the far side. "I won't look."

"Never crossed my mind that you would." He dropped the blanket and rose unsteadily to his feet. His head swam. For a second he thought he was going down. He took a deep breath and held it until the world stopped spinning. He thought about calling out to Maggie for help. It would be worth it to see the look on her face.

His grin turned into a grimace as he pulled on his trousers. The damp cloth clung to him. He might not have broken anything, but he was bruised all over. After securing the buttons, he bent down and grabbed the spare shirt she'd left beside the bedroll. He shrugged into the garment. As he pulled it up his arms he remembered her rubbing him dry. He shook his head. Maggie? Touching him on purpose? Not possible.

He buttoned the shirt. The sensation of his fingers on his chest again reminded him of another touch. A gentle brush of female fingers. He rubbed his jaw. There, too, he almost remembered her holding his face. He closed his eyes and concentrated. And felt the fleeting touch of her lips pressed against his.

"Maggie?"

When he opened his eyes, she stood in front of the wagon. There was no doubt; she wasn't going to look at him if she could help it. She stared at the sky, then the ground. Finally her gaze settled on the second button of his shirt.

He was imagining it, he told himself. She couldn't have—she'd never—not Maggie. The blow to his head must have caused some damage inside. She kicked a log over near the fire. He sat down and took the cup she offered.

"Do you want whiskey in it?" She held out the flask.

"Thanks."

She poured, never raising her eyes above the cup. "This should help."

He took a sip. "It's fine."

"I'm glad." She sat at the far end of the log and studied her hands.

He leaned forward and touched her chin, forcing her to look at him. "Maggie, what the hell is going on?"

Her blue eyes darted back and forth. He was ready for almost anything except the flash of guilt. She licked her lips. The rush of desire at the sight of her pink tongue told him certain parts of his body hadn't been injured at all. He released her instantly and hunched over his coffee.

"I was worried about you," she said softly.

He glanced around their camp. "You did a good job. Sebastian, the fire." He gave her a quick smile. "You learn fast."

"Thanks." She went back to studying her hands. "Colter?"

"Yeah?"

"Tell me about Alexander."

He straightened, instantly alert. With his free hand he rubbed the scar on his shoulder. "Why?"

"You called out his name while you were sleeping. I just wondered. You don't have to say anything if you don't want to."

"We met during the war."

"You said he saved your life."

It was getting better, he told himself. The sights and sounds and smells of the war faded each day. Soon he would be able to ignore the screams of the dying and the calls of the dead. He shook his head to dislodge the memories. All that happened was that the memories remained and the throbbing at his temple increased. He reached for the flask of whiskey and poured the rest of it into his cup. He hadn't eaten since breakfast. He was well on his way to getting drunk. Here's to you, Alexander, he thought, raising his cup to the night sky.

"I was in South Carolina. My horse came up lame, and I ran out of luck. A patrol caught me." He tried to ignore the past, but it came along with the telling. He could smell the damp ground. Seemed like all the time he spent down South, it rained. He hadn't been dry in weeks.

The gray gelding had limped along behind him, his regular breathing the only sound in the night. Even the crickets had been silent.

He'd heard the patrol long before he'd seen them. They would never have seen *him*, except for that damn horse. Something small spooked him and he'd reared up. He remembered the sound of the guns, followed by pain blossoming in his shoulder and thigh. He shook himself free of the memory and stared at the fire.

"I got shot. Thought I was dead for sure. It was raining and I was able to crawl away. I ended up near a plantation. I remembered looking up at that big house and thinking I must have already died. These were the gates to heaven. And here I thought I was heading for hell."

"Don't." She reached out and touched his arm. "You *are* a good man."

"You've said that to me before, Maggie. You don't know what you're talking about."

"You're wrong." She stared straight into his soul. "I know you."

He swore, forced to look away by the intensity of her gaze. He didn't want her prying inside him. He knew what was there. And what wasn't. He pulled his arm free.

"Alexander found me. He was in charge of a group of slaves. Seems one of them had left some tools out and he came looking for them just after dawn." Colter managed a smile. "I remember looking up and knowing the Southerners would be mighty upset to know they let slaves in heaven, same as whites. He told me he would have to turn me in." He rubbed his shoulder again. "I wasn't in any shape to argue. I'd lost blood. I'd taken off my shirt to stop the bleeding." He took another drink and stared at the fire. "But instead of taking me to his master, he carried me out past the plantation to a little house no one knew about. About three days later, when I stayed awake long enough to talk, I asked him why. It was the marks on my back. Alexander said he never turned away a man who'd known the lash."

Maggie's harsh intake of air was the only sound in the still night. It seemed that even the forest creatures had paused to listen to the tale of his sorry life.

"I left as soon as I could travel. But I couldn't forget what he'd done for me. He'd risked his own life. And his sister's. She's the one who cared for me. I came back in a couple of months and asked him to spy. I'd found out who his master was. A very high-placed official, with sons in the Confederate army."

Alexander had known, he told himself, trying to shake the guilt. The other man had known the risks and had chosen to help. But it wasn't the war that killed him, Colter thought. Or his master. It was someone here, up North. Someone in the army.

"He agreed?" she asked.

He nodded. "In return, I would take his sister north. I came through every few months and collected information. Once I gave him a rifle I'd bought. Beautiful weapon. He kept it polished as fine as any lady's silver. He gave me a horse. Siren." He frowned. "Bay mare. I had to let her go when Petty and Gant caught up with me."

"How did Alexander die?"

"When he asked, I brought him north. He wanted to fight against the South, so I helped him join up. When the war was over, he was murdered."

He drained the last of the whiskey. "He's one of the eight men dead. Bound up, shot in the back. Nothing stolen but a rifle. The one I gave him."

"That doesn't make sense. If you were friends, why would you be accused of his murder?"

"No one knew we were friends," he said. "He wanted it that way. Said he didn't want to take favors from anyone. If the killer had known— I was riding to tell his sister about the murder when I was arrested."

She sprang to her feet. "So tell them that you were friends. Surely someone had seen you together. You're a good man, Colter. They would believe you."

He tossed his cup to the ground and rose. "Dammit, stop saying that. I'm a killer, Maggie. I'll always be a killer. I won't change. I'm going to clear my name because I mean to die on my own terms. There is someone who can help. When we reach him and it's safe, you can go. Until then, just stay the hell out of my way."

He didn't know how much of his anger was the whiskey and how much of it was frustration. Not just at his situation and the injustice. Some of his rage came from Alexander's senseless death. He'd suffered the worst slavery had to offer, and he'd survived, only to be shot down by a Union bullet. The rest of his pent-up emotion was Maggie's fault. Her and her damn questions. Why'd she have to be so pretty and soft and smell like flowers?

"Hell," he muttered, and tossed a log on the fire. "I killed him, same as if I pulled the trigger."

"Don't say that. You didn't kill your friend."

His head throbbed. "Why did you save me? This was your chance to escape." God, he hurt inside. Not from being in the river, but from a deeper and far older wound. He wanted to ask for comfort, to reach out and be healed. The weakness made him furious. What was happening to him? He viciously poked the log, nearly thrusting it from the blazing circle.

"It was my fault you fell in the river. I had to save you."

"You think I'm some charity case you can fix with good deeds and a quilting bee. Don't bother. I don't care about you or anyone. I would have left you for dead in the river."

She stared at him. Her throat moved as she swallowed, then she squared her shoulders. "I don't scare so easily now, Colter James. You wouldn't have left me."

"Bullshit. If you once got in my way, you would have been gone. While we're telling the truth let's lay out all the cards. The only reason you risked your precious self for me was because you're afraid to be alone. You still need me to teach you how to survive."

She flinched from the words, but held her ground. "That's true," she admitted. "But I also saved you because it was my fault you were in trouble. I saved you because—" She licked her lips. "—because I wanted to."

He had to turn away. Rage and need and his sworn promise not to hurt her battled inside. Damn lot of good he was doing. He was *trying* to hurt her. And for no reason except he didn't know what else to do with his pain but inflict it on her.

"Go away," he growled.

"Colter."

"Dammit, Maggie. Go away. Leave me be."

He felt her small hands touch his back. She traced thin lines through his shirt, outlining the crisscrossed marks there. He shuddered, but couldn't bring himself to move away.

"Tell me about the scars," she said.

He didn't answer.

"My mother did horrible things to feed my sister and me. I don't have these scars, but I know how they hurt you." She moved closer and pressed her cheek against his back.

The warmth and trust made him ache. He felt her breath on his skin. It wasn't all about sex. It was about something bigger, something that threatened his sanity.

"I'm sorry," she whispered.

He felt a soft pressure through the shirt, as if she'd kissed the raised scars.

"Stop!" he commanded, spinning away. "Leave me alone."

"I won't." She clutched at his sleeve. "I can't. Colter, please. I understand. I know what it's like to be hurt and abandoned."

Perhaps she did know. That would only make it worse. The last thing he wanted was her pity. He stepped around her to the log and sat down. He braced his elbows on his knees and rested his head in his hands. He reached down low for the anger. It was his only weapon.

He looked at her. "You know nothing. You can't even say the words. Your mother did terrible things? No, Maggie, she was a whore. You watched, didn't you? You heard the sounds. They frightened you. They should. I should.

Don't pretend to think you've tamed me."

She blanched. "No. Don't talk like that. Don't say those things to me."

"Are you afraid now? Where are you going to run? I'm all you've got to keep you alive."

She planted her hands on her hips. "You're trying to scare me. It won't work. I won't let you."

He started to stand up, then realized *he* had nowhere to go. She continued to look at him. "What do you want?" he growled.

"Oh, Colter."

It was the way she said his name. The sudden tone of understanding made him uneasy. She walked forward until she stood in front of him. Before he could move away, she crouched down and took his hands in hers. A small smile quivered at the corners of her mouth.

"You have to hurt me," she whispered, "so you won't be hurt yourself."

She clutched his hands tighter and shifted so that she was kneeling on the ground. She leaned forward, her gaze fixed on his mouth. Startled, he could only wait for the touch of her lips on his. But even as he felt the first whisper of her sweet breath, he tossed her aside and rose.

She fell on her hip and elbow. A strand of hair pulled loose from her braid and drifted across her face. Wide blue eyes stared up at him in shock.

"I'm not interested in the fumblings of a virgin," he growled. "When I want a woman, I'll buy one. The way men bought your mother."

# Chapter 26 ══════════════

Colter regretted the words as soon as he spoke them, but had no power to call them back. If he'd meant to hurt her, he couldn't have placed the knife more expertly. Tears sprang to her eyes, but she blinked them away. Color flared on her cheeks, faded, and flared again. She opened her mouth to speak, but no sound came.

It was like watching a beautiful piece of glass fall to the ground and shatter. There were too many pieces for the whole to be reassembled. So it was with Maggie. The broken bits of her newly found confidence flung to the winds. She crawled to the log and sat down, staring unseeing at the fire. Raw pain, more than he could have imagined her feeling, darkened her blue eyes to the color of a storm. Her hands twisted, fingers weaving together, then slipping apart.

Then she reached deep inside and gathered up the scattered parts. Her spine stiffened, her eyes focused, her hands stilled. She tilted her chin and looked at him.

"I admired you," she said. "I knew that while you might choose to keep me alive or kill me, either fate would be merciful. I took comfort in the knowledge that you weren't a bully. I misjudged you. You should have left me to the wolves. At least that end would have been quick."

Even as he marveled at her strength, he felt a giant fist squeezing his chest tighter and tighter. The gunshots, the beatings, nothing compared with the agony of Maggie's bitter stare.

"I'm sorry," he said hoarsely.

"Why? You finally spoke the truth."

*No,* he wanted to call out. For the first time he lied. But he couldn't speak. Words couldn't repair the wound. "I didn't mean those things."

She bent her head and smoothed her skirt. "At least Zachery didn't pretend to be other than he was. I knew from the moment I saw him that he was my enemy."

"Maggie." Colter took a step toward the log. She eyed him warily. "I wouldn't hurt you."

"You haven't."

He'd finally taught her to be like him. To pretend it all didn't matter. If she recalled her other lessons as well, she'd survive on her own.

He made a move to sit on the log. She jumped, but didn't rise. He lowered himself cautiously. Strong, he thought. How did she get to be so strong? Brave and beautiful. And bruised beyond trust. If he could erase those few words, take them back, he'd pay any price. His life. His soul if he still had one.

For that was how deep her wound ran. Past her surface feelings, past her heart, down to the purest part of her being. He knew her fear of men, and could only imagine the strength it had taken to reach out to him. He'd thrown her most precious gift away.

Lies and truth. How often they blurred. He would speak the truth, would reveal his soul, that its darkness might prod her, if not to forgiveness, then to mercy.

"I hurt you on purpose," he said. "Because you hurt me. Here." He tapped his chest. "I don't know how or why. It started when you stood up to me that first day, I think. I've never been around a woman like you. I don't know how to act. It's easier to be dead inside. Safer."

He turned to face her. If she'd been crying, he would have felt better. At least he could have gathered her close and comforted her. But her eyes were dry and her face unreadable. Something else she'd learned from him.

"Did it keep you alive?" she asked, her voice low, giving nothing away. "Being dead inside?"

"Yes."

"I understand."

"I'm sorry," he said.

"It's all right."

She accepted his apology, but it wasn't all right. He knew that. But he didn't know what to do or say to make it better. To take away her hurt. He wanted to—

He leaned forward. She glared at him. Slowly, so as not to startle her, he tucked the loose strand of hair behind her ear.

"Soft," he murmured, his fingers touching the sweet curve of her ear. "Everything about you is so damn soft. No rough edges. Nothing tough or hard on the outside. You hide the strength behind those big blue eyes."

Those eyes held his. Silent questions, he thought, returning her gaze. He had no answers. Only questions of his own about pain and forgiveness, and questions about a soul's ability to heal.

He moved a little closer to her. The questioning look became wary. He stroked the back of his hand against her cheek. So warm and alive. Innocent. He moved his hand lower and under her chin. She bit her lower lip. The flash of white teeth made him smile slightly.

"Maggie." He leaned toward her.

She moved her head back. He glanced down. Her hands twisted together in her lap. He stilled her movements by pressing his palm against her fingers.

He'd lost enough pride to ask for it again. She needed to hear the asking as much as he needed to say it.

"Please," he whispered.

Maggie stared. If he'd tried to convince her with fancy phrases or promises, or even apologies, she would never have forgiven him. It hurt so much. Inside, a giant hole gaped open. She was raw and bruised, as if a herd of cattle had trampled over her feelings. Only it hadn't been a herd. It had been one man. She'd wounded him, too, she knew. She'd seen it when she compared him with Zachery and found the latter to be superior.

Colter wanted her to forgive him. He wanted her to offer herself again. Worse, she wanted to make the offering.

Not because he had hurt her, but in spite of the pain. She believed him when he said he lashed out because of what he was feeling inside; she felt it, too.

His strong hand slipped between hers. Their fingers laced together, squeezing tighter and tighter until she never wanted to let go. He moved closer. She'd kissed him before and it hadn't been so bad. Of course, he'd been asleep.

A shivery feeling rippled through her body. Her breasts tingled, almost as if she were cold, yet an uncomfortable warmth grew between her legs. She pressed her thighs together and looked at Colter. His face was inches away. The rest was up to her. What did she want?

He'd wounded her. Wounded her past all her other pain. Only by the depth of the wound did she see how much she'd come to trust him. With her life. With her feelings. All that was left was her body.

"Please," he repeated, asking for that as well.

She took a deep breath, closed her eyes, and leaned forward the few inches separating them. Their lips touched.

In her chest, her heart pounded so hard, the thundering was all she heard. She didn't move, didn't open her eyes. Fear fought with excitement. When Colter didn't press her, excitement began to win.

She pulled back and opened her eyes. A flush heated her cheeks. She pulled her hands free and covered her face.

"Not so bad," he said. "I've never kissed a lady."

"I've never kissed a man."

He drew in a breath and touched her cheek. "I'm sorry."

She nodded. "I forgive you." She had no choice.

His relief was tangible. He grinned, then the grin faded. "Kiss me again, Maggie."

She folded her hands together and placed them under her chin. "Why?"

"Don't you want to?"

"It's not what I thought," she admitted. "I thought it would be unpleasant."

"Another kiss," he said. "Please."

In all the time they'd been together, he'd never said that word to her. Now she'd heard it three times in a row. She smiled. It was enough to give a girl ideas.

His gray eyes studied her face, tracing each feature as if seeing her for the first time. The intensity made her feel special. Pretty.

"All right." She closed her eyes and pursed her lips.

Instead of kissing her, he slipped his arm around her shoulders and turned her toward him.

"What are you doing?" she asked, opening her eyes.

"Shh."

His other hand cupped her chin, tilting her head up and to one side. Their knees bumped. He shifted on the log and her legs slid between his. Before she could protest their position, he bent down and claimed her lips.

It wasn't like the last time. Her hands clutched at the fabric of her skirt. This time his mouth moved on hers, slowly, back and forth, from side to side. It was wonderful. The hand on her back moved up and down, following the line of her spine. She arched against his palm, and his fingers made small circles that sent warmth flooding through her.

She wasn't sure when, but she'd closed her eyes again. She could smell the scent of his body. She pressed harder against his mouth, wanting to feel even more. He angled his head and returned the pressure. Her hands fluttered up toward him. Could she touch him? Did he want her to?

The hand on her chin moved slowly down her throat. He'd worked hard his whole life. The rough calluses rubbed her skin, but what she would have expected to be uncomfortable felt exactly right. He reached the collar of her dress and continued drifting until he rested on her shoulder.

Yes, she thought mindlessly. This is what she'd wanted. To be close to him like this. But she wasn't close enough. She needed—something. She raised her arm and touched his side. He didn't pull away. She rested her fingers a few inches above his waistband. He felt different from her. Harder. Lean where she curved.

He raised his head. She dropped her hand and blushed.

"I like it when you touch me," he said, their lips almost brushing together.

"Really?"

He nodded. "I liked it when you touched me before, although I don't remember much."

The blush turned fiery. She tried to duck away. He held her in place. "I didn't mean anything," she muttered. "I was worried about you after being in the river and I . . . Oh, I thought you were asleep." How could she have been so bold?

"I almost was. I only remember pieces. Touch me again, Maggie."

His eyes burned with a bright fire. She'd seen flames there before, but only the cold light of a killer. This fire burned with a heat that a few short days ago would have frightened her. Apprehension wasn't far away, she admitted to herself. Still, it was pleasant to be so close to the flames. The danger of the game made her breathing uneven. But she absolutely couldn't touch him like that. Not with him looking at her.

"I can't."

He took her hands in his and raised them to his face. His touch was gentle; she could have pulled away at any time. Instead, she let him place her palms on his cheeks. She felt the hollows and the stubble, the planes and hard lines. He closed his eyes and she traced his eyelids. Then his dark eyebrows. Her fingers discovered the curves of his ears and the steady pulse on his throat. She found the line by his shirt collar where stubble gave way to smoother skin.

He watched while she explored. His hands rested lightly on her shoulders. For a moment she wished he would hold her as he had when they'd kissed. She imagined him rubbing her arms, her throat.

Her fingers returned to his face. She touched the scar on his chin, then fluttered across his mouth. His lips parted. She drew back. He didn't move, but his gaze urged her on. Cautiously, she outlined his mouth, slowly circling around. She touched the open seam and felt the moistness. The tip of his tongue touched her finger. She jumped. It was as if a bolt of lightning had shot up her arm. She brushed the spot again. Again his tongue caressed her finger. Her eyes widened. She would never have imagined— Goodness.

He made a strangled noise deep in his throat and cupped her face in his hands. Before she could catch her breath, his mouth pressed hard against hers. She clutched at his shoulders. He moved harder and faster, his lips probing and demanding. Their chests touched, her breast flattening against his muscled strength. She liked that, she thought, and leaned against him more. Both his large hands moved up and down her back, their speed adding to her sense of urgency. Something was about to happen. She wanted it, wondered what it would be, hoped she wouldn't be afraid.

His mouth parted against hers and she felt his tongue on her lips. This time the bolt of lightning rocked both her arms and halfway down her chest. She gasped. He circled around and around, wetting her mouth. She pressed hard against him. The tingle in her breasts turned into a heavy ache. It mirrored the feeling in her thighs. Every part of her body felt different, as if she were just becoming aware of herself.

She slid her hands behind his neck and touched the silk of his dark hair. The coolness contrasted with her own heat. His tongue continued to caress her mouth. She drew in a deep breath. Like her finger, she thought. She knew the next move. Her tongue to his. She wanted to. But . . .

She dug her fingers into his back and parted her lips. He continued to trace the seam, moving deeper and deeper with each stroke until his tongue touched hers. This bolt of lightning shot straight to her feet. Her soles burned and her toes curled tight.

He cupped her face and thrust his tongue inside. Moist heat circled around, touching everywhere. Wondrous sensations flooded her body. She hadn't known she could feel such things. Wanting, needing, oh, she'd never known what it felt like before. Sparks flew and ignited fires all over. Her arms, her back, her breasts. Yes, her breasts. She pressed them harder against him. In her mind's eye, she thought about him touching her there. Her breasts swelled at the image, the ache becoming more intense. His mouth continued to caress hers. As his tongue swept around she brushed it with her own. More heat, lovely, lovely heat. It rolled through her in great waves that stole the strength from her until all she could do was cling to him.

He retreated. She began to murmur a protest, when he touched her, then retreated again. Follow, she thought. She mimicked his actions, first cupping his face, then tracing his lips. He felt different now. Wet from her. She paused, not sure of what to do, then tentatively moved inside his mouth.

He tasted sweet. Hotter than she'd expected. She explored his mouth. More sensations. Rough and smooth, hard and soft. What had she been so afraid of? she wondered, and giggled. He pulled back.

"So you find kissing me amusing?" he said, his eyes glinting with humor.

She smiled. "Yes. Lovely and amusing."

"Oh, Maggie."

He leaned forward and kissed one cheek, then the other. He kissed her chin and her ear and trailed kisses down to the collar of her dress. The late-afternoon air cooled the moist trail he left behind with each kiss. She moved her head to make it easier, and laughed when he licked the spot behind her ear.

A wonderful gift, she thought, knowing he would never understand what it was she received. A man could still make her tremble with fear, she knew, but now she'd touched one and laughed with him. The memory of these kisses would stay with her always.

"Kiss me again," he demanded.

She did. She pressed against his mouth and swept her tongue inside. She dueled with him. She ran her fingers through his hair and arched up toward him when his hands splayed along her sides. Then he kissed her and she felt as if her bones began to melt, and she wondered if anything would be better than this moment.

His hands moved to her stomach, then higher. She broke away and looked down at the strong hands that seemed to belong there. They'd saved her life. They'd killed for her. Tears sprang in her eyes. His thumbs rested just below

her breasts. She ached for his touch. Safe enough through
the dress.

He moved his hands higher. She ached in anticipation.
She watched as he cupped her breasts in his palms. Instantly, the ache intensified. She closed her eyes, overwhelmed
by the flood of sensation. Surely he could feel her heart
thundering in her chest.

He swept his thumbs across her hardened nipples, then
lingered there, moving slowly back and forth. She knew
she would never be able to turn away from his touch.

Colter bent down and touched his mouth to her right
breast. Through the dress and her camisole, she felt the
heat of his breath.

"You'd tempt a saint," he said as he released her. "We
both know what I am." He straightened and wrapped his
arm around her.

She leaned against his shoulder. "Colter?"

"Hush, Maggie. Don't say anything." He kissed the top
of her head. "Tonight I'll teach you about the weather and
we'll study the stars so you can find your way."

"Thank you," she said. He was still going to teach her
to survive on her own. Knowing that should have made her
happy. She raised a hand to her swollen lips. It didn't.

# *Chapter* 27 ═══════════

Logs crowded together in the river. For as far as he could
see, cut timber bumped along the rapidly flowing water.
Gant reined in the mare and swore.

Major Petty slowed beside him. "Loggers," he said.
"We'll have to go downstream until we find the mill and
cross there."

"Could be miles."

Petty looked at him. "Do you have another suggestion?"

Gant wanted to raise his fist and scream at the heavens.
Why was this happening? He was so close; he could feel
his enemy. Now this. Petty was right. There wasn't any
other choice. They couldn't cross over the logs. In this
wilderness, there wouldn't be a bridge nearby.

Rather than answer, Gant turned the mare and started
downstream. What was he going to do if James got
away? What if he met up with the general? Gant would
be doomed.

Why hadn't he killed Colter James when he had the
chance? He shouldn't have waited. He thought James would
be hanged quick enough. When the trial had been delayed,
Gant had been forced to send in his own men to do the job.
The bastard had killed most of them. One that survived had
confessed that they'd tried to have sport with James first.
Gant had shot him for his stupidity. It's not that he wouldn't
have liked to have seen James raped by a gang of men, it was
that he'd warned his men not to take chances. If they'd gone
in and shot him like he'd told them to, he, Gant, wouldn't
be in this trouble now.

All because some niggers were dead.

He thought about how he'd tied them up first and then
shot them. He grinned. Most of them had begged for mercy. He kicked one like the dog he was. His brows drew
together. Except that one. Alexander. He'd tried to stare
Gant down. His brown eyes had gleamed with contempt.
That's why Gant shot him first. He knew what those men
thought of him, what that man had thought.

Gant glanced over at Petty. The prissy officer would
about shit in his pants if he knew. Gant chuckled. Petty
and those like him believed in the good of their men. Petty
was probably stupid enough to risk his life for one of the
enlisted. Gant knew better.

A command, they'd said. A chance to forget about tracking and hiding out in the South, wondering if each day
would be his last. How he'd hated that. Week after week
in the mud, starving, trying to stay alive, gathering enough
information so that no one became suspicious. The only
good time he'd had was when he'd met up with Zachery
and they'd kidnapped three women and kept them in an
abandoned barn for almost a week.

A command. He grimaced. Niggers. Might as well have
been a troop of pigs and chickens. Everyone knew they
couldn't think or learn. How he hated those brown-eyed
slaves. He'd waited until the war was over to get his revenge.
Not just on them, but on Colter James as well. The man who
had told lies about his character when he'd had a chance
at a white command. James was nothing but a bastard and
a nigger lover. He'd seen him talking to Alexander; he'd
known the rifle was a gift.

He reached down and rubbed the weapon attached to the
side of his saddle, then stroked the mare's neck. *I've got
you now, you son of a bitch.*

They'd been riding beside the river for almost an hour
when he spotted the tracks.

"Hold on," he called, and motioned everyone to stay
back. Gant dismounted and crouched near the ground. A
wagon had passed by within the last day or so. He peered
closer. Left rear wheel wobbled.

"What is it?" Petty asked.

"Tracks." He hesitated. Looks like he wasn't going to get a clear shot at James. Still, a hanging wasn't the worst way for his old enemy to die. As long as he didn't get the chance to say what he knew. Gant didn't like the odds, but didn't see another way out. "I've seen these tracks before. It's a farm wagon pulled by a single horse."

"James?" Petty asked.

"Could be."

"You said that woman had seen him on horseback."

"Without a saddle. If he was going from farm to farm, he'd travel faster leaving the wagon in one place." He walked back to the mare and mounted her. "They must have crossed before the logs got sent down."

"Then we're nearly there," Petty said. "Let's ride, men. We need to make up the time we're losing."

"I don't understand," Maggie said. "If you'd served under Major Petty, why wouldn't he believe you?"

Colter was sorry he'd brought the whole thing up. Once Maggie got her teeth into an idea, she wouldn't let go. "A man says he saw me kill those men."

"But you didn't."

"You're the only one who believes that." He glanced at her. She sat on the wagon seat, her back straight and her chin thrust forward. Even though he knew it was a waste of time, he liked her willingness to defend him. "My word against his."

"But that man you're going to meet knows you didn't do it. Isn't he going to tell them the truth?"

"If he got the message." Colter stared at the narrow path in front of them. He'd sent several telegrams from Chicago, asking the general to meet him in St. Paul. He knew his friend came down from Canada in the spring and stopped in the city to visit his daughter. A slim chance, Colter thought, but the only one he had. With Petty and Gant breathing down his neck once he'd been spotted in Chicago, his choices had been limited.

"Who claims he saw you commit the murders?" Maggie asked.

"Their commanding officer. Gant."

"I thought he'd worked with you as a tracker?"

"He did. For a time. Like I said, I didn't care for him. When he tried to get a transfer, I sent a letter about him and his character. He didn't like that." He remembered his surprise when Alexander had told him the name of his captain. Gant hadn't seemed the type to take on the Colored Troops.

"So why would he lie?"

"Don't know. It was his men who were murdered. I was there that night, for a time. I met with Alexander. Then the general and I rode into town for a—" He looked at her. Better not to tell her all of it. "For a drink. Ended up staying late. When we returned to camp the next morning, the men were dead."

"When they came to arrest you, you told them, didn't you?"

He remembered the ambush outside the camp. Someone had sent eight men to take him. He'd gone quietly. "Didn't get much of a chance. I was waiting for my trial. I told Gant when he came to see me, but he didn't believe me." He frowned. "Then I was attacked in prison. They tried to kill me, so I escaped."

Maggie turned to face him. "What do you mean, they tried to kill you?" She sounded shocked. "Where were the guards?"

He shrugged.

"How can you be so calm about this? You could have died."

He could see concern and fear in her eyes. She seemed genuinely upset. "I'm fine," he said. "Nothing happened."

"Oh, of course not. Nothing at all. What's prison, and men chasing after you? It must remind you of all the times you enjoyed down South. I'm another Alexander. You've saved my life, I've saved yours. You're right. It's very exciting." Her voice shook with the last few words. Despite the warm afternoon, she hugged her arms to her chest.

"Maggie."

"Damn you."

He'd never heard her swear before. He raised his eyebrows.

"Yes, that's what I said. I'll say it again. Damn you, Colter James. If they catch you, you'll hang."

"I know."

"You know!" she shrieked. "That's all you can say? Don't you care? Aren't you worried?"

Sebastian's ears flickered as if he were listening to the conversation. Colter wished he could ask the old gelding for advice. He'd been with Maggie a lot longer than Colter had. Maybe he would understand her better.

"We're all going to die," he said. "It's a matter of when."

"But I don't want you to die." She turned on him and flung herself against him. "I don't want them to get you."

She didn't cry, but her body shook as he held her. He held the reins with one hand and stroked the other up and down her back. "They won't," he said.

"You can't know that." She looked up at him. Her dark and troubled blue eyes probed his, looking for concern to match her own.

"I'm doing everything I can to keep us both alive," he said. "I'm not a fool. I haven't been caught yet."

She clutched his shirtfront. "Leave me. Take Sebastian and save yourself."

"No. I won't put you out in the middle of the forest. You're getting out of this alive. It's bad enough that I kidnapped you. Don't make it worse by sacrificing yourself."

She snuggled closer to him. "I wouldn't have survived the wagon trip by myself. You told me that."

She was right, he thought. She didn't have the money, the supplies, or the skills. But that didn't make what he'd done right.

They traveled along in silence. He studied the thinning trees around them. The number of birds had decreased in the last hour. He hadn't seen a rabbit or deer track all morning. The path had widened about a quarter mile back. Another joined it. Wagon wheels blended together in the drying earth. They were near a settlement.

He would have to leave Maggie to go and buy supplies. And a horse. He was close to his destination. Another day or so and he would reach the Mississippi River. Then she would be free. It would be best for both of them. He could clear his name and she could put all this out of her mind.

Her head rested on his shoulder. He fingered the thick length of her braid. Soft and warm from the heat of her body. Her hands rested trustingly on his chest. He could slide his fingers down her back and cup the tempting curves of her derriere, he thought. She would look up, surprised, but she wouldn't refuse him. He could kiss her, he could touch her. But he couldn't claim her. She wasn't the kind of woman a man purchased for an hour or a night. She was the kind of woman a man married.

Colter still hadn't figured out why people married. Maybe it had something to do with the knot in his gut every time he thought about letting her go. But let her go he would. No matter how big the knot grew. She had her dreams to follow and they would lead her out West. She would find somebody who knew about ladies and what they needed. A man who would keep her safe and never say or do the things he'd done. A man without blood on his hands and unrelenting darkness in his soul. He would walk away and forget about her.

He slowed Sebastian to a halt and secured the reins. Maggie looked up at him. "There's a small town up ahead," he said. "I have to go and get some supplies. I'm going to take Sebastian and leave you with the wagon."

She nodded. "I'll wait."

He hid the wagon behind a clump of trees. He thought about leaving her a gun, but she didn't know how to fire it and there wasn't time to teach her. He pulled the knife from his boot.

"Here," he said.

She took the weapon. "I'll be fine."

After unhitching Sebastian, he mounted the gelding and kicked his sides. They'd gone about ten feet when he turned him and walked back to where Maggie stood. Her dark blue dress, stretched and stained from its constant wettings, hung loosely on her body. Yet she wore it proudly, her badge of triumph over the journey. Gold-blond hair fluttered around her face. She pushed it away impatiently. While he was gone she would probably take down the braid and brush her hair, then secure it again. He would miss seeing her do that, miss the way raising her arms caused her dress to tighten across her breasts, miss seeing the pale line of her throat and the innocence in her eyes as she smiled at him— never knowing how he burned for her.

"Make a fire if you get cold."

"I have my coat. Colter, just go. I'll be here when you get back."

He cursed under his breath. With one quick movement, he jumped down from the horse and strode over to her. He clutched her by the shoulders and pulled her hard against him. Their lips met. He'd thought she might be shy, but she responded with an eagerness that told him she remembered her previous lessons. Her hands clung to his back, the sheathed knife she held pressed against his shoulder blades. She angled her mouth against his and moved her lips back and forth. When he thrust his tongue forward, she opened for him, admitting him into her sweetness.

He hardened instantly. He dropped his hands to her behind and pulled her up against him. Through the layers of their clothing, she probably couldn't feel him, but he felt her. Felt the warmth of her belly and the instinctive rotation of her hips. Felt her hands clinging to him, urging him on.

He knew this kiss would end with her wide-eyed and him hot and ready. But he continued to kiss her anyway. Her tongue swept past his lips and searched the corners of his mouth. She strained to get closer. He thought about touching her breasts, but that would make it harder to stop. He had to stop. Maggie deserved more than he had to offer her. Not just because he couldn't give her what she needed, but because he'd only ever been with whores. He would rather cut out his heart than hurt her.

He took her arms and set her away from him. "Stay safe," he murmured, and led Sebastian out toward the path.

# Chapter 28 ═══════════

Gant stirred the cold ashes. He studied the ground, searching for footprints. There, by the log. A man's. And beside that a woman's—same as at the cabin where Zachery died.

"He's traveling with a woman."

Petty crouched beside him. "Are you sure?"

"Look." Gant pointed. "See how much smaller that print is. Even a short man would have bigger feet. Plus her boots are a ladies' style. You can tell by the heel."

"How far ahead?" Petty asked.

Gant stirred the ashes again. "Two days. Maybe three."

Petty nodded. "We'll ride past sundown. Rest only as long as the horses require. I want to get him before he reaches the city." He walked over to his horse. "We may have to detain the woman to question her. Knowing James, he probably kidnapped her to use her wagon."

Gant smiled. He was finally close to victory. When the time came, he would volunteer to question James's lady friend.

Maggie sat on a log and smiled. Then laughed and smiled again. Colter. Just thinking his name made her feel . . . happy. She touched her fingers to her mouth. Her lips still tingled from his kisses. She felt alive. Every inch of her body vibrated with sensation. The thought of him touching her was enough to make her eyes flutter shut and her mouth grow dry. She wanted him to touch her and kiss her and whisper things to her. The words didn't matter. She just wanted to hear his voice. She hugged her arms to her chest and let her head fall back. He'd only been gone an hour and she missed him.

To pass the time she tried to remember what he'd taught her about different kinds of tracks and how to tell if an injured animal was safe to eat. Her mind reeled from all the information and the lingering effects of his kiss. She licked her lips as if she could still taste him. Sunlight filtered through the budding branches and warmed her body. She inhaled the fresh scent of spring. Wildflowers would bloom soon. The berries would appear and start to ripen. All new and fresh, yet ordinary. So different from the past weeks.

She tried to remember the fear she'd felt when Colter had first taken her prisoner. But all she could think of was the way his smile warmed his face and the crinkles that appeared at the corners of his eyes. She thought about how patiently he'd taught her the ways of the woods. How he made sure she was warm and dry and that they had food. He touched her now. Little touches he probably thought she didn't notice. A quick brush of his fingers to tuck a strand of hair behind her ear. An arm around her shoulders as he sat next to her by the fire. And she touched him back. A lingering caress when he helped her from the wagon. Fingers bumping as she passed the coffee.

"Alice, is this how it was with Edward in the beginning?" she said aloud. "Did he make your heart race? Did your stomach feel funny when he looked at you? Did you want him to kiss you?"

She pulled her knees up to her chest and wrapped her arms around them. It wasn't just about feeling tingly. She also worried about him and those men getting close. What if they caught him? He would never go back to prison. She knew that now. He would rather die. A cold shudder swept through her. He *would* die, she realized. If they caught him before he found his friend, he would make them kill him rather than risk going to jail. She couldn't stand it if anything happened to him. She couldn't possibly live without him. It wasn't about surviving or not surviving. It was about Colter James. Not what he did for her, but who he was.

She loved him.

Maggie jerked her head up. She couldn't. Love him? Love any man? But she did. She felt the love growing inside of her. She didn't care about his past, about the secrets burning so coldly in his eyes. She didn't care about the blood on his hands or the men he'd killed. He'd killed one for her. Then he'd comforted her and made her feel safe and clean again. Despite what he thought about himself, she knew there was goodness in him. He proved it every day they were together. That was why she loved him. Because they'd lived through a test of fire. All pretense had been burned away. She'd seen what Edward had become when he'd been tested with the death of those babies. He'd turned hard and cruel. Colter hadn't. Every day he gentled more. Whatever happened to them, as long as she was with him, she could trust him with her life and her soul. She could trust him enough to love him.

She wanted to run and find him, tell him what she'd discovered. She wanted him to know how she felt. She rose to her feet, then settled back on the log. Would he want to hear the words? He was going to let her go. As soon as it was safe, they would part company. She knew that as surely as she knew she'd come to love him. There was nothing she could say to change his mind. But she had today and tomorrow and as many tomorrows as he would allow her. She would live them with him, knowing that Alice had been right. She *had* found the right man to love.

Maggie sat up and straightened her dress. Colter should be returning anytime. She'd no sooner thought the words than she heard a faint rustling. Before she could become alarmed, he spoke her name.

She walked out to greet him. Instead of sliding around on Sebastian's bare back, he rode a fine black mare with a brown leather saddle. Matching saddlebags bulged on either side of the animal and a bundle had been tied in front of the horn. Sebastian looked more like a pack mule than a horse. Giant cloth sacks had been stacked high on his back and hung down either side of him. Supplies and a spare horse. Some of her happiness faded.

"You all right?" Colter asked as he dismounted.

"Fine. Didn't see or hear anyone."

"Did you start a fire?"

"No. I didn't get cold." Now that he was here, she found herself feeling awkward with him. She stared at the new horse, at the bundles, anything rather than look directly at him. What if he guessed? Would he reject her? She told herself he wouldn't, that he was kind, but her feelings were so new. She didn't understand them herself, let alone know if it was good for her to share them. Besides, by the looks of things, he wouldn't be around much longer.

She leaned over and patted the black mare's nose. "You've bought a horse. You're going to let me go now." It wasn't a question.

"Not here," he said. "It's not safe. When we get to St. Paul, we'll find a wagon train for you to join." He motioned to the burden Sebastian carried. "Those are for you. To help you on your journey west."

She stared at the packages. "Why did you buy them?"

"I've eaten most of your food. Used a lot of supplies." He shrugged and led Sebastian to the wagon.

"Not that much," she said. "There's enough food there to last me—"

"At least to Missouri. Probably farther."

"I can't take these." She frowned. He began loading bags into the back of the wagon. "Colter, stop. I don't have the money to pay for this."

He tossed a sack onto the hay. "I don't want your money."

She had a sudden vision of her mother lying on the bed and a man dropping a silver coin into the dish. She flushed.

"Dammit, Maggie." Colter removed his hat and wiped his forehead. "I don't want that, either."

She tilted up her chin.

"Wait." He reached out to touch her, then dropped his hand to his side. "What I mean is that I don't expect you to pay for the supplies. I want you to have them. If it wasn't for me, you'd be halfway to Missouri by now."

"I might also be dead. You said so yourself."

He grunted and finished storing the bags. After hooking up Sebastian, he led the mare behind the wagon and tied her to the back.

"You aren't going to ride her?" she asked.

"You up to handling the wagon on your own?"

"I'm going to Missouri by myself, aren't I?"

She knew her tone sounded sharp, but she was hurt by Colter's actions. She couldn't say why. Buying her food and supplies she couldn't afford was a generous act. He could have simply let her go on her own and never given a thought to her situation. She tried to figure out what was bothering her. Perhaps it was because he seemed to let her go so easily. There was no sign that he would miss her, even a little.

He pulled the saddlebags off the mare and opened one of them. "Here." He held out a pair of gloves. "I hope they fit. I didn't know the size."

Maggie stared at the gift. Inside, her heart fluttered foolishly behind her ribs.

"Take them," he said gruffly.

"They're beautiful."

"Kid leather."

She could see the fine stitches in the soft-looking material. They were pale brown, almost beige.

"Maggie, are you going to take them or not?" He flapped the gloves at her.

She took a step closer to him and stared some more. Finally she reached out and he dropped them in her palm. She closed her fingers around the smooth leather, then brought them to her face and inhaled the scent.

"Put them on," he said impatiently.

He'd pulled his hat low over his forehead so she couldn't see his eyes or his healing gash. He was pretending it didn't matter, but she knew he wanted her to like the gloves. She drew them on slowly, first her left hand, then her right.

"Perfect," she said as she closed her hands in fists, then opened them again. "Thank you."

She reached up and kissed his cheek, then ducked away.

He coughed. "It's getting late. We'd better get going. Petty and Gant are closing fast. We need to take advantage of the daylight."

Her good mood vanished with his mention of those men. He helped her into the wagon and placed the reins in her hands. Then he mounted the black mare and led the way onto the path. They circled around the small settlement. She looked over at the buildings and houses. It would have been nice to stop, she thought. To take a bath in a tub and eat food cooked on a real stove. She would have the chance when they reached their destination. When Colter found his friend, or after he left her, she would have as much time as she wanted. The realization didn't make her feel better.

They traveled until almost sunset, then made camp. As she started the fire Colter unloaded some of the sacks and sorted through the contents.

"What will you do?" she asked. "When all this is over, where will you go?"

He crouched in the bed of the wagon, searching through one of the bags. "I spent some time in Tennessee. There's a section of land, at the high end of a valley." He rested his forearms on his thighs and looked at her. "I'm going back to buy the land and raise horses. I have my first brood mare." He shook his head. "I had her, anyway."

"The one Alexander gave you?"

"Yeah. Pure bloodlines in that one," he said. He stuck his hand in the bag and withdrew a wooden box. "I bought you this."

She placed another log on the fire and walked over to the wagon. He grabbed the side and vaulted to the ground, then reached in and picked up the box.

"It's small, but accurate. Easy to learn how to use." He raised the lid.

She stared down at the gun resting inside the case. "Why?"

"I want to know that you can protect yourself." He took off his hat and hit it against his thigh. "There's some daylight left. Come on. I'll show you how to use it."

"I couldn't."

His gaze narrowed. "Take it or use it?"

"Both. I don't have enough money to pay you for the supplies, let alone a gun."

"We've discussed this. The gun's a gift. Take it."

His gray eyes hid his feelings. She wanted to believe that he cared for her, that the purchases came from a full heart rather than a guilty conscience.

"When you can shoot, you won't need me at all." He grinned.

She didn't smile back. So that's what it was all about. He wanted to be able to leave her without worrying about her safety. "I'll take the gun," she said, brushing her hands on her skirt and picking it up. It felt cold and heavy. She had to use both hands to point it straight ahead. "But you're wrong about my not needing you."

Colter pretended not to hear her. He grabbed the pistol from her and led her into the forest. It was better this way, he told himself. Better for both of them. She needed the protection and he needed to get the hell out of her life.

He explained how to load the gun, then fired several practice rounds. She flinched with each shot.

"The gun won't hurt you if you handle it right," he said.

"It's not me I'm worried about," she said. "I don't think I can shoot anything. Especially not a person."

"You probably won't ever have to. But knowing you've got the gun will make you sleep easier at night."

Her blue eyes met his. "I've been sleeping fine, thank you."

He knew what she meant and he didn't like it one bit. "You need to take care of yourself, Maggie. You won't always be able to depend on a man."

Her chin raised slightly. "On you, you mean."

"On anyone."

She held out her hand. He gave her the pistol, grips first. She took it, lifted her arms in front of her to shoulder height and fired at the tree. A piece of bark went flying.

"Good. You hit it. Now we'll do it until you're comfortable with shooting."

"I'll never be comfortable with this, Colter. I know how to use the gun. That's enough."

She bent over and placed the gun in the case, closed the cover, and started back toward their camp. He walked after her.

"You have to practice more," he said. "If you make a mistake with a gun, you end up killing yourself instead of your target."

"I don't care."

He caught up with her and grabbed her arm. She tried to pull away. He tightened his grip and turned her until she faced him. She clutched the box to her chest. Tears covered her face. He dropped his hand as if he'd been burned.

"Maggie?"

"Go away."

"What's wrong?"

"Nothing." She started walking again. "I've shot the gun. Just leave me alone."

"Why are you crying?"

She stopped so suddenly he almost ran into her. "Because I've had to learn to shoot, maybe even to kill. Because there are men chasing you and you don't seem concerned. Because I'm afraid of what will happen to both of us if they catch us. What if one of them is like Zachery?" She shuddered, then raised her gaze to his. Moisture glistened in her blue eyes. Dampness added a sheen to her face. Her mouth trembled. "And more than that, more than anything, I don't want you to die."

Her confession hit him squarely in the chest, knocking the air from him. He could only watch her turn and run back to their camp.

He followed her slowly. As far as he knew, no one had ever shed a tear for him. He hadn't known he had that much value. He wanted to believe it was about more than his ability to keep her safe, but he knew better than to fool himself. He was a good hunter and a good protector. She was frightened about being on her own. That was what her tears were really about.

She was already cooking their dinner. An occasional swipe of her hand across her cheek and a soft sniff were the only remaining signs of her outburst.

He stood on the edge of the camp and watched her work. "If there isn't a wagon train leaving St. Paul, I'll make sure you're set up somewhere for the winter."

"Don't bother. I can take care of myself. If someone does something I don't like, I can always shoot them, can't I?"

"Maggie, don't." He moved toward her.

"Excuse me." She ducked around him and tossed some spices into the pot. "I'm cooking right now."

"I'm doing the best I can. What else do you want from me?"

She looked up at him. Her stricken expression caught him like a blow to the belly.

"What's wrong?" he asked. "Is this about Gant and Petty? I won't let them hurt you, Maggie. I swear."

She set the pot on the ground next to the fire. "It's not that. I know you'll keep me safe."

"Then what the hell is wrong with you?"

She rubbed her palms on her skirt, then clasped her hands together in front of her stomach. "From the time I first saw my mother doing those things . . . " She shook her head. "No. You were right. I have to think of it as what it was. From the time my mother became a whore—"

"Stop." His own words came back to wound him. He walked over to stand in front of her. "Don't say that. She wasn't a whore. She was trying to save her children."

"The reason doesn't matter. What I'm trying to say is that I've never been able to trust men. When my sister married Edward, I worried about her. At first he was fine, but when the babies kept coming stillborn, he grew mean. After he beat me, I swore I'd never care about a man, never trust one."

Colter tightened his hands into fists. He wanted to find Edward and rip him apart. He wanted to gather Maggie close and hold her until she forgot her past. He did neither of those things. He couldn't. He could only listen and know the worst was yet to come.

"Then you kidnapped me." She glanced down, then back up at him. The setting sun caught her hair and turned it fiery gold. Long lashes cast shadows on her cheeks. Her chest rose and fell as she took a deep breath. "You terrified me. I only wanted to stay alive, as I'd promised Alice."

He was the enemy. He'd always known, but it was still difficult to hear her speak the words. "I wish I'd never taken your wagon," he said, his voice gruff. "You've got to believe that. If I could do it again, I'd change everything." Knowing what he knew now, he'd probably let them kill him in that prison cell.

She reached out and touched his hand. "That's not what I'm saying. Alice had always told me that one day I'd find a man I could trust. Someone I could look up to and admire. Someone who would treat me well, keep me safe. Someone I could . . ." She squeezed his fingers. "Someone like you, Colter. Someone to love." She blushed, her cheeks staining with faint color.

He stared at her. Better that she should hate him, he thought, fighting the urge to turn and run. It wasn't pleasure at her words that kept him frozen in place; it was that he'd never run from anything in his life.

She smiled. "Don't say anything. You don't have to. I wanted you to know before we parted company. I love you, Colter James."

"Don't love me." She flushed deeper and withdrew her hand. Before she could turn away, he grabbed her arms and held her in place. "Wait."

"I didn't mean to embarrass you," she said stiffly, squirming against him. "While I didn't expect a return declaration, I certainly hadn't planned to upset you."

But the hurt in her eyes told him that she *had* hoped he would return her regard. Once again she had pushed him to the place where only truth would salvage her feelings. He remembered being a young boy and watching families when he visited a nearby trading post. Fathers carried sons on their shoulders. Mothers held daughters' hands. Couples

smiled at each other. He'd felt isolated. He'd known he
would never fit in with these people. No one had cared
about him, or ever would. Now Maggie claimed affection.
Love. It was too late, he thought sadly.

"I can't," he said, holding her tightly, fearing she would
flee if he gave her the chance. "I can't say those things to
you. I don't know what they mean. Don't love me, Maggie.
You don't know the man inside. You don't know what I've
done and seen. It's too dark here." He released one hand
and touched his chest. "Too ugly."

"No." She placed her hand over his. "There's good inside.
I've seen it. Every day you prove yourself to me." She
smiled. "So many times you could have hurt me or left me
to die. You never did. I was always your first concern."
She reached for his other hand. "You've taken a life to
save mine."

"So you're grateful."

"Always, but that has nothing to do with loving you."

"It's all this," he said, raising his arm to take in the forest
and their camp. "We've been together for several weeks.
You think you care because I've saved your life and taught
you how to survive."

"You're wrong," she said.

He knew he wasn't. She might think that she loved him,
but in time she would come to see the feelings for what
they were. Gratitude. He hated the word, but he lowered
his hand to his side.

"*And* you're a fool." She raised herself up on tiptoe
and removed his hat. Then she pressed her lips against
his.

He kissed her back because he couldn't help himself.
He held her close to him because she pressed her warm
body against his and he didn't have the will to refuse. He
cupped her derriere and squeezed because she placed her
hands on his chest and looked at him with a hunger that
made him hard.

Her tongue circled his. He groaned low in his throat
and wrapped his arms around her, trying to pull her close
enough that he could bury his wanting deep inside her.

She responded by clinging to him and pressing her breasts against his chest.

He'd wanted women before, but never like this. If he didn't touch Maggie's body, taste her soft skin, and feel her next to him, under him, moving, calling out, wanting him with the same intensity, he was going to explode. He had to have her now, in the forest, by their fire. He had to take her on the bedrolls where they'd shared their secrets, offered each other comfort and strength. Here, before his enemies forced him to flee, before he had to let her go on to the life she deserved.

He reached for the top button of her dress. His fingers brushed against the softness of her throat. She looked up at him, her eyes wide and trusting. The knot he'd been carrying in his gut for weeks doubled in size.

He had nothing to show for his life, he thought. Not one damn noble deed. It might kill him, but he was going to let Maggie go the same way he'd found her. Innocent.

"What's wrong?" she asked.

"You should see to dinner." He was pleased that his voice sounded normal. He didn't want her to know how much he ached inside. His erection pressed against his trousers. If she glanced down, she would see the visible proof of his desire. But Maggie didn't know enough to look.

"You don't want to kiss me anymore?" She bit her lower lip. "Did I do something wrong? Was I too bold?"

"Never." He stroked her cheek with the back of his hand. "I don't want to scare you. We should stop now."

She stared at his face. Her hands gripped his shoulders. Finally, she nodded. "You have a powerful need," she said solemnly.

He swallowed and almost choked.

"It's all right," she said. "Alice explained it to me once. When a man is close to a woman, he wants to do"—she paused—"those things. What does the need feel like?"

He rubbed his hand over the back of his neck. "We shouldn't talk about this."

"Why? I want to understand." She smiled shyly. "My insides feel funny. Hot, but tingly. I like it when you kiss me. If you want, we could—"

He cut her off. "No, we can't. You're a virgin."

"But Alice said—"

"I don't care about Alice. Maggie, I'm doing my damnedest here to be noble. I'm about to go crazy from wanting you. Don't you know what you're doing to me? I see you every day. You smile at me and I want to rip—" He drew in a breath. "Alice was right. I do have a powerful need. But I don't intend to do anything about it. Start the meal. Now."

The last word came out as a roar. Maggie didn't look the least bit frightened. She nodded slowly, as if she were beginning to understand something important.

She reached up and took his hand in hers. She kissed his rough palm, letting her lips linger on the calluses at the base of his fingers. Flames licked up his arm and through his body, settling into a burning throb at his groin.

"The meal's already started," she said. "In fact, it's cooking just fine. Do your insides feel hot and tingly?"

"Yes," he said hoarsely.

"Show me more, Colter."

"I can't. I've never been with a lady. I wouldn't want to frighten you."

If she'd responded with the slightest hint of fear, he would have been able to gather the remains of his self-control and turn away. Instead, she smiled.

"I'm not afraid of you." She placed his hand on her breast.

# Chapter 29 ═══════════

Maggie trembled at his touch, but not from fear. Memories from her past, the sounds her mother had made, cries from Alice's room, battled with her trust of Colter James. She wasn't completely sure she wanted to be with him, the way a woman was with a man. But she knew he wanted her. She had nothing else to offer him, nothing else he would value.

"Are you sure?" he asked.

She nodded.

Before she could regret her decision, he swept her up in his arms. She gasped and wrapped her arms around his neck. With a single kick, he unrolled the bedding and placed her down on the layer of blankets. When she was settled, he added two logs to the fire.

"Undo your braid," he said, crouching down beside her.

Her heart pounded. She didn't regret her decision, she thought as she loosened the tie and finger-combed her braid. Second thoughts weren't the same as regrets.

The sun began to set. The warmth from the fire chased away the late-afternoon chill. Night creatures began their melody. The familiar chirps and calls and rustles added to her sense of well-being. Those first days she'd feared the forest. Now she knew the tall trees and thick brush offered cover from danger. The animals told her of predators nearby. In a way, the woods were like Colter. He had frightened her at first. She'd run from what she didn't understand. But now she knew him to be a kind and gentle man.

He slid his hands through her hair. Long fingers rubbed
her scalp, then moved to her shoulders. He massaged the
muscles there until her head lolled back and forth. She sat
cross-legged on the blankets. He moved to kneel behind
her, spreading his legs so his thighs cupped her hips. As
he swept her hair over one shoulder she felt his lips press
against the side of her neck. She smiled as he trailed kisses
to her ear. The faintly moist trail tingled.

He repeated the kisses on the other side. Then he took
her earlobe in his mouth and sucked. Her eyes flew open.
She drew in a breath and let it out slowly. Delicious warmth
filled her body, settling in her breasts and melting between
her thighs. She half turned and he eased her back onto
his lap.

His mouth claimed hers. She parted her lips immediately.
His tongue circled around, touching every sensitive spot.
She reached up and stroked his face, running her fingers
along his cheeks and jaw, then moving to the dark silk of
his hair. Her head rested on his arm, his legs supported her
back. His free hand lay on her stomach. While they kissed
she felt her breasts swell inside her chemise. The tightness
at the tips increased. She wanted him to touch her there.

He withdrew his tongue and sucked on her lower lip. It
was better than when he'd done that to her ear. She shifted
her mouth and took his lip in hers. Applying slight suction,
she ran her tongue back and forth along his skin. Beneath
her back, his muscles tightened.

As they traded kisses he began to move his hand up her
chest. She tensed in anticipation. His hand slipped between
her breasts and paused at her collar.

When the first button came free, she realized he meant
to touch her under her clothes. With the second button, she
felt a wave of embarrassment. With the third, she pulled
her mouth from his and clenched her teeth tight. On the
fourth, her breasts began to ache fiercely. As he parted the
cloth she felt a rush of cold air around her upper chest and
throat. His warm hand banished the chill.

While he planted soft kisses on her cheeks and eyelids,
his hand moved around, rubbing gently against her neck,

moving lower and lower. He'd undone the buttons to her waist. Her arms fell to her sides and her fingers curled into her palms. She wanted to open her eyes and look at him. She wanted to run away. She wanted to tell him to hurry.

He stroked the skin just above the lace on her camisole. She jumped. He soothed her with soft words, then spoke her name.

"Maggie? Look at me."

She opened her eyes. The fire still burned in him, hot and bright. Tension tightened the lines of his face.

"We can stop, if you need to. This far and no farther."

A web of control held him stiffly against her. His hand stopped moving. His wrist rested on the swell of her breast. She thought of how Zachery had hurt her with his pinching and squeezing and of the things that men had done to her mother.

Maggie lay in Colter's embrace, feeling the heat of his body and the tenderness of each caress. She reached up and cupped her hand behind his head. She pulled gently until his mouth was inches from hers.

"Don't stop," she whispered. She pressed her lips to his, tasting him, devouring him in a hungry assault that left them both breathless.

His fingers moved lower, slipping under the camisole to touch her bare skin. From the top of her breast, he circled under the soft mound, coming up to hold its weight in the palm of his hand. She exhaled her wonder. With each shift of his fingers, pleasure gripped her tighter in its spell. She had feared pain and embarrassment. Now she arched toward him, seeking more and more of the feel of him on her. Each callus grated deliciously on her sensitized flesh. He moved slowly around and around, touching each bit of her breast. She felt herself swelling against him. Between her thighs, the dull ache deepened. She pressed her legs together, but it wasn't enough.

His finger grazed her nipple. A jolt of heat shocked her. He touched the hard tip again. She whispered his name.

"You like that?" he asked.

"Yes." Her voice was breathless. Nothing had prepared her for the trembling excitement. Her legs felt heavy and weak. Her hands fluttered as she lolled her head back to expose herself more.

He withdrew his hand and raised her to a sitting position, then pulled her to her knees. She felt dazed. He unbuttoned the bodice down to her skirt.

"So beautiful," he murmured as he kissed her neck.

The nibbling caresses made her shiver. She clutched at him for support. He took her arms and placed them at her side, then lowered her dress over her shoulders.

She hadn't thought of being undressed. For a second she stiffened, resisting him as he drew the dress to her waist and freed her arms. She raised her hands up to cover her breasts.

"This far and no farther," he said again.

Their eyes met. She knew this man, she reminded herself. And he would know her in the way a husband knew his wife. She let her hands drift down.

He reached up and tugged on the end of the ribbon securing her camisole. She watched his strong hand as he pulled.

"You're trembling," she said, touching his wrist. "Why?"

"You make me tremble."

She slipped her hands under his and pressed them, palm to palm. He swallowed.

"Don't be afraid," she said.

"I don't want to hurt you." Agony joined the hunger in his eyes.

He knelt before her. Strong, proud. A man who had risked his life for hers. Brought to his knees by something within her. She didn't know if it was her innocence, their circumstance, or some mysterious working of God. She no longer cared.

"I love you," she whispered, and slipped the camisole off her shoulders.

The thin cotton pooled at her waist. She'd never stood exposed before anyone. She bit her lower lip and forced herself to remain still. He stared. Heat flared on her cheeks. At last, when she could stand it no longer, he touched her. Both hands cupped her breasts. His thumbs rubbed her hard nipples, sweeping back and forth, pressing slightly. She swayed on her knees and clutched at him to stay upright.

Pleasure filled her, surrounded her, surging again and again until she thought she might die of it. Lower in her body, pressure built, a need, an urge to . . . to do she knew not what. He leaned close and took one breast in his mouth. The evening air had cooled her skin. The contrast between that and his hot mouth circling her, sucking gently, made her want to cry out. She held her breath to keep silent. He moved from breast to breast. Her released sighs, her touch on his cheek told him when she wanted him to linger and continue the exquisite torture.

Her hips began to move back and forth. Her thighs shook and she sank into a sitting position. He bent over her, stretching her out on the bedroll. He swept her dress to her knees, then off completely. She lay bare, except for the camisole around her waist and her pantaloons. He lay beside her, fully clothed, touching her everywhere. His hands explored her legs, tickled behind her knees. His mouth caressed her shoulders, her stomach. He sucked on her fingers, one by one, from the smallest to her thumb. His teeth nibbled the sensitive pads. He rose up on one elbow and stared at her breasts. He traced patterns with his palm, moving closer to her hard peaks, then he licked each point until she moaned. Her hair grew tangled as she tossed her head back and forth. The soles of her feet burned. She touched his face, his lips, his neck. She undid the first few buttons of his shirt and pressed her hand against his bare chest. The warm hair tickled her.

He stroked the top of her thigh. Her hands grew still on his body. Her eyes opened.

"This far and no farther?" she asked softly.

His teeth clenched together. The hand holding her hair curled into a fist. Her gaze dropped low on his body and she saw a stiff ridge pressing against his trousers.

"This far and no farther," he said.

She sat up and pulled off her camisole. The thin cotton fluttered to the ground. She untied the ribbon at her waist. He stilled her hands and urged her to lie down. He kissed her gently, his tongue tracing circles around her mouth. His fingers returned to her thigh, moving delicately up to her stomach, then down, between her legs.

Instinctively, she tightened her muscles. His hand stilled, but his kiss deepened. She unbuttoned the rest of his shirt. He shrugged out of it and returned to rest next to her. She touched his warm shoulders and back, traced the scar from the bullet. His hand slid down from her belly. This time she forced herself to relax. Over the cloth, he cupped her mound. His middle finger pressed in toward her private place.

A jolt shot through her. She jumped. He pressed again. The ache that had grown so deep and heavy shifted at his slight touch. Her legs parted. He moved his hand under her waistband, over her bare skin to the curls that protected her. He slipped through them and stroked her. Her toes curled as her fingers bit into his skin.

Yes, she thought. She ached more, yet his touch made her want to beg him never to stop. He began to move slowly, cautiously. Long fingers probed inside her. She raised her hips to take more. His thumb brushed back and forth, creating raging fire all through her.

He stopped long enough to strip off her pantaloons and his own trousers. Before she could rouse herself enough to think about being afraid, he knelt between her thighs and touched her again. His fingers played their magic music on her most sensitive spots. She moaned. She had thought the noises coming from her mother and Alice had been pain. Perhaps sometimes, she thought hazily. Perhaps not always.

He leaned forward and caressed her breasts, nuzzling the soft skin, sucking on the hard points. Her hips moved toward him, thrusting her pleasure, her impatience. His hand continued to stroke her, his fingers delving inside, then out, touching that special place again and again.

He whispered her name. She opened her eyes and gazed at him. Desire stripped away all expression except need. She looked at his bare body, his broad chest, muscular arms. She followed the pattern of hair as it narrowed at his waist, became a thin line, then flared into a triangle of dark curls. Nestled at the center, his male organ strained toward her.

It was too large, she thought. Panic flared. She rose on her elbows as if to get away. Instantly, he stopped touching her.

"Don't be afraid," he said.

She stared at him. Suddenly she realized she was naked with him. Alone in a forest. What had she been thinking? She had to get away. Where were her clothes?

"This far and no farther," he said quietly.

She raised her gaze to meet his. Sadness stole his desire. Sadness and regret. She saw his false assumption that he was not what she needed him to be. His pain became hers. It stabbed her with an intensity that took her breath away. She had to comfort him. No. She had to convince him that he was the best of all things.

"I've never seen a man before," she said. "When I saw him, the one with my mother, it was from behind."

Colter nodded and handed her the camisole. She clutched the garment in her hands. She squeezed it tight, then flung it away.

"I'm not afraid of you," she said.

The relief in his eyes made her want to cry. She smiled instead. He reached out and touched between her legs. She moaned softly.

"That's how it will feel for me," he said. "When I'm in you."

She peered at him. "Where does it go?"

He moved his fingers inside of her. "Here."

"Will it fit?"

He smiled. "It will be tight, but yes, it will fit."

"Will it hurt?"

He sobered. "Probably. I've heard the first time is sometimes difficult."

She continued to study his maleness. "It looks hard. Is it painful?"

"Not the way you mean. You don't have to be afraid of me." He touched himself, moving back and forth. "See. Nothing awful."

She pushed herself into a sitting position. Tentatively, she reached out her hand and stroked him. "It's hot."

He nodded, but didn't speak. She wrapped her hand around his smooth hardness. Her thumb and forefinger barely touched.

"Like this," he said, his voice rough. He moved her hand back and forth.

She mimicked the motion. "Is it nice?"

"Yes."

She continued to caress him. He lowered her back on the bedroll and took up a matching cadence between her thighs. Soon the rhythm of his fingers made her breathing come in gasps. Her muscles tightened. He pulled her hand away from him and placed it at her side. She tried to murmur a protest, but couldn't speak, couldn't move, could barely breathe.

Every part of her concentrated on his fingers moving against her. He rubbed faster, yet lighter, while his other hand toyed with her nipples. She raised her hips toward him. She strained upward, as if by pushing, she could ease the pressure building, building to a fever pitch. It made no sense that touching that small place would cause this. Nothing made sense. She tossed her head back and forth. He should stop, she thought, before she broke into a hundred pieces.

As she was about to tell him she couldn't stand it, the trembling increased even more. She hovered on the edge, the pleasure between her legs growing and growing until it built up to an incredible peak. She held her breath. As her foundation began to crumble she felt him press himself against her. Ripples of sensation poured through her. Every part of her body cried out in the release of pleasure. Her breathing stopped for a moment then resumed, slower now as she relaxed.

Between her legs, he pressed in. Her body stretched and quivered around him. He halted suddenly, then gathered himself and pushed on.

The sharp pain brought her up onto her elbows. She blinked him into focus.

"That's the worst of it," he said. "I promise."

She relaxed back. He promised. She believed him.

He braced himself with his hands on either side of her head. She closed her eyes. His thickness filled her completely. When he'd pressed into her fully, he withdrew and pressed in again. She tilted her hips to accommodate him.

Tears filled her eyes. She blinked them away, afraid that he wouldn't understand why she cried. She wasn't sure that she did. Perhaps it was the pleasure he had brought her. Perhaps it was more. She looked up at him. His gray eyes held hers. A tear flowed down her cheek. He leaned forward and kissed it away. He thrust in her again.

"You're so beautiful," he said.

At that moment, naked beneath him, she felt beautiful. He closed his eyes and grimaced.

"Does it hurt?" she asked.

"No." He groaned. "It feels—"

He couldn't speak. What had happened to her was happening to him, she realized. She looked down at the place where their bodies joined and watched him move in and out of her. Then she bent her knees more and urged him closer.

He moved quickly twice, gripped her hips, and held himself deep inside her. His muscles quivered. The cords in his neck tightened. She felt his thighs strain against hers, then relax. He spoke her name and leaned forward to gather her close.

When his breathing had slowed, he raised his head and looked down at her. "You all right?"

She nodded. Those stupid tears were back again. She was afraid he would get angry. Instead, he tenderly wiped her face and rolled onto his side, pulling her against him until her head rested on his chest and her legs tangled with his.

"I'm sorry for crying." She rubbed her eyes.

"It's all right," he said. "Thank you."

"For what?"

He drew his hand through her long hair. "For all of it."

She had to say the words, even if he didn't want to hear them. "I still love you, Colter."

He hugged her tightly to him. "I believe you," he whispered.

Contentment settled onto her. She stretched out against him. The hair on his legs tickled slightly, but it felt right to be here like this. She touched his chest and ran her fingers down to the thick hair above his thighs. She touched his male organ. It was different now, she thought, feeling the smaller shape. Had she been the one to make it so big and hard? Heat coiled in her belly.

"Will we do it again?" she asked.

"If you want to." He tucked one hand behind his head.

He might think she was brazen, but she had to know. "Tonight?"

He raised his eyebrows. "Do you want to be able to walk in the morning?"

"What does that have to do with anything?"

"Ask me in the morning."

# Chapter 30

Gant stirred the ash from the fire. Tiny embers burned red. He looked up at Major Petty. "They were here this morning."

Petty glanced around the open land and slight rolling hills. "How far are we from the Mississippi?"

Gant shrugged. "Less than a day's ride." He studied the tracks leading away. That same wagon, with the wobbly wheel. He peered closer. Another horse rode alongside. "James bought himself a horse. Maybe at that last settlement we passed."

"Mount up," Petty called to the other men. "We'll ride hard and catch them before they cross."

Gant mounted Colter's bay mare. His hands shook as he took up the reins. He was so close. So close to killing him. He swallowed thickly. How close was he to his own death?

They rode for almost an hour, following the trail. Then a second wagon joined the tracks. Three more sets of hoofprints blurred the remaining path.

"People headed for the ferry," Gant said.

Petty frowned. "We'll have to split up. No telling which way they'll be going. They might choose to cross a little farther upstream or down. James wouldn't want to travel with a large group."

Gant slowed the mare and turned her until she walked beside the trail. "Good idea," he said. If he were James, he would do exactly what Petty suggested. Gant sighed in relief. All he had to do was look— He stared down intently.

269

He knew James would go north. He sensed it in his gut. There had to be— Yes! There! A single wagon with a horse following alongside. The wagon had a loose rear wheel.

He cleared his throat and deliberately made his voice sound calm. "Of course James might think he'd be safe in the middle of a large group," he said. "We can't open fire on civilians."

Petty glared at him. "You will *not* be opening fire on anyone without my direct order to do so. Do you understand?"

I understand I'd like to put a rifle shot in your belly, Gant thought. "Yes, sir," he said meekly, knowing his time would come. "Still, I think you should have most of the men follow the main trail."

Petty hesitated before agreeing.

"I'll take Wilson and head north," Gant said. He could trust the corporal. Wilson and Zachery had been friends. Although Wilson didn't share all Zachery's tastes in women, he wasn't above a little mild sport from time to time.

"Whether you find him or not, come back to the main ferry crossing," Petty said. "We'll meet there and go into St. Paul together. I don't want anyone approaching James alone."

Gant nodded. He motioned for Wilson to join him, then he pressed his thighs against the mare and urged her forward. With Petty out of the way, Gant knew he would have a clean shot at James. Wilson would back up his story of James drawing first.

Maggie watched the rickety old ferry move closer to the shore. Some of her apprehension must have showed because Colter glanced down at her and smiled.

"It can't be worse than crossing that river," he teased.

She smiled back at him. The last two days had changed him. She didn't know if it was her admission of love, the fact that their journey was almost over, or the magic they shared together each night, but the dark brooding stranger had disappeared. In his place, a kind, gentle man shared her life. Oh, she didn't doubt that black rage boiled just below the surface, but she wasn't afraid of him. The hunter could still hunt, but only out of necessity.

The ferryman, an old white-haired man, as frail looking as his flat craft, approached. "Two dollars for the wagon. Fifty cents for each horse," he said.

Colter handed him the money. The old man studied the coins, then glanced up at Colter. She saw the fear flare in his rheumy blue eyes and he backed away quickly, tucking the money in a vest pocket.

"You'll have to put 'em on yerself," he said, his old voice quavering. He practically ran to the ferry and climbed on board.

Maggie felt bad. She wanted to tell the man that Colter wouldn't hurt him. She knew he wouldn't believe her. A few weeks ago she would have reacted the same way.

She looked at Colter as he led the black mare onto the ferry. The flat boat with its row of boxes stacked in front swayed with each movement of the river. He spoke with the ferryman about the best way to place the wagon. From her seat on the grass-covered bank, she couldn't hear their words.

It had taken her an entire lifetime to learn to trust a man, she thought, picking absentmindedly at a small white flower. Their time together was slipping away. She tried to hold on to the hours, spending them wisely, drawing out the minutes and telling herself to remember everything. It wasn't working. Whole days passed. They were almost in St. Paul. Then what?

"I'll have to empty the wagon," Colter said, walking toward her. The warm midday sun beat down on them. He dropped his coat beside her. "The ferry is small. It'll take two trips. I want to get the wagon across first."

"Fine."

"You only have to worry about yourself, and the saddlebags with the money."

She smiled at him and held out her hand. He crouched beside her and laced their fingers together. "I love you," she said.

He frowned at her, although his expression was more resigned than angry. "I've told you to stop saying that."

"You can't tell me what to do. I refuse to listen."

"Woman—"

'Woman?' She drew back in mock dismay. "You don't even remember my name? But, sir, last night, you called it over and over again as I—"

He leaned forward and cut off her words with his kiss. At the first touch of his lips on hers, excitement coiled low in her belly.

"You are wanton," he murmured against her mouth.

"It's your fault."

He stroked her cheek. Gray eyes darkened. "Maggie, I do care about you. As much as I can. I want you to know that. When we reach St. Paul, I'll—"

"This wagon ain't gonna unload itself," the old man called fretfully. "I've got a schedule to keep."

Colter smiled at her and rose. "We'll talk tonight," he promised.

She watched him walk away. As she raised her fingers to her mouth she prayed for a miracle. God had listened to her once before about Colter James. The Lord had saved his live. Maybe He'd grant her one more boon and make Colter realize that he loved her and needed her to stay with him always.

Colter unloaded the heavy sacks. When he waved the saddlebags containing the money, she stood up and walked toward him. He handed her the bags. As she clutched them to her chest and traced the worn stamping of his initials, she thought about the first time she'd opened them and considered stealing from him. Now he freely gave all that he had. She sighed. They would talk tonight, he'd said. Would he say what she wanted to hear, or would he discuss arrangements for her safe passage west?

He picked up her music box and set it on the ground, on the far side of the rest of the supplies. He was so careful to take care of everything that mattered to her. She walked over to Sebastian and was patting his face when the first bullet hit the ground at her feet.

Colter dropped the bag he was carrying and spun toward the sound. Two men rode over a rise. Beside him, Maggie screamed. Sebastian reared. Colter reached for the lines and pulled the horse down, then he grabbed Maggie and thrust himself between her and the approaching riders.

He didn't have to get a good look at them to know who they were. Damn, to be so close.

"Get on the ferry," he commanded Maggie. She stood, frozen, trembling. Her face paled and her mouth worked, but no words came out. "Now!" he shouted.

She glanced at him, around at the ferry, then scrambled toward the boat. The old man stood up and began squawking.

"I don't want no trouble. You git." He pushed Maggie off the boat onto the bank. A bullet splashed into the water.

Colter pulled out his gun. "Let her on, old man. I only need the boat, I don't need you."

The man stepped back, bumping into the black mare already on board. Colter pulled out his knife and cut the lines holding Sebastian to the wagon. The men riding closer fired another shot. This one whizzed by his hat. He felt the streak of wind beside his ear and swore. Lucky shot, he told himself. Riding as hard as they were, they wouldn't be able to take aim. He was safe till they slowed.

"Colter, hurry," Maggie screamed.

He jerked Sebastian's bridle and forced the horse onto the ferry. Another shot. The old gelding staggered. Blood spurted from his shoulder. Colter swore. Not now. Not this.

"Take him," he commanded, and thrust the lines behind him.

Maggie grabbed them. He started toward the pile of supplies. He didn't bother glancing at the men riding toward them. They were getting close enough not to miss the next time. He heard hoofbeats slowing.

"Where are you going?" She grabbed his shirtsleeve. "Get back here."

He glared down at her. "I've got to get the music box."

She stared. "No! No! I don't care about that. We've got
to go. Those men will kill you." She turned to the ferryman.
"Get us out of here."

The small man stayed crouched behind a stack of boxes.
"I don't want no trouble. You all git."

Colter took one last look at the supplies. He dragged
Sebastian onto the ferry, kept the wounded horse between
Maggie and the men, leaped back to shore, and pushed off.

He felt more than heard the next shot. He dove on board,
between Sebastian's feet, and rolled to safety just as the
bullet hit the edge of the boat. The black mare reared.

"Get down," Colter ordered Maggie, pushing her until
she lay flat on the wood.

Sebastian began to breathe quickly, each inhale audible.
The old ferry creaked as the man began moving them
across the Mississippi.

"Damn you, Colter James," one of the men called from
the shore.

Colter recognized that voice. Gant. It figured he would
be the one to find him. Colter pulled his rifle out from the
mare's saddle. He had to step over Maggie and around the
crouched ferryman. Two more bullets sailed around them;
one hit Sebastian in the leg. The gelding made a choking
sound, but remained upright. Colter gave him a quick pat
on the head.

"Hang in there, boy," he murmured. "Keep Maggie
alive."

He knew with the big horse in the way, the men on the
shore would have trouble shooting at the passengers. Colter
positioned himself behind the stack of boxes and, for the
first time, bothered looking at the two men and the horse
one of them rode.

"Son of a bitch," he muttered, then stood up. "You bastard," he called.

From the shore, Gant laughed. "She's a beauty, James.
I'll give you that." He raised his rifle. "I'll see you in hell,
old friend."

Colter knew he should duck, but he could only stare
at the rifle. Even from this distance, he recognized the

gleaming wood and the intricate carving. Alexander's rifle. The only thing that had been stolen from the dead men.

His head reeled. Gant? But he was their commanding officer. He wouldn't have killed his own men.

"Get down," Maggie screamed, coming up behind him and jerking at his arm.

Gant aimed. Instead of moving, Colter stuck his thumb and forefinger in his mouth and whistled twice. Siren's ears flickered. She took two dainty steps forward. Gant's shot went wide left. He jerked on the reins. Colter whistled again. The mare reared up and dumped the other man, then she raced down to the river and into the water.

The man still on horseback shot his pistol twice. Even as he fired Gant pulled him down to the ground and struggled to mount his horse. They were still locked in combat when the ferry bumped into the other side of the river.

"Take the black," Colter ordered Maggie. "You." He pointed at the old man. "Help her mount up." He turned back to Sebastian. Blood poured from his wounds; pain darkened his brown eyes. There was nothing to be done for the animal that had saved their lives. "I'm sorry, boy," he said as he raised his pistol and shot the horse between the eyes. The animal fell heavily to the floor of the ferry. The boat rocked back and forth, then settled against the bank.

Siren swam toward him. "Come on, girl," he called. Maggie was already on the black. "You have the saddle-bags?" he asked.

She nodded.

"Then go." He swatted the mare's rump. She jumped forward. Maggie grabbed the saddle horn.

"What about you?"

"I'll catch up. Hurry."

He dug in his pocket and tossed the old man another coin. On the far bank, Gant had claimed the other horse and raced parallel along the shore. Siren heaved herself up on dry land. Colter swung onto her back. The bay mare snorted, as if pleased to have her rightful master back. He squeezed her sides and raced after Maggie.

# Chapter 31 ═══════════

"Who is that man?" Maggie called over her shoulder as Colter rode up behind her.

He didn't answer. She clutched the saddle horn and glanced at him. Her rapidly thundering heart seemed to squeeze tight in her chest. She knew the look on his face, even if she no longer knew the man. In the space of a few minutes her gentle lover had been replaced by the cold-blooded killer. She told herself that they were the same man. This was the Colter she loved with all her being. But it wasn't. She knew that in her heart. She'd lost him to hate.

"Who is he?" she repeated.

"Gant."

"And the mare?" She motioned to the bay racing easily along side her black.

"My horse. He tracked her, as I'd planned. Then the bastard took her for himself. He's the one." His voice sounded grim. He'd lost his hat in their flight. The wind blew his dark hair back from his face. His mouth pulled into a straight line. "He's the one."

"The man tracking you?" She was confused. "But you knew that."

They came to a curve in the path. Their narrow dirt trail fed into a large road. Several wagons moved along, as did people on horseback. A pair of young boys walked over to one side. No one took notice of them as they veered onto the main path. They must be heading for the city, she thought.

Colter drew the bay back to a canter. Maggie sawed on her mount's reins and gradually slowed. When they'd passed two of the wagons and were again alone, he glanced over at her.

"You all right? Shot anywhere?"

"I'm fine." She bit her lower lip. "You said that man was the one."

"He killed them."

The cold rage in his voice made her shiver. "Alexander and the others? How do you know?"

"He has Alexander's rifle. The one I gave him. It was the only thing taken that night."

They cantered around the last wagon in their path. A woman in the front bench nodded at Maggie. She smiled automatically, even as she tried to figure out what Colter was telling her.

"But you said he was their commanding officer."

Colter swore. "Of course," he muttered, more to himself than her. "Just like that coward bastard. His own men. They'd never suspect him. He's the one who found the bodies in the first place. He's the one who accused me."

She cast worried glances at him. The crowd on the road thickened, forcing them to slow to a trot. She kept glancing over her shoulder, but didn't see anything.

"He'll meet up with Petty first," Colter said finally. "We've got at least an hour's lead."

That should have made her feel better, but it didn't. She tried not to think about what was going to happen now. She tried to forget about the fear, about the bullets that had come so close. About Sebastian. She wished she'd had a chance to say good-bye to the old gelding.

They reached St. Paul. The bustle of people and animals, the sounds and smells, the press of the crowds, and the wooden buildings shocked her after her time in the forest. She glanced down at her travel-weary dress and for the first time felt self-conscious about her appearance. Colter circled around the main streets and headed back toward the river.

"Where are we going?" Maggie asked.

"There." He pointed to a group of wooden buildings on the edge of a wharf.

Her stomach clenched tight. "Why there?"

"Steamer."

He couldn't, she thought desperately, pulling her horse to a stop. Colter reined in alongside her. He looked at her, his gray eyes cold and lifeless, as if he were already dead.

"I'm not leaving you," she said.

"You don't get a choice."

He reached down and grabbed the black's bridle and pulled her along behind him. She thought about jumping off the horse and running, but she was afraid he would waste precious time looking for her. Still, she wouldn't be sent away like an unwanted parcel.

As they approached the wharf she saw the big boat anchored alongside the row of buildings. Barrels and stacks of wood lined the wharf. Men in thick woolen shirts and heavy boots moved back and forth, carrying bundles and unloading ships.

"Finally, some luck," Colter said.

He dismounted and tied up the bay. Then he reached for Maggie. She tried to fight him, but he simply grabbed her dress and pulled her down. She clung to him. He brushed her off and moved around her. After securing her horse, he took her arm in one hand and the saddlebags containing the money in the other.

"Move," he commanded.

"Don't make me go," she pleaded. "Not like this, Colter. Can't I stay somewhere safe until you've found your friend? We have to talk."

"Nothing to say."

"But you told me—"

"I was wrong."

He climbed the two steps to the ticket counter. The balding man behind the counter glanced up. "Yes, sir?"

"When does it leave?" Colter jerked his head toward the boat.

"Four o'clock."

"Where's it going?"

The other man sniffed. "There are over twenty stops—"
Colter cut him off. "The final destination."

"St. Louis."

Maggie slumped against him. "How much?" he asked.

"To St. Louis? Cabin or deck fare?"

"Private cabin."

"Twenty dollars."

Maggie didn't even bother to look as Colter slid the coins across the wooden counter. He took her arm and pulled her out of the ticket office. They walked to the edge of the dock, beside the great steamer. People lined up to enter the ship. Colter glanced around, then tugged on Maggie's arm until she followed him to a quiet corner, away from the other activity.

She dragged her feet with every step, but he didn't seem to notice. Despite the warm day, she shivered. She told herself it was the breeze, or the river. She knew she lied.

"I won't go," she said forcefully, raising her chin up and staring at him. "You can't make me."

He released her arm and handed her the saddlebags. "You'll get to St. Louis faster than you would have if you'd gone with the wagon train. The river flows straight down." He tapped the leather. "There's enough money there to get you a decent outfit. Buy oxen, not horses. And plenty of meat. Don't expect anyone to hunt for you." Even as he gave her advice he scanned the wharf. "Damn, I wish we hadn't lost your gun. Buy another one."

She wanted to reach out to him. She wanted to scream at him, beg him, plead with him, anything that would douse the rage in his eyes and allow him to see her again. But he continued speaking, as if she'd never mattered at all.

"Keep the saddlebags close. Sleep with them under you."

"I'm not going," she said again. "I don't want your money." She shoved the bags into his chest.

He grabbed her wrist tightly, squeezing hard. "You'll get on that steamer and get the hell out of here."

"Colter, no. Don't talk to me like this. Please." With her free hand, she clutched at his sleeve. "I know you care about me. I know it. You're hiding or pretending. Those

men are after you. You have to find your friend. I'll wait
here. You can come back to me and we'll—"

"No."

He glared down at her. All gentleness, all hint of humanity, had long disappeared. Cold gray eyes pierced hers. His
mouth pulled into a straight, forbidding line. That same
mouth had touched hers. It had murmured words of comfort, had caressed her body to ecstasy. She stared at the
thin line, then at the hard contours of his handsome face.

"This is what I am, Maggie," he said. "It's what I've
always been. I'm not the man you think I am. I can't
change. I'm a killer. You'll get on that boat and go to
St. Louis because I don't want to see you again."

He couldn't mean it— even as she began to believe it
was true. Tired, she thought suddenly. She was so tired of
it all. The running, the fear, the moments of hope. Her legs
trembled. Tears threatened. She blinked them away.

"You're lying," she whispered, even as she wondered if
she was the one refusing to see the truth.

He dropped the saddlebags on the wooden wharf and
grabbed her shoulders. "You're nothing to me. Get the hell
out of my life." With each word, he shook her.

The tears poured down her cheeks. Her hair loosened and
fluttered around her face.

"Go," he commanded.

He pushed her away from him. She stumbled on the
wharf. He ignored her as she regained her balance, then he
thrust her the saddlebags and pulled her to the gangplank.
A sailor at the bottom gave her a questioning glance. She
looked away and started up the ramp.

All for nothing, she thought dully. She had learned to
love and trust a man who would never care for her or be
able to love her back. She'd been a fool. She'd offered her
heart and begged him to take it, and he'd refused countless
times. She hadn't listened when he'd told her what kind of
man he was. She wiped away the tears.

At the top of the gangplank, she glanced back. Colter
was almost halfway across the wharf. Inside her chest, her
heart swelled. Dear God, she couldn't let him go like this.

"Colter?" she called.

He froze in place.

She ran down the plank toward him. He turned. As she got closer she saw the anguish in his face. He did care! He did! She held out her arms and he pulled her in close to him. His body felt warm and familiar, the only constant part of a world gone mad.

"I love you," she whispered. "I love you. Always. I'm leaving now, because you want me to and because it will make it easier for you. But know that I'll wait forever. In St. Louis. Come find me."

He brought his mouth down hard on hers. So much pain. She tasted his despair. So much suffering. He might die this day, she thought, wanting to hold on to him and never let go.

She touched his face. "Stay safe, my love." She forced herself to smile. "Clear your name, then come to me."

"I can't."

"You must," she said. "I'll be waiting."

He started to protest. She placed her fingertips over his mouth.

"Whatever happens this day, know that I have seen all the blackness inside you. I've seen the hunter, the man who has killed, and I still love you."

He stared at her.

She kissed his cheek, then turned and walked to the boat. When she reached the gangway she looked back, but he was already gone.

Colter untied Siren and the black mare and led them along the street. He glanced at the sky. Another couple of hours until the boat left for St. Louis. Maggie had promised to wait for him there. Those things she'd said about loving him. He shook his head to clear it. How long would she wait? he wondered. A week, a month? He wanted to believe her. What a fool he'd become, grasping at the promises of a young woman who spoke in the heat of emotion. It didn't matter that he could still see her face without even trying, or that he wondered what it would be like not to leave her here, to bring her with him to that valley in Tennessee.

He swore. He had no time for fanciful thoughts. In the spring she would outfit herself and head west. She would find what she wanted, marry someone, and settle down to a life she deserved. A life without him.

He was doing the right thing. He'd seen the look in her eyes, the fear. Fear of him. Of the man he was inside. She claimed to love him, but he knew her love was simply gratitude. Better for both of them to end it this way, he thought, and put her from his mind. At least she was safe from Gant.

When he reached the main street, he glanced around. The Dacotah House was on the corner of St. Anthony and Fort. He asked a soldier for directions, mounted Siren, and pulled the black behind. If the general had gotten the message, then everything would turn out right. If he hadn't— He looked around the busy street and wondered what it felt like to hang.

# *Chapter 32* ═══════════

Maggie hovered by the entrance to the ticket office. She should get back on the boat and leave. It's what Colter wanted. But she couldn't go without knowing what happened to him. Even if he didn't care about her, she had to know that he survived. She had to be sure that he was cleared of the crimes. What if he couldn't find his friend? Maybe she could convince the army officer that Colter was innocent. If she spoke on his behalf, then there would be two voices against Gant. Even if Colter wanted her gone from his life, she couldn't bear to let him hang.

She entered the office and smiled at the man behind the counter. "When does the next steamer leave for St. Louis."

"End of the week."

"Thank you." She left the office. If she missed this one, she would be in town for several days. What would Colter say when he found out? She knew he'd be angry, but she had to take the chance. Better angry than dead.

She stepped into the main road. Even standing on tiptoe, she couldn't see above most of people milling around. Wagons rolled through the muddy street. Soldiers on horseback rode in formation. She had to find him. She closed her eyes and thought. Where would he meet his friend? Where did men go to meet? A saloon?

She bit her lower lip. Edward had spent much time in one whenever they'd gone to town. She knew her mother had found her customers there from time to time. It seemed a logical place to start. How many could there be in St. Paul?

She only had to find the main street and look for the two horses tied in front.

She followed a group of men, staying far enough behind so that they wouldn't notice her. She clutched the saddle-bags tightly to her chest and rubbed the initials stamped in the fine leather. Just tracing them over and over gave her strength.

The men turned. The sign on the side of the building said THIRD STREET. She glanced down at the rows of buildings. Oh, no. Saloons. So many. JOHN B. LAHR read a sign on the corner. Farther down stood EMMERT & HECK. There were more than she could have imagined. And this was only one street.

People stared as she walked slowly down the side of the road. She knew it was because she was a woman alone. The dress didn't help her fit in, she thought, reaching down and fingering the patch. Fear swelled up inside her. She thought about asking for the sheriff's office, but what if the men after Colter had telegraphed ahead? The sheriff wouldn't be willing to help her then. Why would he take her word over an army officer's?

She walked up and down the streets. A man approached her and offered her a dollar. She didn't have to hear his coarse words to know what he wanted. She ran and ran until he was far behind her, then she turned another corner.

The smells of the city invaded her nostrils. Stench from sewage and waste blended with fresh bread and the odor from the corner butcher shop. So many buildings. Her legs grew weary. Saloons and saddlery stores. Printers and doctors. She'd never seen this many people in one place. St. Paul must be the biggest city in all the country.

She walked to the end of a street and peered at the sign: ST. ANTHONY. She turned left. Two blocks down she saw a bay mare tied next to a black. Her heart raced. The horses stood between two saloons. JACOB HINKLE and DACOTAH HOUSE. She looked from one to the other. With a deep breath, she walked to the one with the sign reading Jacob Hinkle and stepped inside.

Cigar smoke threatened to choke her. Men sat every-where in the small, dark room. She clutched her saddle-bags close to her chest and peered into the corners. She didn't see a man who looked like Colter. Had she chosen incorrectly?

Gradually, the men became aware of her. Conversation died as they turned to stare. She started backing up slowly. If Colter were here, he would have seen her.

A hand touched her arm. She jumped and turned. A small dark-haired man with beady eyes stared at the saddlebags. He touched the initials.

"Looking for someone?"

Colter nodded and the general poured him another glass of whiskey.

"You're one lucky bastard," John said. "Gant could have killed you a hundred times over."

Colter frowned. He didn't feel very lucky. "He tried, in prison. He made the mistake of sending a few others to take care of the job."

John raised his glass. "To Alexander and the seven other men. May their souls find peace."

Colter lifted his arm in salute and downed the contents. It burned to his belly, then flared into a comfortable glow.

John tipped his hat back on his head. "I took the liberty of telling the sheriff there might be a little trouble. Good thing I did. Petty had already wired ahead."

"He's thorough, if nothing else." In the distance a whistle blew. "What time you have?"

John pulled out a gold pocket watch. "Five past four."

She was gone, Colter thought. He'd hoped the whiskey or the relief at finding the general would dull the ache. Neither had helped. He told himself he should be grateful. All he had to do was sit here until Petty found him. John would tell his story. Being a retired general added cred-ibility. Colter would prove that Gant was the killer, and it would all be over. He could take Siren and head for that patch of land at the end of the valley, raise his horses, and die a happy man. He frowned. Hell, except for these last few days with Maggie, he'd never been happy in his life. At least he would die on his own terms.

"I did a little checking on Mr. Gant," John said, pulling several folded papers from his wool-lined greatcoat. His bushy gray brows drew together. "Seems our friend is from Kentucky. Signed up on the side of the South, then changed his mind. Might have been a little uncommitted about the cause."

"Explains why he had to wait so long for his command."

"Could be." John smiled. "Could also be that letter you sent me, at the end of your first mission together. I put it in his file."

"Just told the truth."

John folded the paper and stared at him. "You want to talk about it, son?"

"What?"

"Whatever's giving you that hangdog expression. Looks like you lost your best friend." He grinned. "Not that you were ever one for friends. You've got your mare. I saw her out front. She's still the prettiest bay I ever saw."

"Everything's fine," Colter said, angry as hell that the old man could read him so easily. So what if he was thinking about Maggie? He would get over her. He could barely remember how blue her eyes were, or the gold-blond silk of her hair. He grimaced.

"Nice touch, by the way," John said, pouring another glass. "Keeping the bay in plain sight, like a flag ol' Gant'll be sure to rally 'round." He looked again at his watch. "Maybe we should find the sheriff ourselves."

Colter glanced at the door and straightened. "Don't bother. Look." He pointed.

A young officer stood inside the door and looked around the bar. He saw Colter and recoiled visibly. Without saying a word, he backed out of the saloon and ran.

John poured them each a drink. They toasted each other silently.

"I know you're in there, you bastard. Come out now."

Colter's stomach clenched. "Gant," he said quietly.

"We'll wait for Petty," his friend said. "Don't want any accidental shootings."

"No! Stop!"

The sound of a woman's screams brought Colter to his feet.

"What the hell?" John stood beside him.

"He's got Maggie," Colter growled. "Dammit." He started for the door.

"Who the hell is Maggie?"

Colter didn't answer. He pulled out his pistol and headed for the street.

John grabbed his arm. "Killing him isn't going to help your cause. You're already a wanted man."

"He can't hurt Maggie. I don't care about the rest." Their eyes met. "Stay out of my way."

John raised his hands to show he was unarmed and backed up slowly. "You always were meaner than an injured bear."

"Only when I'm crossed."

He walked to the entrance, paused, then burst onto the street, his gun raised. "Let her go, Gant," he said coldly.

Gant smiled. He held Maggie in front of him. Her slight body shielded most of him. He'd wrapped an arm around her throat. His other hand held a gun to her temple.

Colter didn't let himself look at her face or meet her eyes. The panic and fear there would distract him. He concentrated on her position and tried to figure a way to save her without getting her injured. She clawed at the arm around her throat, the saddlebags banging against her chest.

"Drop it," Gant ordered. He pressed the gun harder against Maggie's temple. She squirmed, but didn't scream.

A crowd began to collect. Colter felt John behind him, but didn't turn around.

"It's too late," Colter said, staring into Gant's dark eyes. "I know the truth. I know you were the one who killed Alexander and the other men."

Gant laughed, but it was a false sound. "You know shit. I've got a witness to back me up."

"So has he." John stepped forward.

"You've got Alexander's rifle," Colter continued, never taking his eyes off his enemy. "The killer stole it."

Gant grinned. "Can you prove it was his? Or will only you and I know the truth?"

A man leading a horse broke through the crowd. From the corner of his eye, Colter saw a man in a blue uniform push through to the front. "What exactly is going on here? Gant, what are you doing with that woman?"

"There's your killer," Gant said. "There's James. Shoot him while you have the chance. He'll escape again."

"Let the woman go," Petty commanded, even as he approached Colter. "Captain James, I'm going to have to ask you to lower your weapon."

"No so fast." John stepped forward.

"General." Petty looked surprised. "What are you doing here?"

"Helping a friend." John took off his hat and ran his fingers through his thick gray hair. "Colter James was with me the night of the murder. We went into town and did a little whoring together. Next morning I delivered him back to his tent, drunker than a skunk. I left for Washington. I'd have come back if I'd known he was arrested. He's not the killer. Seems that man there is."

Colter didn't allow himself to look at Maggie. He knew what she'd be thinking about him now. Whoring. Using a woman the way other men had used her mother. Forget her, he told himself. Concentrate. He looked at Petty.

The major stared at Colter. "Is this true?"

He nodded.

"Why didn't you tell this story before?"

"I did. To Gant. I didn't know he was the killer, so I explained what had happened that night. He—"

"Colter!" Maggie screamed.

He jerked his attention back to her. Gant was slipping through the crowd, pulling Maggie along with him. Colter pushed Petty out of the way and went after him. John followed.

"I'll go around to the left," the general said as he slipped through the people.

"Gant, James, I command you to halt!" Petty ordered.

Colter ignored him. He could see Maggie's face as Gant dragged her along. Her eyes flashed with rage.

"Be careful," she called, then squirmed. "Let me go." Gant squeezed her throat tighter. She gasped for breath.

Colter stared at the gun pressed against her. With each step, it wobbled wildly. Gant couldn't watch him, the gun, and where he was going. He saw the muzzle raise up toward the sky and he jumped forward.

His shoulder hit both Gant and Maggie. She cried out. Colter grabbed Gant's hair and tugged his head back. His grip loosened and Maggie fell free. Colter dropped his own weapon and grabbed Gant's wrist. They wrestled for the gun. He sensed more than saw Maggie crawl away. Gant kicked out at him. Colter jerked back, but kept his hold on Gant's wrist. Gant backed up against the railing on the other side of the street. His feet slipped. Colter felt him going down. He twisted harder on his wrist, then fell heavily with his old enemy and pressed both knees into his chest.

Gant pointed the gun straight at his gut and smiled. "I'll see you in hell."

Colter rolled away as the gun fired. It grazed his arm. Pain shot through him, enraging him. He kicked out and the gun dropped to the ground. Gant grabbed for it. Colter jabbed him in the kidneys and got the weapon first. He pressed the muzzle against Gant's sweating forehead.

"That will be enough," Petty said from behind him. "I'm placing you both under arrest."

"No so fast." John approached. "Take a look at these. I've got a signed statement of what happened that night and a telegram from your superior officer clearing Colter James of all charges."

Colter heard the rustling of papers. Gant glared up at him. It would be so easy, Colter thought.

"Fine," Petty said. "Mr. Gant, I'm arresting you for the murder of eight enlisted men. Jackson, ask the sheriff where we can hang this man. James, get up, please. We'll take care of Gant this afternoon."

"No."

"What?" Petty sounded outraged.

Colter didn't care. Nothing mattered except revenge. Not just for Alexander and those other seven men, but for Maggie and what had happened to her.

"I'll see *you* in hell, you bastard." He cocked the pistol.

"No!" Maggie screamed from behind him. She ran over and dropped on her knees beside him. "Don't do this, Colter. Let the army take care of Gant. Dead is dead. Why does it matter who kills him?"

"Kill me," Gant taunted. "You know you want to."

"Don't." She clutched at his arm. "Please. For me. For all that you've been to me. If there is a spark of the man I love inside, if you can hear me, don't kill him."

"Young lady, I'm going to have to ask you to move," Petty said.

"Shut up," John roared. "Colter, don't be a damn fool. You didn't go through all this just to end up charged with murder. The woman's right. Dead is dead."

"Colter?" Maggie squeezed his arm. He didn't take his eyes off Gant's face, or the contempt in his eyes. But he felt her hand, the soft warmth. He smelled the sweet scent of her body.

He rose suddenly and handed the pistol, butt first, to Petty.

Maggie flung herself at him. He stood stiffly in her embrace, allowing her words to flow through him. Over her head, he saw John give him a salute.

"Well done, Captain," he said.

Slowly, Colter wrapped his arms around Maggie and held her as if he would never let her go.


Maggie adjusted the cuff of her new dress. The fine rose-colored wool, light enough for summer, fell over three new petticoats. Underneath, the lawn camisole and pantaloons caressed her skin with each step she took as she paced the parlor of their hotel room. She could see the big tub through the open bedroom door. She'd gotten her wish of a bath, but it hadn't been what she'd hoped for. She'd been too worried to enjoy the hot water and sweet-smelling soap. Colter had been gone for so long.

The door opened and he stepped inside.

"Gant's dead," he said, without looking at her.

He set his new hat on the stand by the door and shrugged out of his jacket. A new shirt and trousers hugged his tall, muscled frame. She could see the outline of the bandage on his arm, but no other signs of his wound. She wanted to run to him and hold him close, but she wasn't sure of her reception. Since he'd put her away from him, after letting Petty take Gant, he hadn't looked directly at her.

"I'm sorry about the boat," she said, picking at her skirt. "I should have stayed on board. But I was worried about you. I had to know that you were going to be safe."

"You could have been killed." He walked over to the window and parted the curtains. "Did you ever stop to think about that?"

"No." She stared at the fine rug covering the wooden floor. "I just—"

"Do you think I wanted your blood on my hands as well?"

He sounded so angry. She had thought he would be happy that his past was finally laid to rest. He was a free man now. Somehow, her heart had foolishly thought he would claim her as his. That he would come in the room and sweep her off her feet with declarations of love. That they would begin to make plans for their life together. She would happily have gone with him to his valley in Tennessee.

"You probably want me to leave," she said.

He didn't answer.

She picked up her reticule. "There's another steamer leaving at the end of the week. I guess I'll get a ticket for that."

Again silence.

Don't let me go, she pleaded silently, staring at his stiff back. She looked at the bedroom and the corner of the bed visible through the open door. She'd thought they might spend this night together in that bed. Perhaps even share a bath.

"I hope you like Tennessee," she said, more to give him time to ask her to stay than because she wanted to talk about his destination. "It's supposed to be very beautiful. You have Siren back, so you can start your herd of horses." She looked back at him. "I guess I should go now."

Nothing. The quiet told her all she needed to know. He didn't want her in his life. She was still in shock, she told herself. She had to be. Leaving him didn't hurt as much as she would have thought. The real pain would come later.

"I'll get another room. When I make my way West, I'll pay you back all the money." She walked to the door. "I'm glad you're safe, Colter. I know you won't come for me in St. Louis. I understand that you don't love me back. I guess I've always known. I'd hoped my loving you was enough. I'd hoped *I* was enough." She turned the handle. "Good-bye."

"It's never been you," he said.

She froze, half out of the room, half in the hall. "What did you say?"

"It's not you, Maggie, who's not enough. I've told you, I don't know how to be the man you need."

She stepped back inside and spun to face him. He looked at her, his gray eyes bright with a fire she didn't understand.

"You've always been enough," she said. "I love you."

He shoved his hands in his pockets. "What about California?"

Hope flared so brightly that it burned in her belly. "Tennessee is fine with me. It was never about the place I was going to. It was about belonging."

"This is who I am. I'll never be anything else."

She took a step closer. "If you care about me, it's plenty."

He took a step toward her. A dark lock of hair tumbled over his forehead. She longed to brush it back, she longed to touch him. But she sensed he had to be the one to reach out. She clutched her reticule tighter.

He moved closer still, until they stood less than a foot apart. He rubbed her cheek with the back of his hand.

"I love you, Maggie Bishop."

"Oh, Colter!" She flung herself against him. His arms wrapped tightly around her and held her close. "I love you, too. Always."

His mouth hovered above hers. "I mean to marry you."

"You say that like you think it will scare me off."

He grinned. "It scares the hell out of me." His smile faded. "I'll be beside you for as long as you want me. I'll share the load." He brushed his lips against hers. "I'll do my damnedest never to hurt you, Maggie."

"I know that," she said. She rested her cheek on his chest and listened to the thundering of his heart. "I've always known."

# Epilogue

"Mama, Mama, look at me."

Maggie turned from the rosebush she'd been tending and waved to her daughter.

"I'm riding Blackie," the little girl called from her seat on the back of the stout pony. Alicia's six-year-old legs stuck out as she bounced around the corral. "I'm a big girl."

"Yes, you are," Maggie said, and stood up.

The spring morning was sweet and cool in the Tennessee valley where they made their home. Behind her stood the two-story house they had built almost six years ago. Three barns led to paddocks and outbuildings. The horse farm prospered with a new contract to provide mounts for the calvary.

"Papa, I'm riding," Alicia said, smiling up at the tall, broad-shouldered man standing in the center of the ring watching her.

"Slow Blackie down, Alicia. Your brother wants to ride with you." Colter walked over to the dark-haired young girl and placed the towheaded boy in front of her. "Hold on to him."

"I will." Alicia wrapped her arms around her brother.

Maggie felt a familiar tightness in her throat. Colter looked so right with his children. He was gentle but firm, a loving parent who had the patience to teach them to ride as well as to read.

She found it had to hard to believe it had already been seven years since he had kidnapped her from the wagon train. After leaving St. Paul, they'd traveled south to this valley. By the time they'd arrived, it had been fall. There had only been time to build a single room before winter. Maggie smiled. How many times had Colter apologized for not providing a better dwelling? She'd told him it didn't matter where they lived as long as they were together. They'd spent that first winter loving each other under a warm quilt. By the following spring she'd been big with child. With Alicia.

"Come see us, Mama," her daughter called.

Maggie picked a single blossom from the rosebush by her front porch. She touched the petals and walked toward the corral. The sweet fragrance drifted to her, reminding her of the day she'd purchased the plants from the nearby general store. The owner's wife had been shocked that Maggie had sent all the way back East for two rosebushes. They had been expensive and impractical. But Colter had understood. He'd been the one to suggest she plant them to honor her mother and sister. The roses had thrived in the rich soil. Their blooms each spring and summer reminded her of the love she'd shared with her family, and the sacrifices each of the women had made for her.

Maggie leaned against the painted railings. Colter moved to stand next to her, never taking his eyes off the children.

"They're doing well," he said, absentmindedly reaching out to stroke her hair.

She smiled up at him. He had more wrinkles by his eyes now, a testament to his frequent smiles. The gauntness had left his face; he no longer listened for the enemy. But sometimes he looked beyond her to a past she couldn't share. Sometimes she held him in the night when the ghosts haunted him. Sometimes she loved him until an exhausted sleep rescued him from the demons. Always she thanked God for him.

"Don't trot," he called to Alicia. "Keep Blackie at a walk."

"How is Siren?" Maggie asked.

"Ready to foal again."

Maggie touched her own still-flat belly. She'd only been sure for the last couple of days. "I'm with child."

Colter glanced down at her. A slow smile pulled at his mouth. One lock of dark hair tumbled onto his forehead. "I know."

Maggie shook her head. "How did you know?"

"Your scent changed. And your body." He leaned close to kiss her. "Last night your breasts were fuller."

The feel of his lips against hers caused a stirring of heat. It didn't matter that he'd kissed her hundreds of times or that they still made love as often as they could steal the time and privacy. Just the touch and nearness of him left her trembling.

They both pulled back and looked at the children. Alicia held her brother securely in her chubby arms. They were happy children. Healthy. She'd borne them easily.

Maggie rested her arms on the top of the railing and handed Colter the rose. "I thought if it was a boy, we would name him after your brother."

Colter spun to look at her. The lack of expression on his face told her he hid great emotion. After seven years she knew her husband as well as she knew herself. Not for one second of their time together had she ever stopped loving him.

"I'd like that," he said, his voice husky.

He took the rose and tucked it into her hair, just above her ear, then bent down and kissed her a second time. The tenderness in his touch brought tears to her eyes.

"They're kissin' again," young Jonathan said.

As Colter pulled her hard against his body, Maggie offered up the prayer she said every Sunday in church. That her children would be blessed with the same happiness she had found, and that she and Colter would continue to love each other more with each passing day. They had made their way through the trial of hardships and found their future together. By learning to trust, she had earned the hunter's heart. By releasing his hold on the past, he had found a haven of peace. It was, they both knew, a miracle.